CODENAME
FIREFLY

Books by **CJ Daugherty**

Night School
Night School Legacy
Night School Fracture
Night School Resistance
Night School Endgame
Night School The Short Stories
The Secret Fire
The Secret City
Number 10
Codename Firefly

As **Christi Daugherty**

The Echo Killing
A Beautiful Corpse
Revolver Road

CODENAME
FIREFLY

C J DAUGHERTY

THE ENEMY IS AT THE GATES

MOONFLOWER

Published by Moonflower Publishing Ltd.
www.MoonflowerBooks.co.uk

1st Edition

Moonflower Publishing Registered Office: 303 The Pillbox, 115 Coventry Road, London E2 6GG

MOONFLOWER

The past is never dead. It's not even past.
William Faulkner

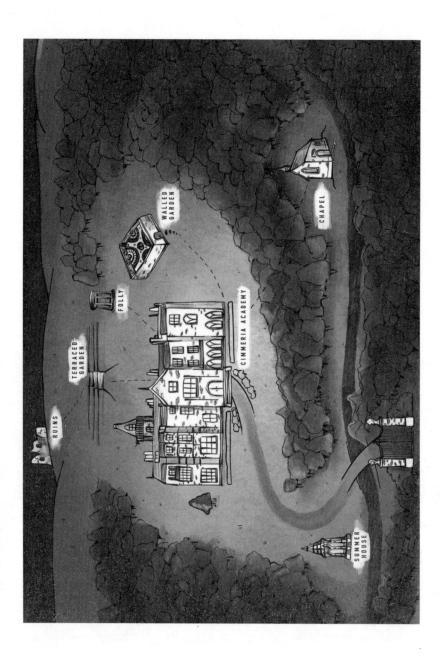

ONE

It was late and Gray was running through the frozen dark. Around her the woods crowded in, thick and threatening, branches stretching out as if to grab her. The moon had disappeared behind the clouds some time ago, leaving her stumbling along a path she could barely see. It had rained all day and now the December night was turning the raindrops to ice.

As she skidded around a bend in the path, the wind picked up, dropping a shower of frozen water from the sodden pine needles, and sending ice down her spine.

With each step, she thought of the people who had brought her to this place. Her mother – the prime minister. Her father – the spy. And the men who'd tried to kill her – the deputy prime minister and a shadowy group of traitors who wanted power at any cost. They had betrayed their own country and they would do it again.

Thinking of them made her angry. Anger kept her warm.

It was the only way she was getting through this.

All she wanted was to go home.

But where was home? Not the prime minister's residence at Number 10 Downing Street where she'd lived until she came here, but the outh London flat she'd shared with her mother before she was chosen to run the country. If she closed her eyes, she could see the comfortable worn rugs and the long navy sofa, cushions flattened into a cosy nest. Her little room on the top floor, with its view of tree tops, chimneys, and red brick houses.

The memory was so strong for a fleeting instant, she could almost smell its toast and marmalade morning scent. Feel the warm sun flooding through the windows on a summer day…

A snapping sound jerked her from her reverie.

Gray stopped and whipped around. Trees towered beside her, dark and inscrutable, fringed by dried bracken turned russet by the cold. Beneath them, nothing stirred.

Some long-buried instinct made the fine hairs on the back of her neck rise. That sound had been made by a person moving carefully. But not carefully enough.

The attack was coming.

Her heart began to race.

There was no time to think. Already breathless, she pelted as fast as she dared down the uneven path, trying to remember everything she'd been taught. But her mind had gone blank. Her chest tightened until she could barely draw a breath.

Sweat stung her eyes and raindrops chilled her face. The thumping of her trainers sounded unnervingly loud in the silent woods – a neon sign flashing an arrow. "Here she is! Here's the prime minister's daughter! Come and kill her."

She glanced to the right and saw something moving in the bushes. A shadow shifting just out of sight.

Above the rasping of her breath and thudthudthud of her heart, she thought she could detect the hiss of disturbed branches as someone closed in.

Panicked now, she turned to look back and instantly tripped over a fallen tree branch. She went sprawling, landing so hard the rough earth scraped her hands and burned her knees. Barely aware of the pain, she scrambled back to her feet and lurched forward. But it was already too late.

A figure clad all in black burst out of the shadows onto the path just ahead of her.

Gray froze.

All dressed in black. A knife in his hand…

She couldn't move. She felt as cold and dead as the winter ground she stood on.

"Leave me alone." The words came out in a breath, lost on the breeze.

But he wasn't going to leave her alone. He advanced on her steadily, his features hidden behind a balaclava, empty hands twitching at his sides.

No knife, she realised, distantly. And then he was upon her.

The second his hands touched her she recovered her voice, screaming so loudly her throat burned. She struggled in his grip, clawing at him, her feet drumming against his legs as he swung her into the air.

"Let me go! Let me go!"

"Jesus, Gray, will you calm down?" a male voice grumbled gruffly in her ear, as he released his hold.

Another black-clad body burst out of the trees.

"What's the matter?" the new person demanded, lifting the fabric covering her face. A shock of white-blonde hair caught the moonlight as Gray's bodyguard, Julia Matheson, looked at her with concern.

11

At the sound of Julia's reassuring voice, Gray began to sob brokenly. "It happened a-a-again."

The man pulled off his headgear. Through her tears, she saw the familiar brooding features of Carter West, the school's security expert.

Producing a water bottle from somewhere, Julia handed it to her. "It's all over. You're safe. Drink this."

Gray took a sip. The liquid cooled her throat and gradually she began to calm.

"I'm sorry," she told both of them. It was freezing, but she felt hot – humiliation burning through her skin. "I got scared."

"It's a process. You'll get better at this. It's only the second time we've tried." The bodyguard's voice was confident, but Gray was uncomfortably aware that Carter had said nothing. His dark eyes were thoughtful, but she read his silence as judgement.

"Well," the bodyguard said. "I think that's enough for tonight."

Nobody disagreed. The three of them began walking back down the wooded path, the air heavy with all the things nobody was saying.

With the two of them at her side the woods didn't seem as frightening as they had a few minutes ago. It wasn't even that dark – the moon had reappeared and stars painted the sky silver.

It never feels so terribly dark when you're not alone.

An icy breeze froze the perspiration on the back of Gray's neck. Shivering, she yanked up the hood of her fleece and shoved her hands deeper into the pockets.

When Julia had come up with the idea of teaching her self-defence, Gray hadn't been keen. Especially after her bodyguard suggested doing the training at night. But the reality had been worse than she expected. She knew the attack was coming, and what she was supposed to do. But each time she panicked.

Ahead of her, Julia and Carter were talking in hushed voices, their heads bent toward each other. Gray held her breath, trying to hear them.

"She panics so fast, Jules," Carter said softly. "Fear completely immobilises her."

The December wind swirled around, ruffling Gray's hood, and drowning out what Julia said in reply. She only caught the end of the sentence: "...she's traumatised. Give her time."

Traumatised. The word was huge, but even that didn't convey the overwhelming fear she felt. Or the way it took over her body. There wasn't a word in the world big enough for that.

Gray trudged along, lost in her thoughts, until they rounded a bend and the branches parted. Suddenly, the huge Victorian Gothic school building appeared in front of them as if springing from the earth, its long rows of arched windows aglow with light, like something out of a fever dream. The imposing four-storey structure had two sprawling wings and a roof that rose into sharp, jutting peaks. At the highest points, tall chimneys thrust up at the sky like fists.

Gray studied it dispassionately as Julia dropped back to walk alongside her. "We'll try again later this week," the bodyguard told her, a perky note in her voice. "But we'll stick to the gym. Maybe if you're not in the dark..."

"...I won't freak out?" Gray finished the sentence for her.

Julia touched her arm. "You'll get there."

She was saying all the right things, but as they crossed the smooth lawn and climbed the steps to the imposing front door with its ancient, elaborate locking system, Gray didn't feel any better. Not at all.

Inside, the air was warm and dry and smelled faintly of furniture polish and wood smoke. The three of them walked across a worn stone floor beneath enormous antique tapestries. The candleholders on either side of the fireplace were nearly as tall as Gray. The entrance hall led to a wide arched doorway and then they were in a grand hallway with oak-panelled walls and oil paintings in gilded frames.

It was past curfew, and they were alone when they reached the main staircase with its carved bannister that curved up beneath a glittering chandelier. Carter stopped at the foot of the stairs. "Have a good night," he told them both. Giving Gray a direct look, he added with unexpected warmth, "Don't worry about tonight. It'll get better. Just keep falling up."

In her rare encounters with him, the school's security director had always been just a little distant, and for a moment Gray was so surprised she couldn't think of anything to say.

She managed to mumble, "Thanks," before he jogged away.

Julia and Gray climbed the elegant stairs, their movements watched by the painted eyes of men in elegant 19th century frock coats and women in fantastic pearl-draped dresses. At the landing, they passed three statues on low plinths in front of towering windows hidden behind velvet curtains, before turning into a second, simpler staircase. This one took them up to a slim corridor lined on either side with identical doors, each painted plain white with a number in black.

It was just after eleven o'clock, and the dorm was a hive of activity – girls running down to the bathrooms and showers, chattering non-stop. They were all too sophisticated to stare openly, but Gray felt their eyes on her back as she and Julia reached the door with the number 326 painted on it. She stepped aside automatically, waiting as the bodyguard opened the door and flipped on the light.

Julia quickly checked the room and then motioned for her to enter.

"Safe as houses," she announced.

Gray attempted a smile, but failed.

Julia's face softened. "Get some sleep, Firefly," she said, gently. "Tomorrow will be better."

Firefly was Gray's codename with the Secret Service agents responsible for protecting the first family. Nobody used it here, except Julia. It had become a kind of nickname.

"You keep saying that," Gray said, dejected.

"Because it's true." Julia rested a warm hand on her shoulder for just a second. "I promise."

After the bodyguard had gone, Gray stood by the bed, thinking about what she'd said. She wanted to believe it. She'd had two weeks of bad days since she came here. Fourteen lonely days.

Blinking back tears, she studied her reflection in the frameless mirror on the back of the door. Her dark, wavy hair was escaping from the ponytail she'd pulled it into an hour ago, tendrils curling loose around her face. Her cheeks were flushed. Her blue eyes glistened with unhappiness.

"Pull yourself together," she ordered.

But the truth was, she didn't know how to do that.

Her phone vibrated and she pulled it from the pocket of her hoodie. When she saw Chloe's name on the screen, her heart lifted, and she hit answer.

Chloe's familiar face appeared, dark hair pulled back in a braid, beaming at her.

"There you are!" she said. "I've been calling all night. I have to tell you what happened today. Are you sitting down? Well, brace yourself – Tyler Bolino asked me to Adrian's Christmas party. Can you believe it? I didn't even know what to say. I mean he's gorgeous, obviously, but he's kind of boring and you know…"

She chatted on excitedly, and Gray let the familiar voice flow over her. Chloe was her best friend back in London. Adrian's parties were the events of the year back at her south London school. His dad was a nightclub owner and concert promoter, and he always made the parties memorable.

If times were normal, she and Jake might have gone, but things were anything but normal. There was no guarantee she'd go home for Christmas at all. And Jake, who might have become her boyfriend if things had been different, was in Leeds. He might never come back to London again.

Finally noticing her silence, Chloe said, "Hey. Are you OK?"

"Yes… I mean, no. Oh, I don't know." Gray forced a laugh. "I just miss you so much. And I hate that I can't be there."

"I miss you, too," Chloe said. "Nothing is fun without you. And now I have to decide about Tyler Bolino by myself, all because of stupid terrorists chasing you away. It's hideous."

Gray laughed again, this time for real. "Go out with him, you idiot. He's cute. You'd be an adorable couple."

"Yeah, but all he ever talks about is rugby."

"So, don't talk to him. Wear him on your arm like a fancy bag. You've had a crush on him since we were fourteen."

Without letting go of the phone, Gray kicked off her damp trainers and settled down on the bed, shaking off her hoodie and dropping it on the floor next to her shoes. Lifting a soft blue blanket off the footboard, she wrapped it around herself, creating a warm nest. The cold that had sunk into her bones began to fade.

At least for a while she could talk to her best friend and pretend she was home, and everything was fine. And that Cimmeria was just a bad dream. One that would disappear in the morning.

TWO

Julia walked down the staircase to the first-floor landing, speaking quietly into the microphone on her wrist. "Firefly in nest." A second later, a male voice emerged from the tiny earpiece discreetly hidden by her straight blonde hair. "Copy that."

She waited, but he said nothing more. No "Thank you." No "Have a good night." Back in London, someone on her team would have cracked a joke or invited her out for a drink. Here, the end of her working day was a cool, emotionless "Copy that."

It wasn't a surprise. After all, she was a walking reminder that the government didn't think they were good enough to protect the prime minister's daughter.

As far as Julia was concerned, the government was right. The school's security guards spent most of their time making sure the students didn't smoke weed when they sneaked out into the woods at night.

It was so odd. The school looked exactly the same as it had when she was sixteen, but things had changed. The students seemed more spoiled now. The staff took safety for granted. There just wasn't the same discipline.

When she'd been a student here… Well. Everything had been different.

It was still surreal to find herself here. This school had lived in her dreams for years. Back then she'd thought – hoped – she'd never see it again.

Life has a sense of humour.

At the base of the stairs, she paused to listen. Everything was quiet. Too quiet. There'd been a time when guards patrolled these hallways constantly, looking for any sign of danger. Now the corridors were left empty all through the night. It felt abandoned.

And yet, as she turned toward her room, something stirred.

It was the slightest change in the air, almost imperceptible, and yet all at once she knew she wasn't alone.

Instantly alert, she tilted her head to listen. At first, she heard nothing but her own breathing. Then, behind that, the low, unmistakeable hum of hushed voices. Rising and falling, like a soft breeze through an open window.

She followed the sound, tracing it down the hallway. When she realised where the voices had taken her, she stopped.

She was standing just underneath the grand staircase. In the faint light, the ornately carved wood panelling looked unbroken. If she hadn't known this school like the back of her hand she wouldn't have seen the door there, its edges worked so expertly as to make it invisible. But she did know it, and she stood just outside it, listening to voices that had once been familiar. They were speaking too quietly for her to make out their words.

Oh well. I don't want to go to bed anyway, she thought as she rapped her knuckles lightly against the door.

The voices stopped.

She turned a small brass handle. The door swung open to reveal a windowless office.

The school's acting headmistress, Allie Sheridan, was perched on the edge of the desk in a very un-headmistress-like way. Her straight, golden-brown hair hung loose to her shoulders. In jeans with the cuffs rolled up to expose slim ankles, and a striped top, she looked very little like someone running a school for a hundred and twenty elite students. Her oval face was smooth and unlined, and her grey eyes watched Julia with caution as she stepped inside.

"Jules." Carter stood near Allie, still in his running gear. "Is something wrong?"

"Everything's fine," she assured him. "I was just passing by and heard voices."

"Was there something you wanted?" Allie's voice had deepened a little since Julia had known her back when they were teenagers caught up in their families' dangerous games. Then, Allie had been the ultimate outsider. Now she was Queen Bee, running the school while headmistress Isabelle le Fanult was in Scotland, establishing a sister school to this one – a job that was taking longer than anyone expected, and one Carter had confided he wasn't sure she'd ever return from.

"I thought we ought to talk about what happened tonight." Julia closed the door behind her and leaned against it, casting a quick glance at Carter. "You were right out there. Gray's struggling."

"She wasn't good," he agreed. "Her fear's getting worse."

"She hasn't been here long though," Allie interjected. "We should give her time. She's been through a lot."

For some reason, Julia found this intensely irritating. Allie hardly knew Gray. They'd barely interacted since the girl arrived.

She'd come here to inform her about what was happening, not be told how Gray had suffered.

"What if we haven't got time?" she asked, her voice sharpening. "After all, things have changed."

Carter's brow creased. "Why wouldn't we have time? She only got here two weeks ago."

"Didn't Raj Patel call you?" Julia asked. "He called me earlier today to give me an update. I assumed he called you too."

Raj was the security expert who ran Talos, the company Julia worked for. Talos provided personal security to the prime minister's family and others in high-profile positions.

"Nobody contacted us. What did he say?" Allie didn't look pleased.

"He said we need to increase security," Julia explained. "The group that attacked Gray are looking for her. He's sure they'll figure out where she is."

"For God's sake." Allie's voice grew tense. "Why didn't he call my office? If Raj has information about our students he should come to me first."

"I guess he came to me because I work for him." Julia's tone was polite but she was secretly pleased she had information Allie didn't.

"That's all?" Carter asked. "He didn't have any information about where they're looking or what they'll do if they find her?"

Julia hesitated. Allie and Carter had been given only the most basic information about the threat against Gray and her mother. The two of them knew there'd been an attack, and that Gray was considered high risk. They couldn't be told everything because they had no government security clearance. The information about the shadowy group that had tried to kill Gray and her mother was top secret. Along with the fact that Deputy Prime Minister John Ashford was in the plot up to his eyeballs. And worst of all, that the Russian government was behind it all.

Only a few people at the highest levels of the British government knew about that. And she had no idea how much Raj would want them to know right now.

"You should call Raj," she told them. "All I can tell you is that he's worried things are getting more dangerous. His sources tell him they're hunting for her. And they're determined to find her."

Carter looked at Allie. "I don't like the sound of this."

Julia studied the two of them. Carter, tall and brooding, his athletic frame always angled toward Allie, as if poised to protect her. And she, in need of no protection, but constantly near him. They were so united, so connected to each other, it was hard to believe she could ever come between them.

I never stood a chance of breaking them apart, she realised. If I hadn't been so young, I never would have tried.

"Me neither." Allie glanced at her watch. "We're going to need a plan. Let's get everyone together in the morning and talk it through. Jules, I'd like you to be there too, if you don't mind."

"Of course," Julia said, crisply. "Happy to help."

"Also," Allie continued, "I don't think we should tell Gray about this."

The bodyguard stiffened. "Why not? I'm not going to lie to her. Trust matters between a bodyguard and the person she protects."

"I understand that," Allie said. "But if she's struggling with fear now, knowing what's going on could make things worse. It's our job to keep her safe. Let's do that, and let her get on with healing and finding a way to settle in here."

Julia bristled with unspoken objections, but the annoying truth was, Allie was right. Gray was fragile right now. And it wasn't like she could protect herself.

"Fine," she said. "We'll hold that back for now."

"Great." Allie's reply was clipped. She said nothing more. The dismissal in her tone was clear.

Julia, who had not stepped far into the room, reached for the door handle. "Well, I'll let you get back to your conversation."

Without waiting for them to say goodbye she stalked away, fuming.

She didn't know why she was so angry. Maybe some part of her had hoped that now they were grown up, she and Allie might get along. But she was starting to learn that time doesn't heal every wound. Some stay fresh and raw forever.

Grumbling to herself, she headed in the direction of the gym. She didn't want to sleep and there was nowhere else to go. No one else to talk to. She might as well go punch something.

She was halfway down the hallway when she heard Carter's voice. "Jules, wait up."

Reluctantly, she turned back. "What is it?"

He stopped a few feet away, a knowing smile lifting the corners of his lips. "That didn't go very well, did it?"

Julia sighed, her shoulders drooping. "I'm sorry. She just gets to me."

"And you get to her. You two are oil and water. I've never understood why." There was no judgement in his voice, but she felt like an idiot all the same. Why had she over-reacted like that?

"I don't like taking orders from her," she said. "She's not my boss."

"You know she doesn't mean to upset you, right? She likes you."

"She has a funny way of showing it. She's barely said ten words to me since I arrived," Julia said, bristling.

"Well," he said, "As far as I can see, you don't talk to her, either."

Julia held up her hands. "Fine. I haven't done all I should. I'll try harder." Her tone said the opposite but they both ignored that. "Anyway, all that matters is keeping Gray safe. I have no problem as long as we agree on that."

"We do agree," he assured her. "But you have to understand, it's been years since we've had any security problems here. That stuff – it's all in the past. Things have been safe for half a decade."

Julia bit back her frustration. There had to be a way to make him see what was happening. The second Gray Langtry had walked through the door of this school, everything had changed. The only problem was, the people in charge had not yet accepted that.

"Trust me, Carter," she said. "The people after Gray and her mother are deadly serious. You have to do more. We all do. People could die. Right here."

She struck her foot against the floor for emphasis, and the sound echoed in the quiet, unguarded hallway.

24

The smile faded from his eyes. "Hey, come on. That's a bit harsh. We're doing everything we can—"

"Nobody's doing anything." She cut him off. "The security system relies entirely on cameras, which are too widely spaced and not monitored enough." She gestured at the empty corridor. "How long have we been standing here? Five minutes? And yet nobody's come by to find out what's going on. Nobody patrols. Nobody checks to make sure the students are safe. Everyone just believes things are fine. Stop believing." She took a step toward him. "Trust me when I tell you, things aren't fine anymore."

Colour rose to his face. "Fine. Maybe we've become a little complacent, but only because nothing bad has happened – we can't fight a war that's not there." Before she could argue again he continued. "Look, I hear you, OK? You have a good point. Things have changed. We need to do better. Allie knows this. Come to that meeting tomorrow and tell the others what you've told me, and we'll come up with a plan." He held her gaze. "We'll fix this, Jules."

The way he said her name sent warmth flooding through her. Years had passed but there still wasn't much better in this world than Carter promising to have her back.

All the argument went out of her. "I know you will," she said. "And I'll be at Allie's meeting. But…" She paused. "Everyone has to understand. Trouble is coming."

"They will," he promised. "Just tell them what you told me."

There was so much more she wanted to say. How she'd missed him. And how much everything that had happened back when they were young still hurt. But what was the point? Saying it wouldn't change anything. They'd dated when they were teenagers. It had ended badly. And it was all a long time ago.

She glanced at her watch – it was well after midnight. "Look, I'd better go. I want to fit in a workout before bed."

Another faint hint of a smile. "Classic Jules. Still pushing yourself to the limit."

"Yeah, you know what I'm like." She forced herself to turn away and open the door leading to the basement gym. But when she glanced back, he was still standing there, watching her.

"You know what? It's really nice to be working with you again," she said, before she could stop herself. Adding, just because it was true, "You look great."

He gave her a slow smile. "Right back at you."

As soon as the door closed between them, she pulled out her phone and dialled Raj's number.

Whatever Carter said, it was clear Raj needed to step in and make sure that Allie understood what was really going on. Otherwise, Gray was in deep trouble here.

THREE

Gray was in a cold empty corridor. A faint blue glow revealed gritty concrete, and bare walls strung with wires and cables. In the distance, she could hear the discordant sound of a symphony being played out of tune and a low rumble of voices, the laughter shrill and malicious.

She stood frozen, staring at the familiar scene.

Not again.

Why did she keep coming back to this place, night after night?

She hated it here.

Some part of her – an elemental protective space deep inside her brain – knew this wasn't real. It was a dream. But that tiny part of her couldn't save her. Not from this. Not with fear curling its talons around her heart and digging in deep.

It felt so real. She could feel the floor rough beneath her bare feet. Hear the changing tune of the music. Notice the goosebumps rising.

Every instinct told her to run, but moving was like walking through glue. It took everything she had to make herself run. And even as she did, a voice in her mind told her it was futile. She'd been here enough times to know there was no way out. But she didn't listen. Couldn't listen. Now that she was moving she ran faster and faster, flying through the shadows, breath scouring her dry throat. But the voice had been right. The hallway seemed to lead nowhere – it tangled and twisted. She kept ending up back at the same familiar stretch of dark corridor.

Horror turned her blood to ice. She knew what would happen next. He'd be waiting. He was always waiting.

A shuffle of feet in the distance. A quick intake of breath, like a laugh suppressed. She spun around, peering into the shadows. A flash of movement in the darkness. And then he stepped into the pale light.

"No," she whispered, and tried to back away, but her feet wouldn't cooperate.

He wore all black and his smile was a flash of rage. The long silver blade in his hand dripped with red.

"I wanted your mother," he said, advancing on her. "But you'll do."

Gray's screams woke her from the nightmare. She sat up in bed, her heart racing painfully, her gaze skittering around the shadowy room.

White-washed floors. Plain pine desk. No killers. No killers. No killers...

She drew in a series of quick, short breaths and let the dream fade.

She sank against the pillows. The nightmares were getting worse and she didn't know why.

She'd thought about telling Julia, but how could she tell Julia that she wasn't even strong enough to get over one attack?

Her parents had made her see a therapist right after the attack happened, but she'd been fine back then. Or so she'd thought. The dreams had come later. And the fear of the dark. The fear of everything.

She let out a long breath and rested her chin on her knees. If she just had friends here – someone to talk to. Someone who wouldn't judge her. But she hadn't made friends yet. This place was as tightly knit as a cashmere blanket.

No one was outright mean to her – people were polite. But most of them had been here for years. She was an oddity to them. Famous, yes. But an outsider.

In the pre-dawn darkness, the loneliness suddenly seemed unbearable – a yawning chasm of emptiness into which she had fallen, and from which she might never emerge.

"I want to go home." She whispered the truth into the empty room. But she couldn't. Because home wasn't safe anymore.

Through the tall arched window the sky was still dark. The alarm clock on the desk told her it was just after six in the morning. Breakfast didn't officially begin until seven-thirty. But she wasn't going back to sleep.

She swung her feet to the floor, bumping against the slippers that were set out for her every evening. This was one of the many weird quirks of this place. Someone cleaned the room each day – made the bed, dusted everything. Then in the evening, someone left slippers out for her and put out an extra blanket. These tiny kindnesses were the only things she liked about Cimmeria. Well, that and the library. She wanted to live in the library.

She put on a soft white robe, tying it tightly around her waist before heading down the hallway to the shower room, which was empty at this hour.

She chose the furthest cubicle, closing the curtain behind her and setting her things on a teak stool before turning the water on scalding hot. She stood beneath the sting of the shower's spray for as long as she could bear. Her muscles ached from last night's failed self-defence training. The scar on her neck ached a little in the heat. It had been weeks since she had been stabbed and the wound rarely hurt now. But it was clearly visible – a vivid line against the pale skin.

When she walked out into the main bathroom a few minutes later, a towel wrapped around her head, it was still empty except for one girl, who stood at a sink brushing her teeth.

Above her school-issued white dressing gown, her long dark hair hung in unbrushed tangles. Gray glimpsed tawny skin and a heart-shaped face before she realised the girl was watching her in the mirror. She quickly turned away.

The girl, though, had no such compunction, and watched with unabashed interest as Gray got out her own toothbrush. Finally, she spat out her toothpaste. "I know this is a weird time to introduce myself, but I've been dying to meet you."

Gray's hand froze, her own toothpaste tube half-squeezed. "Um… You have?"

The girl nodded vigorously. "My dad knows your mum. He told me all about you. I could not believe that bloke tried to murder you. What an absolute asshat."

Somehow, it was impossible to take offense and Gray found herself almost laughing.

The girl was about her age, but smaller and slimmer. Her cinnamon-coloured eyes were her most striking feature – filled with mischief and intelligence. There was something oddly familiar about her that Gray couldn't place.

"Wait a sec." The girl rinsed the toothpaste from her mouth, and dropped her toothbrush into her shower box, which was identical in every way to Gray's. It had been in her room when she arrived, along with a closet full of dark blue pleated skirts, crisp white blouses, and pressed blazers.

The girl dried her mouth with a towel. "I'm Minal," she said. "Minal Patel."

Gray put it together in an instant.

"Your dad is Raj Patel?" Surprise sent her voice up an octave. Raj was Julia's boss. He was so much a part of Number 10 Downing Street it had never occurred to her that he might have a family of his own.

The other girl nodded. "I would have said something sooner but I was too intimidated to even speak to you."

"Intimidated? Why?"

"Oh, come on. You've been in all the papers. You've been to Bijou." Minal sounded so awe-struck at the idea of the trendy nightclub in London, Gray didn't have the heart to tell her she'd only been there once, and it had been disastrous. "You go to those parties," Minal enthused. "You've even got a bodyguard. It's so glamorous. I can't even imagine what it's like to be you. I want to know what it's like to live in Downing Street. To be on TV. To meet the Queen. To be famous. I need you to tell me everything," she concluded. "Every tiny detail."

"OK, but..." Gray held up her toothpaste. "Can I brush my teeth first?"

Minal's eyes widened. "Oh my God, I just totally gate-crashed your bathroom time. I'm going to leave you alone for at least five minutes." She gathered her things, keeping up a stream of chatter as she headed toward the showers. "You know, it's weird. You seem so normal. I thought you'd be a total snob."

This took Gray aback. "Why would you think that?"

The girl paused in the shower entrance, one hand on the curtain. "I don't know. Because your life is so interesting, I guess? Nothing ever happens to me. I want something exciting to happen someday."

She had disappeared into the shower cubicle before Gray replied, her voice too low to be heard over the running water.

"Be careful what you wish for."

Half an hour later, when Gray walked down the grand staircase in her uniform with her book bag over one shoulder, she was still mulling over the conversation.

She hadn't been able to bring herself to tell Minal the truth – she hated being the prime minister's daughter. How could she explain what it was like to be followed everywhere? To not be able to do even the most basic normal thing without a team of security guards at her side?

Until her mother had been chosen to lead the country, Gray had been just like any other anonymous teenager, so the sudden public attention had been overwhelming. The paparazzi were big, burly men, and they had constantly pursued her. Even after everything that had happened – even after she was stabbed and nearly died – bodyguards had been forced to sneak her out of Number 10 to bring her here, using back streets and unmarked cars. If they hadn't done that, there would have been ten photographers outside the gates of Cimmeria Academy, trying to get a shot of her in gym shorts.

As she reached the ground floor, she had a flashback to Chloe glaring at a red-faced photographer who'd held his camera low to try and get a picture up her skirt. "She's sixteen years old, you utter pervert," she'd told him. "You have shirts older than her."

Chloe had acted like her bodyguard long before Julia had come along. If she were here, everything would be different.

Talking to Minal had given her the first glimmer of hope that she could make new friends. More than anything, she wanted people to know she wasn't really the girl they'd seen in the papers. She was more complicated than that brightly smiling invention.

In the dining hall, breakfast was just beginning. The staff were busy setting out platters of food on long tables. Soft morning light filtered through sheer shades over the tall windows, giving the grand, oak-panelled room an ethereal glow. One wall was dominated by a fireplace so big she could easily have stood inside it next to the flames, which crackled merrily. The room was warm, and smelled of toast, coffee, and wood smoke.

Maybe this wasn't home, but she had to admit there was a kind of magnificence about it.

The round tables, each surrounded by eight chairs, were mostly empty. But a few students were already eating – all of them wearing identical dark blue blazers. She thought she recognised a girl with distinctive curly blonde hair at the back. A short distance away, she spotted a lanky American boy who was in several of her classes, a thick book open next to his plate.

Both glanced up at her as she walked in, but turned back to their food almost immediately.

Gray's heart went cold. It was always like this. But maybe there was something she could do about it.

She went to the counter and filled a bowl with cereal and fruit, grabbing some warm toast from a rack. Then she poured herself a mug of tea from a large copper urn and splashed milk into it.

Carrying these, she walked back to the table where the blonde girl sat. As she approached, girl glanced up again and their eyes met. Gray seized the opportunity.

"Hi!" The word came out too loud, firing at her like a shotgun. The girl's eyes widened.

Gray tilted her head at the empty seats and lowered her voice. "Would it be OK… can I sit here?"

There was a brief hesitation.

"Take your pick." The girl gestured at the seven empty chairs surrounding the oak table.

Relieved, Gray set her tray down and pulled out one of the heavy chairs.

"I'm Gray," she said, when she was seated.

The girl smiled slightly. "I know. You're the famous Gray Langtry."

She had a soft, unidentifiable accent. Along with her high cheekbones, and curls that gleamed gold in the light, it made her seem incredibly sophisticated.

"I'm Maya," she added. "Not famous at all."

"It's nice to meet you." Gray tried to look welcoming and open without appearing deranged.

For a while after that, a silence fell while they both ate. Gray had almost finished her cereal before Maya spoke again.

"How do you like it here?" she asked, in that velvet soft accent. "It must be so strange for you arriving in the middle of term. Knowing nobody."

Gray buttered her toast, buying time.

"It's been weird, I guess," she said after a moment. "I miss my parents more than I expected. But it seems like a good place."

Maya gave her an astute look. "I've been here three years now," she said. "I came when I was thirteen, from Poland. I knew nobody. I was terrified. I thought it would be strange being at an English school when English is not my first language. And it was, at first. But now it is home. People accept each other here. I have so many friends. And you will make friends, too."

"I hope you're right," Gray said. "I haven't made many so far."

"You will." Maya sounded absolutely confident. "I promise. You have been through a lot. Everyone knows what happened…" She gestured at Gray's throat where the scar could be seen above the collar of her white blouse. "I think you're brave. The man who did that—" A look passed over her face. "I am glad he's in prison. If anyone hurt me or my family like that, I would want him to go to prison for life."

"Yeah, I'd be one hundred percent OK with that," Gray agreed.

The attacker had been in jail for weeks now but had refused to talk. He wouldn't say who had hired him or why he'd tried to kill her. In interviews with the police, Julia said, he just sat there. Smiling.

"Gray." The voice came from behind her.

She turned to find the headmistress, Allie Sheridan, standing behind her chair. "If you're done eating, I'd like a chat." She nodded at the steaming mug in Gray's hand. "You can bring your tea."

Her light brown hair was pulled back in a ponytail and she wore casual black trousers and a V-neck top. She looked young but there was authority in the set of her shoulders, and the steady way she looked at Gray.

"Sure." Gray stood up. She turned back to Maya. "It was nice to meet you. See you in English class?"

"Yes," the Polish girl said, a smile lighting up her face. "See you then."

As she stood, Gray's eyes briefly met those of the lanky guy she'd noticed earlier at the next table. He quickly returned his attention to the leather-bound book, and yet she had the feeling he'd been eavesdropping on their conversation all along.

There was no time to think about that, though. Allie was already halfway across the dining hall, and Gray hurried after the headmistress out into the wide hallway, clutching her mug of tea.

It was busier now with students heading down for breakfast, and the hum of sleepy voices filled the air as Allie ducked through a low door into the office beneath the stairs, waiting for Gray to pass through before closing the door behind them.

She'd been here once before, on her first day at the school. It was a small room with a faded Persian rug on the floor and two black leather chairs facing the mahogany desk. The only art was a modern painting of three women standing in a circle, hair flowing down their backs, hands touching.

Gray took a seat in one of the leather chairs. There was no obvious place to set her mug except Allie's desk, so she balanced it carefully on her knee.

The headmistress studied her with unnerving interest. "I thought we should have a catch-up. You've had two weeks to settle in now. How are you doing?"

"Fine, I guess?" It was as much a question as an answer.

"I was glad to see you with Maya today." Allie rocked back in her seat, studying her. "I've noticed you often sit alone at mealtimes, and I've been a bit worried that you were having trouble fitting in."

Gray was mortified. Had they all been watching her? The prime minister's daughter who couldn't make friends?

"I'm trying to make friends but I'm still new here. I need time," Gray said, her cheeks burning. "I can't make people like me."

"I actually think you're doing incredibly well," Allie told her.

Gray blinked.

"This is a hard school to join in the middle of term," Allie continued. "Everyone knows everyone else – they're a kind of family. When you're new, it seems as if there's a wall around them and you're outside it."

It was as if the headmistress had read Gray's thoughts. She leaned forward, eagerly, grabbing the mug before it could topple. "Yes. It's exactly like that. They're not mean. They're just kind of … not interested."

"Well, I think they are interested, but they're too shy to say so," Allie told her. "Especially Maya, who you sat with at breakfast. Did she tell you anything about herself?"

"Not much."

"I'm not surprised. There's a lot she doesn't talk about," Allie said. "But I think you should know. She's the daughter of the former prime minister of Poland. Someone tried to assassinate her father last year. I think it's fair to say she knows precisely how dangerous it is to be connected to power." She gave Gray a steady look. "Just like you do."

Gray's jaw dropped. She thought of what Maya had said: If anyone hurt me or my family like that, I would want him to go to prison for life…

"Why didn't she tell me?" she said.

"I suppose it's not exactly normal breakfast conversation. And I interrupted the two of you before you could talk for long." Allie paused. "You know, you will find your place here, Gray. Right now, everyone's a little unsure of how to approach you. But they'll come around. I'm not at all worried about that. What I am worried about is how you're dealing with what happened to you." She leaned forward, resting her elbows on the desk. "How are you sleeping?"

Caught off guard, Gray blinked. "Fine.'

"Nightmares?"

Gray thought of the man in her dreams, his ice-cold smile. "No more than usual."

"You're still having panic attacks, though."

"I guess." Gray shrugged. "I don't like the dark. I mean, that's not so unusual, is it?"

She wasn't certain why she wasn't telling the truth but she couldn't seem to make herself say the words.

Allie watched her thoughtfully. "Jules is worried about you. She thinks you're struggling. I'd like you to talk to someone…"

Gray flinched, knocking over the cooling mug of tea on her knee.

"Bollocks," she swore, jumping to her feet. "I mean… Sorry."

Allie walked around the desk holding a cloth and knelt down to dab up the tea.

"Don't worry. This rug is about seventy-five years old. It doesn't mind a bit of tea."

Her tone was easy, but Gray was still flustered. She balanced the now empty mug gingerly on the edge of the desk.

"I don't want to talk to anybody," Gray said. "It's my right not to talk about it." She stood rigidly, waiting for Allie to argue.

Instead, the headmistress rose to her feet, and turned to face her with no surprise or anger in her expression.

"I get it, I really do," Allie said. "And I'm not going to push you on this. But believe me, I know a thing or two about trauma. And I can tell you that ignoring it won't make it go away. It gets in your head and doesn't let go. Trauma has claws. As time passes, you think you'll get better, but it's always there, hanging around, waiting for its chance." Allie drew a breath. "We will do all we can to help you. All I ask in return, is that you trust me enough to let me know if things are getting worse. Do we have a deal?"

Her description was so right – so close to what Gray herself was learning – that she found herself longing to tell the headmistress about the nightmares. But she needed more time. Time to get to know her. And time to process how she felt.

So instead she said, "It's a deal."

"Good." The headmistress crossed the room with unhurried steps. When she opened the door the normal school soundtrack of voices and laughter flooded in.

"If you need anything – even just to talk to someone – I want you to walk back through this door. Any time at all – day or night. If I'm not here, send someone to find me. I'll come immediately."

Gray gave her a grateful look. "Thank you. That means a lot."

"You're going to be fine," Allie promised. "I have absolutely no doubt about that. In fact, you're going to be better than fine. You are going to soar."

FOUR

As soon as Gray was gone, Allie closed the office door and leaned her back against it, closing her eyes.

She knew Gray wasn't telling the truth about her mental state – she could see it in her eyes. She'd pressed her too hard. Why hadn't she just waited for Gray to come to her? That would have been better. But the conversation with Julia and Carter had worried her enough that she'd thought she had to do something.

After all, Allie had once been the traumatised sixteen-year-old girl in this very office, with a chip on her shoulder and no friends. Back then, she'd had a headmistress with the patience to gradually whittle through her defences. Could she be that person for Gray?

On current evidence, she wasn't convinced.

"Dammit, Isabelle," she muttered. "Come back."

She shouldn't be here at all. She'd only returned to Cimmeria a year ago, when Isabelle phoned to tell her she was going away. That she was burned out. And that she would trust only Allie and Carter to do her job.

At first, they'd resisted. They were fresh out of Oxford University then, and living in London. They'd felt, for the first time in their lives, truly independent. Carter had been working with Raj

Patel at Talos, learning about the security industry, and training as a bodyguard. Allie had had an office of her own in the headquarters of Aurora, the organisation that now owned Cimmeria Academy, among many other things.

The simple truth was, she didn't have to work – she'd inherited tremendous wealth when her grandmother had died six years earlier. But she wanted to run Aurora completely one day. To be, as her grandmother had been, a force for good in the world. So she had been learning multiple roles. It was complicated and technical, but she could see Lucinda Meldrum in all of it – in the non-profit branch, which supported schools all over the world, and the financial side, which was coldly calculated to make as much money as possible. It was the yin and yang of her family.

Back then, she'd had a two-year plan to learn enough to step fully into Lucinda's role. The last thing either she or Carter had wanted was to go back and run the school they'd once attended. But they'd had little choice. Isabelle had been determined to go. Starting a new school in Scotland, where she'd grown up – that had always been her dream. Besides, she had sacrificed a great deal for both of them when they were younger. They owed her.

And so here she was – running a school with no clue how to do it right.

Across the room, the phone rang, and she dashed to the desk, snatching it up. "This is Allie."

"Alyson Sheridan?" The voice on the other end was crisp and official. Female and with a faint Scottish burr that left her wondering, for a confused second, whether it was Isabelle calling.

"Yes?"

"Please hold for the prime minister," it said. And then the line went silent.

Allie had just enough time to whisper, "Bloody hell." And then the line clicked again.

"Ms. Sheridan." The rich, well-spoken voice was familiar from television news coverage. "This is Jessica Langtry. I'm sorry to phone out of the blue, but I think we need to talk."

"OK... I mean, of course. How can I help you?"

She'd never spoken to the prime minister before. Gray's arrival had been arranged by Raj Patel. So this came out of the blue.

The prime minister didn't seem to notice her fumbling for words. "You are responsible for the safety of my daughter, and some information has come to light that I feel you must know. But this information is classified. Before I say more, you must be aware that you'll be bound by the Official Secrets Act. Nothing I say to you from this point on can be shared."

"I understand." Allie's feet carried her around the desk; she dropped into the chair and reached for a pen.

"Good. I'm sorry to tell you the situation is much more serious than you know. I believe you are aware of the basics about the attack last month?"

"I know the man who attacked Gray was caught, and is in jail waiting for trial," Allie said.

"Precisely," Jessica said, crisply. "The problem we have is that he wasn't operating alone. He was part of a wider plot. One involving the Russian government, and very possibly members of my own government working with them in exchange for money and power."

Allie found it hard to grasp what she was being told. Other politicians had tried to have the prime minister killed? They'd collaborated with an enemy nation against their own?

"How is that possible?" She whispered the words aloud, too shocked to stop herself.

"That is a question I would very much like an answer to," the prime minister said. "Despite our best efforts, we haven't been able to find the proof we need to have those involved arrested. They are very good at covering their tracks. Which brings me to the reason for this call." She paused. "I've been given new information that indicates the people behind the plot have changed their focus. Intercepted communication indicates they've decided that I'm too difficult to reach. Gray is a better target. They are determined to find her."

Allie's stomach dropped. Jules had told them something about this last night but this made it sound much, much worse.

"Does anyone know where Gray is?" she asked. "Anyone who might talk?"

"Only her father and me, and Raj Patel, who handles Gray's personal security, along with a handful of Raj's staff," the prime minister said. "But I'm afraid it will be impossible to keep it secret for long."

Allie couldn't argue with her. "The students will talk," she said. "They'll tell their parents, and their friends back home. Christmas break is just ten days away."

"Indeed. I think we have weeks at most before someone tracks her down. Maybe days." The prime minister's voice grew taut. "That is why I'm calling. I am aware that Cimmeria has excellent security, but we need it to be even better. Raj tells me

44

there was a time when your security was enhanced. He said the hallways were patrolled and the grounds watched by guards at all times."

"Yes." Allie's voice was steady. "It was like that when I was a student here."

"Could you do that again?" the prime minister asked. "Could you make the school safe enough to keep out a determined attacker? Someone willing to hurt as many people as it took, in order to kill just one?"

The questions seemed to hang in the windowless room, as if each letter were carved in fire.

This was everything Allie had never wanted to hear. She'd hoped those days were over forever. And yet, deep down, now that it was happening again, it all felt inevitable. As if on some level, she'd always known the bad times were just waiting for their chance to rush back in, and turn her world upside down.

She cleared her throat. "In theory, yes we can," she said. "But it will take us some time to—"

The prime minster cut her off. "I understand that. How soon can you begin?"

Allie wasn't sure how to reply. What the prime minister was asking for would impact every student in the school. It would impact one hundred and twenty lives.

"I'll have to run this by a few other people before I can put changes like this into place," she said, her mind whirling. "This is not my decision to make alone. But assuming they agree, we could start right away."

"Have those conversations," the prime minister ordered. "Do it as quickly as you can. Raj Patel has been authorised to provide you with whatever you need, including additional guards. He will be reachable twenty-four hours a day, and he always has a direct line to me. Let him know if you need anything else at all and I will make sure you have it." She paused. "Raj tells me you are incredibly experienced in these matters. You're my only hope right now. I'm trusting you with my most precious possession. Please keep her safe."

With that, the line went dead.

FIVE

Gray walked down the wide hallway, her hands shoved deep in the pockets of her blazer. She wished she'd been able to tell the headmistress the truth. The things she'd said about the fear not going away had resonated. Her only hope was that this was a stage that would pass, and that she could be her old, confident self again. But that fearless girl seemed a long distance away now. And she didn't know how to get her back.

Her phone buzzed angrily, and she pulled it from her pocket to see Julia's name on the screen.

"Hey," she said.

"You're not in your room or the dining hall," Julia said. Her tone seemed unnecessarily accusing.

Gray stopped walking. "I had a meeting with the Head. I just got out."

"Fine, but you need to tell me these things. I'm not a mind reader. I need to know where you are whenever you deviate from the schedule, OK?"

Gray was baffled. Security had been pretty relaxed since she had arrived at Cimmeria. It wasn't like Julia to check up on her like this, or to freak out if she wasn't where she was expected to be.

"It's not my fault," she insisted. "I went down to breakfast early and she grabbed me." She paused. "And yes, before you say it, I forgot to tell you I was going down to breakfast early."

"Gray. What's my motto?" Julia asked.

Gray sighed, and recited, "It's hard to protect someone if you don't know where they are."

"There you go," Julia said. "And right now you are where, exactly?"

"Ground floor hallway. Not going to get myself kidnapped anytime soon."

"Excellent news. So I can have breakfast without calling in the helicopter gunships?"

Gray rolled her eyes. "I think I can stay safe until my English lesson."

"That's a relief. Check in with me before going on any walks with terrorists, please," the bodyguard said, and hung up.

Gray frowned as she put her phone away. There must be something going on. Julia had tried to lighten her tone at the end, but it hadn't been convincing. She'd been anxious when she first called.

She was standing between two marble statues in the central atrium – one a young woman in a long full dress, her waist squeezed by a stone corset. Her hand rested on the question mark-shaped handle of an umbrella. It struck Gray that in the two weeks she'd been here, she'd never really stopped to look at it. Now she craned her neck to see the statue more clearly. The woman had a sweet face, with wide eyes.

The sign on the base said:

Emma Waterford

Student. Teacher. Mentor.

The statue next to that was of a man wearing round glasses and a long frock coat, which billowed around him as if he were in a frantic rush. In one hand he clutched an open book. In the other, a pocket watch.

His sign read:

Edward Rosenstein

Beloved Professor

It was oddly nice to think of these long dead people once walking right where she was now. Emma with her stately bearing, and Edward hurrying along.

Just then, someone jostled into her and she spun around, half expecting to see Emma or Edward running by. A younger boy she didn't recognise glanced back at her over his shoulder and said, "Sorry! Late for breakfast." And then continued his dash.

It was fifteen minutes until the first class and she could hear the rumble of conversation from the dining hall before she reached it.

Turning away from the last-minute crush, she headed past the kitchens, where the staff were still bustling around the huge stoves. The next room along was the great hall, always ghostly and echoing. Gray kept going past that, too. She didn't stop until she reached the last door on the right.

When she pulled the handle, the door swung open with a soft shushing sound.

The room on the other side was quiet and dimly lit. It had a distinctive smell – smoky and hard to describe, like an exotic incense. She inhaled deeply, relaxing a little with each breath. Worn Persian rugs covered the floor, absorbing the sound of her footsteps. The library was always peaceful at this hour – even the tall librarian's desk, set near the front with a view of the room, was unmanned. The green lamps on the study tables were alight, glowing like jewels. Beyond them, the room stretched out, disappearing into rows of dark wooden bookcases built so high the upper shelves could only be reached with rolling ladders. Overhead, circular metal light fixtures descended from the ceilings on chains.

All the tension in Gray eased as the library folded around her like a hug. Since she first arrived, this had been her favourite place at Cimmeria. She walked between the bookcases, trailing her fingers along the leather and fabric spines, pausing now and then to pull out a volume at random.

There is no better way to escape from the world than by going to a library.

The one in her London school had been brightly lit, with a few low shelves of books and too many rows of computers. But this room felt like a remnant of an earlier time – a time before computers, when books were the centre of everything.

In the history section, a book with "History of Woman Suffrage" embossed on the dark spine in gold leaf caught her attention. It was very old. The pages were soft as powder beneath her fingertips. She turned them carefully, as if they might fragment at her touch, but they were sturdier than they first appeared. Stamped on the bottom of the title page was the year "1889".

The first line was a stunner: "The prolonged slavery of woman is the darkest page in human history."

It was enough to convince her to drop her heavy book bag and lean against a shelf to read. She was absorbed in chapter one when a voice spoke at her elbow.

"You're going to miss your first class."

Gray jumped, and the heavy book nearly slipped from her hands as she turned to see who'd spoken.

It was the tall, skinny guy who'd been sitting at the next table at breakfast. She recognised him from her English class but she couldn't remember his name. It was something that started with a D, like Devon or Dexter.

As she closed the book carefully he glanced at the title, eyebrows rising.

"Elizabeth Stanton and Susan B. Anthony," he read in a flat North American accent. "Are you reading that for history? Because last time I checked we were doing Napoleon."

As soon as he spoke she remembered his name – Dylan.

"It's not for class." Turning, she slid the book back into the empty space on the shelf at her elbow. "I was just interested."

He angled a doubtful look in her direction. "Well, it's a hell of a book to put in a high school library. Actually, most of the books here seem to be way beyond high school students' reading levels."

His lofty tone irritated her. It was like he thought he was much more mature that everyone else here.

"Maybe in America that would be true," she told him, tartly. "But here, we read." Sweeping her bag from the floor she walked away.

Wait a minute," he called, laughing as he hurried to catch up with her. "You can't just say something like that and then walk off without letting a poor Yank defend himself."

When she gave him a challenging stare he held up his hands.

"Look, I'm not going to lie to you. Plenty of people in America don't like reading. But then I'm told the same is true here, or is everyone in Britain basically a genius?"

"I wouldn't claim to know what everyone does with their time," she told him airily as they reached the door. "But people with good sense read."

"Well, Americans wrote that book you were holding back there." He reached past her to open the door before she could do it herself. "So there's that."

They stepped out into a hallway packed with students. Gray raised her voice to be heard above the roar. "That was a hundred and fifty years ago. What have they written since?"

His smile broadened. "Oh, you know. Americans have written a few books over the last century. You might come across one now and then." He seemed to be enjoying this.

Gray hurried her pace but he easily kept up, his long legs taking one step for every two of hers as they merged into the hallway traffic, joining the flow toward the classroom wing.

"How nice that we can walk together," she noted, with irony.

The look he gave her then was almost admiring. "You don't pull your punches, do you?"

"I just don't like being patronised."

He burst out laughing. "And you would never patronise anyone, would you?"

Heat rose to her face. He turned every single thing she said around on her. It was infuriating.

As they passed the statues of Emma and Edward in the atrium and made their way through double-doors into a new hallway, lined on both sides by classrooms, he gave her a knowing look.

"You're that famous chick, aren't you? The politician's kid."

She raised her chin. "I'm not a chick."

"But you're her, right?"

"I'm Gray Langtry, if that's who you were thinking of. I'm not famous for anything but getting stabbed. Who are you?"

"I'm Dylan James," he said. "I'm nobody."

Gray was sceptical. "You're not nobody if you're here."

He stepped back to allow her into the stairwell first and said, "I'm nobody compared to you."

She was no longer sure whether or not he was making fun of her. He was impossible to read. Luckily, they reached the doorway of the English classroom a few seconds later. They were nearly late and the room was already mostly full. There were two empty seats at the back, and one lone seat in the front row.

"Dylan! Over here." A stunning girl with glossy dark hair and perfect skin motioned toward the two empty seats next to her.

Sophie Montgomery had to be the most beautiful student at Cimmeria. Tall and willowy, she wafted through the corridors like a princess through a castle. Other pretty girls constantly clustered around her, hair flowing, teeth flashing, like stars near a sun, happy just to be in her orbit.

Dylan lifted a hand in reply and Sophie's face lit up, her perfect smile brightening.

Of course he's one of Sophie's disciples, Gray thought. That's so typical.

"Oh well. It's been great talking," Gray said, and strode away to the front of the room and its lone empty chair. She dropped her book bag on the floor with a thud.

She knew she'd over-reacted in the library, and she wasn't sure why she had. She could have ignored him, or been distant and polite. Now he could tell everyone that the prime minister's kid was a stone cold bitch, and completely up herself. And he wouldn't be wrong.

Plus, she'd been totally anti-American, and that was probably an international incident for all she knew, given who her mother was.

She was relieved when the teacher walked in and closed the door.

"Settle down everyone." Eloise Derleth was small and athletic, with straight brown hair and trendy glasses. Like all the teachers at Cimmeria, she insisted everyone call her by her first name. It had taken Gray a solid week to get used to this and it still felt weird. The worst was Allie. How could she have a headmistress called "Allie"?

"I trust you all did your reading last night and are ready to sit down and discuss Edna St. Vincent Millay." As she spoke, she wrote the name on the whiteboard in distinctive long letters that curved slightly to the left. "Did you love it?"

The room responded with silence, but she treated it like a rousing affirmation. "Yes, me too. You all had several poems to read, but I'd like to start with First Fig. I need a willing victim…." She paused. "Sorry, not victim. I keep doing that. Volunteer. I need a volunteer to read today. Who's up for it?"

Several hands shot up. Gray, her mind still mulling over the conversation with Dylan, stared at her book, the words meaningless and shifting on the paper in front of her.

Why had she been so mean? He'd seemed arrogant but she could have been misreading him. She'd just lost her temper in an instant. The whole scene had left her feeling unpleasant and guilty.

It took her a second to realise Eloise was saying her name.

"Gray? Gray Langtry? Are you with us…?"

The students behind her tittered. She had the sinking feeling the teacher had been calling her name for some time.

Flushing, she sat up straighter. "Yes?" Her voice was timorous, and the laughter behind her grew louder.

Eloise gave her a meaningful look. "Oh, good. You're awake. I'm afraid it's your lucky day. I've selected you out of an audience of…" She glanced around the room, counting silently. "…eighteen students, to be our star reader." When Gray still blinked at her blankly, she added, "The poem First Fig, one of the three you were assigned to study last night. A poem you undoubtedly stayed up until two a.m. researching. I'd like you to read that one, please."

Slowly, Gray got to her feet, and picked up her textbook.

This day kept getting worse. She should have taken the seat at the back, even if it was next to Dylan Sodding James. That would have been better. Anything would have been better. Prison would have been better.

It took her a second to locate the correct poem on the page. Behind her, the titters had begun again in the awkward silence.

At least the poem was short.

"First Fig," she read aloud. Her voice cracked, and she paused to steady it. "By Edna St. Vincent Millay."

> "My candle burns at both ends;
>   It will not last the night;
> But ah, my foes, and oh, my friends—
>   It gives a lovely light!"

As she dropped back into her seat, someone applauded sardonically behind her, but Eloise silenced them with a fierce look.

"Right. What does it all mean, Gray? What is our poet talking about? Who lights both ends of a candle?"

Gray had, in fact, done her homework the night before. More than that – when she'd first read the poem it had resonated with her. "It means she's working too hard. She's not resting. And the lovely light thing – it's irony, right? It means she's burning out, but the way she's going… it's a beautiful thing. She doesn't care."

"I don't think a poetry reviewer could have said it any better." Eloise gave her a look of pure approval, and Gray felt at least five percent better. "The only way to burn a candle at both ends is to hold it horizontally, which causes the flame to burn more brightly, the wax to melt faster, and the candle to disappear, leaving darkness behind. The metaphor refers to someone who is overworked, overtired, perhaps even giddy with exhaustion – or in love, and not sleeping because of the excitement of a new relationship. They know they need rest. But they don't want to stop." She paused. "Now then, what do we know about Edna St. Vincent Millay, aside from the fact that her name is quite a mouthful?"

A silence fell. "She was a poet?" some wag suggested from the back. Eloise shot him a cutting look.

"Come on, people." She clapped her hands sharply. "Wake up. What do we know about this poet?"

"She was bisexual," a voice suggested.

Giggles rose again and were almost immediately suppressed.

Eloise nodded. "She was indeed. Openly, in fact, at a time of sexual repression. She was out and proud before the phrase even existed. It takes a brave person to do that." She motioned for more. "What else?"

"She was American, wasn't she?" another voice called out.

Gray stiffened. It was Dylan's voice.

"Yes indeed. She was one of our American cousins like others I could name," Eloise said.

As the teacher continued to talk, Gray twisted around in her chair. From the back row, Dylan met her gaze with a look of beatific innocence.

Clearly, she hadn't heard the last of him.

SIX

Somehow, Edna St. Vincent Millay changed the direction of Gray's day. After English, her other classes passed without drama or pain. Right after her last lesson she ran into Minal Patel, who cried out across the crowded corridor, "Hey Gray! Nice to see you with all your clothes on for a change."

As everyone turned to look, Gray burst out laughing. Minal reminded her of Chloe in the best ways. Her personality was exuberant and absolutely everyone seemed to know her. During their short walk down the hallway, at least a dozen people stopped to say hi, to ask Minal questions, or to tell her things, and each time Minal would say, "Do you know Gray?" Or just, super casually, "This is Gray." By the time they reached the end of the corridor, she felt like she'd met half the people at the school.

"Do you want to study together?" Gray suggested, impulsively. "We could go to the library."

Minal grimaced. "I have an extra science lab after this. I should warn you that I'm a complete geek. It runs in my family like a genetic disorder. But will you promise to sit with me and my friends at dinner tonight? It would be so cool."

Gray didn't hesitate. "I'd love that," she said.

"Yay!" Minal bounced on her heels, beaming at her. "So many people are dying to meet you. I'm going to introduce you to everyone." She glanced at her phone. "Gotta go. The lab's all the way upstairs at the other end of the wing. See you in the dining hall at seven."

With that, she shot away whippet fast, her dark hair flying behind her. Gray smiled as she watched her go. No wonder the whole school adored her.

As she strolled from the classroom wing to the main building her steps were lighter. In the atrium she passed two girls she recognised as friends of Minal and they both waved.

"Hi Gray," one of them said, and she could have hugged her.

To her own amazement, she thought she might go and hang out in the common room. She'd avoided it solidly the entire time she'd been here, but right now, she felt like she could handle anything.

When she reached it, the room was crowded and raucous – two students were hammering out a pop song on the piano, as everyone around them hurled jovial abuse. Others were playing board games, or clustered around laptops.

She was on the verge of walking in when she noticed Dylan James sitting by himself at the back, absorbed in a book. Still feeling guilty about how she'd handled things earlier, Gray decided she wasn't ready to face him again just yet.

Alone in the library, she finished all her homework for the day. Only when she was wrapping up did she remember the book on suffrage she'd found that morning. She hurried back to the history section. It was divided by years so it was easy to find her way to the late nineteenth century. When she reached the shelf where it should have been, though, the book was gone.

Gray frowned at the empty space. It was odd that someone had taken that book on the same day she'd discovered it.

Determined now, she headed for the tall desk at the front of the room.

Librarian Erin Walsh, who was shuffling through a stack of index cards, looked up. "Checking something out?"

"Actually, the book I wanted isn't there, and I wondered if it was here for re-shelving," Gray explained.

"I can check that for you," Erin said. She wasn't very old – in her twenties probably. She had a pleasingly broad Northern Irish accent, which suited her elven look, with sleek, dark hair cut just above her ears, and nutmeg brown eyes that studied Gray with interest. "Hit me with a name."

When Gray gave her the information, her brow creased. "I'm sure I checked that book out to someone already. Let me look." She spun her chair around, expertly ending up in front of a set of small drawers. After flipping through the cards she spun around again, holding one up triumphantly.

"Yep. Knew it. A Mr. Dylan James checked it out. You want me to put you on the waiting list?"

Dylan sodding James. Again.

Gray wondered, irrationally, if he'd done this as revenge. He must have seen she was interested in the book. Did he suspect she'd come back for it?

Erin was waiting for an answer.

"Sure," she said. "Put me down."

"Miss Gray Langtry… would like to read," the librarian said to herself as she wrote Gray's name on the card. When she finished, she added it to her stack and said, "I swear that book hasn't been checked out in the five years I've been here. Its new popularity fills my jaded heart with joy."

Gray still wondered why Dylan would check out that book, but as she rushed up the staircase to her room, there was no time to dwell on it. Cimmeria's one inviolable rule as far as she could tell was that everyone had to be inside the dining hall by seven o'clock, or they couldn't eat.

After dumping her books on the bed, she hurriedly brushed the tangles out of her cloud of hair. In the mirror her eyes – almost the same shade of blue as the blazer she wore – looked brighter than they'd been in a while. There was colour in her cheeks.

She'd talked to more people in one day than she had in two weeks. For the first time the school didn't seem hollow and cold to her.

As she hurried downstairs her phone buzzed. She read the text from Chloe as she hurried down the stairs.

I told Tyler I'd see a film with him. If it all goes wrong it's your fault! How's life at boarding school today? Still terrible?

Gray paused long enough to type a quick reply.

Slightly less hideous. Might have made a friend.

Chloe's reply was instant.

Hooray! But if your new friend tries to replace me I'll shred her with my nails.

Gray typed back.

No one can replace you. BFF <3.

Before she put her phone away, she noticed she'd missed another call from Jake.

They'd spoken little since she came to Cimmeria. He'd been settling into his life in Leeds, re-united with old friends and his mum and her wife.

All of a sudden, she missed his voice. His northern unflappability. The way he understood politics better than most adults. His cool, discerning gaze. But he was far away, and she had to figure out how to fit in here.

When she reached the foot of the stairs, Julia was waiting.

Gray gave her a surprised smile. "Hey."

"Hey yourself."

There was no evidence of tension in her demeanour, but Gray gave the bodyguard a curious look. The two of them had established a routine. Gray checked in with Julia first thing in the morning and after classes ended. At night, Julia checked Gray's room before she went in. Up until now, that had been it. Julia had often complained about being bored.

But things seemed to be changing. First there'd been Julia's call in the morning, now the sudden escort.

"Is… everything OK?" she asked.

There was a slight but definite pause before Julia replied. "It's all good. I just thought I'd check in with you. You've been busy today."

The bodyguard didn't meet her eyes and Gray wondered what the truth was, but before she could press for more information they reached the crowded dining hall. At the door, Julia said, "Have a good time. See you after dinner," and disappeared down the hallway, talking quietly into the microphone attached to her wrist.

Gray frowned as she watched her go. She was acting so odd. She'd press for more information the next time she saw her. Right now, she needed to find Minal.

During the day the dining hall was a bright noisy space, but at night it was transformed. The round tables were covered with pristine white linen cloths and each place setting glittered with crystal glasses, heavy silver cutlery, and china plates embossed with the school's crest. Candles gleamed on every surface, and a fire crackled in the hearth. The space was filled with the roar of a hundred students talking at once.

Gray was almost the last to arrive, although a few other stragglers hurried by. It was hard to see the back tables from where she stood, but she didn't want to wander around the room. She was still lingering in the doorway trying to decide what to do, when the history teacher August Zelazny strode up to her, his narrow eyes glittering with disapproval.

"Well, are you coming in or guarding the door?" he barked.

Casting one last desperate look around, Gray said, "I… I'm waiting for someone."

He gave an elaborate look at his watch. "I suppose you're aware students are required to be on time for dinner, and on time means seven o'clock. And on time also means sitting in your chair."

"Yes," she said, a bit tetchily. "I know."

He fixed her with a piercing look. "It is seven o'clock. Are you sitting in your chair?"

The room was growing quieter, as those closest to the door scented a drama.

"No... sir," she said.

"Well then, you need to sit down." Zelazny was growing irritable.

Just then though, a voice called out.

"Gray! Over here!"

She looked up to see Minal waving frantically from a table on the far side of the room. Relieved, she left the teacher behind and raced across to her.

"You just saved my life," Gray said, sliding into the seat. "Zelazny was about to arrest me. I think I owe you my first-born child in return."

"Eeuw." Minal wrinkled her nose. "I don't want anyone's kids, including my own. I'm going to be a career woman, with a fancy car and a house with no plastic in it."

"I would have kids." It was Maya, who Gray had sat with at breakfast. She was sitting across from Minal, her blonde curls tamed into a wavy bun. "But I'd prefer kittens."

"Babies are weird looking."

Gray followed these words across the table to where Sophie Montgomery watched her with interest. Her dark hair had been tucked behind a perfect pale ear. "Every baby looks like an alien,"

Sophie said. "It doesn't matter what the parents look like. Even famous people have alien babies. I don't want one of those."

"None of you are ever going to be allowed to babysit for me," a stylish boy with a shock of straight brown hair and smooth tawny skin announced. "Babies are gorgeous."

"You don't have a uterus," Minal informed him. "You are allowed no opinions about babies."

"Prejudice." He shook his head. "It's everywhere."

"I just really want a cat," Maya said to nobody in particular.

Gray tried not to stare at Sophie, who glowed among them like a perfectly cut jewel.

Minal held up her hands. "Everyone, this is Gray. Gray, you already know our resident cat-lady Maya, I think?" Maya inclined her head. "And this is Sophie, who thinks babies look like aliens. And Kyle Sindal, who is horrified by all of us."

"Nice to meet—" the boy began, but Sophie spoke over him before he'd finished, still watching Gray with steady curiosity.

"At last, a celebrity in our midst." She angled forward, resting her perfect chin on a slim hand. "We've had lots of politician's kids here but never a prime minister's. What happened to you – that must have been absolutely terrifying. Is that why they sent you here? For safety?"

Her accent was old money, "ab-so-lootleh," and the questions were way too personal. Gray felt illuminated in her gaze, a tiger in the crosshairs of a millionaire's hunting rifle.

Her mind went blank. "I... uh..."

Before she could think of an answer, a familiar American voice said, "Oh good! You saved me a seat." Dylan James slid into the chair next to Sophie, and looked around at the circle of faces. "What did I miss?"

"Crikey. You shaved that close." Kyle glanced at the door, which was solidly closed.

"Oh, come on." Sophie rested a possessive hand on the American's shoulder, her lips curving up. "Dylan makes his own rules. He could get away with murder. Even Zelazny loves him."

With an amiable shrug. Dylan set a book down on the table at his elbow. Gray didn't have to look at it to know what the title would be.

"I was reading in the common room, and lost track of time." He tapped the leather cover. "It's a history book so Zelazny gave me a pass."

"If it was about Napoleon he'd give you an award." Minal's tone was dry. "The man is obsessed."

"He once saw me with a book about Napoleon and talked to me for ten minutes." Maya shuddered. "Napoleon is not a hero in my country."

"He's not a hero here either," Minal pointed out.

"I hear he's big in France, though." Kyle reached for a crystal jug of water which sat on a gleaming silver tray and poured himself a glass. "Very popular."

While they bantered, Gray shot a surreptitious sideways glance at Dylan. Sophie still had her hand on his lean shoulder. He was listening to the others with a wry smile on his lips. They made an annoyingly pretty couple.

A brief silence fell and Sophie filled it. "I realised today it's less than two weeks until the Winter Ball and I completely panicked. I'm not even remotely ready."

She addressed this to everyone at the table, but somehow Gray had a feeling her target was Dylan. He looked away, as if not really listening. But Minal and the others brightened.

"It should be good this year – I hear the invitation list is immense," Minal said.

"Once again I have no date," Kyle sighed. "Always the bridesmaid. Never the bride."

"You like that guy Ben in your history class," Minal dug her elbow into his ribs. "He's super cute. You should ask him."

"Maybe." He sounded unconvinced.

"Do it," she insisted. "You'd be the cutest couple."

"I don't even know if he plays for my team," he reminded her. "It's not as easy for me as it is for you."

His tone was gentle but pointed, and Minal put an apologetic hand on his arm and gave it a light squeeze. "I'm sorry. I'll shut up now."

"What about you, Gray?" Sophie asked. "Do you have a date?"

Gray, who had been trying not to think about the annual dance since she got to the school, winced internally. She had no intention of going.

"Haven't really thought about it," she said, shrugging.

"Me neither." Dylan turned to her and changed the subject. "So, has Zelazny given you detention yet?"

"Not yet." Her brow creased. "Is that a thing with him?"

The others made pained faces. "He's a real ball buster about The Rules," Kyle explained. "One wrong step and…" He slashed a finger across his throat.

Minal passed Gray the water jug. The heavy pitcher sparkled as she lifted it to fill her glass.

"Which rules in particular?" she asked, as she filled her glass.

The others gasped.

"Oh, come on." Kyle stared at her. "You must have read The Rules. They were in your information packet. They are the actual Bible of Cimmeria Academy. Or at least the Magna Carta. Everyone has to memorise them."

Across the table Maya was nodding seriously. "They're very strict."

Gray vaguely recalled a stack of papers she'd been handed by her mother the week before she'd arrived at Cimmeria. There'd been so much going on back then, she'd barely glanced at it before shoving the pages into her suitcase.

"Not exactly," she confessed. "I didn't realise it mattered."

"She hasn't read The Rules." Kyle looked around the table in disbelief. "She just… didn't read them."

"You should probably read them," Minal advised.

"You could just get your bodyguard to tell you what they are," Dylan suggested. "She went to school here after all."

"She went here?" Minal sounded surprised. "What year?"

Gray stared at Dylan. She'd never told anyone her bodyguard had once been a student here. Julia had asked her to keep the information to herself.

"How did you know that?" she asked.

At that moment the double doors at the far end of the room swung open, and black-clad staff strode in, carrying trays of food. Everyone was instantly distracted.

"Thank God." Kyle sagged back in his chair. "I thought they'd decided to let us starve this time."

"It's roast chicken tonight," Maya observed, with relish.

Sophie leaned over to whisper something in Dylan's ear, and he smiled, turning to talk to her quietly, making it clear he had no intention of answering Gray's question.

It seemed to her the two of them looked like a matched set – Dylan long and lean, with warm brown skin and high cheekbones. And Sophie, tall and elegant. They belonged in a celebrity magazine, not a boarding school.

Minal made a joke as platters of bronzed chicken, steaming heaps of emerald broccoli and vivid orange carrots – were set on the table. Gray smiled, but her mind was still on the question Dylan hadn't answered.

One way or another, she intended to find out how the hell Dylan James could possibly know something she'd never told a soul.

SEVEN

After dinner, they trooped out toward the common room, talking and laughing. The others, still astonished that she hadn't read The Rules, kept peppering Gray with real and false requirements. ("You must be in your room by eleven." "You must brush your hair 100 strokes before bedtime." "You must wear a purple scarf on Wednesdays.") She was laughing helplessly as they joined the crowd gathered at the front looking for a space, but every seat was already filled.

"It's packed." Sophie wrinkled her aquiline nose. "Let's go somewhere else."

"The library?" Gray suggested.

"We don't want to study," Kyle scoffed.

For a second, silence fell as they all considered their options. Then Sophie glanced at Minal. "Let's go to the chapel."

"Yes." Minal bounced excitedly.

"Sounds good to me," Kyle agreed. "Has anyone got any booze?"

"I've got a bottle I can bring," Sophie said.

"I've got some doobage." Kyle tapped the breast pocket of his blazer.

"It's a party, then," Sophie declared. "Everyone grab your coats and meet at the edge of the woods in five minutes."

Dylan, who along with Gray and Minal had remained silent throughout this, followed them back into the hallway. He said nothing as they climbed the stairs to the first floor and separated, the boys heading right toward the boys' dorm stairs, and the girls left. But somehow Gray got the feeling he disapproved of the plan.

Gray, too, was conflicted. If she told Julia what they were doing the bodyguard would insist on coming with her, and that would ruin everything. Of course, there was no pressing reason to tell her, really. The grounds were perfectly safe. A huge fence surrounded the school and the gate was kept locked at all times. What danger could there possibly be?

The thought made her feel better about not telling Julia the truth. The chapel was in the woods behind the school building. They'd just go there and come back again. No harm. No foul.

In her room, she grabbed her coat, and paused in front of the mirror to smooth her hair and reapply lip gloss. Her chest buzzed with a pleasing mixture of excitement and nerves.

Studying her own blue eyes in the mirror, she paused. She didn't need to read The Rules to know that going out to the chapel at night to drink booze was undoubtedly a violation of about a dozen regulations, not to mention laws. If she got caught, her mother would be livid.

But I won't get caught, she reasoned. No one will ever know.

The others clearly did this all the time. If they got into a lot of trouble for it, they wouldn't be so blithe about it.

She'd be fine. They would all go and have a good time. And then she'd come back to her room without Julia ever knowing.

Her mind made up, she switched off the light, closed the door behind her, and hurried down the stairs, pulling on her coat as she walked.

When she reached the entrance hall, with its worn stone floor and tall candle holders, it was empty. The students were all in the common room or the library, the staff were cleaning up after dinner, and the teachers had retired to their own rooms. There was no one around to watch her tentatively try the front door handle. No one to object when it swung open and let in a freezing December breeze that made her shiver. The air carried a frosty wintery scent of pine needles and cold earth and the promise of adventure.

She stepped out into it eagerly, and closed the door behind her.

Aside from a few lights at the edge of the building, the grounds were unlit. Across the gravel drive, a long expanse of lawn spread smoothly into the shadows. Beyond it, the woods were a dark blur.

Gray shuddered. She hated the dark. The idea of making her way across to the woods by herself made her stomach churn. But she couldn't pass up on this party because of a childish fear.

Anyway, she couldn't go yet. First, she had to deal with Julia.

Retrieving her phone from her pocket, Gray scrolled to her number and pressed the call button.

The bodyguard answered on the first ring. "What's up, Firefly?"

Her cheerful voice sent a shard of guilt into Gray's heart. But she wasn't going to change her mind now.

"Just checking in."

"How was dinner?"

"It was good." Gray forced a light note into her voice. "I'm heading to the library to work on my history essay, and then I'm going straight up to bed. There's no need for you to wait up, really."

She must have been convincing, because Julia said, "Well, if you're safe and snug in the library, that's fine. I'll go down to the gym and get a workout in. But call me when you're ready to go up to bed, I'll walk you up."

"Cool. Have a good workout." Gray kept her tone light but her shoulders slumped as she put the phone away.

"You sure you want to do this?" The words, which emerged from the shadows at her right shoulder, sounded for all the world like the voice of her conscience.

She turned to see Dylan James leaning against the school wall, watching her with hooded eyes. He must have been there the whole time.

"Bloody hell," she spluttered. "Are you stalking me or something? Why are you everywhere all of a sudden?"

Even in the dim light she couldn't miss the slight smirk. "Oh come on, get over yourself. You're not that famous. I'm on my way to the chapel just like you."

This managed to be devastating and disinterested in equal parts. Gray was glad he couldn't see her face reddening in the dark.

"All I was saying is," he continued, "since you haven't read The Rules yet, let me assure you that drinking alcohol on campus is frowned upon."

"I know that," she snapped, stung. "And I'm not going to drink. I'm just going to hang out."

"And you think it's a good idea to lie to your bodyguard?" His eyebrows rose. "Wasn't there some kind of problem a couple of months ago? Some sort of attack?"

She glared. "That's my business."

He considered her for a long moment, his expression inscrutable. Then he shrugged. "Well, I'm going that way, too. We might as well walk together."

"Oh so, it's wrong for me to break The Rules but it's fine for you. That makes sense." The words burst out, driven mostly by embarrassment. He'd already started walking away, and his reply floated lightly back to her on the cold breeze. "Last time I checked, I wasn't the daughter of the prime minister."

Gray listened to his footsteps crunching on the gravel drive, uncertain what to do. She didn't want to go anywhere with him. But if she didn't go with him, she'd have to walk through the darkness to the woods by herself.

Swearing under her breath, she set off in his wake.

They headed across the long curved drive, and then a minute later reached the manicured lawn, soggy from earlier rain.

It was the first time they'd been alone together since dinner, and Gray decided to take advantage of it. "How did you know Julia went to school here?" she asked accusingly. "I didn't tell anyone that."

His back was to her so she couldn't see his expression. There was a pause before he replied. "I guess I heard something about it."

"Who?" Gray let doubt ring in her voice.

He turned to look at her. "I overheard her talking to Carter West. It was really obvious they knew each other back when they were students here."

"Really?" Gray couldn't hide her surprise. Julia had told her she'd been a student at Cimmeria and that she'd moved to another school when she was seventeen, but she'd never mentioned knowing Carter, or anyone else.

"Yeah, it was kind of clear they hadn't seen each other in a long time." He thought for a second. "It was kind of awkward actually. Like, maybe they'd left things on bad terms or something, and now they were sorry."

"Huh." Gray was at a loss for words. Now that she thought about it, Julia and Carter did work together really well. They had an easy connection. It would make sense if they'd known each other in the past. And yet Julia had said nothing.

Maybe I'm not the only one with secrets.

"As far as I can tell, she knows everyone here." He dropped back to walk beside her, pulling his jacket tighter against the freezing breeze. She could see his breath as he spoke – puffs of pale steam against the dark night. "She talks to Zelazny like they're old pals. And she definitely knows Eloise, the English teacher. The only one who doesn't seem to like her is Allie."

Gray felt suddenly embarrassed about how little she knew about her bodyguard's life. Julia had been basically her only friend since she got here and yet Dylan had noticed more about her than she had.

"Guess I missed all that," she admitted, kicking a stone across the grass. "I need to pay more attention."

He gave her an interested look. "Don't beat yourself up. I mean, someone tried to kill you. You left your school, your family, your friends. You'd be forgiven for not noticing everything going on in your bodyguard's life right now."

For once, he didn't sound smug or insulting. In fact, if she didn't know better she'd think he sounded almost… sympathetic? But that had to be wrong.

"Maybe," she said. "But she's also my friend."

There was a pause before he replied. "Well. Next time you see her, ask her." With that, he strode ahead again.

Gray gave his back a baffled look. She couldn't figure him out.

She trudged behind him, her school-issued leather Oxford shoes sinking in the soft turf. There was almost no wind but it was getting colder. In three weeks it would be Christmas and the term would be over. Would she go home? Or stay here alone, for safety? Her parents hadn't made their minds up yet.

She didn't want to think what it would be like to be alone in this big building over the holidays.

While they'd been walking, the clouds had cleared. To distract herself, she tilted her head back and looked up. The sky was alight with stars.

"I never knew there were so many," she said.

"So many what?"

"Stars."

Dylan followed her gaze, his steps slowing. "Yeah, they're something else." He glanced at her. "Guess you're a city kid, like me."

"I've always lived in London," she said. "Where are you from?"

She expected "New York" or "Los Angeles". Something flashy.

He smiled, his head tilted back as he gazed at the star-filled sky. "Houston, Texas.'

"Really? I wouldn't have thought you were Texan," she said, not hiding her surprise.

"Why? No cowboy hat?" His tone was lightly mocking.

"Something like that, I guess."

"I left mine back home," he told her, and suddenly she thought she could hear a faint southern accent. "Texas is a modern place these days. Lots of shopping malls. Lots of SUVs. Not as many horses as you'd think." He lowered his gaze to meet hers. "It isn't like the movies."

"Well, that's disappointing," she said.

He laughed, and Gray found herself smiling.

"Tell you one thing, though. It's a hell of a lot warmer than this place," he said, shivering, and the two of them began walking again.

As they neared the edge of the woods, Gray heard voices ahead. She began to hurry toward them but Dylan touched her arm.

"Wait. Are you really sure you want to do this? You could still go back, you know."

It was such an odd thing to say. As if she were about to walk too close to the edge of a cliff.

Her brow creased. "I'll be fine," she assured him. "I'm only staying an hour. Nothing will happen. Why are you so worried?"

He hesitated, and she got the feeling there was something he wanted to tell her. But in the end, all he said was, "Be careful."

"I'm always careful," she said, and ran ahead to meet the others.

EIGHT

As Gray passed the treeline, the silvery glow of starlight disappeared behind the canopy of branches, and the night grew darker. In the shadows, she could make out a cluster of figures standing near the path. Minal, the smallest, waved at her.

"Sorry we're late," Gray said, running up to her.

Kyle was next to Sophie, her white cashmere coat ghostly in the darkness. Maya, tall and sleek in a dark coat, studied something on the tree trunk next to her. Sophie had eyes only for Dylan, and she crossed the wooded path to whisper something in his ear.

Kyle, his jacket too light for the frosty weather, was hopping up and down to keep warm. "Thank God. Now, can we get going? It's as cold as a Tory's heart tonight." He shivered, blowing on his fingers.

Minal elbowed him hard. He gave her a baffled look. She frowned, shooting a significant glance at Gray.

His eyes widened as he realised what he'd said. "Oh, bollocks. Sorry, Gray. I didn't mean your mum."

She shrugged it off. "Don't worry. I've heard worse."

"Let's get going," Sophie said, impatiently. She and Dylan took the lead, walking side by side. Minal and Maya fell in behind them, but Kyle hung back to apologise again.

"I'm such an idiot. I shouldn't have said that. I just forgot who you were for a second." His warm brown eyes were filled with contrition.

"It's really alright," she assured him. "I'm used to it. It doesn't bother me."

"I hope you mean that. It's weird but, now that I kind of know you, you're not Gray the famous daughter anymore. You're just... Gray."

Her heart swelled. This was what she'd hoped for. Here inside the protective fence, with no paparazzi, no insulting news stories, no threats, no violence – she could just be herself again at last.

"It's cool," she said, as they moved into the darkness. "Anyway, I'm not sure I agree with my mother on politics."

"That's got to be awkward at home," he said. "Wouldn't it be totally weird if you joined another party? Would your mum ban you from Number 10?"

Gray thought about her mother inviting Jake to their flat as a surprise for her, even though his dad was the head of the Labour party – her worst enemies.

"In the past, maybe," she conceded. "But she's changed in the last few months. Now she'd probably invite all my communist friends over for tea and cake, and they'd totally like her. Even Stalin would love my mum if he got to know her."

"Now Stalin..." Maya's voice floated out of the shadows ahead of them. "He did not have a heart."

"This conversation is so random," Minal said. "I love it."

"If you had to choose between Stalin or Genghis Khan for prime minister, who would you choose?" Dylan called back over his shoulder.

"Genghis Khan," everyone chorused.

"Stalin was hot when he was young, though," Minal pointed out.

"Psychopaths always are," Sophie told her. "It's the same with all apex predators – wolves, tigers, lions, eagles – they're all beautiful. That's how they get away with eating you."

"Yeah," Kyle agreed, "While they're eating your heart you just lie there going, 'Take it, you gorgeous thing. I don't need it.'"

Their laughter echoed off the trees, drowning out the rush of the wind through the branches. It was freezing cold and yet Gray felt warm and light. It occurred to her that she wasn't afraid at all, even though they were deep in the darkness now.

For the first time she wondered what she was really afraid of. Was she really scared of the dark? Or of being alone?

"How far is it to the chapel?" she asked Kyle.

He gave her a puzzled look. "Haven't you been there before?"

She shook her head. "I meant to, but it's been so cold and rainy since I got here."

"Hasn't read The Rules. Hasn't been to the chapel." Kyle ticked her offenses off on his fingers. "It's like you spend all your time studying or something."

She couldn't tell from his tone whether he thought this was a good thing or a bad thing.

"Don't worry, Gray," Sophie called back. "We'll corrupt you."

"She doesn't need corrupting. She's been to Bijou," Minal reminded her.

"She's thrown up in front of Bijou," Kyle corrected her.

"Oh God." Gray covered her face with her hands. "You saw that story?"

"I adored that story." Sophie told her. "You're a hero to me. If you're going to be famous, be famous and decadent."

Minal glanced back. "Your mum must have been furious."

"I was grounded forever," Gray confessed. "Like, until I came here, I was grounded the whole time. Technically I'm still grounded, as far as I know."

By now, they'd reached a stone wall, ancient and pale. Gray's eyes had adjusted to the dark, and she could see it ran for a long distance alongside the footpath, broken only by an arched wooden gate, blackened with age.

"Here we are," Minal called running up to it. When she pushed it, the gate swung open without a sound.

"Thank God." Kyle hurried after her. "My teeth are chattering."

"It's not that cold." Maya's tone was dismissive.

"You're used to it," he said. "Poles are hearty stock. I'm a fragile English flower."

Maya swept through the gate, her blonde head held high. Kyle appealed to Minal. "It's cold out here, right? It's not just me?"

"It's chilly," Gray agreed, supportively.

"I love the way Maya says whatever she thinks," Sophie confided, lowering her voice and leaning closer. "She's so brutal.

I aspire to being that blunt." Her breath smelled faintly of alcohol, and Gray realised she'd already been drinking. She wondered if the others had too.

She hadn't had a drink since that night at Bijou when she'd drunk too much and thrown up in the street in front of the paparazzi. It had put her off drinking ever since.

On the other side of the wall a short path led across a clearing to a small stone chapel with a high peaked roof. Gravestones and tilted stone crosses softened with age loomed from the shadows around it. Dead winter grass curved black against the pale stone.

"Spooky, isn't it?" Dylan appeared at her side as the others walked ahead. "This place gives me the creeps."

"I love it," Minal said, approaching the chapel door. "It appeals to my inner Wednesday Addams."

"You really are her, though," Kyle told her. "You have a heart of pure goth."

"Aw, thanks." Minal looked genuinely touched.

The door handle was a heavy iron ring, and she grasped it with both hands, turning it with effort. As the door swung open, revealing nothing but darkness, she said, "I hope someone remembered matches." Her voice echoed. *Matches…matches…*

"I did." Kyle pulled a small box from his pocket, holding it up as he walked in behind her.

The others followed, chattering and laughing, but Gray hung back. Now that she was here, it felt wrong. This was an actual church. Somehow she'd envisioned an ex-chapel. One that didn't feel religious. But this was the real thing.

Dylan turned back to look at her. "Bit late to back out now."

"I'm not backing out," she insisted. "I'm just thinking."

She lingered in the doorway. Ahead, a glimmer of light flared, and the others cheered.

"You could think inside, where it's warmer," he pointed out.

"Fine." Gray stepped in, and the door latched behind her with an icy clang of metal against metal.

It was immediately clear there was no electricity. The others used Kyle's matches to light candles in tall holders and simple iron candelabra suspended from the ceiling. In the flickering light, the small nave came to life.

The walls were covered, floor to ceiling, with paintings. Not just ordinary paintings, though. These were ancient and faded with time. In the dancing flames, she saw chaotic pictures – a bird, a dragon, a tree – and words. Poems or stories.

It was almost too much to absorb, and Gray turned slowly to take it all in, her lips parted with surprise.

"Wild, isn't it?" Dylan said. "This place blows my mind. I think it might be older than my country."

"My dude," Kyle said from across the room where he was lighting the last candles, "This place is seven hundred years older than your country."

"Alright, alright," Dylan chuckled. "There's no need to rub it in."

"The chapel is older than the school building," Minal explained to Gray. "By a lot. There used to be a small village here – there are still some stone cottages left around. They were all on the property of a wealthy landowner. Eventually his house became the school. Check this out. This is my favourite." She pointed at the painting of a dragon, scales clearly drawn on its back, soaring toward a white dove, which, wings spread wide, barely escaped its claws. "The dragon represents the devil."

"But you mustn't miss the school motto." Sophie pointed languidly at the words above the door.

Gray squinted at the faded shapes of the painted letters.

"Exitus acta probat."

"How's your Latin?" Kyle asked, blowing out a match.

"Awful," she admitted.

"It means 'The ends justify the means'."

"That… is not how mottos are meant to work," Gray said.

"It's all about winning, darling," Sophie called from a pew where she'd stretched out, her feet propped up on the back of the pew in front of her. She held up a small bottle of amber liquid. "Anyone want some? Dylan?"

The American student shook his head, and stayed beside Gray.

It looked like dismissal, and a frown darkened Sophie's features, but then Kyle dropped onto the pew next to her and held out his hand. She passed him the bottle and he took a drink. When he'd finished, he blew air from between pursed lips. "Whiskey. The drink of queens."

After handing the bottle back, he pulled a rolled cigarette from his breast pocket and retrieved his matches, lighting up. Instantly, sweet-sour marijuana smoke drifted through the air, chasing away the lingering scent of dust and incense.

Sophie held the bottle out in Gray's direction. "Interested? I mean, I know this isn't exactly Bijou but…"

Gray hesitated. One part of her was tempted to lose control for a while. Take risks like she used to. But then she thought of her father's voice when he finally told her the truth about what was going on. "We're trusting you with this information," he'd said. "And we're counting on you to help us. We think you're mature enough to handle this."

"No thanks." She kept her tone light. "I'm not great with booze, as you might have guessed from reading the papers. I tend to throw up on everything."

"Maybe you just haven't tried hard enough," Sophie suggested. She turned to proffer the bottle to Maya, who sat down on the pew in front of her, and took a ladylike sip, wrinkling her nose at the taste.

"I'm great with booze," Sophie said, her eyes on Dylan as Kyle handed her the spliff. She took a lingering drag, blowing out the smoke in a velvety cloud that swirled around her. "Very, very good at it. Years of practice."

Still, Dylan didn't glance back at her. Instead, he stayed near the wall. Minal, Gray noticed, was ignoring the three on the pews and staying near the two of them as they examined the ancient paintings.

"Look at this one." Dylan pointed at a painting of a tree. The tangled mass of roots beneath it formed the words "TREE OF LIFE" in curved and twisted letters. The paint was chipped in the middle, Gray noticed, as if someone had hit it with something.

"I know I sound like a typical Yank," Dylan said, "but this place is incredible. We're standing where people have stood for nearly a thousand years. Where they sang and prayed."

There was something charming about his genuine enthusiasm. Gray, who had grown up with castles and ancient churches, and who had been dragged to historic houses and gardens by her parents since she was small, was inclined to find it all dull without actually looking at it. Seeing it through his eyes, she realised how extraordinary it was.

"I hadn't thought of it that way," she admitted, watching the way the paintings seemed to move and shimmer in the dancing flames of the candle light. "It's really beautiful."

"Did you know Henry VIII came here once?" Minal asked. "He may have stood right where we are."

Dylan shook his head. "That's so wild. This country – even this school – it's like walking through history."

As he spoke, Gray observed him surreptitiously. His hair was cropped short, emphasising the angular lines of his face. He looked older than sixteen, she thought – more like eighteen. But that might just be because he had an air of maturity. A kind of knowingness she couldn't quite identify.

Sensing her gaze, he glanced over and caught her looking. "What?" he asked, with a half-smile.

"Nothing." She looked away, her gaze flitting to the window next to his left shoulder. Through the thick glass, she could see trees swaying in the breeze. There was an enormous yew tree in the churchyard – its roots so old they rose out of the earth, bending and curving like arms.

Someone was standing beside it.

She stepped closer to get a better look. On the other side of the window, the shadowy figure broke loose and moved stealthily away.

"Is someone else meeting us here?" she asked, trying to see where the person had gone.

"No. Why?" Instantly serious, Dylan stepped closer. "Did you see someone?"

"Maybe. I'm not sure. I thought for a second..." She squinted into the darkness. There was nothing beneath the tree now except shadows. "Never mind. It was probably nothing."

"Don't doubt yourself. What did you see?" The intensity in Dylan's voice took her aback.

"It's just... it looked like a man," she said.

He spun on his heel and headed for the door. "Stay inside," he barked with sudden authority, talking fast. "Nobody leaves this building."

Gray stared at him with her mouth open. Before anyone could recover enough to ask questions, he crossed the stone floor and disappeared outside, slamming the old door.

"What is it?" Sophie called from the pew. "Are we being invaded?"

"I'm not saying it's aliens," Maya giggled. 'But it's aliens.'

The bottle they were sharing was half empty now.

"He's so masterful," Kyle sighed. "I'd do anything he said. I'm not moving a millimetre."

"You fancy him so much it's tragic," Sophie said.

"Yeah, well, so do you." He reached for the bottle.

Minal turned to Gray and said quietly, "Did you really see someone out there?"

"I thought I did. But it's so dark outside. It could have been branches." She pressed her face against the cold glass.

Outside, she saw Dylan hurrying between the gravestones, his head tilted down as if searching for something in the dirt. When he neared the yew tree he crouched low, reaching out to touch something. He looked up, scanning the trees around him. Then he moved in the same direction the shape had gone earlier.

"What's he doing?" Minal stood beside her.

"I don't know," Gray said.

The door flew open with a bang. They all jumped.

Dylan strode back in.

"We have to go," he said firmly. "Now."

NINE

The others exchanged baffled looks. Sophie didn't lift her legs from the pew in front of her.

"But we just got here," she protested. "It's supposed to be a party."

"I'm confused now." Maya twisted around on the pew to see Dylan better. "What exactly did you see out there?"

"Nothing to worry about. But I think we need to go all the same." There was a carefully controlled edge to his voice that set off warning signals. Gray knew that tone. Julia used it when there was something she wasn't telling her. Something bad.

"If you didn't see anyone, why can't we stay?" Sophie demanded petulantly.

"Because Gray saw something where there should be nothing," he said evenly. "And someone tried to kill her five weeks ago, so I think she should go back, and I don't feel comfortable leaving anyone out here alone."

"They arrested that guy." Sophie gave Gray a resentful look. "Besides, she's perfectly fine now. You're fine, aren't you, Gray?"

"Sophie." Dylan's voice was stern.

Kyle got to his feet with a shrug. "We might as well go back. We're nearly out of booze anyway."

Maya stood as well, and followed him to the door. "Maybe she saw a ghost. I've always believed the woods are haunted."

The two of them stood beside Gray and Minal. Sophie watched this migration but didn't move a muscle. They all turned to her.

Dylan gave her a meaningful look. "Are you coming or not?"

In the candlelight, Sophie's eyes glittered like chips of ice.

Gray found herself holding her breath, waiting to see what the other girl would do.

After a long second, Sophie dropped her feet to the floor with a thud, and rose. With her head held high, she strolled regally across the nave.

"I hate it when a party ends early," she said, shooting Gray a frosty look as she joined Dylan at the door.

Gray's heart sank. Whatever inroads she might have made at Cimmeria today, she had a feeling she'd just lost Sophie Montgomery forever.

One by one, they trooped out into the night until Minal stopped in the doorway. "What about the candles?"

Dylan, who had already been heading for the gate, stopped. "Damn, I forgot. Would you mind blowing them out? I need to keep everyone together out here."

"On it." Minal dashed back into the building.

"I'll help," Gray said, and ran after her before Dylan could stop her.

Inside, Minal climbed up on a pew to blow out the candles on the fixture hanging from the ceiling. She made sure the others were out of earshot before leaning over to ask quietly, "What exactly did you see out there?"

"It was just a shadow," Gray told her as she blew out the candles in the tall, metal holder. "But it kind of looked like a man. I can't be certain, but somehow I got the feeling he'd been watching us."

After that, Minal didn't ask any more questions. They both worked fast. One candle at a time, the room descended into darkness. When the last flame went out, Gray could suddenly see nothing at all.

"It's really dark," she said. Her voice echoed eerily off the stone walls.

Remembering what Maya had said about ghosts, she shivered.

"I can't see a thing." Minal's voice seemed to come from everywhere. Seconds later, there was a thud, and Minal's voice again. "Ow."

After that, silence.

Irrational fear gripped Gray's heart. "Minal?" she called, her voice too loud.

A scuffling of feet against stone made her jump. And then Minal spoke. "Over here. Be careful – I nearly killed myself on a sodding pew."

Gray stepped cautiously toward her voice, hands outstretched. At first she felt nothing but cold air. Then, to her relief, the warm solidity of the other girl's hand. Clinging to each other, they made their way to the aisle and then across to the door.

As they rushed outside, the wind picked up, rustling through the branches of the trees with an ominous, low roar. Graves jutted from the earth like rotting teeth. Shivering, Gray scanned the churchyard for signs of the man she'd spotted from the window. She could see nothing in the darkness, but all the same, she wanted to get out of here.

You could call Julia, a voice in her head whispered. But then she'd have to admit that she'd lied.

No, she decided. She wouldn't call the bodyguard. All they had to do was get back to the school building. Besides, she wasn't sure she'd really seen anyone. The tree branches were swaying in the growing wind, sending shadows swooping. The whole thing could have been a trick played by shadows.

Dylan had gathered the others at the gate, and she and Minal sped over to where they were huddled together. Only Sophie stood apart, her expression as cold as the icy breeze.

"It's got colder," Kyle informed them. He looked pale, his teeth were chattering.

Sophie gave a brittle laugh. "You just haven't drunk enough. I can't feel a thing."

Gray noticed she still held the bottle of whiskey. She wished someone would take it away from her.

"We should move fast," Dylan told them, ignoring Sophie. "Kyle? Are you sober?"

Kyle tried to walk a heel-toe straight line along the edge of the footpath, and promptly lost his balance.

"Ish," he said.

His brow furrowing, Dylan motioned for him to come closer and turned to Minal. "I'm going first, and I'd like you two to come last, is that OK?" His tone was deadly serious and, for once, Kyle didn't make a joke in reply. He and Minal nodded. "If you see or hear anything coming up behind us, don't hesitate," Dylan said. "Shout as loud as you can."

"Got it," Minal said.

Dylan turned to Gray. "I need you to stay close to Sophie and Maya. They've both had too much to drink. Try to keep them moving."

"I'll do my best," she said, heading toward the two girls.

As she passed him, he called after her. "Gray?" She glanced back. "Don't go off the path."

An odd undertone in his voice sent her heart into her throat. He was genuinely worried. She could sense it. Whatever he was telling them, he must have seen something out there.

A high-pitched whine of panic had begun to buzz inside her head and she ordered herself to stay calm. She had to keep it together. Just until they got to the school. She couldn't have another panic attack. Not now.

Dylan set off first. The others followed in a jagged line. His attention was on the path ahead. Behind Gray, Minal and Kyle took on their roles with uncharacteristic seriousness, scanning the trees for trouble.

Maya was quiet, her eyes on the dark forest around them. Only Sophie, who still carried a bottle in her hand, seemed oblivious to the tension.

"I don't understand why we have to do this just because of her," she complained, waving the bottle at Gray before passing it to Maya.

Gray wanted to shout at the Polish girl to stop Sophie from drinking. She'd obviously had too much. But Maya didn't lecture her. She shrugged and said, "I guess it makes sense to be careful. Besides, it's getting late."

Now that she'd started, though, Sophie showed no interest in stopping her complaints. "She's ruining everything. Who does she think she is? No one likes her mum anyway. She's a fascist. Everyone says so."

Gray drew in a sharp breath.

"Sophie…" Kyle's voice held quiet disapproval.

"Oh please, everyone just shut up." Sophie rolled her eyes. "You're all so boring."

At that moment, Maya tripped over something and stumbled, dropping the bottle, which spilled the last of its contents onto the ground.

Sophie stared at her in disgust. "Typical," she grumbled. "Now we haven't even got that." She stormed after Dylan, visibly fuming.

Maya glanced over her shoulder and gave Gray a conspiratorial wink as she slid the empty bottle into her pocket.

Gray tried to smile but her lips seemed to be frozen. She was hot with embarrassment and cold with fear all at once. The worst part was, Sophie hadn't been wrong. This was her fault. None of this would be happening if she hadn't come to this school and brought danger with her.

She wanted to tell them all how sorry she was for ruining things, but before she could find the words, a sharp cracking sound split the silence.

"Shh," Dylan hissed, lifting one hand as he slowed his steps.

"What now?" Sophie sighed.

Dylan stepped closer to the trees, peering between the branches.

"There!" Kyle said, pointing. In the distance, a shadow shifted. A sudden crashing sound made everyone jump. Branches swayed as something – or someone – raced through the trees, just out of sight. It moved fast, and with intent.

In Gray's mind an image flashed of a man all in black, holding a knife. She tried to scream but she couldn't make a sound. She couldn't draw a breath. Dylan turned to speak to her, but she couldn't make out what he said.

She heard him say her name as if from far away. "Gray? Are you OK?"

"She's white as a sheet." Minal's voice came from the bottom of a well, hollow and cold.

Dylan grabbed her shoulders and shook her once, gently. She heard herself give a moan of fear.

"Gray," he said, his voice urgent. "We have to go. We can't stay here"

"Please. I know what to do." Gently, Maya pushed Dylan out of the way, and moved in between them.

"Gray, can you breathe?" There was concern in her blue eyes. Gray tried to tell her to run as fast as she could. To get out of here. But she couldn't form a word. The world around her began to fall away.

Without warning, Maya raised her hand and slapped Gray's cheek hard.

It stung like fire. Gray drew in a sharp, startled breath. And then another.

The haze began to clear.

"Breathe again," Maya ordered.

Gray breathed.

"Better now?" Maya's blue eyes held hers steadily.

"Yes," she whispered, as feeling returned to her hands and feet.

"Take my hand." Maya gripped Gray's fingers and looked up at Dylan. "She's fine."

Whatever Dylan might have been thinking, it didn't show on his face. He said, "Kyle, stay with Sophie. Minal, keep close to Gray and Maya. Everyone stick together. Nobody leaves the path."

Minal gasped. "Over there! It's on the other side now." She pointed to the left. Gray spotted a blur of movement as something rushed through the woods, moving parallel to the path.

Dylan turned to them, his face deadly serious. "Run."

They all took off.

Gray ran without any focus but Maya's hand was tight around hers, pulling her forward, keeping her on the path. She didn't dare look back but she heard the others panting, and the pounding of their feet. A crashing of branches that could have been them or someone else. A cry ahead as Sophie stumbled, and then Kyle's voice urging her to keep going, keep going. The path seemed to stretch endlessly until Gray's breath burned her lungs. Tears stung her eyes, and she could hear someone sobbing. It took a moment more to realise that she was making the sound herself.

At last, the branches parted and the school building appeared ahead of them, huge and solid, the windows ablaze with reassuring light. Gray saw figures on the grass ahead – people walking toward them.

C J DAUGHERTY

"Help!" Minal called, racing ahead and waving her arms. "Help us!"

Gray wanted her to stop. It was too dark to see their faces. They could have been anyone. She slowed her steps, pulling Maya back. She heard the other girl say something in Polish, and then in English as if remembering who she was talking to.

"It's OK. They're our people."

The figures were running toward them. As they neared, Gray saw it was Carter and Allie, along with Julia. The bodyguard raced up and pulled her free of Maya's grip without ceremony.

"What the hell happened?" she asked, almost angrily, searching Gray as if looking for wounds. "We've been looking for you everywhere."

"We were at the chapel," Dylan told her. "Someone followed us."

"Who?" Allie demanded.

"We didn't get a good look. Whoever it was, it was a man, shoes about size 10," Dylan said, quickly. "He watched us through the windows, and followed us back here."

Shoes about size 10? Gray stared at him. How could he know that?

Minal and Kyle exchanged puzzled looks as if they were wondering the same thing, but Dylan's attention was fixed on the adults.

Carter glanced at Allie. "No guards were scheduled to patrol out there," he said.

"That doesn't mean it's an intruder," Allie insisted. "It could be a teacher. Or a student."

"Maybe," he said. But his voice was doubtful.

Julia had heard enough. "Everyone inside the school now," she snapped, turning to the students.

They didn't need to be told twice. They all rushed for the front steps. Gray's legs felt rubbery with fatigue, but it didn't matter. Julia grabbed her shoulders, hustling her across the gravel drive and up the front steps into the building, shielding Gray's back with her own body. They were inside in seconds.

In the entrance hall, the students huddled, confused and panting. Sophie wrenched her hand free of Kyle's grip. Her cheeks were bright red, her black hair tangled, her eyes angry. Nearby, Minal clutched her ribs, trying to catch her breath. Maya leaned against the wall, arms folded tight across her torso.

Four guards dressed in black thundered past them and out the door. Julia motioned the group of students down the hallway. "Common room," she ordered.

Stunned into silence, they trooped down the hallway behind her. Even Kyle seemed unable to think of anything funny to say.

The common room was nearly as crowded as it had been when they'd left it. Nobody looked up from the board games and computers that held their attention, as they gathered stray chairs together until there was space for all of them.

Julia didn't sit down. "Stay here," she ordered. "I've got to find out what's happening outside."

As soon as she was gone, Kyle turned to Dylan accusingly. "Size 10 shoes? You lied to us back at the chapel. You saw something out there. And apparently you also like, measured it."

The American student gave him an apologetic look. "I didn't want to scare you guys, so I didn't say anything. But there were footprints outside the window in the mud. Size 10, give or take. Same as mine."

Gray stared at him. "So I didn't imagine it?"

"No, you didn't," he told her. "Someone was out there." He met her eyes. "And they were watching us."

TEN

After leaving Gray and the other students safely in the common room, Julia raced back down the corridor toward the front door. Her hands felt icy but her steps were steady.

In her earpiece she could hear the voices of security staff searching the grounds.

"Earth disturbed in the churchyard…"

"No sign of intruders in quadrant eight…"

"No sign in quadrant seven…"

You won't find them, she thought, grimly as she raced down the front steps. They're too good for that.

She located Allie and Carter standing with August Zelazny outside the front door, their expressions grave.

"They haven't found anyone?" she asked, although she already knew the answer.

"Not yet. But it looks like it was one person, probably a man, working alone," Carter told her. "Dylan was right about the footprints."

Allie looked at Zelazny. "You're sure it couldn't have been a guard or a student?"

The history teacher shook his head. "No guards were in the area. As far as we can tell, it wasn't a student either. We've done a headcount – everyone's inside."

Allie looked from him to Carter. "Then who was it?"

"We're working on that part," he said.

Allie stared at the point where the shadows of the forest met the darkness of the sky. "We must be missing something. Nobody could get in here. It had to be a student."

Julia couldn't believe what she was hearing. "Oh, come on, Allie. You know they can get in. We've seen them get in before. All of us have."

The words came out more sharply than she'd intended and Allie bristled. "We've improved security since you were last here, Jules. We have cameras everywhere. Alarms." She held up her phone. "If anyone even touches that gate this lets me know. We've had one intrusion this year and it was Sophie Montgomery's bloody boyfriend. Other than that, nobody has tried in years."

"Well, they're trying now. And they're succeeding." Julia gestured at the empty grounds around them. "How many security staff have you got working tonight? Five? Covering what? Ten acres? Fifteen? Including woods and hills and miles of fences." She took a step closer. "You need to wake up. Someone got in. I warned you this was coming. And you didn't believe me. Now it's here."

Allie's face reddened. "Sod off, Jules!" she snapped. Turning on her heel and stormed into the building.

Zelazny looked from Carter to Julia, eyebrows rising. "Guess I'll go talk to those five guards," he said, before heading across the grass toward the woods.

Seeing the mutinous look on Julia's face, Carter sighed. "I'll talk to her."

Julia's lips tightened. "No. Let me do it."

She ran after Allie into the school, her feet flying up the familiar stone steps and into the warmth of the entrance hall. The building was quiet – the students had been told to stay either in their rooms or in the common room. Any teachers not helping with the search outside were in their own residential wing.

She spotted the headmistress outside the great hall.

"Allie, hold up," she called. "We need to talk."

With clear reluctance, Allie stopped. "Look," she said, as Jules reached her, "I'm sorry I spoke to you like that. I was out of order. But I genuinely believe you're overreacting. We can't say for certain it even *was* an intruder. We'll question the staff. Maybe it was a teacher out for a run."

"A run." Julia gave her a look of incomprehension. "This person pursued them through the woods. Dylan said they were almost taunting them. Would a teacher do that? You saw their faces. Those kids were scared."

"There's no indication anyone came over the fence," Allie insisted. "None of the sensors were triggered. The gate stayed shut. We've got someone checking the CCTV for any sign of intrusion. If they find it, we'll know. But without that…"

"You and I both know that wouldn't prove anything." Jules said. "Allie, think about it. What if someone studied your security system and knew where the blackspots were on your CCTV coverage? They could come over that fence and leave no trace. If they're good, you wouldn't realise your system had been defeated until they were long gone."

"Don't lecture me about my school," Allie said hotly. "You just got here two weeks ago and suddenly you're an expert? Who the hell do you think you are?"

"I am an expert, actually." Jules kept her voice even. "I'm a professional bodyguard hired by the prime minister to protect her daughter. Knowing everything that could go wrong is my job. And I'm telling you that something has gone wrong. Very wrong."

Allie flinched. "Come on Jules, that's not fair. We're protecting Gray. Like we've protected students for years."

"It seems to me you haven't had to protect anyone in a long time. Forgive me if I don't trust you to protect Gray."

"And forgive me if I don't think this has much to do with Gray Langtry," Allie retorted.

A sheen of ice fell on their already cold conversation.

"What does that mean, exactly?" Julia asked.

"I think this is about what happened six years ago," said Allie.

Julia drew in a breath.

What happened six years ago. When her parents dragged her out of this school at seventeen, threw her into another school where she knew nobody. Six years ago, when she left Carter behind, and Allie stepped into her place. Six years ago, when her life fell apart.

"Fine. Let's do this." Julia folded her arms. "You've treated me like your enemy ever since I got here because of what happened when we were teenagers. And yes, that bothers me. I wish it didn't, but I'm only human."

"That isn't true," Allie insisted.

"Isn't it?" Julia gave her a steady look. "Well then, humour me. I didn't leave Cimmeria because I wanted to. My parents made that decision. I had no control. They packed my things and sent a thug to drag me out of here."

"I know that." Allie's tone was stilted.

"Do you, though?" Jules stepped toward her, dropping her arms. "Do you really? Do you know that I was sent to a school where I knew nobody? I was completely alone. I'd left my boyfriend and all my friends behind. Nobody returned my messages. I was completely cut off. And then..." Julia's voice trailed off.

"And then your boyfriend ended up with me instead," Allie said.

"Yes." There was a long pause. And then Julia said, "And that broke my heart."

The two of them regarded each other with a complex mixture of suspicion and regret. The anger evaporated from their conversation.

Allie let out a breath. "I always felt terrible about that time," she confessed. "We were so young and so scared. Life seemed just to happen, somehow. But we didn't mean to hurt you. I've thought about it many times – how hard it must have been for you. And I want you to know that... I regret that."

The pain Julia had held onto for all those years eased just a little. It was like setting down a weight she'd carried for a hundred miles.

"I'm not going to deny it hurt like hell but..." She paused. "I guess I got over it a long time ago. I've had a life since then. A good one. And I'm good at what I do. Honestly, Allie, I'm not saying this to score a point. I really do know more about this than you do. And you have to believe me when I say, the people who tried to kill her are coming for her again. They will find her. And they'll hurt anyone who gets in their way."

Allie met her gaze. "What do you need from me?"

"I need to look at your rota of security guards and see if we can have more of them on the ground for the next couple of days until we can get more people out here to help us," Julia said. "We need to bring back patrols of the grounds and the school building. The guards need to be experts on the students and the staff – we need them to recognise an unfamiliar face in an instant."

"We can do that," Allie said. She looked away for a long moment before continuing. "I'm sorry I've been so cold to you since you came back. It's just that it all came from out of the blue. But I know that's no excuse." She rubbed her forehead with the fingers of one hand. "You know, I didn't ask to run this school. This isn't what I wanted to be doing with my life. And now it feels like, as soon as Isabelle left, it all came crashing down around me. I guess…" She faltered and then met Julia's gaze. "I just didn't want you to see me fail."

"Then let me help you," Julia urged. "Your security team isn't as good as it could be. Let's put together a better one. I can do that for you. Carter can work with me."

"Done," Allie said.

"There's one other thing." Julia braced herself before completing the thought. "Raj and I – we think it's time to bring back Night School."

"Jules, no." Allie looked shocked. "Things can't be that bad. Can they?"

"See it as a precaution. Other students could benefit from self-defence training. I've been researching the most at-risk people here. Maya, for instance – her family is still being targeted by extremists. And Kyle – his family has had threats. We could do the training three nights a week. Keep it quiet. Nobody need know. A few instructors."

There was a long silence. Allie's reluctance was so tangible, Julia thought she could feel it around her like a cold breeze.

Finally though, she said, "I'll decide tomorrow, OK? I really need to call Isabelle, and talk to Zelazny and Eloise. This has all been happening so fast. I want to know what they think before we do anything."

"Of course," Julia said. "In the meantime, Raj is sending some guards down to help."

"Great," Allie said. "We could use the help. And Jules – I really will think about Night School. It's just hard to believe we have to do this again. I worked so hard to get away from this stuff." There was a hint of despair in her voice.

"I know," Julia said. "But we'll get through it. Whatever it takes, we'll fix this."

The two women studied each other for a moment, an ocean of memories passing between them. Of themselves as young women, fighting side by side, for something they believed in.

"I'm glad you're here right now, Jules," Allie said, quietly. "I truly am. It's good to have you home."

ELEVEN

When Gray came down the next morning, Julia was waiting at the foot of the stairs.

Gray eyed her warily. She hadn't seen her since the bodyguard had hustled her into the building the night before and ordered her to stay put.

The students had stayed in the common room for an hour while the grounds were being secured. Aside from those who'd been at the chapel, no one had a clue what was happening. There'd been an announcement about a small fire in the kitchen and that they were to remain where they were – a deception everyone had accepted.

Now, dressed in jeans, a black leather jacket and sunglasses, the bodyguard offered only an affectless "Good morning," before turning to escort her to the dining hall. Without being able to see her eyes, Gray couldn't gauge how angry she was, but the icy silence was worse than a lecture. Everything Julia wasn't saying reverberated in Gray's mind as she struggled to find a way to make this better. But the words died in her throat.

There were no excuses. She'd lied. Again. And that was that.

Shame is a hollow feeling.

"Is there any news?" Gray asked, after a moment. "Did you find anyone last night?"

"No luck. We're confident there's no one in the grounds now. It's all been thoroughly searched. But we still don't know who it was. Or what they wanted."

Julia delivered the news with no emotion.

At the door of the dining room, they stopped. To Gray, Julia's dark glasses seemed to reflect blank disapproval as she said, "I have to go to London today for a meeting with your mother. I would appreciate it if you would stay close to the building until we figure this all out."

Gray's heart twisted. If her mother knew what had happened at the chapel, she'd be furious.

"Can I ask... What are you going to tell her?"

"Don't worry," Julia said, coolly. "There are more important things to worry about right now than whether or not you were honest with me."

With that, the bodyguard turned and began heading down the hallway. Gray watched her go, her hands clasped anxiously in front of her. After a few seconds, though, she ran after her.

"Julia," she called. The woman stopped and turned back. "I'm sorry. I shouldn't have gone." Gray's words tumbled over each other. "I thought I was safe here. I didn't think I was taking chances, I swear. I just wanted to make friends. That's all. I wanted to fit in. And I knew if I told you the truth you'd come with me and then I'd lose my chance. It was stupid of me. I'm sorry."

Slowly, the bodyguard removed her sunglasses to reveal blue eyes underscored by shadows.

"I thought you'd be safe here, too," Julia said. "And I'm sorry you were frightened last night. I'm going to try to fix this, but to do that I need to be able to trust you. You can't lie to me again, do you understand? I can't do this without you."

"You can trust me," Gray promised fervently. "I won't take chances again. I get it now."

The bodyguard held her gaze for a long moment. Then she nodded. "I believe you. Thank you for your apology. Now, stay safe until I get back. And that's an order."

It was the shortest lecture Gray had ever received for lying, and also the one with the biggest impact. She hated that she'd let her bodyguard down. If it took her whole life to do it, she was going to become the kind of person Julia respected. Somehow, she was going to earn her trust.

There wasn't much time to think about how she'd do that because as soon as she walked into the dining hall, Kyle and Minal pounced on her.

"We've been waiting ages." Minal shoved a cup of coffee into her hands, as they hustled her over to a table. "Have this. We thought you always came down early. We rushed down to find you as soon as we woke up. We need gossip."

Before she'd even sat down, they began peppering her with questions.

"Wasn't last night amazing?"

"Who do you think chased us?"

"Wasn't Dylan so cool? How did he know how to do all that?"

"He was like an actual cop off an American TV show. Like Cimmeria Police Academy, or whatever."

Finally Minal shushed Kyle, and asked, "What did Julia say? Does she know who it was?"

"She didn't say much." Seeing the disappointment on their faces, Gray added, "She's going to London to meet my mum and talk about what's happened. That's pretty much all I know."

"Your mum is going to freak out," Kyle told her. "Mine too. The school is going to be in all the trouble. It's supposed to be super secure. I mean, our parents pay a fortune so we can, like, not get kidnapped in the chapel."

Minal grew serious. "If someone really got into the grounds, my dad is going to lose it. He put in the security system himself and he swears it's the best in the country. Someone must have really messed up if this guy actually got in." She gave Gray a worried look. "They're not going to pull you out of here or anything stupid like that, are they? I mean, nobody got hurt."

Her words sent a chill through Gray – until now, she hadn't considered the possibility that her parents might make her leave the school after just two weeks. But it wasn't out of the question.

"I don't think so…" she said, but the other two didn't miss the uncertainty in her voice.

Kyle looked horrified. "You can't leave. You only just got here! You've brought glamour and excitement to our world, and they can't rip that away from us. I will throw myself in front of the car if they try to take you," he said, theatrically.

"He'd do it, too." Minal gave him an affectionate nudge. "For the drama."

"I feed on drama," Kyle agreed. "That would keep me full for a week."

Their exuberance was contagious, and Gray found herself smiling despite everything.

"You don't have to stop cars. I'm not going anywhere," she said. "Number 10 isn't safe. And if someone can find me here, they can find me anywhere they send me."

There was a dark note to her voice but the others were too excited to notice.

"Who do you think it really was outside the chapel?" Minal asked, looking from Gray to Kyle. "I mean, maybe it wasn't an intruder. It could just have been a creepy student."

"It could be a reporter," Gray said. "Back in London they followed me everywhere I went."

It wasn't a pleasant thought. If the reporters found her, everyone in the world would soon know where she was. But Kyle looked thrilled.

"If it's a reporter, do you think they got pictures of us smoking in the chapel? The scandal would be shocking. Think of the headlines: 'Wealthy Teens Go Wild'."

Gray was less excited about that prospect. "I'm not sure. I think if it was a reporter they would have stopped us and asked questions. I don't know why they wouldn't say anything. Whoever it was, he just stood there. And then it was like he... I don't know. Disappeared."

"It must be crazy being chased by paparazzi," Minal said. "Is it really like on TV? Are they all, 'Gray, over here! Pout for me, baby'?"

Gray didn't smile. "It's like that, only big men asking gross questions to try and upset me. It's kind of disgusting."

"Well, that's disappointing," Kyle said. "I'd hoped it was more fun."

"That's why I don't think it was them. Last night it was like…" She paused to find the words. "It was like we were running from a ghost."

"I hope it wasn't someone who wants to hurt you or your mum." Minal's face clouded. "I don't understand why someone would do that."

"People would do anything for power." Gray recognised Maya's elegant European accent before she looked up to see her standing next to them, holding a mug and a plate of food, her curls tamed into a ponytail. "It is the worst part of humanity, in my opinion."

She looked a little pale, but none the worse for wear as she took the seat next to Gray, and frowned at the empty table in front of her. "You have no food."

"Oh bollocks. That's our fault. We haven't given her two seconds." Kyle jumped to his feet and turned to Gray. "I'll get you something. What do you want? Toast? Bacon? Toast and bacon?"

"Toast and bacon, please," Gray said. "And more coffee."

"On it." He ran to the tables at the end of the room, where food was stacked on heated trays and kept warm on covered silver salvers.

"Are you OK after last night?" Maya's eyes searched Gray's face. "It was a shock."

Until then, Gray had been distracted by Kyle and Minal's exuberance. Now the memory of the way she'd frozen on the path, and Maya's calm slap to her face, flooded her with embarrassment.

"Yes… uh… I'm fine," she said, flushing. "I'm sorry about that…"

"Don't apologise," Maya interrupted before she could say more. "Anyone would be afraid after what you've been through. It is normal. I am always afraid when I'm home. Not here, normally. But last night was bizarre. I was afraid, too."

Emboldened by this revelation, Gray said hesitantly, "I've been meaning to say – Allie told me about what happened to your father. That people tried to kill him."

Minal shot a surprised look at her, but Maya only nodded.

"Many times." She wrapped her hands around her mug, her expression darkening. "Like you, we have bodyguards at home. Although it is less now that he has left power and there's nothing more to take from him."

Gray leaned towards her and lowered her voice. "How do you deal with the fear? Since the attack I've been so scared. For me and for my mum. The world feels out of control."

Maya regarded Gray. "It's not exactly dealing with it. It just seems as if, first the fear controls you, and then, after a while, fear becomes something you can control. It's as if fear becomes part of the furniture of your life. A chair you sometimes trip over, and then remember, Oh, yes, that's fear. Here to trip me up. Nothing new there." She paused and added with new emphasis, "You must never let it stop you from living. Living your life is how you defeat fear. It's how you win. Learn to kick the chair out of your way and keep moving forward. That's the trick of it."

Gray longed desperately to learn how to kick fear away. And she wondered if she ever would.

"But if someone is looking for her here," Minal interjected, "it's understandable to be frightened. I was scared shitless out there last night."

"Perhaps." Maya's brow creased. "We don't know for certain who was there, and it is best not to panic before you know what you face. For now, we must be calm, and practical. If there's something to worry about, the teachers will tell us."

Kyle dashed back across the room and slid a plate holding a bacon sandwich in front of Gray, replacing her mug with a fresh coffee so quickly it never had a chance to spill. When he sat down again, he noticed their serious expressions.

"What did I miss?" he asked. "Was it good? I always miss good things."

Before anyone could explain, though, Sophie walked into the room with the smooth stride of a gazelle.

They all fell silent, watching as she piled fruit and yoghurt into a bowl, before wandering over to join a group of similarly beautiful girls on the other side of the room, ignoring all of them as she passed.

"She's angry," Maya observed.

The humour left Kyle's oval face. "Last night was definitely not Sophie's jam. All she wanted to do was get high and make out with Dylan. But he was only interested in Gray as far as I could see. She was furious even before things hit the fan."

"She can't think…" Gray stared at him. "That's insane! It wasn't like we were flirting. We were talking about art and history. Minal was talking to him, too."

"Well," he said, "I'm pretty sure that's not how Sophie saw it."

"Dylan did seem very interested in you," Minal agreed, apologetically.

"I thought so too,' Maya said. "He never left your side."

"That's ridiculous." Gray's face went hot. "I don't like him. We don't like each other. He's always patronising me."

But she kept thinking about the way he'd looked at her when they were talking about the wall paintings. He hadn't patronised her then.

"Sophie's hard work. I'd let it go," Minal advised. "Avoid her until she gets over it."

Maya took a thoughtful bite of toast as she considered this. "Everyone has their demons. Sophie's demons are unique. I will talk to her."

Gray shot a surreptitious look at the dark-haired beauty, who had not spared them the slightest glance. "Who is she anyway?" she asked. "Why is she like this?"

Kyle glanced over to make sure Sophie couldn't hear before saying in a low voice, "Her dad is a venture capitalist billionaire. He's a complete bastard. He made a fortune buying this chain of clothing stores and then shutting it all down, firing everyone, stealing their pensions. He bought, like, three yachts after that. Her mother was this Malaysian beauty queen – Miss World or whatever. They were married for about five years, and then, when Sophie was three, he took off with wife number two. He set up this huge trust fund for Sophie and seems to think that's parenthood, done and dusted. Last summer she tried to get in touch with him, to have some sort of relationship. Only, when she got him on the phone he told her, 'I don't have time for this. You need to accept that I'm not father material.' She took a handful of sleeping pills with some of her mum's vodka and ended up in the hospital having her stomach pumped after the maid found her on the floor."

"Bloody hell." Gray said, stunned.

"Yeah, her dad's a total douche canoe," Minal said. "The whole thing really messed with her head. She was nicer before that happened. Ever since, she's been crueller. And much less happy."

Throughout all of this, Maya had been quietly eating her breakfast. Now she pushed her plate back and announced, "She's putting up walls to protect herself from anyone else who might want to hurt her like her father. But being hurt is no excuse for hurting other people."

Remembering something, Gray turned to her. "Last night, you dropped that bottle on purpose, didn't you?"

Maya shrugged. "She drinks to dull the pain. She's too young to do that. I don't like to watch it."

"She's an icon," Kyle said, regretfully. "But she's also a messed-up drama bitch." He glanced at Gray. "Watch your back around her. If she can't be your beautiful friend, she'll be your beautiful enemy. And she can do damage."

His words filled Gray with dread. How could she have enemies when she'd only just started to make friends? This was the last thing she needed right now.

TWELVE

Dark clouds were gathering over London when Julia steered a government-issued car into an unmarked car park on a quiet Westminster lane. The lot had a clear view of the gilded ornate gates of Buckingham Palace, but when she stepped out of the car she didn't head toward the sturdy palace. Instead, she turned in the other direction, to an unremarkable security gate where a police officer in a bullet-proof vest stood, a compact machine gun strapped across his chest.

Jules scanned her pass against an electronic reader and then held it up for him to double-check. His eyes moved from the image on the card to her face and then, with a nod, he stepped back and opened the gate.

After she'd gone through security she made her way through the warren of government buildings to a narrow path leading to Downing Street.

A small clutch of photographers stood across from the famous door with its lion's head knocker and the simple number 10 gleaming white against the black. Before she'd even reached the low step, the door swung open and another police officer stepped aside for her to enter.

"Name please?" he asked when she was inside.

"Julia Matheson, to see the prime minister."

His polite expression never wavered. "I'll call up for you."

While she waited, Julia placed her phone in a numbered cubbyhole on a polished wooden shelf near the door, and then stood near the guards.

When Gray had been living at Number 10, Julia had been given a card that gave her full access to the building without a single question or check. Those days were definitely over.

One of the door guards glanced up from his computer screen and said, "You can go up, Ms Matheson."

Julia crossed the black-and-white tiled floor to the long, familiar corridor leading into the heart of the office building. It was just before noon and the hallways teemed with office workers and security, everyone walking double-speed and talking a mile a minute. She departed the throng to climb a staircase that curved up past portraits of former prime ministers.

She was halfway up when Raj Patel appeared, hurrying down to meet her.

"Good of you to come in for this," he said. He was slim but muscular in a charcoal grey suit that stretched tight across his shoulders. "I'm sorry to drag you in, but the prime minister is extremely anxious about what happened last night."

"She should be," Julia said simply.

"You're convinced someone's been on the grounds? It couldn't have been a misunderstanding?"

"I'm sure of it."

Raj swore under his breath. "Gray's not even been there three weeks," he said, as they reached the landing. "I thought we'd get more time than this. How did they find her so quickly?"

"Either they figured it out on their own – there are only so many boarding schools – or someone talked," she said.

"One of the staff?" he guessed.

"Or the teachers. Or the students to their parents." She shrugged. "It was never going to stay a secret. The only thing that matters now is, are we ready?"

"That's what we're here to talk about." He gave her a warning look. "She wants to pull Gray out."

"Of school?" Julia was aghast. "And put her back here? Where the threat started?"

"Or in another school."

She could see his disapproval in the tense line of his jaw. He looked as tired as she felt. Nobody was getting enough sleep right now.

"You think this is as stupid as I do, yes?" she said.

"It's a terrible idea," he told her. They'd reached the heavy door leading to the prime minister's office; he reached for the handle. "I need you to talk her out of it."

The small waiting room on the other side of the door was empty. The secretary glanced up as they came in. "Ah, Mr Patel. Miss Matheson. She's waiting for you." She gestured at the door to her left.

Straightening her jacket, Julia followed Raj through the door, closing it behind them.

The prime minister's office was a large, light-filled space with a row of windows protected by blast-proof curtains that pooled on the floor. In an explosion, they would billow like sails, holding broken glass and other projectiles in their folds. Like so many things, the curtains appeared fragile, but were as tough as iron.

Jessica Langtry stood up from her seat behind a large walnut desk. Her highlighted hair, cut to the nape of her neck and neatly styled, caught the light. "Raj, Julia." She gave a tight smile. "Thank you for coming." She motioned for them to sit in the leather chairs facing her desk and walked around to join them, taking a seat on the matching sofa. "Clearly, we have a situation on our hands."

"Yes, it's disturbing," Raj said. "But we were expecting this. She was always going to be found."

"But like this?" The prime minister's brow creased. "Chased across the school grounds in the dark? How on earth did he get in?"

Raj nodded at Julia. She cleared her throat. "We found footprints outside the chapel where Gray and her friends were when they saw him. We are quite certain it was one man acting alone. We know where he came over the fence, and we've adjusted the cameras and the sensors so that if he uses the same spot again we'll get him."

Even though she'd observed the state of Sophie Montgomery and smelled the quite obvious marijuana smoke on Kyle's jacket, she decided to keep the finer details of Gray's chapel outing to herself. None of that mattered right now.

"Do you have any idea yet who it was?" Jessica asked. "Did the camera catch anything?"

Raj answered that one. "Unfortunately, we can't identify him at this time, Prime Minister. He chose a good spot to come in, between two cameras, shielded by branches. We found climbing equipment outside the wall, and evidence – broken branches and so forth – on the inside. It looks like he walked as far as the main school building, and then backtracked through the woods again, possibly after spotting Gray and her friends heading to the chapel. He may have followed them from the moment they left the school building."

For the first time, Gray's mother looked genuinely shocked. "He got that close? My God, Raj. She could have been killed."

"Our people were always nearby," he assured her. "And the kids reacted very well. They protected each other and ran straight back for help."

The prime minister stood abruptly and strode to the window, her back stiff. When she turned around, her face was creased with worry.

"I have to say I'm deeply concerned about Gray remaining at the school," she said. "We have to assume this person was part of John Ashford's group. The fact that he eluded the security on the fenceline and then avoided capture indicate this person was highly trained. I don't believe the school can protect her from a group with those capabilities. I believe she's too exposed."

"Prime Minister." A note of caution entered Raj's voice. "We have to accept that any school she goes to will not be safe for long. She will be discovered. Word will get out. And Cimmeria is very well protected…"

"So well protected that my daughter was pursued through the woods by an unknown assailant last night." A steely note entered the prime minister's voice. "I know it's impossible to protect her here, but I do not like her being in danger so far from home. As you know, Raj, I didn't want to send her away in the first place."

"I completely understand." Raj's tone was measured. "As you know, my own daughter is at Cimmeria, and I worry about her as well."

"Of course you do." Jessica inclined her head slightly. "And it does comfort me that our daughters are together."

Julia spoke up. "Actually, Minal was with Gray at the chapel last night."

If she didn't know him as well as she did, she might have the missed the slight flicker in Raj's expression as he absorbed this information. She hadn't thought to tell him this fact earlier. But all he said was, "I see." Then he turned back to his boss.

"Prime Minister, we've got Julia on the grounds, along with the school's existing security team, which is run by Carter West, a very capable young man I trained myself. I'm sending more of my agents out there this week to work with him on tightening up any loose edges. We can protect her."

Julia jumped in. "We're expanding patrols to include the woods now, as well as the fence line. With your permission, we'd also like to give certain students – including Gray – training in self-defence, so they're prepared if this happens again."

"Self-defence. My God." Jumping to her feet, Jessica stalked across the room to the white marble fireplace, then turned to fix the two of them with a look. "Is that really necessary?"

"It is not unusual for young people who could be victims of kidnapping to have this type of training," Raj assured her. "It's very straightforward. And it can make them safer."

Julie marvelled at how Raj made it all sound so normal.

Jessica listened, her expression telling them little about what she might be thinking.

"What does Gray know about what happened last night?" she asked.

"We haven't told her much," Raj said. "Only that it's under investigation."

"What are you going to tell her?" she asked, fixing him with a steady look.

Raj and Julia exchanged a glance.

"I don't think we should tell her the truth," he said. "If she knows the same group is after her again, and that they got this close, I think she could backslide. She's still recovering from the attack in Oxford."

Jessica turned to Julia, who'd stayed silent. "What do you think?"

Julia hesitated. "I hate to lie to her," she said, honestly. "As her bodyguard, I need her to trust me. But telling her the truth right now…" She paused. "I think it would shatter her."

The prime minster rubbed her fingertips against her forehead. "Fine. Don't tell her. Let's give her some peace for a little while longer." When she dropped her hand, she didn't look happy. "I have to say, neither of you has convinced me Gray will be safe if she stays at Cimmeria Academy. Far from it. I'm less certain than ever that we've made the right choice."

Raj opened his mouth but Julia spoke before he could say a word.

"I think you know that neither of you is safe anywhere."

The prime minister's face hardened but Julia kept talking, her voice steady and determined.

"Out of all the places Gray could be, I believe Cimmeria is the best. We can't promise nobody will come over that fence again. It stretches for more than five miles through dense woods. But we can improve security enough that no one can get close to Gray. We can have a security plan for her. I will make sure she understands the risks. But also…" She held up her hands. "She has a right to be a normal sixteen year old girl. I'm going to see to it that if she wants to go out with friends at nine o'clock at night, she can at least do that without fear."

Jessica held her eyes. In that long, expressive look, Julia sensed all the emotions she kept bottled up inside her heart. Yes, she was the leader of the country, but she was also a worried mother who loved her daughter.

"I know you care for her," Jessica said. "You've risked your life for her. And I am hugely grateful to you. All my instincts are telling me to get Gray out of there – and you must understand why. But you make a good case."

She turned to Raj. "I want you to give Julia whatever she needs to secure the school. More guards. More equipment. Wrap that building in chain mail if you have to."

"Absolutely." He paused before asking, "And the self-defence training we discussed for the most at-risk students – what do you want do about that?"

"Start it immediately," Jessica ordered. "If they're going to be there they need to learn how to defend themselves." She looked back and forth between the two of them. "I don't like this. My instincts tell me to bring her home. I'm counting on you to take care of her. If I keep Gray at Cimmeria you must protect her."

She turned her focus to Julia. "Whatever it takes, whatever you need – I'll make sure you have it. Just… Please. Keep my daughter safe."

THIRTEEN

Even before Julia had returned from London, Raj called Allie and gave her the news. Alone in her office late that afternoon, she began typing the memo she needed to send to the teachers to get them ready for the changes that had to happen now.

"More guards will be coming from London over the next few days. In addition, self-defence training will begin this week for a group of hand-selected students. We would like to keep this from the other students, to avoid causing jealousy or concern. To that end, the training will be conducted at night, in the basement gym or elsewhere on the grounds …"

Someone tapped on the office door, and her fingers stilled on the keyboard. "Come in."

When Carter walked in, her muscles relaxed a little.

"Hey." His dark eyes searched her face. "What's wrong?"

Abandoning the memo, she got up from the desk and walked over to him. "How do you always know when something's wrong?"

"Because I know you."

She put her arms around his neck, pressing her face into the crook of his shoulder. He'd been out checking on the workers

127

adding more security cameras to the fence, and he smelled of fresh air and pine needles.

"Seriously," he said, pulling her close. "What's the matter?"

"I've got to start up Night School again and lie to Gray Langtry, and I feel like a monster." Her voice was muffled against the fabric of his jumper.

"Orders from her mother?" he guessed.

She nodded, without lifting her head. He folded her in his arms.

"I don't want to be a grown-up today," she said. "I hate it."

"It sucks," he agreed.

"All that girl needs is honesty and love and time to heal, and she's going to get none of it. I'm going to give her lies and pain and I'm going to teach her krav maga and kick-boxing."

"And when you were her age, how much did that hurt you?" he asked.

There was a moment's silence.

"Shut up," Allie said.

Carter's laugh was a low rumble against her cheek. "I know you don't like lying, and I'm sorry you have to do it. But the training will empower her. The lies are her mother's idea, not yours. And the truth will come out someday, probably sooner than we think. She'll be okay. You're not a monster, you're a hero. Stop worrying."

Allie lifted her head to blink up at him. "How do you always say the right thing?"

He gazed down at her. "Because when I do, sometimes you look at me like that. And it's the best."

She raised her lips to his. His hands slid down her back. She could feel the warmth of him against her, melting away the ice the phone conversation had left behind. Seven years since their first kiss and still, each time he held her it felt like home.

Her lips parted as she tasted the salt of him. She felt his chest rise as he took in a quick breath. His arms tightened around her, muscles like iron.

Her hands flattened against his back and he lifted his head, looking down at her breathlessly. "I didn't lock the door."

Allie gave a light laugh. "We can't do anything in Isabelle's office. It's like church."

"Damn." He gave her a rakish smile. "I want to pick this up later in our room. Right where we left off."

"It's a date." Allie brushed a kiss against his shoulder. "Now, you have to excuse me. I need to finish warning the staff we're about to become a fortress."

Fifteen minutes later, she walked down the hallway with Gray beside her. It was uncanny how much the girl reminded her of herself at that age. With her thick wavy hair and those blue eyes she looked different of course, but her impulsive decisions, and her stubborn determination to survive – those were traits they shared.

"Is everything okay?" Gray asked, watching her warily. "I feel like I should apologise for what happened at the chapel. I shouldn't have gone. It wasn't right. But I didn't drink or…"

"Look, it wasn't against The Rules or I'd be giving you detention right now. And trust me, you do not want Cimmeria detention – it's very old-school. But, this is about something else." Allie motioned for Gray to sit in one of the leather chairs facing her desk. She took the chair next to her rather than going behind her desk, and turned to face her. "I just want to give you an update on what we know about the person you saw out there."

Gray's face darkened. "Do you know who it was? Have you caught them?"

Allie didn't miss the way her hands gripped the arms of the chair, or the tension that tightened her face.

"Not yet," Allie said. "But we know more about them."

"Did they see me at the chapel?" Gray asked.

Without showing any of the reluctance she felt, Allie gave her the agreed story. "We don't think so. We know they made it as far as the edge of the woods, where we think they hid in the bracken and watched the school. That's probably where they were when you and the others went out to the chapel. They must have seen all of you heading into the woods and followed. We don't think they got close enough to know it was you."

Gray's face looked white and pinched. "Who was it? Someone who wants to hurt my mum?"

"We believe it's a photographer from one of the tabloid newspapers," Allie said. "One of the fence cameras got a partial image of a car registration plate, and Raj's team traced it back to him. We can't be absolutely certain of course, as he managed to stay off camera. But it's a pretty good indication of who we're dealing with."

Gray was still watching her, as if looking for any hint of deception. "You really don't think it's the people who want to kill my mum and me? You think it's just press?"

"That's what Raj thinks, and it makes sense to me," Allie lied.

Gray sagged back in her seat, relief suffusing her features. "I was so scared it was starting again. That they'd found me." Abruptly though, she sat up straighter, a new fear filling her. "But they will find me. The photographer will put the pictures in the paper…"

Allie held up a hand to stop her. "Apparently he didn't get any clear images of you. He may not have even known it was actually you who was there. It was very dark, and then he was chased away before he could see more."

"So… you think I'm safe?" Gray asked the question hesitantly. As if the idea of safety was too much to hope for.

Allie bit back a sudden burst of fury. It was so unfair. Gray was just a girl trying to live her life, and the world was determined to judge her, assess her, damage her, even kill her.

But all she said was, "We think so."

Eager to avoid the need to come up with ever more complex falsehoods, she talked quickly. "All the same, we're bringing in more security. And there are a few things we would like you to do, as well. In particular, self-defence training. I know you've been doing some work on that with Julia. We want to enhance it."

Gray's posture stiffened. "Why? If it's so safe, why do I need to learn that stuff?"

"It's just a precaution," Allie assured her. "In case it ever happens again, your mother thinks it would be best if you acquired certain skills."

"Certain skills." Gray sounded disgusted. "If she's so concerned why doesn't she learn how to fight?"

Allie fixed her with a look but Gray didn't back down. "I'm no good at it," she insisted, growing heated. "I don't know how to fight and I don't want to learn. It's ridiculous."

"It is ridiculous," Allie agreed. "You should never ever have to do this. But the truth is, you had two bodyguards and an entire police force trying to keep you safe in Oxford and you still nearly died in that attack. The best security in the world only has to blink." She snapped her fingers. "And someone can slip through. You know that better than anyone. This way, if one of us blinks and someone gets close to you, you'll know basic self-defence. You'll be trained in evading capture." She leaned forward, holding Gray's gaze. "You'll be able to fight back."

Gray wasn't sure she'd ever be any good at fighting, especially given that even the slightest threat seemed to completely immobilise her.

As if she knew what she was thinking, Allie's tone softened. "How are you sleeping?"

Gray's face went carefully blank. "Fine."

"And the panic attacks? How often are they happening?"

Gray looked away. In the silence, they could hear voices in the hallway outside, the faint sound of shouts and laughter.

"I can't stop them," she confessed. "I don't like the dark. I don't like being touched without, like, my permission. I don't like being surprised. Every time it happens… it happens."

There was a moment's quiet after she spoke as Allie considered how to respond.

"Everybody gets symptoms after a trauma like that," she said, finally. "Those feelings are little echoes of the fear you felt. The thing is, those echoes can't be ignored. They won't get better

on their own. And they could get worse. That's what worries me."
She thought for a moment before adding, "You know, I once went
through something similar to what happened to you."

Gray looked at her with surprise.

"When I was your age, I was attacked," Allie revealed. "I
could have died. A close friend did die. But I survived, and I got
stronger. And I swear to you, Gray, you will, too. You will get
through this. I want to help you."

Their eyes locked. Something passed between the two of
them in that moment – shared pain and loss.

"I hope you're right. I want to get better." Bright tears
glittered on Gray's lashes. "I'm so tired of being afraid. Sometimes
it feels like fear owns me. I'd do anything to make that feeling go
away."

"I know that feeling so well," Allie said. "But I'm going to
teach you how to fight back. If you let me help you, I swear to you
the day will come when nothing will ever scare you again."

FOURTEEN

The next morning when Gray woke up, an envelope lay on the floor of her room near the door. The thick white paper had only one word written on it: GRAY.

Still groggy with sleep, she picked it up. Turning it over, she studied the neat, no-nonsense handwriting. The envelope was sealed with red wax with the Cimmeria crest pressed into it – three castle towers, three keys, two crossed swords.

Carefully, Gray broke the seal. Inside, she found a thick card that looked very much like a formal invitation.

'You are invited to be part of a select group of students for training in self-defence. Report to Training Room 1 at 22:00 tonight. Be on time. Workout gear will be provided for you. This group, the training you receive, and the information you are told during training sessions are secret. You may tell no one. Anyone found to have broken this Rule faces expulsion from the group.'

Gray turned the card over, but the back was blank. The note was unsigned.

She read it through again, as if she might have missed something in the sparse text, but it was all very simple.

Nervousness swirled in the pit of her stomach. Training had gone so badly with Julia and Carter that the idea of trying that again but with even more people to watch her fail was horrifying.

As she showered and dressed, she could think of nothing else. What if she froze again in front of everyone? Would the others be better at this stuff than she was? The two nights with Julia and Carter were all the training she'd ever had, and they'd been disastrous.

But, what if Allie was right? What if learning to defend herself made the fear go away?

She'd risk anything for that.

A short while later, she joined the flow of students heading downstairs to breakfast. Minal caught up with her just as she reached the ground floor, where Julia stood waiting for her, and the two of them walked with the bodyguard, Minal bounding like an excited kitten and chattering about the history assignment Zelazny had given them.

Nothing in her demeanour indicated that she'd received an invitation this morning to secret self-defence training. She seemed perfectly normal. But maybe she was good at hiding things. After all, her dad was Raj Patel.

Gray had spoken to Julia last night when she had come back from London, but the bodyguard had told her little about the meeting with her mother. All she'd said was, "It was just a security meeting. Nothing to worry about."

Now the bodyguard smiled indulgently at Minal's description of the history teacher as a "Napoleon Fanboy", and even volunteered the information that he'd been obsessed with Napoleon back when she was at school here, too.

"His love for Napoleon is real," she said, as they reached the busy dining hall.

Gray noticed with interest that the bodyguard was no longer hiding her connection to the school. Minal didn't miss this either.

"When were you a student here?" she asked.

"I left about six years ago," Julia kept her eyes on the crowded hallway as she spoke.

"Really?" Minal gave her an interested look. "My sister, Rachel, was here back then. Did you know her?"

"I knew Rachel very well," Julia said. "We were friends."

As Minal exclaimed over this and demanded incriminating stories, Gray observed her bodyguard curiously. She hadn't missed her emphasis on the word "were".

One day she would ask Julia what had happened back then, and why she seemed to have such mixed feelings about the school.

At the door of the dining room, Julia left the two of them, and Gray and Minal joined the throng filling their plates.

When they reached their usual table, Dylan was already there with Kyle and Maya. She searched their faces for any sign that they, too, had received a secret invitation this morning, but everybody seemed perfectly normal. She wanted to ask but couldn't bring herself to do it. The invitation had been so unambiguous about the need for secrecy.

None of them seemed anything other than perfectly normal. Minal was bubbly. Kyle made acerbic jokes. Maya sipped her coffee and occasionally commented in that velvet voice.

For his part, Dylan barely glanced at her. Whatever Sophie or Kyle thought they'd seen, there was absolutely no indication that he was remotely interested in her. If anything, he showed even less concern about her existence than before, as he smiled at something Minal had said and sipped a strange-looking smoothie.

"Dude, your diet is way healthier than it should be," Kyle observed. "I admire this, while not replicating it myself." He gestured at the sausage and egg sandwich on his plate.

The American shrugged this off. "I went for a run this morning, so I'm feeding my muscles right now."

"You've been for a run already?" Kyle gave him a look of sheer horror. "What time did you get up?"

"I usually get up at six." Clocking Kyle's expression, Dylan laughed. "Dude, don't look at me like that. I can't help that I don't sleep much. I ran up to the castle ruins today while it was still dark. Came across a few deer, grazing under a tree. I got this close." Dylan held his hands a small distance apart. "I'm such a city boy, I still get excited about stuff like that."

Maya smiled over the top of her coffee cup. "That was lucky. The deer around here are very shy. They avoid people completely."

"These didn't seem to mind," Dylan said. "I must have stood there staring at them for ten minutes. They were so beautiful."

"Mmm," Kyle said, wistfully. "Venison stew."

"You're a monster," Minal scolded.

"I can't help it if deer are delicious," Kyle insisted. "I see both sides of them – they're pretty *and* tasty."

None of them seemed to notice Gray's distraction as she sat quietly, searching for clues as to which of them would be in this new secret group.

For the rest of the day she tried to focus on her lessons, but her mind kept returning to the invitation hidden in her room. By the time her classes ended, she was worn out from pretending, and told Julia she was going to study in the library until dinner time. Even there, in her favourite room, where the rugs hushed the sound and the rows of table lamps glowed green, it was hard to focus.

At one point, she got up to search for a reference book on the shelves near the back and noticed Dylan James sitting at a table in a corner with Sophie Montgomery. The two of them were talking quietly, their heads close together. Neither of them noticed her.

Her heart tightened, and she hurried away before either of them could see her.

When she got back to her table she stared at her book, but the words swam across the page like fish.

Why did it bother her, seeing them together like that? It wasn't any of her business.

She couldn't answer that question. All she knew was that it did bother her.

After that, she couldn't concentrate. She was heading for the door when the librarian called her name.

"Gray Langtry." Erin held up a hand. "I've got a book for you."

Gray walked over to the tall desk, with its tiny old-fashioned cubbyholes and long narrow drawers filled with index cards. Erin slid a familiar looking leather-bound book across the desk. The title on the cover in faded gold read History of Woman Suffrage.

"I've already stamped it for you." Erin said, adding with stern admonishment, "Take good care of it."

"I will," Gray promised, tucking it carefully in her bag with her notes.

As she turned to go, she heard the sound of running feet. Sophie raced past, dark hair flying, her face flushed and angry.

"Hey now, the racetrack is in Cheltenham," Erin called, disapprovingly.

The girl didn't spare her a glance, slamming through the door and disappearing into the hallway.

"It's like talking to a wall," Erin sighed, as she gathered an armful of books for shelving.

By the time Gray walked out into the hallway seconds later, Sophie was long gone.

As she trudged up the stairs a few minutes later, the heavy bag thumping against her hip, she found herself thinking about the glimpse she'd had of Sophie and Dylan. Now that she thought about it, Sophie hadn't looked happy.

When she reached her bedroom, she switched on the lights and set the bag down, taking out the heavy old book. The leather binding had been worn soft by a hundred years and thousands of readers. She turned the pages gingerly, scanning the words. But she couldn't focus. She kept thinking about Dylan looking at her in the chapel, with candlelight reflected in his eyes.

Impatiently she closed the book and set it on the shelf.

Outside the arched window it was already dark. In a few hours, she'd know who else was in the secret group. She'd know what the next steps would be.

That was all she should be focusing on. She had to stop thinking about Dylan James.

FIFTEEN

Just before ten o'clock, Gray ran down the main staircase. She was late. It wasn't yet curfew and the hallways were still busy. Students ran past her heading upstairs, talking and laughing.

To her relief, the first person she saw when she reached the ground floor was Julia. The bodyguard was standing near the headmistress's office, looking at something on her phone. Instead of her usual blazer and jeans, she wore snug black exercise gear. Her straight white-blonde hair was pulled back tightly.

As if she'd sensed Gray's presence, she glanced up, and gave her a look of surprise. "Aren't you supposed to be training?"

"I'm going there now," Gray said.

"You better hurry," the bodyguard told her. When Gray still didn't move, she shot her a look. "You don't know where to go, do you?"

"Where even is Training Room One?" asked Gray, holding up her hands.

With a sigh, Julia slipped her phone into her pocket. "Follow me."

The two of them headed down the wide hallway. Julia moved fast, ignoring everyone around them until they passed two guards Gray didn't recognise – one was a dark-skinned woman, athletic and tall. The other was a man with ruddy skin and a muscular build. They seemed to be studying everyone's faces with intense interest.

"Who was that?" Gray asked, when the guards were behind them.

"Raj sent them to help out. You're going to be seeing a lot of new security from now on. They've also enhanced the computer systems and the CCTV." Shooting Gray a sideways glance, the bodyguard added, "Basically, you can chill, Firefly. The cavalry has arrived."

She stopped in front of an unmarked door Gray had never noticed before. On the other side of it, steps led down from the ground floor to a cellar level. Unlike the main staircase, these steps were simple, utilitarian. A bare fluorescent strip light sputtered overhead. The air smelled faintly of dust and sweat.

"It's down here?" asked Gray, dubiously.

"Yep." Julia cast a glance at her watch. "We'd better move faster."

Gray had to race to keep up as she sped down the steps to the narrow corridor below. Halfway down it, Julia stopped, and pointed to a door on their right. "Changing room there." She pivoted, pointing to her left to a door bearing a single word: ONE. "Training room there. You'll find gear inside. Choose anything that fits. Do it fast. Being late won't be forgiven, even on your first day."

The changing room was a large open space lined with benches, above which hooks were mounted. Black exercise leggings and matching tops hung from all of them. Trainers and socks had been lined up in descending size on the bench below, from the largest to the smallest. There were gaps where it looked as if people had already taken shoes and clothes. Several dark blue Cimmeria uniforms hung from hooks as well, but revealed nothing about who their wearers might be.

Rushing now, she fumbled through the exercise clothes until she found a set that looked like her size. Hurriedly, she tore off her blazer and white blouse, stabbing them onto an empty hook before yanking the long-sleeved top over her head. It was a little too big but it would do. The leggings fit better, but she was in too much of a rush to care much how anything fit. She kicked her shoes off, heedless of where they landed, and grabbed a pair of black trainers in her size. Hopping on one leg at a time she yanked them on, before hurtling out of the room without waiting to tie the laces.

She raced out of the room and across the corridor to the training room, and shoved the door open so hard it slammed into the wall behind it with a bang, revealing a dimly lit cube of a room painted the colour of coal dust. Thick exercise mats covered the floor. A small crowd had gathered at the centre. She caught a glimpse of Minal, looking puzzled, and next to her Maya, distinctively tall and blonde.

"You're late." The voice was female, unforgiving. It stated the allegation flatly, not seeking an explanation. The speaker was a slim young woman with straight brown hair that almost brushed her narrow shoulders. She looked no more than twenty years old, maybe younger. She had accusing brown eyes and a smooth oval face, and she wore black exercise gear, similar to the clothing Julia had on.

"I'm sorry," Gray said.

The woman gave her a look of incomprehension as if she'd spoken in another language. "And your shoes are untied," she noted.

"Yes... I..." Gray fumbled for something to say. A whisper of muffled laughter swept the room before she found the words, "I'm going to tie them."

"All students should be appropriately shod at all times in this room," the woman announced, raising her voice and giving the rest of the students a stern look, as if they'd all been thinking about coming in with shoelaces trailing.

Reddening, Gray crouched to tie her laces. From her low position, she scanned the room. She couldn't see Julia. Along with Maya and Minal, she saw Kyle and two tall, patrician boys – one with dark hair and the other blond. They had different colouring but their faces were similar enough for them to be brothers. Next to them stood a stocky, muscular guy she didn't recognise, as well as a girl from her English class, whom she'd sometimes seen with Sophie Montgomery.

Then, to her horror, she realised who was standing next to the girl.

Sophie Montgomery, her dark hair pulled back into a thick braid, long, perfect legs encased in flattering leggings, was watching her. When their eyes met, Sophie's lips curved up and she gave a slow, pitying shake of her head, before turning away.

Gray felt sick. What the hell was Sophie doing in this group?

"OK then." At the other side of the room, Allie stepped forward. Gray hadn't seen her in the shadows.. "Welcome everyone. This is the first step toward taking back control, and learning to protect yourselves."

Gray straightened as Allie turned to gesture at the young woman, who was listening to this with her head cocked slightly to one side.

"This is Zoe Glass. Zoe will be overseeing the training programme. She's a former Cimmeria student who has come back specifically to help us. She's highly skilled in self-defence, and we are very grateful to her for taking time away from graduate school to help."

There was real affection in her voice, but Zoe just nodded.

"Everyone here has been hand-picked to be part of this group because of danger your families face." Allie's gaze fell on Gray. "Some of you have already faced real violence in your lives. Not because of anything you've done – because of who you are. Here in this room, we intend to make you less vulnerable. Less of a target. More of a fighter."

Gray's embarrassment faded as the words washed over her. She wondered why the others were here. What danger had Kyle faced? Or, for that matter, Sophie? The biggest threat she faced seemed to be a bad manicure.

"Surprise is the greatest weapon in any arsenal. Nobody must know what you learn here. The names of the people in this group must remain secret." Allie's voice grew cold. "Anyone who breaks this rule will be removed from this group and never re-invited. And that is a promise."

A sound like a sigh passed through the small crowd.

"Otherwise, the process is simple." Allie held out her hands. "Follow the rules. Have faith in yourselves. Try things that scare you. In this room, you will learn to be brave."

She was looking at everyone in the room, but Gray felt as if those words were just for her. Being brave again was all she wanted. She would do anything to have that.

The crowd shifted and she noticed Dylan standing in the shadows at the edge of the group. Somehow she knew it was him even before she made out his features.

He was staring at Allie, transfixed.

"Right then. Let's get started," the headmistress said. "Zoe? They're all yours."

The younger woman stepped forward. In contrast to the eloquence of the headmistress, her approach was blunt. "Before we do anything you need to warm up, so we're going on a run. I'll lead the way. Divide into pairs – it doesn't matter who with. You just need a running partner. Let's go."

Without waiting for them to absorb her rapid-fire commands, she darted across the room to the door Gray had crashed through moments earlier, and disappeared.

For a surprised second nobody moved. Then Minal called, "Run after her, you guys. We'll lose her."

Everyone rushed at once, instantly forming a bottleneck at the door, laughing and complaining until they tumbled out into the hallway and hurried after the trainer.

Sophie brushed by Gray on her way to the door and whispered, "Graceful entrance there, Gray." With a scornful laugh, she walked over to where Dylan still stood by the wall.

She said something to him, but he shook his head and said something Gray couldn't hear.

Sophie shrugged and followed the others into the hallway.

Gray hung back, waiting for her to leave. Dylan crossed the room to join her. "No rest for the weary. You don't want to be left behind."

"I just don't want to be crushed to death," she said, but she followed the others at a slow jog. When they reached the corridor she could see the crowd racing after Zoe, who was now far ahead. Amid the crowd, she saw Carter and Erin also running with the students.

"I have no idea where we're going," Gray said.

"Me neither," Dylan said, as if this were perfectly normal. "Should be interesting, wherever it is."

Gray kept waiting for him to take off and catch up with the rest of the crowd, but he seemed to be in no particular hurry.

"I don't know about you, but I've been trying to decide why everyone's been chosen," he said, as they followed the corridor around a bend. "You're the easiest one to figure out. But some don't make any sense. Like those two guys." He pointed at the two tall patrician boys she'd noticed earlier. "I wonder what they're doing here?"

"What about you?" she asked impulsively. "Why are you here?"

"I've been wondering that myself," he said. They were nearing the end of the corridor but Zoe showed no sign of stopping. "Seriously. Where is she taking us?"

Gray noticed that he'd dodged the question. But, ahead, the other students had begun running up a set of low steps and out through a door.

"We better hurry," Dylan said, quickening his pace.

The two of them were the last to run out into the cold night. By the time they came through the door, the others were already speeding across the lawn.

The December breeze was icy against Gray's skin, and with regret she remembered the black fleece jacket she'd left hanging on the hook in the changing room. Still, soon she was sweating despite the cold.

It had been nearly five weeks since the attack in Oxford. Aside from the brief training attempts with Julia, she'd hardly done anything physical since then, and it showed. By the time they reached the soft grass of the lawn she was already winded, and the others were far ahead.

As he jogged at her side, Dylan wasn't even breathing hard.

"You don't want to run with me," she warned, breathlessly. "I'm going to be really slow."

His expression didn't change. "Zoe said to run in pairs. We're a pair."

Gray didn't know what to make of him. He was so confusing.

The others were almost too far ahead to make out now. Gray thought she saw Minal, her dark ponytail swinging, at the end of the jagged line of students. Beyond them, the forest loomed, its darkness reaching out as if to absorb them.

Only then did she realise where they were headed. Straight into the woods. Where the man had followed them only two nights ago. Where she'd had a panic attack.

And she had no choice but to follow them.

SIXTEEN

The first strands of fear tightened around Gray's chest, making it harder to breathe.

I can't do this, she thought, as the others began to disappear beneath the trees. I'm not ready.

"Hey, how's your neck?" Dylan asked abruptly. "Does it hurt?"

This question was unexpected. Nobody mentioned her injury so openly. Sometimes she noticed people glancing at the scar, still livid against her fair skin. But nobody said anything.

"It's OK," she told him, panting. "Doesn't hurt."

"You should be careful, though." He gestured ahead. "They won't expect you to keep up."

She didn't know whether to be grateful or embarrassed that he'd noticed she was struggling. Still, there wasn't time to think about it – they'd reached the first trees at the edge of the woods.

But Dylan had distracted her, and her panic receded.

As they entered the forest the air changed, growing thick and filling with the scent of soft, loam-rich soil. Their footsteps seemed louder here, echoing off the tree trunks.

"I love these woods," Dylan announced. "You know, this is some Grade A Robin Hood shit you've got going on in this country."

Despite everything, an irrepressible laugh burst out of Gray. He flashed a quick smile.

He kept up a running commentary on the trees around them, guessing what kind of pine they might be, and generally distracting her as the path moved deeper into the woods.

Even when they reached the stretches where the branches formed a roof and no moonlight penetrated, her anxiety didn't overwhelm her. Her lungs burned but her footsteps adopted a steady beat – left… right… left… right. Like a heartbeat or a ticking clock.

Dylan stuck by her side. If he'd wanted to, he could have taken off and left her far behind. Yet he stayed beside her. She found his presence strangely reassuring. As if nothing bad could happen while he was beside her.

"Look at that, we're turning now." He pointed to where the last of the students had turned left onto a side path, disappearing behind browning ferns and tall brush. "Starting the loop back. She's keeping the run short."

"Thank God… for that," Gray said between gasps of air. Her legs felt unsteady and sweat ran horribly down her spine.

"Come on. Let's see if we can catch the others for the last bit." He motioned for her to speed up.

"Or not?" she suggested. But he was already powering ahead.

It took everything in her to summon more speed, but she did her best, and they weren't far behind the last few students when, ten minutes later, they all poured back into the building, breathless and sweating. When they reached Training Room One, they all collapsed on the floor mats, panting. Even Sophie was sweating.

Gray landed next to Kyle and Minal.

"That's enough of that," she heard Kyle murmur to himself. "All trained now."

"If anyone wants to kidnap me," Minal said, "I'll go willingly. Just don't make me run again."

Gray didn't have enough breath left to speak. Her chest ached and her legs were rubber bands.

But the night wasn't over yet. Zoe had more in store for them.

"Good. You're warmed up." She stood at one end of the room, her arms crossed. "It's time to get started."

The students groaned.

The trainer strode across the room until she stood at the centre of the cube with bodies around her, like a general at a bombsite. Ignoring their state of collapse she said, "We're going to start with very basic self-defence moves. I need a volunteer for the demonstration." She looked around the shadowy space, her gaze alighting on Dylan – out of all of them, he was the only one still standing. "You. You'll do."

He walked across to her, stepping over Kyle in the process.

"I can die happy now," Kyle announced.

Still on their backs, Gray and Minal giggled. Gray turned her head far enough to whisper to them, "You could have told me you were in this group too."

Minal smiled. "It's a secret, you idiot."

Zoe frowned at them. "Everyone up. You need to be looking to learn anything."

Slowly, the students stumbled to their feet. When they were all watching, the trainer turned to Dylan. "Do you know any self-defence?"

"A little," he said. "I did some training in the States."

"Fine." Zoe gestured at her throat. "I want you to grab me around my neck. I'm going to throw you down. I don't want to hurt you so please just go with the movement. You will land on your back. Don't be afraid."

The students tittered. Zoe was no more than about five foot four, and slim. At nearly six feet tall, Dylan towered over her. The idea that he'd be afraid seemed absurd.

But all he said was, "You got it, boss."

She stepped in front of him, showing him where she wanted him to place his hands. He had to bend slightly to wrap his left forearm around the base of her throat, where he gripped it with his right hand. The hold looked unbreakable.

Zoe looked out at the group of watching students. "Here's how you do it."

Taking one step forward with her left leg, putting him off balance, she dropped her weight, and then pulled him hard to the right. And just like that, Dylan was on his back on the thick matting.

A gasp swept the room.

He looked up in genuine surprise, that quickly changed to a wide grin, until he shook with laughter.

"That was amazing."

She accepted this compliment with a small shrug, and held out a hand to pull him up, telling the group, "I want you all to practise this move."

When the students just stared at her doubtfully, she added impatiently, "It's three simple steps. A four-year-old could do this."

"That would be some four-year-old," Minal muttered, as everyone began to talk at once.

"Your running partner is your training partner," Zoe announced above the noise. "Work together."

Gray's heart kicked. So Dylan would train with her, too.

She watched the other students fall into pairs. The darker of the two tall boys had ended up with Maya – they seemed well matched, Gray thought. Sophie Montgomery was with the blond boy, who looked like his brother. She barely spoke to her partner, and Gray saw her casting angry glances at Dylan, who didn't seem to notice.

"I want to know who everyone is," Gray whispered to Minal.

"I'll tell you later," Minal promised.

Julia, Carter, and Erin melted out of the corners to help – Gray had been too tired to notice them before now. Along with Zoe, they each took on two pairs of students, gathering them at the edges of the mat and talking them through the movements.

Julia motioned for Gray, Dylan, Kyle and Minal to come with her.

"Right. Minal and Kyle. I'm going to walk you through this first. Dylan and Gray, watch and learn."

"I'm a lover, not a fighter," Kyle informed her, earnestly.

"I can break you of that," the bodyguard assured him.

Gray stood beside Dylan as Julia demonstrated the basic legwork. "You use your body weight as a weapon in this move," Julia explained. "If you do it right, you could throw someone twice your weight into the gutter."

She demonstrated where Kyle should place his arm across Minal's throat.

"The element of surprise is important in this move," Julia told Minal. "Don't give away when you're about to drop him." Turning to Kyle she added, "Try not to fight it when she flips you. We're just learning how to do the move, not how to resist it. That will come later." She stepped back. "Go on. Give it a try."

Kyle, who looked queasy, said, "Sorry, sorry, sorry," as he gingerly placed his forearm across Minal's throat.

"You're the nicest attacker ever," Julia told him, dryly. "Now look, when she flips you, don't panic. The padding is soft. Your landing should be…"

Without warning, Minal dropped her hip and shifted her weight as she'd been taught, pulling Kyle's arm. He flew over her shoulder, landing on his back, where he lay gasping.

Julia stared at Minal.

"You said the element of surprise was important," Minal reminded her.

For once, the bodyguard appeared speechless. "I… Yes. I did."

Minal beamed at her. "It worked perfectly!"

"You thug," Kyle groaned. "I think you broke my spine."

"Move your toes for me," Julia said, crouching beside him.

His trainers wiggled frantically.

Her eyebrows rose. "Your spine is fine."

"I'll be the judge of that," he grumbled.

Minal held out her hand to help him up. "No hard feelings?"

"I am going to stab you in your sleep," he said. But as soon as he was vertical, his normal enthusiasm returned.

"Seriously, I've got to learn how to do that move. There are about twenty guys in my old school I'd like to use it on," he told her. "Show me how you did it."

Minal began walking him through it, bubbling with enthusiasm.

"You two practise carefully," Julia warned them, before refocussing on Gray and Dylan. "Gray, I'm a little worried about your neck. I don't want you to injure yourself trying this."

Gray rubbed a hand across the left side of her throat, where the scar was smooth beneath her fingertips. "It hasn't hurt in a while," she said.

"All the same, I don't think I want Dylan to flip you. We'll make you the flipper."

By now, the two of them knew what to do, and Dylan walked around behind Gray as Julia reminded her of the moves Minal had just tried. He put his left arm across Gray's throat, keeping it loose enough for her to breathe, and gripped it with his right.

She could feel the hard muscles of his chest against her back, the warmth of his skin against hers. His breath soft against the side of her face.

Only then did she realise that this was almost exactly what the attacker in Oxford had done. He'd stood exactly like this, holding her, with a knife in his hand.

She froze, staring at Julia.

The bodyguard held her gaze. "Yes. This is the same move he used that night. That's why we're doing it. Now, listen to me. If you panic, you stay the victim. But if you learn how to flip Dylan right now, nobody will ever do that to you again. Do you hear me? You will have control again."

Gray tried to speak but the words wouldn't come. Her chest contracted, tightening around her lungs. But she forced herself to breathe slowly. To keep thinking. She could this. She had to do this. She wanted control. She wanted to be brave.

Drop your shoulder, swing your hip. Pull. Drop your shoulder, swing your hip. Pull... Silently she reminded herself of the moves she had to do.

Dylan waited patiently, his arm across her throat.

Closing her eyes, Gray dropped her shoulder and swung her hip, pulling his arm at the same time with every bit of strength she could muster.

It wasn't as smooth as Zoe's move, or as quick as Minal's, but Dylan fell, right where she wanted him to.

Gray stared at him in disbelief as he grinned up at her.

Julia pulled her into a bear hug. "You did it, Gray. You really did it."

Gray threw her arms around her, dizzy with exhilaration and relief.

For the first time, it seemed the fear that had dug its claws into her weeks ago was beginning to let go.

SEVENTEEN

"Allie. Allie. Wake up."

Allie blinked, and the cold, dark bedroom swam into view.

"What is it?" Her voice was hoarse. She'd been deep in a dream.

Something told her it was very late. The air had the heaviness that only happens at two in the morning, when sunset and sunrise are both far away.

"Someone's on the grounds." Carter was already dressing, his muscular torso pale in the moonlight that filtered through the window as he pulled on his trousers. His back formed a near-perfect V-shape when he straightened.

He hadn't turned on any lights, but he didn't need to. They both knew this small cottage like the backs of their hands. It had been their home for eight months – ever since Isabelle asked them to come back, saying she needed time away.

"Just one intruder or more?" Allie asked, throwing off the warm duvet, and swinging her feet to the floor. She shivered as the cold bit her toes. The little stone cottage was sweet and private, with roses climbing up over the roof. But it was certainly not well heated.

"At least two, maybe three." His voice was tight. "They tripped the new warning system when they came over the fence. The night watch called as soon as it happened."

Allie processed this quickly, grabbing her black running gear from the dresser. "Is anyone out there now, looking for them?"

"There are four guards on duty. Everyone else is being called in." Carter's dark head bent as he laced his trainers. "In five minutes we'll have sixteen people out searching the grounds."

Five minutes, Allie thought. Too slow.

Apprehension swirled, turning her stomach to acid.

"Where's Julia?" she asked, yanking a black thermal top over her head. "Does she know?"

"They called her right after they called us." He shrugged on his jacket, patting the pockets automatically, before reaching for his comms system, which was charging on a table near the bed. He placed the earpiece in his right ear, and slid the microphone over his wrist.

"I'll meet you out there." He headed for the door. "I'm heading for sector two."

They'd long ago divided the rambling, wooded grounds into security sections. Sector two included the chapel and the stream, where the intruder had ended up last time. It made sense for him to go straight there.

"I'll find you," she told him. "Stay safe."

In the doorway he paused, his dark eyes holding hers. "Always."

As the door closed, Allie dialled Julia's number.

"Allie," the bodyguard answered, her voice terse.

"Firefly?" Allie asked, pulling on her jacket with one hand as she talked.

"On my way to her now. How bad is it?"

She was running. Through the phone, Allie could hear her feet pounding on the stairs.

"Two, maybe three," Allie told her. "Location unknown."

Julia swore softly. "I knew it. I knew they'd come back."

"Me too. Keep her safe. Follow the plan," Allie said.

They both hung up.

Allie exhaled and sought the inner calm that kept her nerves steady in bad times. It was a method she'd developed when she was very young, and she practised it as she pulled on her shoes and jacket, checking the pockets for a torch. She grabbed her phone and put on her own comms system, switching on the earpiece to hear the voices of the guards.

"Nothing in sector one."

"Footprints in sector five, just beyond the main drive. Looks like two adult males. Heading west."

West, Allie thought. Toward the school building.

Jules had to be with Gray by now. She would call in as soon as she got her to the safe room. But Allie wouldn't wait for that.

She threw the cottage door open and headed out into the frozen night at a run.

Overhead, a pale winter moon hung low over the grounds. The cottage was surrounded by a low stone wall. Ahead, the fishing pond where she'd skinny-dipped as a student glimmered silver, a faint skein of ice frosting the edges.

When she tore through the little wooden gate, the frozen grass crunched beneath the soles of her trainers. Each intake of breath brought in ice. Each exhale created a cloud that hung in the air for a full second before evaporating. The cold bit into her face, but she barely felt it as she sprinted in the direction of the school building. She should have been going to meet Carter in sector two. He was expecting her. But Jules was all alone in there.

"I'm following their footprints in sector two." It was Carter's voice in her ear. "Tracing their path toward the school. Looks like they came into the grounds in three, and crossed into two. Made it to the chapel and then I lost them on the footpath where ground's too firm to keep footprints."

Allie activated her microphone without breaking stride. "I'm on the path now, heading for the main building. No sign of them."

"Everyone remain in your sectors in case they backtrack," Carter ordered. "Allie has the main path."

There was no wind. Everything was so still. The moon was nearly full – bright enough to create tiny pools of pearl-grey light where it dappled through the tree branches. The ice-cold air felt clean and pure in her lungs. But someone was on the grounds. And she sensed them like a virus in an otherwise healthy system.

But where? In the woods around her, nothing stirred. Wherever they were, they weren't here.

Still nothing through the comms from Jules. She should have had time to get Gray to safety by now. Why hadn't she said anything?

Something was wrong. Very wrong.

Suddenly, her heart went as cold as the December night. She began to run harder, her voice shaking as she spoke into her microphone.

"I'm heading for the main building. I think they're inside."

EIGHTEEN

It was the third night in a row Gray had slept without nightmares, and she was burrowed deep into the dreamless dark when Julia shook her shoulder.

"Gray. Gray. Wake up."

Gray squinted at her blurrily. "Julia? What is…?"

The bodyguard didn't let her finish the question.

"Quick. You have to get up." She grabbed Gray's dressing gown from the hook by the door and thrust it into her hands, pulling her to her feet at the same time. "We need to hurry."

Her voice was barely above a whisper but Gray could hear the tension in it.

Adrenaline rushed into her veins like caffeine as she stumbled to her feet and yanked the soft robe over her shoulders.

"What…?" she tried again but Julia gripped her arm.

"Later. Right now we have to move."

Gray's robe billowed around her as the bodyguard pulled her down the dark corridor, past closed bedroom doors.

Still confused by her sudden awakening, Gray followed numbly. The floor was ice under her bare feet and her stomach felt tight. She asked no more questions. Clearly something had happened. Something bad.

Still holding her arm, the bodyguard opened a plain door. Behind it, Gray saw a winding staircase, lost in deep shadows.

Julia pulled a flashlight from her pocket and switched it on. The old stone stairs gleamed in its glow, as white as bones.

"Stay right behind me," she hissed.

The two of them descended the dark stairs rapidly, their feet scuffing against the dusty steps while ahead the flashlight's beam juddered and danced against the scuffed walls.

Gray's feet grew numb, and she trembled – whether from fear or the cold, she wasn't certain. But she kept moving, following Julia's unsteady light.

She could hear nothing but her own blood rushing through her ears, and the harsh rasp of her breath. The air smelled of dust. Ahead of her, the bodyguard moved with quiet urgency down, down, down.

Gray wanted to ask what was going on, but she didn't dare.

When they reached a narrow door, the bodyguard held up a hand, motioning for her to stop. She switched off the torch, plunging them into darkness that made Gray's heart stutter. Then she opened the door and peered out. There was more light on the other side – a soft glow.

Motioning for Gray to follow, the bodyguard stepped through it. Clutching her robe tightly, Gray followed.

They emerged into the wide ground-floor hallway, just outside the kitchen.

As always, a few lights were on, illuminating the space. It all looked perfectly normal. The sprawling kitchen smelled faintly of rising bread. Everything looked just as it had after dinner last night. It seemed perfectly safe.

Catching her eye, Julia pointed silently down the hallway.

Gray knew better than to speak now. The two of them ran in that direction, their feet nearly silent on the polished oak floor.

Gray kept thinking she heard someone behind them, and she'd spin around only to realise it was her own breathing she could hear.

Julia never looked back though. She moved like a panther, low and silent, down the hallway to the last door on the right. Pushing it open, she hustled Gray in, and closed the door behind them, locking it.

Gray looked around the shadowy library, bewildered.

Julia switched her flashlight on again. The torch beam danced off the ruby wool of the Persian rugs. It was the first time Gray had ever seen the room without the green table lights lit up in rows. It felt strange without them. Dangerous.

Taking her arm again, Julia hurried her past the librarian's desk, beyond the first few rows of bookcases, stopping in front of an elaborately carved oak panelled wall. As Gray watched, she pulled out a small bunch of keys, which jangled in the quiet as she slid one into a nearly invisible keyhole.

A door opened, where there had not been a door three seconds earlier.

Gray had time to see a tiny cubicle before Julia dragged her inside and shut the door, turning the key to lock it. She switched off her flashlight.

Inside, it was terribly dark. Gray's heart pounded against her ribs.

The bodyguard spoke softly. "Firefly secure." There was a pause, and then she said, "Copy that."

"Julia," Gray whispered. "What's going on? Please."

"Two seconds," said Julia.

Gray could hear her moving. A fluttering sound of fabric against fabric and then, after a few endless moments, a click.

An overhead light came on, blindingly bright. Gray flung up a hand to cover her eyes, stumbling backwards in the process, banging into a desk that was right behind her.

"Sorry," Julia whispered, reaching out to steady her.

Slowly Gray lowered her hand, taking in the strange, vividly painted room. The space was small – barely big enough to hold a desk and a leather chair. But that wasn't the interesting part. The interesting part was a mural that covered the entire wall. It showed angels with silver wings, on a green hillside beside a river. They were hovering above villagers who'd gathered to meet them. The villagers all carried long swords, which they held hesitantly, as if thinking the angels might not be on their side.

It was so bizarre, Gray found it hard to believe it was real.

Maybe I'm hallucinating, she thought.

But everything else in the room made sense. The desk. The chair. She could see that the bodyguard had taken off her jacket and was stuffing it against the cracks around the bottom of the door.

"What is this room?" Gray asked, bewildered.

Julia replied without looking up from her work. "It's a study space used by sixth formers. There are a few of them back here. We chose this as a safe room in case someone got into the grounds."

"Someone is on the grounds?" Gray's voice rose.

Julia turned to face her, motioning hard for quiet. "There's an intruder," she whispered. "The guards are searching for them now. We're perfectly safe here, I promise."

"How did they get in?" asked Gray. "Where are they? I don't understand."

Julia gave her a measured look. "Guards are searching for them right now. I'm sorry – I need to listen." she motioned at her ear.

Gray shivered and pulled the dressing gown tightly around her, bottling up the questions she wanted to ask. How could someone have got in after last time? Hadn't they increased security?

Everyone kept telling her she was safe and yet this felt the opposite of safe.

She found herself rubbing her thumbnail back and forth across the side of her index finger – nervously sawing at herself to quell the fear that swirled in her chest.

Occasionally Julia spoke quietly into the microphone on her wrist, but her words were opaque and meaningless. "Understood." "Confirm." "Copy that."

As the minutes ticked by, she lost track of time. It might have been hours or only minutes. Blessedly, Julia left the flashlight on, providing a narrow beam of light, and Gray found herself staring at tiny details on the strange mural – the ornate handle on a sword, or a flower carefully painted at the edge of the stream. She tried not to think about what might be happening outside and why it was taking so long.

At last, though, she noticed sounds from outside. First a thumping noise, and then, faintly, voices.

She jumped to her feet and reeled away from the door but Julia held up her hands.

"It's OK. It's our people."

Someone knocked softly three times against the door. Gray heard a muffled male voice from the other side. "Jules. It's us."

Julia unlocked the little door and it flew open. Allie and Carter stood on the other side, their faces flushed from the cold night.

"We just wanted to check on you." The headmistress sounded breathless. "We're still searching."

"Is the building safe?" Julia asked.

"They've searched the ground floor and they're now working up floor by floor," Allie told her, with a quick glance at Gray. "We've found evidence they made it inside. But we think they're gone now. Anyway, this floor is safe – we checked it ourselves. You can come out." She stood back.

Cautiously, Julia and Gray stepped out into the main library. Gray found that, now that she was safe, she'd begun to tremble.

"You really think they're gone?" she asked.

"I found the spot where they came over the fence," Carter told her. "It looks like they hid a car in the woods – we found the tyre tracks. So we think they're gone. Just to be safe, though, we're searching every room."

"Maybe it was that photographer again," Gray suggested. "He could have come back…." Her voice trailed off as she saw the blank faces around her.

The three adults exchanged looks she couldn't read.

"We have to tell her now." Julia's voice was firm. "If you don't, I will."

"Tell me what?" Gray asked.

There was a long pause. It was Allie who spoke in the end. "The other night at the chapel, we don't think it was a photographer."

Gray's stomach dropped. "You don't? But you said—"

"I know what we said." The headmistress looked tired. "I think we were wrong. On multiple levels."

"So…" Gray surveyed the three of them uneasily. "Who was it?"

Carter spoke first. "This was a professional job. Whoever came in tonight, they were well trained. They had studied the grounds, they knew where to go and what to do. We think this might have been a test to see how our security system reacted. This was no photographer."

Gray's heart contracted. "It's them." She looked at Julia. "It is them, isn't it? They know where I am."

The bodyguard's face was taut. "We think it's them."

"But we will keep you safe." Allie crossed to where she stood. "We kept you safe tonight. And we will do everything in our power to protect you from now on."

Gray looked at her sadly. "They got past my mother's security in Oxford. How will you stop them here?"

For a second nobody replied. But when Allie spoke again her voice was firm. "There's a lot you don't know about this school. But one thing I can tell you for certain is that the people who work here are very good at protecting our students. They won't let anyone hurt you. We have a plan. Things might get rocky for a while, but whatever happens, we are going to protect you."

Gray could tell she meant every word. Her voice was fervent.

Still, she kept thinking about Oxford. And the knife in the dark.

NINETEEN

Gray slept very little that night. It was after three in the morning before the building was declared safe, and after that, sleep didn't come. The next day she felt groggy and hungover.

The others, of course, knew nothing about the break-in. Julia had warned her to keep it to herself. "We don't want people to panic," she'd said.

But it was hard not telling them. It felt like a kind of lie.

Knowing a terrible secret is like having a little piece of poison in your pocket.

Without any idea of what Gray had been through, all day long the others wanted to talk about night training, and how exciting it had been.

"I flipped Minal four times," Kyle boasted.

She gave him a withering look, "Only because I let you."

Maya was more circumspect. "It was useful to learn but I hope I never have to use the training in real life," she said. "I'm not sure it would be as easy."

"Agreed," Kyle said. "But did you see that guy David? The one with Caitlyn? He's so hot. I would definitely flip him any time."

Gradually, they took Gray's mind off the hours spent hiding in the dark. After all, she'd done well in night training, too. She'd flipped Dylan three times. By the third try, she hadn't frozen when Dylan's arms encircled her neck. The feel of his body against hers hadn't reminded her of a killer – it just felt warm and solid. He'd been incredibly patient as she figured it out, never criticising how long it took her to get into position or to summon the courage to make the move.

"You're getting better at this," he had told her as she helped him up.

"Thanks," she'd told him. "You make a nice victim."

They'd worked well together. He had a way of making things that were very difficult seem easier. Before Julia had woken her to hurry her downstairs, she'd felt amazing about it. Powerful and more confident. Perhaps that was why she wasn't as stressed out as she might have been by what she'd learned last night. Somehow, she felt like she'd grown stronger in the last twenty-four hours. Now she felt ready to fight back.

There was just one flaw, really, to the night training group.

"What is Sophie doing in it?" Kyle wondered. "It's supposed to be our super-secret thug life but it's hard to focus when she's glaring at us."

It was lunch break, and Maya, Minal, Gray, and Kyle had gathered at their usual table in the dining hall. There was no sign of Dylan.

"Kidnap target." Maya said it bluntly, as she speared a bit of pasta with her fork. "She told me once that she has bodyguards when she travels because someone tried to kidnap her a few years ago to get money out of her father."

"Oh, wow," Gray was shocked. It was impossible to imagine perfect Sophie dealing with the same hard realities she herself faced. "I had no idea."

"Her life is a mess," Kyle said, not without sympathy.

"I think I'm just in the group because my dad wants me to get more fit." Minal popped the last of her sandwich in her mouth. "It's basically forcing me to exercise."

Gray turned to Kyle. "What about you? If it's not too personal – why are you in the group?"

"Oh, it's all a bit embarrassing." He pushed his empty plate away. "Basically, my father testified against a dodgy man in a trial a few years ago, after a lot of people lost money in some messed up investment. The dodgy man went to prison and threatened our family. So my parents sent me here."

"Don't worry." Minal put her hand on his shoulder. "If the dodgy man comes, I'll protect you."

"Four times," he reminded her, laughing. "I flipped you hard."

The moment lightened, and soon they were all joking and teasing each other. But Gray's gaze kept returning to Sophie, who sat with a group of beautiful girls across the room, her lips curved in an indulgent smile as they chattered around her.

Maybe we're more alike than you know, she thought.

With training in the evening now scheduled three nights a week, there was less time for homework. As soon as classes ended that day, Gray headed straight for the library to try and catch up. She was relieved to find everything normal there again. The green table lamps glowed reassuringly, and Erin was at the desk.

Instead of settling in at her usual table at the back, she found her feet carrying her past the first rows of bookshelves to the heavily carved oak panelled wall. Even though she knew it was there – after all, she'd seen it open with her own eyes – she couldn't find the door to the study space where she'd hidden the night before.

"Hey, are you OK?" The male voice came from behind her, and Gray spun around.

Dylan stood by a shelf of books. His backpack and notes lay on a table a few feet away. She must have walked right by him without noticing him.

"I'm fine," she said. "Why?"

"I just found out about what happened last night," he said in a low voice. "I can't believe it."

Gray was caught off guard. How could he possibly know?

"What do you mean?" she asked, buying time.

"Come on. I know someone came looking for you," he told her. "I overheard a couple of the teachers talking about it. That must have been really intense."

Gray glanced around to make sure no one could overhear. "You can't tell anyone. They don't want everyone to freak out."

Dylan motioned toward a table piled with books. "Sit with me. We should talk."

"Talk about what?" Gray asked, as she took the chair across from his.

"Is it true that the guy made it to the school building?" he asked.

She hesitated. But if he knew the basics already, there wasn't much point in keeping the details from him.

"All they told me was that he got in, but then went out again," she said. "They caught him on camera, but his face was covered."

Julia had showed her the camera images that morning – a man, moving swiftly out the back door of the school with his head down. He was tall and strongly built, wearing a black jacket. The sight had made Gray's blood run cold.

"I'm sorry, but nobody should get that close to you," Dylan said flatly. "I think your security blew it."

Gray bristled. Julia had rushed to her room in the dead of night to save her. He knew nothing about that, but of course he had opinions.

"Allie and Carter say they've got it all under control," she said evenly. "I believe them."

His straight eyebrows drew together. "Look, all I know is my last school had an attempted break-in and they caught the guys in five minutes and arrested them. Whoever got in here last night wandered around for God knows how long and then left without getting caught. We don't even know who they were or what they got up to while they were here. That's messed up, Gray. You could have been killed."

He wasn't entirely wrong. "It's not the school's fault though," she said, after a beat. "Carter told me these were professionals."

She saw a flicker of interest in his eyes. "What did he mean by that?" he asked. "How were they professional?"

"He thought they were trained."

He thought for a second. "It would make sense if they had military training, I guess, given how far they got. But if that's the case…" His voice trailed off.

Gray motioned for him to continue. "If that's the case, what?"

"Nothing," he said. "Just, if that's the case, they won't make the same mistakes again. They've tested the security system twice now. They know how it works. They'll adapt." He held her gaze. "Next time they come in, they won't set off any alarms."

It took a second for her to find her voice to reply. "Look, don't say stuff like that, OK? This is my life we're talking about. Things are hard enough as it is."

He held up his hands. "I'm sorry. You're right. I was just angry that they didn't catch them. That was thoughtless of me."

"It's OK," she said, but the seeds of fear he'd planted were now growing.

Why hadn't they caught whoever it was? How did they get away with guards everywhere and cameras all over the fence?

"At least you're not the only one with this kind of craziness going on," he told her, probably to comfort her. "Maya told me her parents sent her to school in England after they received a warning that someone was going to kidnap her from her school in Poland, take her to Russia, and kill her there."

"My God." Gray was horrified. "I knew things were bad, but she never told me how bad."

"She doesn't talk about it," he said. "Then again, how much of this stuff do you talk about?"

It was a good point. Very perceptive.

She studied him curiously. "What about you? Do your parents get threats?"

"My dad's the first black attorney general in Texas. What do you think?" There was irony in his voice, but something else too. Something deeper and more painful that his tone was trying to disguise.

"Honestly! What is wrong with the world that people just can't accept each other?" she asked, genuinely bewildered. "I don't understand anything. All we have to do is live together and be kind to each other. But everyone just wants to blow up the world because it's not exactly the way they want it to be. I don't get it."

"You're preaching to the choir on this one." He studied her with interest. "You know, you've got interesting views, for the daughter of a Conservative prime minister."

"Well I'm not my mother," she said, flatly. "I mean, don't get me wrong, I love her and I respect her. She's the strongest person I know. But I am my own person. With my own opinions."

He tilted his head. "You say that like it's obvious, but I know a lot of kids with political parents and most of them have the same political opinions. You're a pretty strong thinker to disagree with someone like Jessica Langtry. I have to say, I don't agree with her politics but I admire her as a person. You have to be as strong as hell to be a female prime minister."

Gray smiled. "You sound like my friend Jake."

"Who's that?" he asked, instantly.

Was it possible there was a hint of jealousy in his voice?

"Jake McIntyre. His dad is—"

"Tom McIntyre? Leader of the Labour party?" His voice rose as he put the pieces together. "His son is your friend?"

She nodded. "We went to the same school and, yeah, we're friends."

He gave a low whistle. "What does your mother think of that?"

"She wasn't thrilled about it at first," Gray admitted. "But Jake's a good person, and eventually she came around."

"So I remind you of Jake McIntyre?" he sounded bemused.

She nodded. "He's really interested in politics, like you. It's almost like his hobby. I've always tried to avoid it. It's my mum's thing, not mine. And besides, whenever we talk about it, we argue."

An older student walked by, whistling under his breath. Gray waited until the sound of his tuneless song faded before speaking again.

"I don't know why I don't agree with her," she said, slowly. "It just seems like what I see in the world and what she sees – it's not the same." She paused to think it through. "Like, I know she really wants to make things better for people. She genuinely cares. But people are so angry at her." She let out a long breath. "I don't know. It's really hard to say 'You're wrong, Mum,' when you're sixteen, and your mother is in charge of the entire country. It seems easier not to talk about politics at all."

He was watching her with an odd expression.

She blushed. "I'm sorry. That sounded stupid."

"Actually," he said, "I was just thinking how wise you are. How beyond your years wise."

"Oh." She was flummoxed by the unexpected compliment. "I mean, thanks. I guess."

"It's the truth," he insisted. "You're making your own path in the world. That's the best anyone can do, as far as I'm concerned – cut their own path and walk down it. Don't let anybody change your direction. Take your own journey."

He'd said she seemed wise beyond her years but she felt the same about him. Sometimes he sounded more like a parent than a student.

Most of all, Gray liked the way he always seemed to hear things people said. Really hear them. Maybe that was why he knew more than anyone else about what was going on. He just… listened.

"It must be weird for you being here." She gestured at the room around them. "I mean, so far from home."

"I love it here," he said without hesitation. "It's a fascinating country. You know where I live, we spend a whole year of high school studying Texas history. One entire year. And Texas joined the Union in 1845. Before then it was a Republic for about five years, and before that it was someone else's land. And we don't spend much time studying its native history. Basically, we've got a hundred and fifty years of Texas." He tapped the table with his fingertip. "There are books in this library older than that. I'll bet this building is older than that."

She gave an apologetic wince. "It's a lot older."

"That's what I'm talking about." He held out his hands. "There's more history in a random British living room than my

177

entire state. And it's kind of, I don't know… I guess it's humbling to realise that my country has been around for what seems like five minutes to most nations. I'm learning humility here. And learning about history. It's inspiring."

"I like that," she said. "I take it for granted sometimes. The old buildings, the history. But then to us, America looks so exciting. It's like things are always happening there – big things. I guess it's just that seeing things from far away, you get a different view."

He smiled at her then, a genuine smile, and Gray felt strangely warm, all the way to her fingertips. Their eyes met and held.

A weighty silence fell. Gray couldn't think of anything intelligent to say. Her mind seemed to be suddenly tangled up in his cheekbones, his brown eyes, the lean wrists visible below the rolled up sleeves of his sweater.

She must be misinterpreting things. Because otherwise, she was developing a crush on Dylan sodding James. And that was the last thing she needed right now.

TWENTY

Gray hurried down the hallway, not entirely certain where she was going or why she was hurrying. A man stood on a ladder fixing something on the ceiling and she veered around him without a second glance, barely aware that he was there. The conversation with Dylan had rattled her. She couldn't have a crush on him. What about Jake? There had been a moment in London when it looked like something real might happen between them, but then it had all just ended when she came here. Was it OK to like someone else now? Or was it cheating? And what did it matter? Dylan was probably in love with Sophie anyway.

This had to be exhaustion talking, she told herself. She'd hardly slept last night. But somehow, even she didn't believe that.

She was so lost in her own thoughts it took her a moment to notice Julia standing in front of her.

"Firefly." The bodyguard's voice was hoarse. Gray could see the tiredness in her face as she asked, "Where are you headed in such a hurry?"

"Nowhere," Gray admitted.

"Good. I'd like you to come with me. I want you to see something."

In truth, Gray was glad to have somewhere to go. She needed to sort out her thoughts about Dylan, and for that she needed to be somewhere he wasn't. It was hard to think when he was around, being beautiful and distracting.

She followed Julia beyond the trio of statues in the atrium and then through the double doors into the classroom wing. The last lessons had ended some time ago, and the rooms had a hollow abandoned feel. Their footsteps echoed as they ran up the stairs to the third floor.

Only then did Gray think to ask, "What's up?"

Julia smiled. "You'll see."

This floor was out of use by teachers and students, as it was due for refurbishment. Unlike the rest of the building, which was well maintained, these rooms had a run-down look – paint peeling on the window frames, wooden floors scratched, and white walls scuffed and dirty. An abandoned chalk board had been shoved against a wall, where it stood gathering dust. Through open doors she could see rows of empty desks, neatly aligned, and beyond those, windows through which the watery daylight was fading.

It was only four o'clock, and already the winter night was closing in.

When they neared the end of the corridor, Gray began to hear the distinct sound of human activity – footsteps shuffling, things being moved.

Finally, when they reached the last door on the left, Julia stopped.

"Here we are," she said, and pushed it open.

On the other side, the room was alive with activity. All the school desks had been removed and replaced by long tables, on top of which stood an array of humming computers. Five screens flickered with constantly changing CCTV feeds of the school's corridors and fenceline. A guard in the all-black uniform of Talos Security sat in front of them, his eyes moving from one image to the next. Over his shoulder, Gray could see busy corridors and the common room, crowded with students. That switched suddenly, replaced by the dining hall where the staff were preparing for dinner, draping white linen cloths over the tables.

More guards sat in front of other computers or gathered in small groups, talking quietly. One wore headphones, and talked steadily into a microphone.

"This is Gold Command," Julia announced. "The new headquarters for security at Cimmeria Academy. Raj sent a crew down this morning to upgrade the security system. They've been installing more tech all day. More equipment is coming this evening. By tomorrow, we'll have every inch covered."

Gray watched the images flickering on the screen. Someone was playing the piano in the common room, then the screen flickered and showed the busy main hallway, with students walking in groups, laughing and talking.

"I wanted you to see this so you could understand that last night won't happen again." Julia's voice was firm. "We are all working as hard as we can to make sure of that."

At the far end of the room, Allie and Carter stood talking to Zoe Glass and two guards. Allie waved them over.

"Welcome to our new HQ, Gray," the headmistress said, before turning to Julia. "Jules, there's someone here who wants to speak with you."

The two guards turned around.

"Hey," Riley said, his broad, tanned face breaking into a grin. "It's been a while."

"Bloody hell." Julia stared at the man who had been her Talos partner before she left London. "When did you get here?"

"Twenty minutes ago," he said. "Heard you could use some spare hands."

The two of them exchanged a quick, awkward hug, patting each other's shoulders a little too hard.

Riley turned to Gray and held out his hand. "It's nice to see you looking so well. Settling in OK?"

She nodded, shaking his hand a bit stiffly. She didn't know Riley as well as Julia, but she liked him. He'd always been there when she needed him although she got the impression he didn't always approve of her.

"It's great," she said. "Thank you."

"Except for last night, I guess?" he said.

Her smile faded. "Yeah. Except for that."

"Well, that's why we're here." He winked at Julia. "They've called in the real guards at last, eh?"

She rolled her eyes, but Gray could tell she was glad to see him.

"Once you're settled in we should have a coffee," Julia told him. "I'll bring you up to speed."

The guard next to him was listening to this exchange with amused interest. She had a curvy figure, thick dark hair, and animated brown eyes.

"Oh, hey, I forgot." Riley turned to her. "This is Cameron Perez. We worked together on the investigation in London. Raj sent her to help out."

"I've heard a lot about you," Cameron told Julia. "Riley and Raj are big fans of yours."

"It's a lie," Riley deadpanned.

When Cameron smiled, deep dimples appeared in her cheeks, giving her an impish look that Gray instantly liked.

"Well, I hope I don't disappoint." Julia said it mildly, but Gray could tell she was flattered.

Cameron turned her attention to Gray. "I've heard a lot about you, too. I'm going to do my best to help get the guys who are after you."

"OK," Allie interrupted, drawing them back to the matter at hand. "The security is in place. We have fresh recruits. We've been throwing around a lot of ideas – whether we should keep the school open or close it down. If we keep it open, should we have business as usual, or change things up?" She glanced around the circle of faces. "I think we're all agreed that the school should stay open, and classes should continue as usual?"

Everyone nodded.

"Winter Break starts in just a few days," Allie explained to Julia and Gray. "After that we have a long break when we can take a look at security and make sure we're doing everything we can to keep the students safe. It doesn't make sense to shut down before then." She drew a breath. "The other big issue, though, is what to do about the Winter Ball. After what happened last night, I propose we cancel it."

"I agree," Julia said. "Security will be a nightmare."

Riley and Cameron looked between the two of them. "OK, fill us in," Riley said. "What's a Winter Ball?"

"It's a big fundraiser held every year on the last day of the term," Julia explained. "Alumni come back for it. Lots of bigwigs. It raises a lot of money for the school and the charities it supports."

"How many people?" Cameron asked.

"We're expecting a hundred and fifty this year," Allie said.

Riley gave a low whistle. "That would be a lot of people to watch."

"It's not just how many people," Julia told him. "It's which people. The prime minister is invited, members of Parliament, junior royalty, lots of CEOs. It's a big deal."

"And it's happening next week?" Cameron looked doubtful.

"I think we should cancel it," Carter said, decisively. "Too risky."

"You don't want to be obvious, though. People would ask questions," Riley said. "We're trying to keep all of this low key. Has it ever been cancelled before?"

"I don't know." Allie glanced at Carter, who gave a slight shrug. "We could come up with an excuse. Problems with the heating or something."

Gray listened as they talked through the different ways they could cancel it, how they would handle it. It was odd – until this moment, she hadn't thought much about the ball. She hadn't even thought she would go, though her mother had made her bring a dress just in case. Now the thought of cancelling it made her unbearably sad.

It was mostly an adult affair – only senior students got to go, and it was a big privilege. They'd all been looking forward to it. The first time she'd ever spoken to Minal and Kyle, they'd talked about the ball.

Still, she knew it made sense not to hold it. After all, it had been a fundraiser in Oxford that John Ashford had targeted last time. He'd used the chaos of the party to try and get his assassin close to Gray and her mother. Close enough to nearly kill her.

But then an idea came to her so suddenly she found herself speaking aloud.

"Don't cancel it," she said.

The others fell silent.

"I'm sorry?" Julia gave her a puzzled look. "What did you say?"

"Don't cancel the ball." Gray looked at the adult faces around her. "Use it."

Carter gave her a puzzled look. "Use it how?"

"Ashford targeted my mum at a fundraiser in October. What if…" Gray paused, looking for the words. "What if we could get him to do it again? Only this time we could be ready?"

"I don't think so," Julia sounded dubious. "That's far too dangerous."

"Hang on a minute." Cameron looked at Riley. "She has a point. If the prime minister is coming and we know he's likely to target her, we could set a trap."

He considered this, his brow creasing. "It's not a bad idea. We've already got the school wired from top to bottom, and he can't possibly know that."

She nodded. "We've also got an enhanced team of security guards, and he won't know that either."

"If we give him a goal like that…" Riley said.

"… it would give him a focus," Cameron finished his thought.

Allie held up her hands. "I'm sorry, could somebody fill me in here? A focus for what?"

Cameron turned to her. "We think these attacks against the school are going to continue," she explained. "This is a state-sponsored group, with Russian money and Russian expertise. No matter how we adjust the security they'll get through eventually because they know how to defeat every system we can come up with for a place like this. What we need is to draw them to us on a night when we're expecting them. Then we can catch them in the act. Expose them. Reveal the truth. That's the only way to get rid of them."

"You want to use the Winter Ball as bait?" Carter asked, frowning.

"It's a high-risk plan," Riley conceded. "But if this party is what you say it is, Ashford would find it irresistible."

"It would be catnip for him. I absolutely guarantee you he'll show up," Cameron agreed. "We could prepare behind the scenes – bring in more guards. More equipment. Disguise it in party supply vans. They would never have a clue what we were doing." She turned to Gray. "I like the way you think."

There was excitement in her voice, and Gray found her own pulse starting to race. If they could do it – if they could prove who was involved and make it public, then all of this might end.

"It's not just guests, though. The senior students will be there too," Allie pointed out. "Everyone sixteen and over will be there. How will we keep them safe?"

"But the younger students go home the day before," Julia reminded her. "We only have about fifty students here that week."

"Fifty is still a lot," Allie said.

"Maybe we could get that down," Julia said. "Send more of them home. Keep a core group so it's not obvious. A smaller group we could protect."

"Keep the ones who are doing night training," Gray suggested. "Then it won't be as obvious that the other students aren't there. No one coming to the party will notice there aren't as many students as usual."

Julia glanced at Allie. "It could work," she said quietly.

"There's a lot we can do to make it safer," Cameron told them. "We can cut the invitation list in half for example, and replace most of the guests with undercover security. We won't go into this half-cocked. We'll be ready."

"Cameron's specialty is strategy and risk assessment," Riley explained. "This is what she does all the time."

"So – wait." Allie held up her hands. "Tell me how this would work. It will be the Winter Ball but only sort of? And how will we get this all together in just a few days? The dance is next Thursday."

"The idea would be to fake it all," Cameron explained. "Make it look like a normal party, but really the whole thing would be a trap. Guards at every entrance disguised as guests, police on standby. When they make their move toward Gray or her mother, we arrest the attackers. Take it to the security services, or make sure the papers get hold of it and expose John Ashford's involvement." She clapped her hands together once. "Game over."

A long, silence fell.

"It could work," Carter said, finally.

"It's dangerous," Allie replied.

"Doing nothing is a risk too," Julia reminded them.

There was a pause.

Allie met Gray's eyes. "And you're really willing to be part of this? We'd be putting a target on your back."

"But you'd be here to protect me," Gray pointed out. "And we can't keep waiting for them to show up whenever they want to. This way we're inviting them. We have the control."

That seemed to seal it.

Allie turned to Cameron. "Put a plan together, flesh it out. I need to see how this would work and how we can keep the students safe before I decide."

"You got it, Guv," Cameron said, cheerfully.

Gray suppressed the urge to cheer. They were going to do it.

Now the night training really needed to get moving. They had only a week to get ready.

TWENTY-ONE

"You're back." Zoe Glass stood at the front of Training Room One, frowning at the ten students clustered in front of her. "I didn't think you'd come back."

Kyle watched her with fascination. Minal whispered to herself, "I love her." Maya was more circumspect, observing the trainer with caution.

Next to them, Gray bounced on her toes, eager to get started. She hadn't told anyone about the meeting she'd gone to or the things she'd learned about the Winter Ball. Allie and Julia had sworn her to secrecy, at least for now. They had to pitch it to her mother first and get her approval.

She was excited about the plan – and the potential to free herself from fear at last – but she didn't like the way the secrets were building up, one by one.

She scanned the room for Dylan, finding him in what was becoming his habitual spot at the edge of the group, leaning casually against the rough wall, his eyes on Zoe. At the sight of him, energy hummed through her body.

As she turned back, she met the dark gaze of Sophie. Her long hair was braided, her makeup was perfect. But there was something in her expression – a kind of wounded anger – that made Gray look away quickly.

She thought of that scene she'd come across in the library – Sophie talking to Dylan, and then storming out. Since then she hadn't seen them together.

Maybe they broke up?

Despite everything, the thought filled her with lightness. And something like hope.

Across the room, Zoe was telling the group, "We're going to start the same way. Run with the same partners as last time. You have to run to warm up before we try anything new," she explained, adding with a hint of defensiveness, "It's standard." When nobody moved, she pointed at the door. "You have to go."

This time there was a more orderly process to getting out of the door. The students arranged themselves in pairs as they jogged down the corridor.

"My sister told me Zoe's getting a doctorate in physics and she's not even twenty years old," Minal revealed, as they made their way to the door. "She says she's a genius. I think she's so cool."

"She's strange in the very best ways," Kyle agreed.

As they entered the corridor, Gray turned to look for Dylan only to find that he had materialised beside her. He'd clearly been there long enough to hear what Minal said.

"I've been trying to figure out why they chose her to lead this instead of Julia or Carter," he said.

"Because I'm the best." It was Zoe. She'd run up behind them while they were talking. Now she cocked her head to one side and studied them with bright, bird-like eyes. "You're running too slowly. Stop talking."

With that, she shot by, sprinting to the end of the corridor, her steps fluid and fleet.

The three of them exchanged looks.

"Come on, partner," Minal said, nudging Kyle. "Let's get moving."

"Running is not my superpower," he complained. But the two of them were soon speeding after the trainer.

"I have to find my partner," Maya said, looking ahead. Gray saw Seb – distinctive for his height and dark hair – stop to look back for her.

Maya's face lit up, and she raced to join him.

Dylan and Gray were last again.

"Guess you're stuck with me," she told him.

He shot her a sideways glance. "I can think of worse people to be stuck with."

Gray's heart skipped.

As they went through the door out into the cold, she zipped up her jacket without slowing down. This time she was prepared.

She was breathing hard already, but she made herself run steadily and they kept up with the others, staying just behind Kyle and Minal.

"You're getting faster," Dylan observed.

"Working on it," she said, breathlessly. "Don't want to be last… forever."

They crossed the frozen lawn, the grass crunching beneath their feet as they headed straight for the woods.

He ran steadily, his expression alert but his body relaxed, as if this sort of movement were his natural state. Gray thought fleetingly about telling him about the plans for the Winter Ball, but she couldn't. Not yet.

Zoe seemed to be setting a slightly slower pace tonight, keeping them clustered near her. The other trainers were running with them, spaced throughout the group. Carter and Julia were both there among the runners, and Erin ran just behind them.

"They're keeping an eye on us," Gray said.

"Yep," Dylan agreed, glancing at Erin over his shoulder. "It's about time."

In the darkness of the forest the changes became more obvious. Julia moved closer to Gray, running just ahead of her. Erin moved closer behind her. Carter ran up to join Zoe, sharing the lead.

It looked to Gray like a planned manoeuvre, and she could see Dylan following their movements with interest. When they reached the place where they'd looped back the night before, Zoe ran right by it.

"They're changing up the route," Dylan noted. "Smart move. Staying unpredictable."

After that, they didn't talk much. Gray focussed on avoiding fallen branches or holes in the path. She was already tired. Her lungs had begun to burn.

Getting in shape was going to take some time.

She was relieved when, five minutes later, they took a side path to the right, looping back. But the new path was narrower and rougher than the main route. The group slowed down and stretched out to run in single file. Julia stayed ahead of Gray. Dylan dropped behind her.

Gray had to pick her way along the path, trying not to twist her ankle in the dark.

Somewhere in the distance a fox barked – a mournful, eerie sound that set Gray's nerves on edge.

Why had they gone this way? It seemed much worse than the previous route.

She wanted to ask Julia, but the bodyguard stayed ahead, her attention entirely on the dark woods around them. Occasionally she spoke into her microphone, but her words were too quiet for Gray to make out.

In the distance the small path intersected with what looked like a road. It took Gray a second to realise it was the school's main driveway. The path had looped around to it, somehow.

Relieved, she increased her speed. She wanted out of these woods and off this path.

As the students poured out of the woods and onto the drive, those ahead slowed, and then stopped, clustering together on the wide sweep of tarmac. They were looking at something Gray couldn't see.

Julia ran back to her side, holding out one hand to slow her.

"What's going on?" Gray asked. The bodyguard shook her head, the worried look on her face deepening. Dylan walked on her other side. All of them were peering ahead, trying to see what had stopped everyone.

The students ahead were exclaiming and milling, staring at something to the left.

When they stepped out of the woods, the reason was immediately clear. The school's tall iron gate stood wide open. Something hung from the spikes on the top and swayed in the icy breeze, ghostlike in the dark.

Gray stared at it. "Why is the gate open? What is that?"

Zoe, who had run to the gate, wheeled around and sped back to them.

"Everyone back to the building," she ordered the group, raising her voice. "Now."

Gray saw her give a look to Julia as she passed – an ominous warning of a glance.

Still, for a split second nobody moved. They were all staring at that dark, open gate, and the fluttering silvery fabric impaled on the top of it.

"Move!" Julia shouted, jarring them into action. They stumbled away from the gate. Slowly at first, but then faster.

All the adults began shouting orders. "Move, move, move," Carter called.

"Faster," Zoe urged.

Soon they were hurtling at full speed, their feet thudding against the ground.

Julia and Dylan flanked Gray, matching her stride for stride.

"What was that?" Gray asked.

"Not now," the bodyguard said tightly. "We need to get inside."

Fear as cold as the winter night settled on Gray's shoulders, and she turned to make sure Dylan was close, only to find he was right behind her, his face set and watchful.

"Keep going!" Zoe ran alongside the group, herding them like sheep.

For once, Gray found speed when she needed it, and she flew across the cold earth until they neared the building and the surface turned to gravel, crunching under her feet.

Julia spoke into her microphone. "Firefly on drive. Nearing building."

As she finished saying the words, a group of dark-clad security guards emerged from the school, running at full speed in the other direction, their steps quiet but fast, their faces hidden behind black masks that covered their noses and mouths.

The students poured through the open door into the basement. This time, there was no collapsing in the training room. No jokes about tiredness. Instead, they huddled together at the centre of the room, whispering in shocked tones.

"What was that about?" Minal asked, looking wide-eyed from Gray to Dylan to Maya. "Did you see what that was, hanging on the gate?"

"It looked like a dress..." Maya sounded uncertain. "Or a curtain?"

"The gate could have malfunctioned," Kyle suggested. "We have a gate at our country house and it never opens when you want and always opens when you don't."

"Does it put on its own clothes?" Minal asked doubtfully.

"Good point," he said.

Across the room, Julia, Erin, Carter and Zoe were talking in hushed voices. Their sombre faces spoke volumes.

Gray couldn't seem to shake the chill of the night from her bones.

Catching her eye, Dylan tilted his head away from the group, and they stepped to one side. Across the room, Gray saw Sophie notice this, her expression darkening. But then she turned her back on the two of them and stepped closer to her training partner, smiling up into his eyes.

Dylan didn't seem to notice any of this. When they were away from the others he spoke quietly. "First last night. Now this."

"Someone got in again, didn't they?" she said.

"I think so."

"Quiet." It was Zoe's voice. The cluster of adults at the end of the room had dispersed. The training instructor faced them, her expression calm and fearless. "I will not lie to you – that was bad. The gate shouldn't have been open. The school's in lockdown while the grounds are searched."

A worried murmur swept the small room. Zoe raised her voice to be heard above it.

"You're safe in here. I swear to you. And lockdown is no excuse not to train. In fact, it's a very good reason to learn to protect yourself. Find your partners. I'm going to teach you how to fight. If anyone comes in here, I want every one of you to know how to kick their arses."

That was oddly comforting, and the students divided into pairs.

Zoe walked them all through a new kind of movement, showing them how to punch someone who grabbed them from behind, how to kick someone who approached from the front, and how to elbow an attacker who came from the side. Gray forced herself to focus, but her mind kept wandering back to that open gate, trying to figure out what it meant.

It was clear she wasn't the only one finding it hard to concentrate. Seb ended up with a black eye when Maya misjudged the angle and elbowed him in the face.

Erin dashed to the kitchen for ice while Maya knelt worriedly beside her partner.

"I'm so sorry," she kept saying. "I'm so sorry."

"It's fine," he insisted, even as the eye swelled shut. "It doesn't hurt."

"Pay attention," Zoe ordered, glaring at other students, as the two of them moved to the side of the room. "This is serious."

Gray, Minal, Dylan and Kyle worked with Julia again. She calmed them, saying, "We'll just take it slow. I know it's not easy to focus."

She'd barely finished saying the words when the door flew open. Gray glanced up, expecting to see Erin with an ice pack. Instead, the person who walked in was Allie.

Ignoring everyone, she motioned for Julia and Zoe, who sped across to her. The three spoke quietly. After a moment, they all turned to look at Gray.

Her stomach dropped. She sensed Dylan's body tensing next to her as Julia motioned for her to come over.

"We need a moment," the bodyguard told her quietly.

"Sure." She followed the Julia and Allie out of the room, nerves fluttering in her chest. Behind her, she heard Zoe urging the others to get back to work.

Allie led the two of them across to the girls' changing room, and walked straight to a bag that sat on a bench.

"I need you to look at something for me," she told Gray.

As she spoke, Julia stepped closer to Gray's side, as if to shield her from an incoming blow.

The headmistress picked up the bag and reached inside. "This is what was hanging from the gate. I just need to know if it's yours."

She pulled out a length of grey-blue fabric, the colour of a stormy sky.

Gray didn't have to look at it closely to know it would have a full skirt and a wide-cut neck. Or that the fabric would be the kind of silk her mother loved for its shine. The two of them had picked it out together just before she'd come to Cimmeria. She'd planned to wear it to the Winter Ball.

"It's mine." The words came out in a whisper. Her throat was so tight she could barely speak. She turned to Julia, searching her face for an explanation. "How?"

The bodyguard's face was carefully blank, but Gray could see fury in her eyes and the tight lines of her jaw.

"Where was the dress kept?" Allie asked. "And when did you see it last?"

"I-i-in my c-closet," Gray stammered, fear catching up with her as she realised what this meant. "And I don't know when. A few days ago? Last week?" She turned to the bodyguard, disbelieving. "Julia... They got in my room?"

The bodyguard squeezed her arm and turned to the headmistress. "How did this happen? Do we know?"

"We think they might have taken the dress last night," Allie said tightly. "CCTV shows no one getting into the grounds tonight."

Gray stared at the dress, her stomach churning. Something was wrong with it. It looked broken, somehow. It fluttered strangely in Allie's hands.

"What did they do to it?" she asked, reaching one hand out but not touching it.

Long rips split the delicate fabric of the once perfect garment.

Allie looked at Julia before she replied.

"Someone slashed it to pieces."

TWENTY-TWO

Gray didn't want to go back to training that night, but Allie and Julia insisted. For the next hour, she moved woodenly into the positions she was told to take, did everything she was asked to do, but through it all, her mind was focussed on that dress and what it meant.

After she stumbled through a series of easy movements for the third time, Dylan asked quietly, "What's wrong?" But she shook her head grimly and tried again. His eyes followed her with concern, but he didn't ask again. She was grateful to him for that.

Gossip buzzed around them as the others speculated about what was going on.

"I heard Zoe say the other students are all being kept in the common room and library while they search the building," Minal whispered, when Julia stepped away to take a phone call.

"Are they telling them it's another kitchen fire?" Kyle's eyebrows rose. "They're going to need more fire extinguishers."

It was a relief when Zoe announced training was over and the building was safe.

The instructors escorted the students to the dormitories. When they reached Gray's room, Julia closed the door and turned to face her. "OK, I know this looks bad, but I don't want you to be anxious. You are safe. I promise."

Gray was getting tired of being told how safe she was.

"How did they know which room was mine?" It was the question that had tormented her ever since she'd seen the remains of her dress. "They got that dress out of that wardrobe." She swung her arm at the offending piece of furniture. "How did they know?"

"I just don't have the answer to that," Julia said, after a brief hesitation.

"I don't understand." Gray's tone was accusing. "How can you tell me I'm safe when they can just walk through that gate?"

The shock she'd felt when she first saw the dress had turned to fury now.

The bodyguard looked away. When she spoke again, her tone was measured. "I don't blame you for being upset. It looks like they made it to the girls' dorm a few minutes after I got you out last night. We have CCTV showing a man in the hallway. He's hiding his face so we can't identify him. But… he seemed to know which room was yours."

Bile rose in Gray's throat and she swallowed hard. "How could he possibly know that?"

Again there was a pause as Julia sought the right words. "Either they've been doing long-range surveillance using something like drones or…" She paused, as if bracing herself. "Or someone's helping them on the inside."

Gray's breath caught in her throat. "Someone? Like who?"

"We are running security checks on everyone here," Julia said, an answer that wasn't an answer. "But there are lots of possibilities. Teachers. Cleaning staff."

"Security guards." Gray finished the list for her.

"I'd bet my life it wasn't a guard," Julia said. "We are all thoroughly checked. I think it's someone innocuous. Someone you wouldn't look at twice. Someone who belongs here."

"A teacher," Gray guessed, searching her face.

"It has been known to happen." There was bitterness in Julia's voice, and she took a breath before continuing. "Tonight wasn't about hurting you. Tonight was about making you afraid. Don't let them do it. Don't let fear take over."

"How the hell do I do that?" Gray's voice rose. "That man stood right where I am now. If you'd been five minutes later coming to get me…"

"But I wasn't," Julia reminded her, firmly. "I got to you first and I always will."

They stared at each other across the small room. Gray desperately wanted to believe. She wanted to think she was safe. But she was beginning to forget what safe felt like.

When Gray didn't speak, Julia continued, "I've taken the room next door. For the next couple of hours I'm going to help patrol the grounds, and after that I'll be literally three steps away from you. If you need me, all you have to do is shout." She held Gray's gaze. "I will protect you. I promise."

There was some comfort in the idea that she would be so close, but Gray couldn't let go of the facts. Someone had been in here. They'd touched her clothes. Seen the pictures of her with Chloe she kept on her bookshelf next to the desk. They'd seen all of her personal things.

The thought made her angry, and anger cleared her mind.

If there was one thing she'd learned this year, it was that half the battle of surviving is believing you can do it. Two hours ago she'd believed. She needed to believe again.

She would keep learning to fight, keep learning to protect herself. She would decide who she could trust and she would keep them close. Then she would kill anyone who tried to hurt her or them.

She would not let fear defeat her.

"There's a guard downstairs keeping watch," Julia said, heading for the door. "If you need him, shout and he'll come running. Or call me." She held up her phone. "And I will."

After the bodyguard had gone, Gray stood for a moment, staring at the room. It didn't feel cosy or safe anymore. It felt tainted.

Grabbing her toothbrush and a towel, she headed to the bathroom. All she wanted was time to think, but she'd timed it wrong. It was packed with girls gossiping excitedly. From listening to them, Gray quickly gathered they'd been told about the break-in, but also assured it was nothing to worry about. And they had taken that to heart.

"It's probably Sophie Montgomery's boyfriend again," a girl in pink pyjamas said dreamily. "He broke in last year, remember? He's so hot."

"Do you think he would do that again?" Her friend's eyes were wide. "That is so wild."

"It's true love," the first girl assured her.

Gray made a face at herself in the mirror but said nothing and continued brushing her teeth as the others chattered. It was good news that they didn't associate what had happened with her, anyway.

Mostly they seemed to find it all thrilling.

Sophie herself turned up just as Gray was finishing at the sink.

"Was it Matthew?" the girls demanded, fluttering around her. "Did he get in? Did they catch him?"

The tall, dark-haired beauty seemed to find it all amusing. "If he got in, nobody told me. But it would be just like Matt. He's always doing ridiculously romantic stunts. And he's climbed the fence before. He's so athletic."

She glanced at Gray.

"Oh hey, Gray, you must know. You're so connected here. Was it Matt?" she asked. The girls fell silent and turned to where Gray had stopped in the doorway. "Or was it one of your mother's friends looking for you again?"

Sophie may have been bitchy but she wasn't stupid.

"I have no idea," Gray said, coolly. "But I certainly don't know why anyone would climb a fence to meet you."

Holding her toothbrush, she swept from the room, ignoring the scandalised gasps and giggles behind her.

She heard Sophie say, "Guess I struck a nerve," and laugh before the door closed.

The scene replayed in her head as she got ready for bed, muttering to herself and slamming the pillow down unnecessarily hard. She was so tense that when her phone buzzed it made her jump.

Glancing at the screen, she saw Jake's name glowing at her.

For a long few seconds she held the phone in one hand. There was so much she wanted to say to him but it would be hard to explain what was going on. And then there was Dylan, and her confused thoughts about him.

She dropped the phone on the desk without answering.

When it stopped vibrating, she climbed into bed. A minute later though, it buzzed again to let her know she had a voicemail message.

When she hit play, the first thing she heard was the sound of music and voices, a kind of deafening rumble of noise. Someone laughing near the phone but not into it – a girl's voice saying, "Don't be daft." Then Jake's voice with its flat Manchester accent, more loudly, "Gray, it's me. We keep missing each other. I'm really sorry, things are just so—" He stopped and the sound became muffled. She heard him tell someone, "Just a second. I'm talking to my mate." And then a girl's voice, pouty, "You're always on your phone."

Then Jake again into the receiver. "Can't remember what I was sayin'. But I hope you're doing well. You need to come up here and see for yourself. It's all happening. I'll try and call you later. Take care."

The party sounds cut off abruptly.

Gray set the phone down and wrapped her arms around her knees. Five weeks ago, she and Jake had raced across Parliament together, looking for clues that would tell them who was trying to kill her mother. They'd been a team.

She didn't feel like she was on his team anymore. Maybe that was OK. Maybe she had a new team.

She climbed out of bed and pulled on her dressing gown. After sliding her feet into her slippers, she opened the door to peek out. The hallway was empty. The other girls had gone to their own rooms.

Quietly, she stepped out and closed the door behind her. Then she tiptoed down the hall.

She tiptoed past three doors, stopping in front of the fourth. She tapped softly.

On the other side, she heard a whisper of voices, and then the sound of feet on the floor.

The door opened a crack and Maya looked out. She had a pale cream on her face, and her dark blue pyjamas made her skin look like milk. Her hair, pulled up on top of her head, formed a halo of golden curls.

"Oh good, it's you," she said with relief. "I thought you might be a guard. Come in. We're gossiping."

When she stepped back, Gray saw Minal sitting on a kilim cushion on the floor. She was in her robe, her hair pulled back by a white head band. She had some thick cream on her skin that gave her a ghostly sheen.

Before Gray could ask, she gestured at her face. "Things are never too dangerous to do a face mask. I may be scared, but my pores are not afraid."

Gray laughed, stifling it with a hand across her mouth. This was what she needed. To talk to people who understood.

"Where's Julia?" Maya asked as she walked in to join them.

"She's searching the grounds," explained Gray. "There's a guard downstairs in case we get scared."

"I'm scared." Minal raised her hand. "I've been scared for two days."

"Sit down." Maya motioned Gray toward the bed.

As she sat down, Minal handed her a plastic pot. "Face mask," she explained. "It's so good. It will make you feel better about everything."

For a second Gray hesitated, but then she thought, Why not? I might as well do something fun.

Gray dipped her fingers into the cool white cream, sniffing its calming scent before smearing it on her skin.

"Here." Minal passed her a small mirror.

Maya sat at the other end of the bed, pulling her feet up and tucking them under her as neatly as a cat tucking in its paws.

Her room had the same plain walls and white-washed wood floor as Gray's, but the bookcase was filled to overflowing with books with interesting spines, and there were several framed pictures on the walls, most of them modern art in vivid colours. It smelled faintly of some subtle, smoky incense. A vivid crimson rug brightened the floor.

As she applied the mask, Minal gave her a look. "You have gossip. I can sense it." She motioned with her fingers. "Tell us everything."

"Sophie's letting everyone think it was her boyfriend breaking in because he's so desperate to see her," Gray announced.

"She would." Minal rolled her eyes. "Anything for attention. Plus, she's sick with jealousy about you and Dylan, and she doesn't want anyone to notice."

"Yes, especially since she and Dylan are over," Maya said. "If they were ever truly together."

Beneath the mask, Gray's face went hot.

"I heard that, too!" Minal said. "Something about a scene in the library."

"I heard one of her friends talking about it," Maya said. "She said Dylan told Sophie he didn't want to lead her on. He said she deserved someone better." Maya glanced at Gray. "I think he's been trying to get rid of her ever since you arrived."

"Spill," Minal ordered. "What's going on?"

"I can honestly say: nothing," she insisted.

"He wants something to happen though," Maya assured her. "The way he looks at you."

"It's dreamy," Minal concurred.

Gray wondered if the mask might melt.

"Well, Seb looks at you like that too," she said, hoping to distract them.

Maya gave a small smile. "Seb is lovely."

"Although you tried to kill him tonight," Minal reminded her.

Maya covered her face with her hands, instantly smearing them in cream. She got up and retrieved a box of tissues from the desk, returning to the bed to begin removing the mask.

"He's very forgiving," she said, waving their giggles away.

They talked for a while about boys and training, before the conversation turned to the incident earlier that evening.

"Seriously – what was tonight about?" Minal asked. "The guards looked freaked out."

"They did not expect it," Maya agreed. "They thought the equipment would protect us."

Gray took a deep breath. "There's something I have to tell you."

They both looked at her.

"It was my dress on the gate," she revealed. "Someone stole it from my wardrobe last night."

"Last night? But how? And why did they hang it up there like that?" Minal asked.

Maya answered before Gray could. "A message." Her voice was flat. "Someone wants you to know they can get to you. It's classic."

"How did they get the dress though? And how did they open the gate? Carter and Allie are super strict about those controls," Minal said.

"They think it was hacked," Gray told them.

Minal's jaw dropped. "My dad's going to freak out. He just sent in all these tech guys to put in the new cameras and equipment this week. How did we get hacked so quickly?"

"If this were home, I'd say it was Russia. They are extremely good at hacking. But it can't be." Maya looked at Gray. "It wouldn't make sense for it to be them."

"It does make sense though," said Gray.

It was time, she decided, to tell the whole truth. They were just as threatened by all of this as she was. Besides, they were her team now. And she trusted them.

Talking fast, she told them what almost no one knew – about the Russian plot to kill her mother and replace her with John Ashford, the deputy prime minister. "My dad says the Russians are behind everything. Ashford works for them. The Russian spies – I can't remember what they're called. It's not the KGB anymore. It's something else. Different letters."

"The FSB." Maya's voice was toneless. "That's what they're called." She had gone very still. "Are you sure? That's what your mother said?"

Gray nodded. "They're in charge of it. But really powerful British people are working for them. Getting money from them. Getting help from them."

Both girls stared at her.

"Does my dad know about this?" Minal asked.

"Your dad's running the whole investigation," Gray told her. "But they can't do anything until they have more proof. The people involved are really good at covering their tracks. Until they make a mistake, there's only so much anyone can do. It's our word against theirs. And they're getting closer. Your dad thinks they want to try again – to kidnap me. Or worse."

"This all makes sense," Maya said, with a kind of grim finality. "This school has many children of politicians and elite British families. If they can hurt us, then the Russians will see that as a kind of victory. They hate Britain. But then, they hate everyone who isn't Russian." She turned to Gray. "They are a bad enemy."

Gray met her eyes. "Dylan told me about the threats against you. Was that the Russians too?"

"They were involved. They wanted to scare my father so he would do what they wanted."

"Now they want to scare my mother," said Gray. "For the same reason."

"What a bunch of dicks," Minal declared. "Why are they harassing you guys? You're not your parents."

210

"We're easier to reach than our parents. This is how blackmail works." Maya turned to Gray. "You said they stole your dress last night?"

Gray nodded. "Last night someone got over the fence in the middle of the night. They set off an alarm, and the guards chased them out. I was taken to a safe room. We think that was when they took the dress."

Minal looked horrified. "They were up here while we were sleeping? Why didn't someone tell us about this?"

"They were afraid of scaring you." Gray turned to Maya. "I'm sorry. Allie made me promise not to tell you. But I think you should know the truth."

"If they came twice in one week they are serious," Maya warned. "And they think they can act with impunity."

"Looks to me like they can. We've spent half the night locked up, and now we're huddled together scared to death." Minal folded her arms tightly across her torso. "I'm calling my dad tomorrow. He has to do something."

"I hope he can help." Maya's tone was bleak. "Because the Russians are relentless. And they won't stop until they get what they want."

TWENTY-THREE

The next day, life at Cimmeria took on a new intensity. The changes were unmistakeable from the moment the students walked down the stairs from the dorms. More guards patrolled the corridors, their cool eyes scanning the faces of everyone they passed. A cold, wintery rain misted the windows, but those who were brave enough to go out found black-clad guards patrolling the woods and the fence line. When the daylight faded at four o'clock, the infrared lenses of night-vision cameras glittered red on the walls and fences.

The teachers reacted to the new situation by piling the students with homework. Suddenly, everyone had long essays to work on and vast reading assignments to complete. No amount of complaining or pleading would get the instructors to acknowledge how unreasonable the workload had become.

Gray thought she knew why – it was Friday. Normally, weekends were filled with parties in the woods and in the dorms. Those would be a nightmare for security. It would be much easier to protect the school if everyone was in the library.

Still, at the end of her history lesson, she stared aghast as Zelazny scrawled an assignment on the whiteboard.

"ESSAY – 2,000 WORDS – BATTLE OF THE THREE EMPERORS."

The students groaned. Each letter was a black slash shredding their weekend.

Minal slid down low in her seat. "Two thousand? He can't be serious."

"I've already been assigned a thousand words on Virginia Woolf for Monday," Gray said glumly. "This makes 3,000 words I've got to write in two days. How am I supposed to do that?"

The marker still in his hand, Zelazny turned to face the increasingly resentful students without a hint of sympathy. "The deadline is fixed and cannot be moved. This counts toward your final marks. I suggest you learn how to prioritise your time."

Afterwards, the usually boisterous mood in the hallway was subdued. When Kyle caught up with Gray and Minal his expression was stormy.

"The teachers are demented," he announced.

"Yours, too?" Minal glanced at him.

"I've got, like, four essays due on Monday." He held up his hands in despair. "There would need to be four of me to get this done. I need to be cloned."

"It's like they actually want us to spend the whole weekend in the library," Minal groused.

"It's cruel and unusual punishment," Kyle agreed.

"Haven't they heard of the Geneva Convention?" Minal demanded.

"Don't tell them. They'll make us write 2,000 words on it," Gray said.

As they followed the crowd streaming to the library, she looked around for Julia. She hadn't seen the bodyguard since breakfast. They'd only had a fleeting chance to talk then, and Gray wanted to know more about what the searchers had found, if anything. Or if they'd identified any of the intruders.

They'd barely settled at a table at the back when Sophie walked in. She gave Gray a long, amused look before sitting gracefully at a table near the front with a large group. She leaned over to whisper to them, casting obvious glances in Gray's direction.

"Her new best friends." Kyle tried to sound unbothered but Gray suspected he was sad to lose Sophie; he admired her and she'd dumped him like last year's shoes.

Minal flipped the pages of her history textbook. "Ignore her. She got her precious feelings hurt. She'll get over it."

"Oh, please," Kyle muttered, opening his chemistry book with a thump. "To have feelings you have to have a heart."

This made them all laugh.

"What's so funny?" Dylan walked up, his leather satchel slung over one shoulder. His blue and white striped tie was loose and slightly askew, and he'd slung his blazer over one shoulder. Somehow he made the Cimmeria uniform look cool.

"Kyle's been explaining the strange biology of Sophie Montgomery to us," Minal explained.

"Oh, that."

He glanced briefly in her direction before quickly looking away. Gray wondered if the two of them had really been together. And if he'd really broken up with Sophie because of her.

All the chairs were occupied at their table so he dragged one over, placing it casually in the space next to Gray.

Gray's heart kicked, but she kept her expression neutral.

As he sat down, she noticed Sophie give them a long unreadable look, before turning back to her friends, her shoulders stiff.

"Have you heard anything about what's going on? Did they find anything else overnight?" Minal asked him.

He gave a slight shrug. "I don't know much. I heard two guards talking. One of them said it was a quick strike. The gate was hacked from outside, making it swing open. Alarms went off everywhere and the guards came running. It must only have been a minute or two before we got there. He said if they'd stayed any longer we would have run right into them."

"The whole thing is really scary," said Minal. "I called my dad this morning. He said it was the best hack he'd ever seen. They walked right through about eighteen firewalls. He's sending in more people tomorrow to help."

Dylan turned to her. "Your dad's with that big security company, isn't he? What's it called? Talos, right?"

She nodded. "They put in the cameras."

"Whose dress was that, anyway?" Kyle asked. "It's such a weird thing to do, hanging it out like that. Like a flag or something."

Minal and Gray exchanged a look.

"It was mine," Gray said.

She told Dylan and Kyle what she'd already told the others.

As Kyle and Minal began an animated conversation about clothes stealing and break-ins, Gray gradually became aware that

Dylan wasn't saying anything. Also, now that she thought about it, he hadn't reacted at all to this revelation.

He knew already, she realised.

He always seemed to know things he shouldn't know. It didn't make sense. He was just a student like everyone else. Wasn't he?

Later, when there was a quiet moment, he turned to her and said softly, "Maybe you should go home."

The others were still talking and hadn't heard him speak. Gray stared at him, shocked and a little hurt.

"Why?" she asked, unable to hide her confusion.

"Because they're getting closer." His voice was barely above a whisper; she had to lean nearer to hear him. She could smell the soft scent of the soap he used – something green and fresh. It was distracting, especially given what he was saying. "It's not safe for you."

"I came here because it wasn't safe at home," she whispered.

"Were you safer there than you are here?"

"I ended up in the hospital," she reminded him.

He held her eyes for a long moment, as if there was something else he wanted to say.

"What are you two whispering about?" Minal demanded from across the table.

Gray turned back to her books, her face flaming.

"Homework," Dylan said, turning his attention back to his book.

"Mm-hmm." Minal gave them a look of pure disbelief.

Dylan ignored her. His focus was on the notebook in front of him. He wrote something on a clean sheet of paper. When the others were distracted, he turned it so Gray could see. In his distinctive narrow writing, she read: "We need to talk. Meet me later."

Before she could reply, her phone vibrated. She glanced down to see the name on the screen: Jake.

She couldn't ignore him this time. Clearly, he'd noticed her silence as much as she'd noticed his.

Holding her phone, she stood up. "I have to take this."

She ran across the room, shoving open the door and hitting answer at the same moment. "Jake?" Her voice was breathless.

"There you are." He sounded surprised. "I thought I'd missed you again."

"I'm here."

"Is everything OK? I haven't heard from you in a while. I called last night."

She leaned against the wall, closing her eyes. "I'm sorry, things have been crazy here. With work and lots of stuff."

"Oh, sure. Well… how's it going?" he asked. "Are you making friends at all?"

Dylan's face flashed through her mind: smooth brown skin, high cheekbones, that easy smile.

"I am," she said, feeling instantly guilty. "Raj Patel's daughter is here and she's nice. And then there's Maya – her dad was the prime minister in Poland, and we kind of have things in common."

"Oh… that's good."

There was a pause. Gray could hear music in the background, and voices. Like he was in a café.

"How about you?" she asked. "Are you still liking it up north?"

"Yeah, I'm great, ta," he said. "Busy, you know. Trying to deal with the new school, meeting old friends again. But it's good. It's a lot more chilled out living here than it was with my dad. My mum's been great."

There was an awkwardness to the conversation, as if they didn't have anything to talk about. Which didn't make sense, given that they hadn't spoken in over a week.

Again, she noticed the music on his end of the line, and voices.

"Where are you?"

"At a coffeeshop near my school with some mates." His voice brightened. "You'd love it. The frozen mocha here is epic. They have gigs at weekends. You'd really like it up here, Gray. There's so much going on – music and art, and all that."

Gray wanted to agree. The only problem was, she simply couldn't imagine going to a coffeeshop with friends. To do that, she'd need a security sweep first, and two bodyguards to accompany her. Everyone would stare the entire time.

She could never experience normal life the way he did. Not for a long time. And that truth seemed to expand the distance between them from a narrow divide into a vast chasm.

She swallowed hard.

"Sounds great," she said.

"Come on, Jake. Hurry up." It was the girl's voice again in the background, laughing. "Everyone's waiting."

She heard him put his hand over the phone, and the muffled sound of him telling the girl, "I'm coming. Just a minute. I've got to finish this call."

She was certain that same girl had told him to hurry up last night, too.

"Sounds like you better get going," she said.

"Yeah, I need to get a move on." He hadn't noticed the chill in her tone. "We're all going to a party later. My mate Mike's got a car and he's driving us. I'm sorry – he hates waiting."

Gray didn't want to know any more. Didn't want to know who Mike was. Didn't want to know the girl's name. Didn't want him to tell her what wonderful friends he was making. Besides, he didn't have to say anything. She'd never heard him sound so happy.

"Well, have fun. It was great talking," she told him.

"Yeah. You too! Good luck with everything."

With that jaunty goodbye, the line went dead.

Gray stood for a long second, looking down until the blank screen of her phone blurred.

The emotion she felt was so unexpected it took a second to identify it as jealousy. She was so jealous. Jealous of the coffeeshop, and the friends dragging Jake off to some place she could never imagine going. Jealous of the unidentified girl with laughter in her voice.

Letting the wall take her weight, she dropped her head into her hands, taking a steadying breath. There was nothing for her to do but let him go.

He was already gone anyway.

"Everything OK?"

Her head jerked up. Dylan stood next to her, watching her with concern. "I don't mean to intrude," he said, holding up his hands. "You just looked a little beat."

"Beat." She tried the word out. "I think that about sums it up."

"Call from your mother?" he guessed.

Gray shook her head. "Sort of ex-boyfriend. Ish."

"Oh. It was that kind of call."

"Yeah." She glanced down at the blank phone screen. "It wasn't great."

"I'm sorry." To her surprise, he sounded like he meant it. "Do you want to talk about it?"

"There's not much to say." She put the phone in the pocket of her blazer. "We were never really together. Things just sort of happened. Now, I guess they're kind of... un-happening. He seems really happy without me." She stopped herself from saying any more. "I'm sorry. I'm fine, I promise."

"I know you're fine," he said. "But that doesn't make this stuff any easier. And being here can't help. So far from the real world. It's like being cut off from reality." He bit his lip. "Look, if there's one thing I know for sure, it's that you won't be alone for long. The guys are going to be lining up to ask you out. You wait and see."

But as she held his gaze she knew one thing for certain – she didn't want all the guys to line up. She wanted him.

At that moment, a girl she didn't recognise came down the hall, calling her name.

"Gray Langtry?"

Her knee-high leather riding boots marked her out as a prefect. Only they were allowed to wear their own shoes. Everyone else wore school-issued Oxfords.

"Yes?" Gray said, frowning.

The girl cocked her head to one side, her blonde ponytail swinging over her shoulder. "The headmistress wants you in her office. Right away."

TWENTY-FOUR

"What did you do?" Dylan asked, glancing at Gray.

"Nothing," she insisted defensively.

They were walking down the wide oak-panelled hallway. Cold winter sun slanted through the tall windows ahead of them.

"If you didn't do anything wrong, why is the headmistress summoning you to her office right now?" he pressed. "Please tell me you got around to reading The Rules at some point."

"Seriously, I have no idea what she wants," Gray laughed.

"Yeah, that could be it." He put his hands in his pockets and strode along beside her. He looked a little distracted.

"So – this is none of my business, but I heard you and Sophie kind of broke up?" She kept her voice casual.

He looked at her with what appeared to be genuine surprise. "Word's out already, is it? That was fast."

"Actually, I saw you in the library. I was looking for a book. And then Sophie ran by me…" She let her voice trail off.

"Yeah, she was not happy with me that day. Or now, for that matter. The thing is, we weren't ever together. Not really. She wanted to be together and I kept telling her I didn't think it was a good idea. But no is not her favourite word." He rubbed his cheek ruefully. "Now I guess she believes. And she is not happy about it."

"Oh, right." Gray kept her tone neutral but inside she was skipping.

He's not with her! He never wanted to be with her!

Actually, it was hard to believe anyone didn't want to be with Sophie Montgomery. Purely on a looks basis, of course. And hadn't she just told Chloe a few days ago that she should go out with one of the Bolinos solely because of how he looked?

"So... Don't take this the wrong way but, why didn't you want to go out with her?" she asked. Hating herself for needing to know.

He gave her a sideways glance. "Let me just check – I'm allowed some privacy here, right? Or is that not a thing in England?"

She held up her hands. "Sorry... sorry. It's none of my business. I take it back."

"It specifically isn't any of your business," he agreed. A moment's silence passed, and then he said, "Fine. If you must know, she's not my type."

"Oh, right," Gray said.

"I mean, don't get me wrong – she's stunning to look at, but I don't like her bitchy act," he said, as if she'd asked for more information. "She's better than that but she can't seem to stop. Anyway..." He gave a small shrug. "I have other reasons, too."

Other reasons. It was terrible how everything he said got her hopes up and told her nothing at the same time.

At some point they had stopped walking. They were standing outside the great hall. Gray heard activity in the normally silent room, and she peered in through the open door to find staff had moved the tables to the sides of the room and were polishing the floor and dusting the oak panelling.

"They must be getting ready for the Winter Ball," she said, mostly to herself.

Thinking about it made her stomach tighten. Maybe they'd find proof about John Ashford. Maybe she'd finally be free of the danger that had followed her for months.

Dylan followed her eyes. "Oh yeah. Guess that's coming up." He gave her a look. "Isn't your mom coming for it? I thought I read that somewhere."

"Yeah, she'll be there." The two of them resumed their slow walk toward the staircase.

"Doesn't really seem like a great idea to have a party right now," Dylan mused. "You should probably skip it."

Gray stopped walking again. "Why?"

"Because it's not safe." He gave her a puzzled look. "Not after this week. And by the way, where's your bodyguard right now?" He glanced around the quiet hallway as if Julia might suddenly appear.

"What's that supposed to mean?" she demanded, instantly defensive. He was always going on about Julia, as if everything that went wrong was somehow her fault.

"I'm just saying, she isn't with you when she should be." He kept his tone reasonable. "Last night, for instance. Why did she let you get so close to danger again? You practically ran right into the guys trying to get at you."

"You don't know anything about it," she said hotly. "She's the best bodyguard I've ever had. Most of them just push me around or act like I'm a problem for them to solve. Julia treats me like an adult. Anyway, if I called her right now she'd be here in 30 seconds, and if you want me to test that theory just say the word."

"Alright, alright. I'm sorry. I didn't mean to overstep. He held his hands up. "It's just been a bit messy the last few days and I don't like it."

"Well, I'm not wild about it myself," she snapped. "But it's not Julia's fault."

For a while after that they walked in silence.

"You have to understand," Gray told him, after the quiet had stretched out for too long, "She risked her life for me. I trust her."

He paused before replying, "It's her job to risk her life for you. But I get what you're saying."

She shot Dylan a sideways glance. "Did you have a bodyguard back in the States?"

"For a while." He tensed. Just a little, but she noticed it. "After the threats against my parents got kind of specific, they assigned me a bodyguard. His name was Mike. He was a great guy. A military veteran, young and smart. We used to have great conversations when he'd pick me up after school. He'd shoot hoops with me when I got bored. I wasn't supposed to go anywhere but sometimes he'd take me to Starbucks and get me an iced coffee just to shut me up."

When he didn't immediately continue, Gray said, "What happened to him? He couldn't come with you to England, I guess."

Instead of answering, Dylan said, "One day, I begged him to take me to the mall. I wanted to get a present for my mom's birthday. I could have just ordered something off the internet but I knew the perfect thing and I knew where to go. We would be in and out in ten minutes. Nobody would ever know. I'd been to that mall a thousand times when I was growing up. It was safe." He gave her a helpless look. "It was always safe."

All the sounds of the school seemed to recede until it was just the two of them, completely alone with his memories.

Gray didn't want to ask, but she had to know.

"What happened?" The words came out as a whisper.

"It was August. Must have been a hundred and ten degrees in the shade." He looked through her as if seeing that afternoon, the blinding Texas sun. "We got into the car, he blasted the A/C the way he always did. I cranked up the radio. We made it to the stop sign on the corner. Someone stepped out from behind an SUV holding a rifle. Mike saw him and floored it. It was so loud. The music. The air conditioner. The gunshot. It all became one thing." He blinked, and a muscle flickered in the tight line of his jaw. "We crashed into someone's front yard. The man took off running. He was a drunk idiot, mad at my dad for being alive. Shouldn't have been able to hit anything with that much alcohol in his system. It was just a fluke that the shot was so accurate. Bad luck. Really bad luck." He lowered his gaze to meet hers. "Anyway. That's why Mike isn't here."

Gray's heart ached for him. If anything like that were to happen to Julia, she couldn't bear it. There was a connection between a guard and the person they protected. A bond as strong as love. Or honour.

"I'm so sorry," she said softly. "He sounds like a wonderful man."

He glanced at her and then looked away. But when he spoke again, his voice was steady. "He saved my life. So when you tell me Julia saved yours, I get it. OK? I understand that kind of trust."

They stood there at the edge of the grand hallway, looking at each other – really looking. Slowly, his hand reached for hers. He threaded their fingers together. His touch sent electricity through Gray's entire body.

She felt as if she finally understood so much. Why he was here. Why he was conscious of what the guards were doing. Why he was so calm when things went wrong.

"Gray…" he began, but then he seemed to stop himself. His fingers tightened on hers and then let go. "You're going to be late for your meeting."

Gray could see the main staircase from where they stood. Allie's office was directly underneath it. But she didn't move.

"Look," she began, but he shook his head, giving her a faint smile.

"We can talk later. Neither of us is going anywhere, right? You can't keep the headmistress waiting." He took a step back. "I'll see you at dinner if not before."

Without waiting for her to respond, he turned and headed back toward the library. For a few seconds, Gray stayed where she was, watching that loose-limbed stride, his hands shoved into his pockets.

With a sigh, she turned and made her way to the door under the stairs. After a brief hesitation while she determinedly put him out of her mind, she knocked lightly against the carved shape of an acorn worked into the fanciful oak panelling.

"Come in," Allie's voice called.

When Gray walked in, the headmistress was standing beside her desk. A man stood next to her.

For a second, with her mind still tangled up in Dylan's story, she couldn't seem to accept what was right in front of her. She stared at the man in disbelief. He looked exactly the same as the last time she'd seen him – wavy brown hair with threads of silver just beginning to work through. A thoughtful face, with the slightest shadow of stubble on his jaw.

His eyes, the same ocean blue as her own, brightened when he saw her.

"There's my girl," he said, standing up.

That broke the spell.

"Dad!" She raced across the room and threw herself into his arms.

TWENTY-FIVE

"Hey." She felt her father's laugh against her cheek like a rumble of thunder. "It's only been a few weeks since you saw me. You can't have missed me that much."

When he let go she stepped back, searching his face worriedly. "Why are you here? Is anything wrong? Is Mum OK?"

"Everything's fine," he assured her. "She sends her love. She'd have come herself but she's…"

"…busy." She finished the sentence for him. "I know."

For once though, there was no resentment in her tone. The last few months had brought home just how much pressure her mother was under. As prime minister, her government, her career, and her life were constantly on the line.

She smiled at her father. "It's enough just to see you."

Allie picked up her phone and headed for the door. "I'm going to leave you two to talk. I'll be back in a few minutes. Take your time."

When she'd gone, Gray's father gestured at the two leather chairs, and the two of them sat down.

Gray couldn't stop beaming at him. "This is the best surprise. I thought you were still out of the country."

"I got back a few days ago." Some of the happiness left his face. "That's why I'm here. I wanted to check in and make sure they were taking good care of you."

"Mum told you about the weird stuff that's been happening, didn't she? And now you're freaking out." She gave him a knowing look.

"She mentioned there'd been a couple of incidents." His eyes searched her face. "How are you holding up? That's a lot to deal with."

"I'm actually good," she said. "I mostly feel bad that I've brought so much trouble to the school. Everything was fine until I got here."

Even as the words still hung in the air, she realised what he was here for. She met his gaze. "I don't want to go home, Dad."

The flicker of surprise in his expression told her she'd guessed right.

"Well, that's what I came to ask you," he conceded. "Your mother and I have been talking and we want to make sure you're in the right place."

"I thought so." Gray turned in her chair so she could look at him directly. "I've thought about it too, especially after what happened last night. But the problem isn't Cimmeria. The problem is me."

It was so strange. Two weeks ago, she would have given anything to go home. Now, things felt completely different. The only thing she knew for certain was that she was getting tired of running away. This school was going to give her the chance to stand her ground and fight.

"But two attempts in two days," her father said. "They got into your room. That's hard for us to accept."

"It's hard for me, too." Gray paused, searching for words that could explain how she felt. "I know that you want to protect me. But at some point I have to learn how to take care of myself. I think this is the time. And besides – I've got Julia. I've got an army of guards here. I'll be fine."

Her father studied her as if he were seeing her for the first time. "When did you get so smart?"

She smiled. "I was always smart. You just weren't paying attention."

But the light moment passed quickly, and his expression grew serious. "I want to talk to you about this party. Raj told us about the plan."

Gray's stomach dropped. "You and mum have to let the plan go forward," she pleaded. "It could be our only chance to prove Ashford is behind all this."

"I'm not saying it's not a good plan. I'm saying it's bloody dangerous." His voice sharpened. "I'll run the risk of letting you stay at a school that's doing its best to protect you, but I'm not comfortable letting my daughter be used as bait." He held her gaze. "John Ashford is dangerous, Gray. You know that better than anyone. He's already tried to have you kidnapped. He was prepared to see you dead. I can't let you take this kind of risk."

"I know it's dangerous." Gray took a breath, trying to hide her frustration. She needed to stay calm if she was going to convince him to let her do this. "Look, they're working on a plan for the party, and I know they're going to surround me with security. They're talking about replacing half the people at the party with Talos guards. I don't have all the details but I know they're going to protect me."

He didn't look convinced.

Gray paused. She kept thinking about the silvery remnants of her dress hanging like a warning signal from the black spike of the gate.

"We have to do something to stop John Ashford or one of these days he's going to hurt mum," she said quietly. "You know it as well as I do. Let them try this plan. Let me help them. Let's finish this once and for all."

"I don't know," he said stubbornly, "Your mother—"

She interrupted him. "Mum needs to let me grow up, for God's sake. I'm not a baby anymore."

He gave her a level look. "I was going to say, your mother wants to let you do this. She wants the party to go ahead. I'm the one who thinks it's too dangerous."

"Oh."

This was a surprise. Her mother had always been the one who treated her like a baby. Her father… well. That was more complicated. She had always been close to him, but for the last few years his work for a British intelligence agency had taken him away from home for months at a time. During those months, she'd stopped being a kid. Maybe he'd missed that.

"I know you want to help," he said. "Your mother is convinced you can handle it. I'm not convinced."

"Dad," Gray said. "You know she's the prime minister, right? Maybe you should trust her to make some decisions."

There was a pause, and then he gave a low chuckle.

"This isn't funny," he said, growing serious again.

"I know." She reached across to take his hand. "I love you. And I don't want to scare you. But I genuinely believe I can handle this. Mum will be there. All of Raj's guards will be there. They'll have my back. And if we can end this thing – isn't it worth trying?"

He watched her so narrowly that for a second she thought he'd refuse. Then he held up his hands.

"Fine. How I thought I could stand up to both your mother and you, I can't imagine. But I'm going to work with Raj on the plan, and I reserve the right to pull you out of this if I think it's too dangerous, agreed?"

"Agreed." She said it without hesitation. Because she had the feeling that, with her mother on her side, she couldn't possibly lose.

"Right then. Let's get everyone in here and take a look at this plan," he said, walking to the door.

Ten minutes later, Allie, Carter, and Julia were assembled in the room.

"I've been talking about this with Raj," Gray's father said. "There are some things I want to go over."

Carter spread a map of the grounds out on Allie's desk, and explained the plan.

Most of the invited guests were to be told the party was being limited in numbers because of emergency construction work at the school. They would be quietly uninvited and replaced by security officers in disguise.

"How many students will be there?" her father asked. "That's the part I'm nervous about."

"Ten," Allie said. "We've hand-selected them and they're being trained in self-defence."

"I'd rather there weren't any there at all," he said.

"It would be too obvious if there were none," Allie said. "Ashford might notice."

"That's what Raj says." He didn't sound convinced but he let it go and turned back to the map. "Where are the guards going to be on the fence line?"

"We'll post guards at the school gate, and at strategic locations around the grounds. We'll put them here and here." Carter pointed at two sections of the fence. "These are the locations we know they've identified as access points. I don't think they'll come in that way again, but it's worth protecting them."

"Fine." Gray's father studied the map. "The prime minister will arrive late. She's usually late, so no one will be surprised." He glanced at Gray with a hint of a smile, before growing serious again. "Everyone else should have arrived by then, so you ought to be completely ready. Julia and a team of bodyguards in disguise will keep a close watch on Gray throughout the party. The prime minister will bring her security coterie with her." He glanced at Allie. "Have you heard from John Ashford yet?"

She nodded. "He RSVP'd yesterday."

"Good." Gray's father looked coldly pleased. "Everyone needs to keep their eyes on Ashford. We can't let him slip away unnoticed, even for a moment. The second he heads for the door, that's your signal. Trouble will come. He won't want to be in the building when it all kicks off. He'll call in the attack and he will get out of there."

Carter frowned. "When he leaves, do we follow?"

"Keep one person on him, just in case," Gray's father advised. "Keep everyone else watching the access points. We need to get Gray and her mother out of there as soon as they arrive."

He studied the map for a long moment, his expression intense. "I don't think they'll come over the fence this time," he said. "I think they'll come right in the main gate – either using a hack or brute force. They've already been on the grounds enough to know their way around. I believe they'll come mob handed, planning to smash and grab." He looked at Julia. "You need to have a plan in place to get Gray and the students out of the ballroom and into hiding fast. We must keep the students out of the line of fire. The guards hidden among the guests will take care of everything else."

"Don't worry about me," Gray said. "I can help get the students out of the way."

Her voice was confident. Seeing the plan laid out like that, she was sure everything would be fine. It looked so simple. How could it go wrong?

"Mr Langtry, if you think Ashford will leave before it all happens, how do we prove he's involved?" Allie asked.

"Call me James," he told her, with a slight smile. "We might as well be friends if we're going to stop Ashford together. We'll have cameras everywhere. We will capture every car registration, every face. Somewhere in that information we'll find a direct connection between the attackers and John Ashford. Something he can't lie his way out of."

Gray, who had only found out her father worked for the spy agency MI6 a few weeks earlier, was fascinated to see this side of him. Now she could see the razor edge to his intelligence, and the ruthlessness of the trap he was setting for Ashford.

When he walked out of the school a little while later, she held his hand tightly. It was only five o'clock, but it was already dark. The cold air made Gray shiver as they walked down the drive, their feet crunching on the pale gravel.

He stopped beside a blue sports car Gray had never seen before.

"Is this yours?" she asked, surprised.

He gave a rakish smile. "The government's letting me borrow it."

"Dad," she asked, after a brief hesitation, "Do you think we're doing the right thing?"

He considered this seriously. "I've met men like John Ashford before," he said, after a moment. "And I know the people he's working with. He wants ultimate power. The only way to catch him is to show him the keys to the kingdom." He met her eyes. "That's you. He won't be able to resist trying to take it all. It's dangerous, sweetheart. Very dangerous."

She shrugged. "Everything is dangerous. I can handle it."

"God, you sound like me." He pulled her into a tight hug. "You stay safe," he ordered. "Or you'll find yourself grounded again."

Gray smiled against the rough wool of his jacket. "I promise," she said.

Despite her brave words, it was hard to let go. Hard to watch him get into the car and pull away.

She felt very alone as she stood in the cold watching the car drive into the woods, its red tail lights gleaming through the trees before they disappeared, consumed by the darkness that surrounded her.

TWENTY-SIX

The weekend crawled by. The students were buried in last-minute work, so there were no end-of-term parties in the dorms, and no sneaking out for cold nights in the chapel. As the teachers had surely hoped, everyone was in the library all day.

It wasn't until Sunday night that Allie broke the news about the Winter Ball.

Standing near the huge fireplace that dominated one end of the dining hall, she said, "Can I have your attention please? I'm afraid I have some disappointing news." Slowly the rumble of conversation faded, and the students all turned to look at her. "I'm sure you've all seen the people working in the building over the last few days. These are engineers who've been studying a problem with the heating. It's been made worse by this long cold spell, which means the system has been working very hard. They say they can't fix the problem before Christmas. Because of this, we must cut back attendance at the Winter Ball this year in order not to overtax the system. I'm very sorry to tell you no students will be invited to the ball this year."

A shocked murmur swept the room. Allie raised her hands to quiet it. "I know senior students will be disappointed, and I'm very sorry about that. However, we believe this is necessary so that you can all come back to a warm building after the holidays. I'm sure you can understand how important this is. The good news is, you all get to go home two days early this year. I've already informed your parents, who are making arrangements to collect you this Wednesday. The assignments you're completing now will be your last of this year. I hope that's some consolation."

It had been easier than she expected. The promise of an early release from school had sweetened the bad news enough for them to accept the fairly weak explanation for it.

The hard part came later that night, when she and Zoe told the night training students the truth.

As soon as the students were assembled in Training Room One, Zoe gathered them around her.

"We're not going for a run tonight," she said. "Instead we've got something to tell you."

The students exchanged nervous glances but waited quietly. Gray, the only one who knew this was coming, looked nervous, her hands clenched at her sides.

Zoe continued, "As you all know, there have been security breaches lately. We believe those have been attempts to kidnap or intimidate Gray."

Everyone turned to look at Gray, who kept her eyes on the trainer.

"We think they're going to try again on the night of the Winter Ball," Zoe told them. "And we need your help. We're setting a trap for this group. We need students to be at the ball or they might notice something's wrong. We want you to be there."

As a puzzled murmur swept the room, Zoe motioned for Allie to take over.

She explained the basics of the plan. That they would all pose as normal partygoers. They would keep an eye on each other, but they'd be hustled out at the first sign of trouble.

"We don't want you to fight – you don't have enough training yet. You're going to be there to ensure nobody notices anything is wrong." She scanned their faces. Kyle and Minal looked excited, Dylan looked concerned. Seb and Alex looked intrigued. Maya looked aghast.

"This is fully voluntary," Allie told them, keeping her eyes on Maya. "If you don't want to do it, you can go home on Wednesday with the other students. No one will blame you. This is a big decision. Let Zoe know before you leave tonight whether you're in or out."

As Allie left the room she paused in front of Maya and said quietly, "Don't be afraid. We're going to look out for you."

Maya didn't reply.

Her partner, Seb Longford, looked from her to the headmistress in confusion, but Allie didn't pause to explain. This was for Maya to decide on her own. Allie didn't linger to hear her final decision.

Having seen their expressions as she spoke, she expected three students to drop out – David, the German exchange student, who surely didn't want to get involved in this. Maya. And Sophie Montgomery. That would leave them with seven students.

Would that be enough to ensure Ashford didn't notice something was up? Maybe. But maybe not. There was so little time left. So little room to manoeuvre. It was just days until the dance. The plan had come together very quickly. Too quickly to troubleshoot it. Too quickly to be certain.

When night training ended that evening, she returned to the training room to find Zoe waiting for her in the shadowy room where both of them had trained when they were students. With her slight figure in dark exercise gear, and her straight hair pulled back from her oval face, Zoe looked as young now as she had back then. But Allie knew she was the most intelligent person in this building.

She'd been taking college lessons at thirteen when the two of them first met. She already had multiple college degrees and she was only twenty. Her Asperger's was part of her unique personality. She was the bravest person Allie knew, and she trusted her completely.

"How many are dropping out?" Allie braced herself for bad news.

She was so conflicted about this. She really wanted no students there, but she needed at least some or it could all fall apart.

Zoe looked at her. "None."

"None?" Allie couldn't believe it. "No one dropped out? Not even Maya? Or Sophie?"

"Not even them," Zoe said. "Sophie said, 'I bought a fabulous dress and I intend to wear it.'"

The words came out in Sophie's rich contralto, and a laugh burst out of Allie so unexpectedly she covered her mouth to contain it.

"OK, I should have anticipated she'd go for the fashion angle. But..." She shook her head, "Zoe, they've hardly had any training at all."

"They're not ready. They've learned five things and they're still working on those." The younger woman's face darkened. "I don't like this. There's not enough time. It's not like us when we were younger. We could protect ourselves. They can't."

"I know." Allie considered this. "We need a solid plan to keep them safe on the night of the party. I'd like you to work on that part. I can assign a few guards to help you. But they need a safe place they can get to quickly."

Zoe paused to think, her smooth face bright and bird-like. "The old cellars?"

"Yes." It was a good idea. The oldest part of the school held rambling, ancient cellars much older than the rest of the building. They were unused. "It's cold down there, but they'll be safe. Can you get them ready?"

Zoe gave a quick, tight nod. Their eyes met.

"I thought this would never happen again," Zoe said.

"So did I."

Throughout the weekend, Allie was also busy with plans for the ball. There was a huge amount to do. Things people could see. And things they couldn't. The party was Thursday night.

Isabelle had managed this every year, but Allie had no idea how she'd done it. There was so much to deal with.

The party might be a sham, but that couldn't be obvious. Ashford had been to the ball before; he knew what to expect. If anything felt off, he could cancel the attack and they'd be back to square one. The school had to look as beautiful as it always did at this time of year. All weekend and into Monday workers were out in force, lacing the trees along the curved drive with nets of lights. Inside, thick garlands of pine and red berries were draped on the grand staircase and along the edges of the oak panelling, tied into place with bows of ruby velvet. Ornate silver candelabra were polished and arranged on every marble table. Crates of champagne were delivered.

On Sunday morning a lorry arrived at the gates, bearing a huge Nordic pine tree. It took ten people to unload it and carry it into the building, where it was raised in the atrium. The whole building smelled of pine needles. Decorating the tree took five members of staff that entire afternoon.

The students, oblivious to the dangers that lay ahead, were filled with excitement as slowly, the rambling Victorian building was transformed into a Christmas wonderland. Through it all, Allie fielded questions about budgets, about broken lights. About how many guards to have and whether or not they should be armed on the night of the ball. About whether enough canapés had been ordered for the guests.

The dizzying mixture of the critically important and the trivial required huge patience and calm she hadn't realised she possessed.

All the students' parents had to be contacted and pick-ups arranged for Wednesday, when most would be leaving. She roped in some teachers to help with the calls, but it still took most of Monday morning to notify everyone.

By Monday afternoon, her phone must have rung a hundred times, always with tiny fires to be put out. When it rang again just before five o'clock she snatched it off the desk without even glancing at the screen.

"This is Allie," she said, her eyes on the spreadsheet in front of her.

"Allie." The voice was familiar. Male and very refined, silken and cloying. She recognised it even before he identified himself. "This is Nathaniel St John. We need to talk."

She was so surprised that for a split second her lips moved but no words came out.

The last time everything had gone badly at Cimmeria, Nathaniel St John had been behind it. He'd kidnapped students – even tried to kidnap her when she was sixteen years old. He'd only stopped when she, Isabelle, and Raj had offered him money and power none of them wanted for themselves.

The gasp of surprise was quickly followed by a burning rage.

"What the hell are you doing calling me?" she demanded. "How did you get this number?"

"I know you don't like me, and I understand why." He spoke with the cool deliberation she remembered far too well. "I did things I'm not proud of. I am aware of my mistakes, and I have done my part to make up for it. For one thing, I've kept my distance from you. You have not heard a whisper from me in six years or more, have you?"

"It hasn't been long enough," she snapped.

"It may surprise you to know I agree with you on that. In fact, I've put this call off for longer than I should have. But I can delay it no more. I have information you need."

"I don't know what you're talking about," she said. "Why are you calling me? What information could you possibly have?"

"I understand the Winter Ball is going ahead, ill-advisedly," he said. "And it is my understanding also that you have invited John Ashford. Again, a very poorly considered decision, in my opinion."

Allie drew in a sharp breath. Nathaniel knew about Ashford. How? Was he involved?

She chose her words carefully. "Yes, the ball is going ahead," she said. "And Ashford might be coming – I don't have the list in front of me."

His response was instant. "Don't let John Ashford anywhere near the school, if you value it."

Allie stared across the office, her mind working. Somehow Nathaniel knew about the threat and Ashford's involvement in it. He knew about the ball. He knew everything except how much she knew. That at least was a card she could play.

"What is this about, Nathaniel?" she asked. "I don't know why you'd call me out of the blue and tell me who to invite to my parties."

"Don't you, Allie?" His voice grew tense. "Don't you know why I'm calling? Let me make it easy for you. I'm calling because of Gray Langtry. Because Ashford wants to use her to get to her mother. Because he's working as a Russian agent and this is how he intends to climb the slippery pole to unimaginable power and wealth. He has no morals. He will stop at nothing and you are giving him the girl on a silver platter if you invite him to the Winter Ball."

He knew everything.

There was no point in pretending she didn't know, too.

"I'm sorry," she said. "How do you know this?"

"I know because I know," he said. Then, as if he knew she wouldn't accept this non answer, he said in a tone of exasperation, "You know who I am and how I work. I make deals, and I'm not picky about the deals I make. Ashford's been trying for months to get me involved in this. He's promised me anything I want. To be an MP. To be in the House of Lords. And as part of this contemptible charm offensive, he told me his plans. Or at least enough about them for me to gather that he's coming for Gray and her mother. At the Winter Ball."

Allie realised she was holding the phone in a death grip, her knuckles pale. She made herself loosen her hold.

"Why should I trust you?" she demanded. "You've never done anything but try to harm me and this school. Forgive me, but I don't see you as some public-spirited Samaritan, desperate to save the prime minister."

"It's not about the prime minister." There was an edge to his voice. "It's about the country. Jessica Langtry can look out for herself, but if Ashford succeeds in his plan, our nation is in peril. Our democracy. I believe in fighting for what you want. I have no problem with back door deals. But this? A Russian puppet sitting inside Number 10 Downing Street? No. I can't be part of that. It disgusts me." He paused before continuing. "I'm many things, but I am not a traitor."

Silence fell, as Allie quickly thought it through.

First of all, he was lying. There had to be personal gain involved or Nathaniel would have nothing to do with it. He couldn't care less about democracy – he'd sell the whole country out if there was profit in it.

Still, he was against Ashford. He knew a lot of people in power. And she could use that.

"Right," she said, pulling a sheet of paper and a pen closer to her. "I'm listening. Tell me everything you know."

TWENTY-SEVEN

For the students in night training, the news about the Winter Ball wiped Christmas from their minds in an instant. The term was nearly over, and they were all supposed to be going home on Friday, but nobody talked about that. They were focussed on what might happen on Thursday night. Kyle kept saying they should change the name from Winter Ball to Wrecking Ball, given what it was doing to everyone's nerves.

Ever since Allie had told them the plan, they'd talked of nothing else. For Gray, it was a relief in a way – she was glad to have people to discuss it with. Mostly they were excited about it, or at least intrigued. The worst affected was Maya. She seemed quiet and withdrawn, but whenever anyone asked her what was wrong she changed the subject.

It had become a habit for the group to meet in the library after class to power through their homework together, encouraging each other not to get distracted. This was how they'd managed to meet their impossible deadlines over the weekend. Helping each other, and staying focussed.

On Tuesday, they had little work left to do, but they met at their usual library table out of habit. Minal had her last science lab of the term, so she wasn't there, but Kyle, Dylan and Gray were all in their usual places as soon as classes ended. Maya hadn't come to study on Monday afternoon. For a while, Gray thought she had decided to skip today as well, and the thought troubled her.

But the Polish girl arrived twenty minutes late without explanation and took a seat at the far end of the table, across from Kyle. Her timing was bad. Kyle was in an exuberant mood, and chatting excitedly.

"Trust the Russians to ruin a good party," he said, turning the pages in his chemistry book. "They're probably cross because it's not tacky enough for them. Not enough gold lamé." He paused before adding, "To be fair, that's a valid criticism."

Dylan watched Kyle with amusement. Maya stared fixedly at her history text book. Gray noticed her hands were clenched in her lap and wished he'd stop talking, but he was on a roll.

"Maybe if we told them we'd invited a bunch of hookers and coke dealers," Kyle continued cheerfully. "Then they'd leave us alone because it fits some sort of Russian standard for hideousness—"

"Is everything a joke to you?" Maya snapped, shooting him a blazing look. "Are you incapable of seriousness?"

Kyle blinked at her, his lips forming a perfect "O" of surprise.

"I… I'm sorry?" he said, recovering his power of speech. "Who pissed on your pierogis today?"

"It's not funny." High spots of colour rose to Maya's pale cheeks. "There's nothing funny about any of it. People could die. There could be bodies in this room in three days' time. These people are murderers. You don't joke about death, do you?"

Kyle shrugged. "Well, actually—"

"Stop it, Kyle," Gray snapped, before he could finish whatever he'd been about to say. She turned to Maya. "We're all making jokes to try and cheer ourselves up. But we know this must be terrible for you after what your family's been through."

Kyle drew a breath as if he was about to defend himself, but she shot him a warning look fierce enough to make him think again.

"I've been worried about you," Gray told Maya. "We all have. What are you going to do?"

There was a long pause before Maya answered.

"I've just been speaking to Allie." She looked around the table with wounded dignity. "I told her I wanted to go home. I don't feel safe here anymore. I don't want to stay for the ball. I want to go now."

This shocked even Kyle. He stared at her, aghast. Everyone began talking at once.

"You can't," Gray insisted.

"Don't go just because I'm a twat," pleaded Kyle.

Dylan, who'd been silently observing all of this, said, "Don't be hasty, Maya. Let us help."

The Polish girl held up her hands to silence them. "Don't worry. My parents refused. My travel has to be done with extra security and it's all arranged for Friday. They believe I am safe. So I will stay here and accept my fate." She turned to Kyle. "But I will not listen to you make jokes about something this serious. People have died. They could kill us."

Furiously, she began stacking books, her face tense with a mixture of hurt, anger and fear.

"Maya, wait." Gray got up and walked around to stand beside her. "Please stay. Kyle didn't mean it."

"I didn't," he agreed, contrite. "Please don't leave. I feel terrible."

Maya stopped moving. Her long, pale fingers rested on the stack of books as if it alone held her up. Wild blonde curls tumbled down around her high cheekbones, and her blue eyes filled with unshed tears.

"I'm so frightened," she told them, her lower lip quivering. "My parents sent me here to get me away from those people. It's as if I can't escape. They will find me wherever I go. And what did I do? I did nothing. I am not anyone's enemy."

Gray put her arm around Maya's shoulders, but it was Dylan who replied first.

"I know that feeling," he said. "But you can be safe here. We'll help each other. Protect each other. That's what we've all been trying to do."

"I wish I believed that." A tear traced a line down her cheek and she didn't seem to notice. "It's Gray they're coming for really, isn't it? Why can't *she* go home? We would all be safer if she wasn't here. I'm sorry, Gray. But it's true."

Stung, Gray withdrew her arm and let it fall back at her side.

Kyle looked outraged, but Dylan kept his gaze on Maya. "You need to focus on how you're going to stay safe. How's your training partner? What's his name... Seb, right? Do you trust him?"

Maya nodded, her lips tight. "Seb is very good. His father was a general in the British Army in Afghanistan. The extremists there still have him on a list. He knows how bad things can be."

"Good. Then you have someone you trust." Dylan stood up. "Do you want to talk somewhere quiet?"

Maya, who was calming down now, nodded eagerly. "I would like that."

Gray and Kyle watched as the two of them walked across the library, their heads close together, talking quietly.

There was a moment's silence before Kyle spoke, his eyes on their retreating backs. "At risk of saying entirely the wrong thing twice in five minutes – what the hell was that about?"

Gray watched the pair disappear through the door, still talking.

"I mean, that was weird, right?" Kyle glanced at her. "Not the part where I made Maya want to move back to Poland forever just to get away from me. Or the way she was totally insulting to you. But the way she and Dylan acted. Like he was her guru or something."

"I get it," Gray said. "Dylan has this way of listening, and that's what she needs right now. I can't help because I'm the reason she's so scared. And you're too funny to be comforting."

"That is true," he conceded. "My wit can be a difficult burden to bear."

"Kyle, you know she's terrified of the Russian government, don't you?" Gray chided him, gently. "They tried to kill her and her parents."

"I know." He looked down. "I didn't mean to upset her, honestly. It's just, humour is how I deal with things that I can't deal with, if you know what I'm saying. I do care. And I didn't mean to upset her. Everything's so tense right now. It's all so scary."

It was the first time she'd ever seen him be completely serious. All the light left his face, and he looked drawn.

"Even I thought about going home, to be perfectly honest," he said, glancing up at her cautiously. "I don't want to get killed. I'm only sixteen, and I'm too beautiful to die."

It was a weak attempt at a joke and neither of them smiled.

"You're not going to die," she said, automatically. "None of us are."

"Well, you nearly did. And Maya nearly did," he reminded her. "And these same guys were behind both attempts. So it's not beyond the realm of possibility, right? I mean, we feel untouchable. But people our age die. It just happens."

Their eyes met.

"I hope you don't go," she told him. "I feel better about things when you're here."

"Right back at you." His brow creased. "You know Maya didn't mean it, right? About it being your fault. It isn't. We're all potentially you. Any one of us could be targeted because our parents upset someone. I'm glad you're here. And I'm glad you're my friend." She reached out and took his hand. He squeezed her fingers, his face reddening. "Anyway. I'm not going anywhere. I'm staying here to see this through." He glanced at the door. "And don't worry about Maya. I'll apologise. She'll have to forgive me. I'm too adorable to stay mad at for long."

After they talked a while more, he left to track down the Polish girl and commence a charm offensive. Gray stayed where she was, pretending to read, but her mind kept returning to Maya's words. She had come to see her as the wisest member of the group.

The one most likely to be right. The fact that she was so frightened sent a stab of worry through her.

If Maya thought the plan wouldn't work, Gray had to consider the possibility that she was right. And if she was, they were all in a lot of trouble.

TWENTY-EIGHT

The next day, the students began leaving for Christmas break. All day long Audis, Teslas and Bentleys came and went, engines purring. The rumble of suitcase wheels against the hardwood floors formed the backdrop to the day. For Gray there was a melancholy to it all. The whole school was bright and festive. Lights twinkled on the huge tree in the atrium and on the smaller tree in the common room. Baubles and velvet ribbons garlanded the staircase. Everything looked beautiful, but by midday the building began to feel hollow.

When she came downstairs at lunchtime, her steps echoed. Most of the students were gone now – eager to get home and on with their holidays. But in the quiet she heard a muffled sound she couldn't place. It took her a moment to realise someone was crying.

There was no one outside the dining hall or common room. Everything seemed abandoned. It was only when she looked in the opposite direction that she noticed Sophie. She was standing just inside the entrance hall, hugging one of her friends tightly.

"You'll be fine," her friend told her. "If you're not fine, come to mine. Mum won't mind."

"I know," Sophie whispered. But tears traced straight lines down her smooth face.

After a moment her friend – Gray couldn't remember her name, she was just one of the very pretty girls Sophie was always with – extricated herself from the taller girl's arms.

"I have to go. The driver's waiting."

Sophie stepped back with clear reluctance, as if it took all her strength to make that one step. The girl said something Gray couldn't hear, and then ran out to get into a sleek black car.

Gray heard the car shift into gear, and the crunch of tyres on gravel. Still Sophie didn't move. She just stood there, staring at nothing. Her shoulders were hunched and her hands clenched and unclenched at her sides. Her breath seemed to come in heaving waves, as if she were making herself breathe. Forcing the air through her body.

In that instant, she didn't look like a billionaire's perfect daughter. She looked like a lonely girl.

Feeling as if she'd stepped into a private moment, Gray wasn't quite sure what to do. But she remembered what she'd learned about Sophie's life – about her uncaring parents and the kidnap attempts.

Hesitantly, she walked toward her.

"Sophie?"

The other girl must not have heard her coming, because at the sound of her name she spun around, long hair flying. Her skin was red from weeping. Mascara smeared black beneath her eyes. When she saw Gray, her expression morphed from hurt to defensive in an instant.

"What are you doing, sneaking up on me?" she demanded.

"I wasn't," Gray said. "I just thought I heard something."

"And now I guess you want to make fun of me for being the one student with nowhere to go at Christmas. The only one whose parents won't even send a maid to pick her up." The anger drained from Sophie's face and she burst into tears, holding up a hand as if to fend Gray off.

"Hey," Gray said, softly. "I wouldn't make fun of you. There's still a chance I might have to stay here over Christmas, you know."

Sophie drew in a shaky breath. "Yeah, but not because your parents don't love you."

"No," Gray conceded. "Not because of that."

"Oh God." The other girl's nose was running and she put her hand against it. "I'm a mess."

Gray dug in her pocket for a tissue and held it out to her. "Here."

"Thanks." Grudgingly, Sophie accepted it from her, and wiped her face, gazing in horror at the black smears on the soft white of it. "I must look like shit."

"You look…" Gray sought the right word. "…sad."

"Sad." Sophie gave a humourless laugh. "That's about the state of it." She looked at Gray as if seeing her for the first time. "You just can't know what it's like. I mean, I know your life is messed up, and that we're doing all this stuff because some random Russian wants to kill you. But you have a home to go to. I haven't gone home since last Christmas. That was the last time I saw my mother."

Amazed at being the person receiving confidences from Sophie Montgomery, Gray decided just to go with it.

"What happened last Christmas?"

C J DAUGHERTY

"My mother gave me a Mulberry bag and a pair of Manolo Blahniks that make me six hundred feet tall. And then she introduced me to Mario, her fiancé." Sophie's voice grew bitter. "Mario is barely ten years older than me. He's got an impressive six pack. And he's going to take my mother for everything she's worth. Which I told her." She held out her hands, taking in the empty entrance hall with its unlit candles and cold fireplace. "And that was the last time she let me come home. It seems Mario is more important to her than I am. She's spending this Christmas with him in the Seychelles. And there's no room for me there. She's sure I don't mind staying here where my friends are."

Ever since Gray had arrived at Cimmeria Sophie had done everything possible to make her unwelcome. And yet, in that moment, Gray's heart went out to her. Terrible parents make terrible children. And Sophie's parents sounded awful.

"I'm sorry," she said, with real feeling. "You don't deserve that. I wish there was something I could do."

"Well, your stalkers are making things a little better for me, to be fair," Sophie said. Seeing Gray's blank expression she explained, "The night training. I really like it. I mean, I know it's dangerous and it's all because people might kidnap us, but there's something about it that makes me feel better. You know?"

"Actually, I know what you mean," Gray told her. "It makes me feel stronger. Like I have control."

"Exactly!" Sophie grew animated. "Like, we do it for two hours and afterwards I'm completely wrecked, but while we're doing it I feel powerful. Like nobody can ever hurt me again."

A kind of understanding passed between the two of them. Gray wondered if there was a chance the day might come when she wouldn't loathe Sophie and vice versa.

"Look, it's lunch time," she said, impulsively. "Do you want to get something to eat?"

There were no classes today as the term was technically over. Allie had arranged for the ten night training students to have an afternoon training session, but it didn't start until two. Until then, they were free.

Sophie gave her a look Gray couldn't quite read, but then shook her head. "I need to clean up my troll face. But thanks. And I guess I'll see you at training later."

Gray was surprised to find she was a little disappointed. She would have liked to have talked to her more. There were things she could tell her about her own parents – about being grounded forever and feeling cut off from her family. About her awful stepfather, Richard, and how he'd ruined everything.

Basically, she didn't want to be Sophie's enemy anymore. She had enough enemies as it was. And it seemed to her that Sophie needed more people in her life that she could trust.

People who wouldn't leave her alone at Christmas.

At dinner that evening, the teachers joined the night training students, along with the whole security team and the Talos guards. Even so, the huge room felt cavernous and empty.

The night training students sat together. With ten of them crowded at a table meant for only eight, it was the first time they'd felt like a team in the truest sense of the word.

The fact that they were the only students left at the school gave the evening a sense of intimacy – as if they were the only young people left in the world. They'd been training together for over a week now, but they'd never really talked as a group. They were always too busy. Now, though, they found themselves sharing facts about their lives, the dangerous little secrets that had brought them here.

Sophie looked as perfect as ever. When she'd first arrived, she'd given Gray a discreet nod, but that was the only indication of their earlier conversation.

In addition to Gray, Sophie, Maya, and Minal, there was Caitlyn, a tiny girl from Northern Ireland, with wavy brown hair and huge eyes that dominated her heart-shaped face. She was shy in real life but ruthless in training. When Gray commented on this, Caitlyn explained that she'd studied martial arts since she was five years old.

"My parents thought it was cute to put me in one of those little white outfits. By the time I was twelve, I was a black belt," she confided. "It turns out I just really like kicking things."

Her parents had been targeted with death threats after her father testified against an organised crime gang that had threatened his Belfast business. "They put a bomb under my dad's car," she explained, as calmly as if she were discussing what to have for dessert. "It didn't go off but he got the message. After that they sent me here."

On the boys' side, there were Kyle, Dylan, David, and the two tall brothers, Alex and Seb.

Alex – at seventeen he was the elder of the two – explained that they'd both been in boarding school most of their lives, after their father took over running military operations in Afghanistan.

"That's when the threats started," he said, simply.

Seb picked up the thread, "The guys behind it were obsessed with sons. They kept telling our parents they'd kill us, and nobody would be left to carry on our family name." He looked at Alex. "If they knew where we were, nobody here would be safe."

Alex glanced at Gray, "That's why we get it, you see? What you're going through. We understand."

Caitlyn's partner was a muscular German exchange student named David. He was the son of a German politician who'd been targeted by right-wing extremists. The only person in the group more physically fit than Dylan, he was also one of the top students in their year. He spoke English with barely a trace of an accent.

"For me it's a matter of practicality," he told them. "If you let bullies scare you they'll never stop. You have to stand up to them."

"That's what it feels like for me," Dylan agreed. "I want to be here because I want to see their faces when they realise we're ready for them."

There was an angry undercurrent to his words. Knowing what she did about his life, Gray thought she understood why. It seemed to her, they all had reasons to be angry. And reasons to stay here and fight.

Maya was conspicuously quiet through that conversation, although Gray thought she didn't seem as upset as she had been in the library the day before. In training last night she'd been vicious, taking out her frustration on a punching bag, and then practicing self-defence techniques as if her life depended on it.

"What do you all think about tomorrow?" Gray asked, during a quiet moment. "Are you scared?"

Maya gave her a steady look but didn't reply.

"Well, I'm a little concerned that I need a new tux," Kyle joked. When nobody laughed, he shrugged and muttered, "Read the room, Kyle."

"It's going to be weird," Sophie said, when no one else spoke.

"Yeah," Minal agreed. "They haven't even told us what to expect yet. It's just 'Here's how you kick people. Now go be afraid.'"

"It'll be fine." Dylan sounded confident. "We just have to stick together."

All their training sessions took on an added tension as the hours ticked by and the Winter Ball grew closer.

That night, as the students stretched out on the exercise mats in preparation for their two-mile run, Gray found herself looking at Dylan out of the corner of her eye. She knew so little about him. And the more she noticed, the less sense any of it made. She felt as if she needed to know the truth about him. It was necessary if she was going to rely on him tomorrow night.

He glanced up and their eyes met.

"What?" he asked.

There was so much she wanted to ask him. "How do you know all the things you shouldn't?" "How did you end up my partner?" "Are you who you say you are?" But there were too many people around, and it was pointless anyway. He'd kept his secrets up to now. There was no reason for that to change.

"Nothing," she said, and bent back into her stretch.

Zoe clapped her hands. "Listen, everyone." Standing next to her was Cameron the Talos bodyguard who Gray had seen with Julia quite a lot lately. She held a sheet of paper in one hand.

"Before we run tonight, I'm going to show you the hiding places for tomorrow," Zoe announced flatly.

A worried murmur swept the room. Gray and Minal exchanged glances.

"It's the plan." Zoe sounded exasperated. "Cameron will explain."

She stepped back and the young guard took her place. "The plan for tomorrow night is simple," Cameron said. "We need you all to be at the party by eight o'clock. There are no special rules for this – just be your usual beautiful and happy selves. Dance, have no more than one glass of champagne…" She paused to give them a stern look. "In general, just be as normal as you can. You must stay in the great hall or the dining hall or in between the two for the duration of the event. We need you to keep an eye on your partners, watching out for each other, and notifying one of the guards if you see any sign of trouble or if anyone goes missing. Is that all clear?"

They all nodded.

"You will have comms devices on the night like the ones we wear." She held up her wrist to reveal a small black band hidden beneath the sleeve of her top. "You will have earpieces so we can contact you if we need to give you orders. If you hear the words "Code 9" that is your cue to get the hell out of sight. We will only use this code if absolutely necessary, so if you hear us say it, this is what you do." She ticked the steps off on her fingers. "Step one: find your partner. Step two: move quickly but safely out of the crowded areas following the paths Zoe and I are about to show you. Do not attract attention. Step three: get to a safe space and do not come out again."

She fixed them with a cool look. "Do not contact us and tell us where you are – our lines of communication may not be private on that night. Do not call any other student or your parents and tell them where you are for the same reason. Stay quiet. We will come and get you when it's safe. Agreed?"

The students exchanged glances, before replying somewhat uncertainly, "Y-yes."

She glanced around. "Any questions?"

Seb spoke first. "What do you mean, the lines might not be private?"

"It's entirely possible the team coming here that night will have the ability to intercept and track all our communications," Cameron said bluntly. "We don't know for certain that they will, but they might. To be safe, don't use your phones. It could lead them right to you."

That silenced the students. Everything they learned about the plans for tomorrow night made it all seem more dangerous. More real.

"Right then," Cameron said, as the questions stopped. "We're going to show you where to hide."

TWENTY-NINE

Zoe headed toward the door. "Follow me and pay close attention. This is the only time you're going to be shown these spaces. Memorise them. The key is that you must get out of the way if things go wrong, and stay hidden until we assume full control."

"I'm going to be wearing a new dress," Sophie said, hurrying after her. "These places won't be dirty, will they?"

Zoe cocked her head to one side. "Yes," she said. And walked away.

After a brief moment of hesitation, they followed her into the corridor in near silence. Dylan fell in beside Gray as they made their way down the hallway.

That sense of needing to know the truth about him was still nagging at her. She had to ask him. Somehow she needed to get him alone.

Ahead of them, Zoe stopped to open an unmarked door, revealing a dark, narrow passageway. She hurried in, motioning for them to follow.

"Whoa," Kyle said. "How did I never notice this was here?"

Gray felt much the same. They'd run down that hallway many times, and she'd never noticed the door.

The narrow passage was dimly lit – the only illumination came from wall-mounted fixtures that flickered unpleasantly, throwing twitching shadows on the walls and threatening to leave them in total darkness. It was much colder than the main corridor they'd just been in, and smelled of old dust.

"This cellar is all that's left of the original manor house," Zoe said, her voice echoing off the stone walls and floor. "It's been unused for so long it's not on the modern blueprints. Follow me. Please keep up."

"Oh God, I'm already getting dirty." Sophie brushed dust from her leggings with disgust.

"Hey," Dylan whispered, nudging Gray's shoulder lightly.

She glanced back at him with a frown.

"What's wrong?" he asked.

"Nothing," she whispered.

"Something's going on," he insisted. "You're very quiet."

"I'm concentrating on memorising my path."

"Oh, is that it?" he said. "Because I thought it might be something else."

"Then you thought wrong."

"Come on," he said. "I can tell something's going on."

She slowed down and gave him a steady look. "I'm just ready for the truth."

His brow furrowed. "What's that supposed to mean?"

Ahead, the hallway opened out into a kind of small room, shaped like a church vault, with low, arched stone ceilings, and columns in every corner. The only light came from a few bulbs in ancient glass lanterns, dust-covered and dotted with the papery corpses of insects. Zoe stopped in the centre.

"This is the heart of the old cellars. This is where we want you to come tomorrow night when we tell you to run. There are three ways to get here. The way we came tonight, and the two other routes I'm about to show you. Down here, there are dozens of places to hide."

She motioned behind them, and they shuffled around to see a row of old oak doors.

"Oh, this isn't creepy at all," Minal said, shuddering.

Zoe ignored them, and gestured at the doors. "All the doors down here are kept unlocked. They lead to small rooms. Keep the lights off. Get in one of those rooms, settle in and stay still until we come down to get you. You may have to wait hours, so be ready for that."

"Hours?" Sophie sounded indignant. "You cannot be serious."

For once, Gray had to agree with her. She didn't like the idea of huddling down here in the dark for hour after hour.

Zoe headed down another corridor. "I'm going to show you the other entrances, so that no matter where you find yourself on the night, you will have a way to get down here if you hear us say 'Code 9.'" Her voice faded as she moved ahead and the students followed.

Gray slowed her steps, allowing herself to fall behind, knowing Dylan would stay with her.

"Gray, come on." He walked beside her, watching her with a perplexed expression. "We have to talk about this. I feel like I've done something to upset you, but I don't know what it is. Please tell me, so we can work it out."

"Fine then. We'll talk about it. Let's start with the truth." Her tone was challenging, and she saw the surprise flare in his face. "How do you know things only guards and teachers should know? Are you really who you say you are?"

He still looked baffled. "Come on. You know who I am and why I'm here. What is this about?"

"How do you know so much about what happens here? How do you know so much about me? Was it really an accident that you ended up as my partner? Who are you, really?"

He drew a breath to say something but then paused, his eyes on hers. She could see something new in his expression, a kind of regret. Or confusion. Whatever was going on – whatever the truth was – he wanted to tell her.

"Look," he said, "it's complicated."

"My whole life is complicated," she said. "You know that. I can handle complications. I just want to know the truth."

Again, she saw that look in his eyes. A longing, almost.

The air between them thickened. The space seemed to compress.

"Gray." He breathed her name, and a shiver went down her spine. "I can't…"

She stepped toward him, until she could feel his breath on her cheek.

"You can," she said, quietly. "You can tell me anything."

Their hands brushed, and she felt his fingers move against the outside of her hand, sending electricity through her skin. She couldn't seem to wrench her gaze away from his. She was no longer at all certain what they were talking about. She was lost in his eyes.

"There are some things I can't tell you," he said. "But you can trust me."

"That doesn't make sense," she said. But her fingers were still holding his, and she was conscious of the warmth of his skin against hers. The soft touch of his breath on her cheek.

He stepped closer. "Listen—"

"There you are."

They both spun around to see Minal standing across the stone-walled room watching them with interest. "Zoe sent me back to get you. She thinks you're lost."

"Sorry, it was my fault. We were talking." Dylan's voice was easy, as if nothing had happened.

But Minal gave Gray a significant look as she walked over to join her.

"What was that about?" Minal hissed.

Gray shook her head and mouthed, "Later."

The others were waiting at the end of the narrow, dark passageway. As soon as they arrived, Zoe motioned impatiently for them to follow.

"Keep up," she ordered.

For the next ten minutes, the trainer walked them through a number of escape routes, opening doors they'd all walked by a thousand times without ever noticing, to reveal old staircases and hidden nooks.

Throughout it all, Gray and Dylan paid intense attention to her, virtually ignoring each other. It was as if they'd come too close to a flame, and now they were avoiding the fire.

Gray was uncertain about what that moment in the cellar had meant. Dylan was so hard to read. But there was no time to think it through or make rational decisions before the surreal subterranean tour ended, and Zoe was leading them out of the school for a warm-up run.

Gray found herself dropping back from the others, half hoping to get away from Dylan for a moment and just run by herself, allowing herself time to think. But whatever she did, he matched. If she sped up, he increased his speed. If she dropped back, so did he.

He was so determined to stay with her. To look out for her. Suddenly she couldn't take it.

"Just tell me," she demanded, not slowing down. "Why are you here?"

He stopped, and she did too, as the others disappeared into the darkness ahead of them.

"I'm at Cimmeria for the same reason you are," he said, breathing hard. "Because I have to be." He reached for her hand, threading his fingers through hers before she could stop him. "I'm here now, in these woods with you, because I want to be."

Gray held his gaze, her lungs tightening so completely it was hard to breathe. "I don't understand who you are."

He pulled her closer, and she felt her feet move toward him.

"Yes, you do," he whispered, his breath against her mouth. And then his lips were on hers and her hands were free of his, and reaching around his neck to pull him closer.

And in that moment she did know exactly who he was. He was the one person who could make her forget to be afraid. The person who always seemed to have her back. The one whom – surely – she could trust.

271

His mouth was firm and demanding, taking away what little air she had left. His chest was hard against hers, his arms tight and strong, cradling her against him. He tasted of salt and something sweet, like honey.

She felt dizzy with the closeness of him. The confidence of his kiss.

His tongue teased the edges of her mouth until she opened to him, breathing in his breath, her hands clenching the soft fabric of his jacket.

She felt hot from her toes to the top of her head. Desert hot. And she clung to him, as if he were the only thing that could sustain her, pulling him closer and closer.

He responded to every touch; his breath hitched when her hands flattened against his back. She felt every touch like a flame against her skin. His lips trailed burning kisses across her jaw.

After a moment though, her rational mind broke through the heat, and she pulled herself free, gasping for air.

"We can't," she said, breathlessly. "They'll be looking for us."

His eyes searched hers. "Is that really why you want to stop?"

Was there anything he didn't see?

"It's one reason," she said.

"What's the other reason?" he asked.

Gray bit her lip, still sensitive from the kiss. "I need to understand you. I need the truth."

"Gray, please." She saw that conflict in his eyes. "There are things I'd like to tell you but now isn't the time. Just believe me when I say: I'm on your side. I swear it."

There was no deception in his voice. No duplicity at all.

"I believe you," she said. "But you have to tell me what's happening. I need to understand."

"You will. I promise." He reached for her hand, his fingers warm against hers. "You can trust me, Gray."

His voice was steady and utterly believable. And as they hurried their pace to catch the others, Gray wanted to believe him. The kiss had set her body aflame. The touch of his hand had set every nerve buzzing.

And yet she was sure he was hiding something from her. Something important.

THIRTY

Julia stood in the corridor outside the girls' changing room waiting patiently for Gray. Training had run on for a long time, and it was already eleven o'clock.

She rested her back against the scuffed white wall behind her and rubbed her eyes. She'd had no more than a few hours of sleep for days.

At least, she told herself, the party was tomorrow. By this time the next day, they'd know what Ashford's thugs had planned. And hopefully they'd have gathered enough evidence to put that man in jail for a long time.

Then she could rest.

Just across the hall, the door to the boys' changing room opened. She glanced up as Dylan James stepped out. His school uniform had been put on haphazardly, and his shirt was only half buttoned, revealing a smooth, well-muscled chest. He held his blue-and-white tie loosely in one hand.

"Hi Julia," he said casually, and made to walk by her, but she stepped into his path.

"Wait a minute. What happened out there? You and Gray fell way behind. You're supposed to make sure she doesn't drop back. It's not safe out there."

"It was nothing," he said, with an uninterested shrug. "She was just running a little slowly tonight. She seemed distracted. Must be about the ball."

"Oh really. Because Zoe told me you disappeared earlier tonight in the cellars as well. Was Gray distracted then too?" Julia fixed him with a no-nonsense look.

"That was my fault. We were talking and I lost track of time." His eyes were wide and guileless, but she didn't believe him. It hadn't been so very long since she was a student in these halls, disappearing unexpectedly with boys, and the reasons were rarely innocent.

"Be very careful," she warned. "Gray's only sixteen. She's actually quite innocent, despite the newspaper articles you might have read. And she's relying on you to protect her. We all are. Don't get distracted."

His expression hardened. The boyish look disappeared and suddenly she was faced with an irritated young man.

"Don't make assumptions, Julia. It's never a good idea. You'll almost always be wrong."

"I'm rarely wrong, actually," she retorted, her temper rising.

He didn't hang around to argue the point. Instead he broke into a jog and headed toward the stairs, signalling an end to the conversation. His voice floated back over his shoulder. "Good night, Julia."

As she watched him go, his steps fluid and swift, Julia hoped nothing was going on. Maybe she was being over-protective. Dylan hadn't put one step out of line since he'd joined them. He'd done everything they'd hoped for and more. He'd been great with Gray.

But why had the two of them disappeared together twice in one night? It could be innocent, or he could be taking risks they couldn't afford.

Just then, the door to the training room opened and Cameron stepped out with Zoe.

The three of them gathered briefly. "They're doing better," Zoe said. "But I need about four weeks to get them ready for Thursday night."

Julia gave her a tired smile. "I think you've worked miracles. They've all improved. Did you see Sophie Montgomery tonight?"

"She's really good," Cameron agreed. "When you convince her to stop worrying about what everyone thinks, she's a natural fighter. Lots of aggression there."

"Well." Zoe yawned hugely. "I'm tired."

They said goodnight and she headed away with typical briskness.

When she was gone, Cameron eyed Julia critically. "You look shagged out. Are you still staying up every night keeping watch on Firefly?"

"Yeah, but it's fine. Just one more day before we head back. I can sleep after that."

The other woman considered this. "Actually, I just got word I'm not working tonight and I've got the morning off tomorrow. Do you want me to come up and keep watch for you? You can get some kip, and I can make sure Gray's safe."

Julia desperately wanted to say yes, but she hesitated. "I hate to ask you to do it after you pulled a night shift last night."

Cameron waved this away. "I slept until noon. I'm on a night schedule anyway. Guess I might as well stick to it."

"Well, if you really don't mind." Julia couldn't hide her relief.

"You got it. How should we do this?" Cameron tilted her head. Her thick curly hair, freed from the band that held it back when she was working, flowed to one side gracefully. "You could take my room and I could take yours?"

Cameron's room was in the teachers' wing, about as distant from Gray's room as you could get in this building. The idea of being that far away if something went wrong made Julia instantly uncomfortable.

"Actually," she said, "I can sleep through a hurricane if I know she's safe. If you don't mind, I'll just sleep on the bed, and you can have the rest of my room. It's right next door to Gray's." She paused. "I'd like to stay close to her, you know? Just in case."

"Understood." Cameron looked at her watch. "Meet you upstairs in fifteen? I need to get some stuff from my room first."

"That would be perfect."

The idea of sleep – real sleep – filled Julia's heart with anticipation. Her body craved it. She hadn't dared sleep for days – not since the first break-in. She was certain if she were ever truly unconscious something would happen to Gray.

The other guard ran off to collect her things. Julia watched her easy athletic stride. She was touched that Cameron had noticed how tired she looked. And that she was sacrificing her night off to help out.

Behind her the door opened, and all five girls poured out, talking quietly. Until recently, they'd been in two distinct and separate teams – Gray, Minal and Maya had been on one team, and Caitlyn and Sophie on the other. But that seemed to be thawing. This was a good thing. They'd need each other over the next twenty-four hours.

For Ashford's group Gray was the real prize, but if they couldn't get at her, any one of the others could be targeted to make a point.

Julia straightened. "Alright ladies, it's after curfew. Let's get upstairs."

Exhausted from training, the girls didn't talk much as they made their way upstairs. By the time they reached the girls' dorm, the little hallway lined with arched white doors was quiet. Everyone else had already gone to bed.

Julia did a quick check of Gray's room and then left her to get ready for bed. Closing the door behind her, she turned right and walked one door along. She paused before she turned in, and looked down the hall toward room 301. The arched white door looked exactly the same as it had when it had been her room, seven years ago. She knew if she walked in, the furniture, made of sturdy oak and pine, would be the same as well. Nothing changed here. And yet she was completely different.

The sensitive, bossy prefect she'd been back then was gone. She'd been humbled by life. Brought down by the reality of who her parents were, and her own desire to be nothing like them. She'd given up a lot to become who she was now. To have this job.

"No regrets," she whispered to herself. It was the mantra she'd used to get through tough nights as a soldier. When you know you're doing the right thing, it makes the loneliness easier to take.

Turning away from the past she opened her own door. Her room had been cleaned in her absence. Soft white slippers had been left out, and an extra blanket folded over the end of the narrow metal bed.

Julia kicked off her shoes and lay down on top of the covers. She'd wait until all the girls were done in the bathroom before she went to brush her teeth. Sharing a bathroom with teenagers was a bit exhausting.

She must have dozed off because the next thing she knew, the door was swinging open.

In one fluid motion she leapt from the bed, landing solidly on her feet with her fists raised.

Cameron, holding a laptop case and a thermos of coffee, regarded her with bemusement. "Didn't you hear me knock?"

Embarrassed, Julia lowered her hands to her sides. "Sorry. I guess fell asleep."

"You wake up like a soldier." Cameron bustled in, setting her laptop bag on the desk. "My brother was in the Army. He was the same. Slept on top of the covers. Woke up looking for a fight."

"Does he still do it?" Julia asked. "Or has he got over it?"

"He never got over it. He died." Cameron said it flatly.

Julia winced. "Oh God, I'm so sorry. I blundered right into that."

"Don't worry, you weren't to know." Cameron unzipped her bag, and pulled out a silver laptop Julia recognised as one of the Talos-issued secure computers. She had one exactly like it tucked away in her desk. "I'm the middle child. Marcus was the youngest. I loved him very much. But bombs don't care about families."

Julia could have kicked herself. "I'm so sorry. I would have liked to have met him," she said.

"He'd have loved you." Cameron smiled, her sadness lifting. "He had a thing for blondes. So do I, for that matter."

Julia wasn't entirely sure what to make of that. Was she joking? Or was she flirting?

But the other woman had turned back to her computer, and she couldn't read her expression.

"You should get into bed," Cameron said, typing something. "I'll sit here and do some work. And don't worry about Firefly. I'll stay alert."

Still trying to decide what she'd meant by the blonde comment, Julia grabbed her toothbrush and held it up. "I'll go get cleaned up. Back in five."

The bathroom was empty, and Julia took her time getting ready. Her mind was on Cameron. Her eyes the colour of cinnamon, and her capable hands.

Julia had never dated a woman, but she'd thought about it many times. Her relationships with men had always been unsatisfactory. Carter had been the only one she'd really cared for and that had ended disastrously. Besides, she'd been seventeen. As a grown-up, she'd never made a relationship work. She'd always blamed herself for this fact. Her job involved long hours and lots of travel out of the city. Worst of all, she couldn't tell anyone the truth about what she did. And that put a barrier between her and normal people.

She spit out the toothpaste and met her own blue eyes in the mirror with a look of incomprehension.

"What the hell are you doing?" she asked. "Focus on your job."

This was the exhaustion talking, she decided as she gathered her things. She wasn't here to flirt with bisexuality or whatever it was she was up to right now. She was here to protect Firefly and to guard her from any attack. Everything else – everything – was a distraction.

All the same, when she walked back into her room and saw Cameron at the desk, her heart gave a little kick.

Cameron turned to look at her. "By the way, I love what you've done with the place," she said, gesturing at the blank walls and empty shelves. "It's cosy."

Julia laughed. "I haven't had time to fix it up. And I don't think I will." She put the towel and toothpaste away and got out the T-shirt that she liked to sleep in. "All I want to do is get the evidence we need to put Ashford and his Russian cronies away. Then I can go back to London to my own flat and sleep in my own bed. Get sushi from the place on the corner after work, and pick up a latte on my way to the tube in the morning."

"Living the dream." Cameron said, as Julia pulled off her top and threw it in the dirty clothes bin.

In the Army she'd dressed and undressed in front of enough people to make her completely unselfconscious about it. Suddenly, though, she was hyperaware of Cameron's gaze as she slipped her bra off and threw it after the top. She found herself pulling in her stomach, and trying not to look ungainly as she tugged off her leggings.

"How many brothers and sisters do you have?" she asked, to distract from the sudden nerves that swept over her.

"There were three of us," Cameron said. "Now there are two. My big sister Amelia lives in Canada now. She's a midwife. Loves it there. I don't know how she can deal with all that snow, but it doesn't seem to bother her."

Julia wondered if her sister had the same warm eyes as Cameron. And then brushed the thought away.

In a blue top and sleeping shorts, she sat down on the bed. "You must miss her."

"Sure. You sort of get used to it though, I guess." Cameron thought about it. "I mean, it is weird going from having brothers and sisters to almost being an only child. Christmas feels strange. I try to work that day. Stay busy." She leaned back in the chair. "What about you? Brothers and sisters?"

"Only child," said Julia. "And I don't talk to my parents. So I'm with you on the weird Christmases thing. I've worked pretty much every Christmas since I was nineteen."

"An estranged only child." Cameron looked intrigued. "What could have made that happen? Only children are usually super close to their parents."

"Not my parents," Julia said simply.

"Gotcha."

There was a pause, and then Cameron said guiltily, "Confession. I looked you up. I know your dad's that investor, and your family's super rich." She made an apologetic gesture. "Did you really walk away from all that cash?"

Julia considered her response. She could lie – or at least make up something believable and then change the subject. But for some reason, she didn't want to. She wanted to tell the truth.

"My parents never really wanted a child. I didn't know them well. I was at boarding school most of the time. When I did go home there were nannies, au pairs, tutors – anyone except them. Eventually I stopped going home, and just stayed here."

"Here?" Cameron's gaze sharpened. "You went to school here?"

Julia nodded. "Until I was seventeen. Then they transferred me to a school in Switzerland. I didn't want to go – they forced me to do it. They didn't even talk to me about it. They sent a driver to get me." Even after all these years, her voice was bitter. "I stayed there until the day I turned eighteen, and then I walked out the door and never looked back. I joined the army. Spent four years there, and when I got out, I took a job working for the government. Then I went to work for Raj." She shrugged, pulling the blanket tighter around her. "Now here I am."

"So, wait... You could have had all the money in the world – unimaginable wealth. But instead, you've supported yourself since you were eighteen." Cameron considered this, watching her with interest. "You are something else, you know that? I mean, you might be insane. But I respect you for living the life you chose. It's hard for someone like me – I grew up in a little flat in Hackney. My dad was a builder, my mum was a teacher. With three kids, they really struggled. It's hard to imagine walking away from a fortune like you did."

"You'd do it though, if it was the only way to be free," said Julia, without hesitation. "You'd give up anything."

"I wonder." Cameron was still studying her with an intensity that made Julia flush. "You know, when I said I had a thing for blondes, I meant it."

Julia's stomach dropped. She wanted to say something charming and insouciant, but she'd never really been any good at flirting.

She cleared her throat. "Did you?"

A smile teased the corners of Cameron's lips. "And I'm trying to figure out if you like girls like me. Or if you like girls at all."

Julia's throat went dry. Desire and nerves made her whole body tingle.

"I don't know." Her voice was low. "I've never dated a girl."

"Well," Cameron said, and there were volumes contained in that one syllable. "Would you like to try?"

To her own absolute surprise, Julia found the answer to that question was easy.

"I would, actually," she said.

Cameron smiled, the perfectly symmetrical dimples in her cheeks deepening.

"See, that's who you are," she said. "You're brave as hell." She glanced at her watch. "Now get some sleep. I'll be here to watch your girl."

Julia leaned across to where Cameron sat in the chair. For just a second, their fingers touched.

"Thank you," she said, feeling that touch in every part of her body.

Cameron shivered, as if she felt it too. But all she said was, "Any time. Now rest."

Pulling her hand free, she stood up and walked across the room to turn out the lights.

THIRTY-ONE

The day of the Winter Ball dawned clear and bitterly cold. Inside, a fire blazed in the dining hall inglenook, and the students were conspicuous by their absence. There were no classes that day, and they weren't required to come down at mealtimes. Some slept until noon, relishing the freedom.

For Gray though, sleep had been elusive. She woke early enough to see the sun rise, melting the December darkness into shades of apricot and molten gold. For a while she lay in bed, studying the world through the old arched window, torn between conflicting emotions. The upcoming party hung over everything like a threat. It should have been the only thing on her mind. But something else made her body tingle with anticipation and excitement, and occupied the spaces of her mind that should have been filled with fear.

That kiss.

Even now, with everything about to happen, it was as if she could still feel the imprint of Dylan's lips against hers. Sense his hands warm against her back.

It had been nothing like any kiss she'd ever had before. In ways she couldn't fully explain, it had felt more real. More grown-up. There'd been an unspoken promise of more. More than kissing.

More than hands on her back. It had been a serious kiss. So serious it had swept the anxiety from her mind, and left her thoughts confused.

It was hard to focus on what really mattered when more than anything else she wanted to kiss Dylan again.

But there was no sign of him when she came down to breakfast, which was stranger than dinner had been, in the echoing and empty dining hall. And he didn't appear in the common room, where most of the remaining students gathered later that afternoon.

Minal and Kyle sat with her, both of them so filled with nervous anticipation they couldn't stop talking. As they bantered, Gray's gaze strayed repeatedly to the doorway, hoping to see Dylan walk in. But it remained stubbornly empty.

"Are you even listening to us?" Kyle demanded, tugging her sleeve. "We're so funny and fascinating and it's wasted on you. Who are you looking for anyway?"

"Dylan." Minal gave Gray a shrewd glance. "Right?"

"I haven't seen him all day," Kyle said. "Honestly. You give people one day off and it's instant anarchy."

When Minal didn't respond to his joke, he glanced over to find her still staring at Gray. "What's going on? Why are you eye-stalking Gray?"

"Because I want to know what happened last night." Minal's stare grew more pointed. "I saw you two in the cellar and something was going on."

"What are you talking about? Something was happening where?" Kyle looked perplexed. "Are you both on drugs? And if the answer is yes, can I have some?"

"No, we're not on drugs. As for where – in the cellar when she and Dylan disappeared," Minal told Gray. "Come on. Give it up. What happened?"

"Dylan and I kissed." The words burst out of Gray, as if they'd been bottled up for too long. "Just once. That's it."

Kyle sighed.

"I knew it." Minal bounced on the sofa. "True love. I can smell it like cheese. Long kiss or short? Tongue or no tongue? Commitment for marriage or keeping it casual?"

"I don't know!" Laughing, Gray held up her hands. "And would you keep your voice down?"

"You and Dylan will make a perfect couple," Minal enthused. "I'm so glad you finally kissed."

Gray heard a sharp intake of breath and turned to see Sophie standing in the doorway, her eyes wide.

She jumped to her feet. "Sophie! I…" But she couldn't think of anything to say.

"You're with Dylan now?" Sophie sounded disbelieving. "He chose you over me?"

"It wasn't like that," Gray insisted, although it kind of was, in a way. "It's just…"

But Sophie wasn't going to give her the chance to come up with a confusing explanation.

"Is this why you were nice to me?" Sophie demanded, her voice quivering. "Because you knew you had Dylan and you were laughing behind my back?" She gave Gray's figure a scathing up and down look. "Why would he want you, anyway? Your father's nobody and your mother's basically a fascist."

"Sophie," Minal said reprovingly.

But the other girl didn't stay to debate. She turned on her heel and stormed out.

In the silence that followed, Kyle and Minal exchanged glances.

"Don't listen to her," Kyle told Gray, raising his voice so Sophie could hear from down the hall. "She's so jealous it's disgusting. Her mother has never done anything more interesting than wear a bikini with high heels."

"Don't," Gray cautioned, putting out a hand to touch his sleeve. "She's going to be here all alone over Christmas. And then Dylan. I think she's really depressed."

"Her parents are the worst," Minal agreed. "But she shouldn't talk about you like that."

"Actually – you're going to hate me – but, I was going to ask if she could go to yours over Christmas," Gray confessed. "I wondered if your mum would mind."

Minal wrinkled her nose. Gray couldn't blame her. The idea of spending Christmas break with Sophie Montgomery would be daunting for anyone.

"Would she even say yes?" Kyle sounded doubtful. "She's so messed up right now."

"There's only one way to find out." Gray thought of the pain she'd seen in Sophie's expression. "Either way, she can't be alone. I'm worried about her."

"I'll pop my head into her room," Minal promised, with a sigh. "You'd better not – she might bite yours off." She glanced at her watch. "Right. Well, I think it's time to start getting ready."

Kyle made a show of checking the time. "At five o'clock? The party doesn't start until eight."

"Are you mad? We'll barely have enough time as it is. It'll take me three hours just to do my hair," Minal informed him, as she and Gray stood up.

"Well, it'll take me about ten minutes to get ready so I guess I'll just amuse myself." Kyle waved one dismissive hand. "Be gone, out of my sight. But meet me at eight o'clock on the landing."

Gray started to walk away but then turned back. "Kyle," she said, "Thanks for standing up for me."

His expression softened. "Nobody talks to my famous friend like that."

"You want to come to my room to get ready?" Minal suggested, as she and Gray climbed the stairs. "Bring your stuff. What time is your mum coming? My sister will be early. She's literally always early. Honestly, I know the Russians are coming but I still think tonight is going to be fun. I mean, scary and threatening, but also fun. Oh my God – I can't believe we're the only students who get to go to the Winter Ball this year. We are special."

As the two of them dressed and chatted, the mood was a curious mixture of silly and serious. In some ways, it was hard to believe anything bad would happen, even though Gray knew better.

After her dress was stolen, Gray's mother had sent her two possible replacements. One in dark blue with a ballet neck and long sleeves, and the other a paler blue, with a nipped-in waist and a deep V-neck. When she tried on the latter, Minal said, definitively, "That one."

Gray studied herself in the mirror – the colour brought out the blue in her eyes, and the cut made the most of her figure. It made her look so grown up.

She found herself smiling. Trust her mother to find the perfect dress with absolutely no time to spare.

While Gray was trying to smooth the tangles out of her hair, Minal ran down to check on Sophie and found her getting ready with Maya and Caitlyn. "As calm as if nothing ever happened," she told Gray, when she returned. "They've got biscuits in there too. We stupidly did not acquire food."

"Next time we'll know better," Gray promised. Although the nerves fluttering in her stomach would have made eating hard.

When Gray was ready, she helped Minal curl her hair into dark waves.

"I missed one piece there," Gray told her, pointing at a section of hair on the back of Minal's head and grabbing the heated tongs. "Let me fix it."

"You know, just because you might have to fight off a bunch of evil wankers doesn't mean you shouldn't look pretty at the start," Minal declared, as Gray wound the silky strand around the wand.

Gray dropped the curl and stepped back to study Minal, the wand still in one hand.

"You look stunning," Gray told her. And she did. Her short dark red dress had a full skirt and a high neck that transformed her into a goddess. Her cinnamon brown eyes were highlighted with gold shadow, and her hair hung in thick curls.

"And you look amazing," Minal said.

They considered themselves in the mirror beside the door. Gray smoothed the fabric of her skirt. The wide, graceful neckline of the dress suited her, but also exposed her scar, a slash of pale red against the cream of her skin.

"I know I should be proud of my scars," she said, touching the line. "I know scars prove you're a survivor. But it's hard to get used to."

Minal stood next to her. "No one will notice your scar in a dress like that," she assured her. "They'll only see how beautiful you are."

Gray wanted to believe her, but all the same she kept trying to cover the scar with her hair.

"Wait." Minal dug through her bag until she found a rhinestone necklace and brought it over to her. "Try this."

Tentatively, Gray clipped it around her neck and stepped back, studying her reflection.

"Oh, perfect," she whispered.

The necklace caught the light and glittered, making it almost impossible to see the scar.

Just like that, the past was gone.

Ten minutes later, the two of them strolled down the narrow steps from the dorm wing, talking excitedly – forgetting momentarily about the dangers the night might hold. At least for a few minutes, they were just two girls, on their way to a party.

When they reached the landing at the top of the grand staircase, Kyle was leaning against a marble plinth. He wore dark sunglasses, a dinner jacket, and black tie – a combination that transformed him into a stylish, sophisticated young man.

"Oh my God. Kyle," Gray exclaimed as they neared.

Looking up, he smiled and held out his hands. "My bitches. May I just say you look fantastic?"

They fell on him, smothering him in kisses.

"Don't call us bitches. But also you look so hot," Minal told him, wiping lipstick from his cheek with her thumb. "You're going to pull tonight and we'll never hear the end of it."

He straightened his tie with a flick of his fingertips. "That is the plan."

Hooking arms, they walked down the stairs, silk rustling, laughing and teasing each other. The sound of jazz rose up to meet them over the collective voices of the partygoers already gathered below.

Maybe terrible things would happen later. Or maybe not. Either way – first, there was the party.

THIRTY-TWO

Just before eight o'clock, Allie stood on the front steps. It was below freezing, but she wore no coat over the long black dress that left her shoulders bare. Her hair was pulled back with a gold band, and a pair of antique diamond earrings sparkled like ice chips against her neck.

The sky was moonless but the lights in the trees were like tiny silver flames, creating a glittering fairy-tale landscape that lit up the dark woods. Torches blazed around the parking area, setting everything aglow.

A Mercedes rolled up the drive between the torches, tyres crunching on the gravel.

The door flew open the second it stopped, and a tall young woman with dark wavy hair jumped out of the driver's seat. Beneath her unbuttoned cashmere coat, she wore a burgundy dress that suited her tawny skin and curvy figure perfectly.

"Allie, you're going to get frostbite," she chided. But she laughed as she said it and ran up the stairs to pull her into a hug. "It's so good to see you. I can't believe you're still here. Isabelle is torturing you."

The one person who knew the truth about how Allie felt was Rachel. They'd been best friends since they were sixteen years old.

"I've missed you so much," Allie said. "Please come and work with me and make my life less lonely."

"Not for a million pounds," Rachel told her cheerfully. "How's my little sister? Has she burned the place down yet?"

"Minal is doing beautifully," Allie assured her. "All her teachers love her. She's nearly as clever as you."

Rachel didn't look convinced. "Well, all I can say is, I hope you keep her away from those torches."

As they talked, another woman had climbed out of the car and walked over to join them. Slim and small, she had straight brunette hair that brushed her shoulder-blades, and elven features. She waited patiently until Rachel let Allie go before stepping up to give her a kiss on each cheek.

"It's lovely to see you; it's been ages." Her French accent was like a layer of silk on her words.

"Nicole, you look stunning." Allie stepped back to admire the amber dress that clung to her figure.

"She's always perfect," Rachel said, with a fond glance at her girlfriend. "French women are born with style." Turning back to Allie, she grew serious. "We got your email. I can't believe this is happening. Can we help?"

"I hope we won't need you," Allie told her. "We've got twenty guards, including Secret Service on the grounds. You've just driven past fifteen cameras. The police are on call. But honestly, I don't know. These guys are dangerous. I just want everyone to be prepared."

Rachel draped an arm around her, the fabric of her coat soft against Allie's bare shoulder. "Let's go inside and talk it over. I simply can't believe John Ashford would take the kind of risks you're talking about. It's so brazen."

"He's not working alone," Allie told her. "He feels protected."

"That's treason, surely?" Nicole said.

"Yes, but first we need proof," Allie said as they walked into the school, past candles burning in holders as tall as a man. "It's the one thing we haven't got."

They made their way into the oak-panelled hallway toward the grand, sweeping staircase. As they did, a small woman in a tuxedo perfectly tailored to fit her figure came the other way. Her straight hair swung toward her chin, giving her the avant-garde air of a 1920s film star.

"Oh my God – Zoe?" Rachel exclaimed, rushing toward her. "You look amazing."

The trainer accepted hugs from Nicole and Rachel with pleased patience, and said, with formal politeness, "Thank you. You look nice, too."

"You do look pretty fabulous, Zoe," Allie agreed.

Zoe gifted her with a rare smile and explained, "I wanted to wear something I could run in."

"Dad told me a little of what's going on, but he's so cagey on the phone, I only got bits," Rachel said. "How bad is everything, really?"

"Disastrous." Zoe's answer was succinct.

Two waiters in white aprons hurried by, heading toward the great hall, and Allie motioned for quiet.

"Come to my office and we'll tell you everything," she said, leading them toward the office under the stairs.

"I can't believe this is your office now," said Rachel.

"Me bloody neither." As the others chuckled, Allie opened the door and ushered them in.

"You've changed it!" Rachel exclaimed, looking around the office with its mahogany desk and comfortable leather chairs.

"Just the rugs and the art," Allie said. "Although I'd like to get rid of that desk. It takes up half the room." She gestured vaguely. "Sit, and I'll tell you everything I couldn't put in the email."

The four of them talked for twenty minutes, by the end of which Rachel and Nicole were suitably subdued.

"Why didn't you tell us all of this earlier?" Nicole asked.

"I didn't want to drag you back into this world if I didn't have to," Allie told her. "And we don't know how secure things are, to be honest. They could be intercepting emails and phone calls. We're all getting paranoid."

Rachel and Nicole had taken the two chairs facing her. Zoe was perched on a cabinet nearby, her head cocked as she listened.

"And tonight? Are the kids ready for what might happen?" Rachel asked.

"No," Zoe assured her without hesitation. "We need four more weeks."

"We've only had a few days to prepare," explained Allie. "They're learning fast but no one learns that quickly."

Zoe said, "We've taught them to hide. That was my idea."

Nicole glanced back at her. "I think that is best. They hide while the experts fight. And the prime minister?"

"She's well protected. And she knows everything," Allie said.

"She knows she's bait?" Rachel asked.

"It was her idea to come. She thought it would be the one thing that would draw them out. Get them to make a mistake."

"Brave woman," Nicole observed.

"They tried to kill her daughter," said Allie. "She wants revenge."

Someone tapped on the door and she motioned for quiet. "Yes?"

The door opened. Carter stood on the other side in a jet black dinner jacket that emphasised his broad shoulders and narrow waist.

He smiled broadly at the new arrivals. "Hi Rach. Nicole."

The two raced over to hug him. "You always could rock a tux," Rachel said, admiringly.

He grinned at her. "It seems like ages since we all got dressed up to hang out together."

"Because it has been ages," Nicole said. "We've all been so busy. It's absurd we don't see each other more."

Allie's phone rang, and she answered it brusquely. "Yes?" She listened as the others kept chatting. When she ended the call, she stood up.

"The guests are starting to arrive," she announced. "It's showtime."

As they headed for the door, Rachel put an arm around Allie. "This is so much like old times, it's giving me goosebumps."

"Tell me about it." Allie leaned her head against her best friend's shoulder. "I've had déjà vu for weeks."

They walked out into the hallway in a close group. Carter and Rachel hugged and chatted, while Allie and Nicole laughed at something Zoe said, but then Rachel looked up the stairs, and her smile froze.

"Jules," she said. "You're really here."

The bodyguard stood frozen on the steps, watching them. She wore a beaded, one-shoulder dress that shimmered when she walked. Against the lake-blue fabric, her pale skin and white-blonde hair seemed to glow.

After a brief hesitation, she continued descending toward them, her shoulders stiff. "Hi Rachel. It's good to see you."

Allie held her breath as Rachel, who hadn't seen Jules in six years, walked toward her. "My dad says you're doing amazing work. He's so impressed with you." She held out her hand. "It's been a long time."

For a second, Jules stared at the hand as if it were a mirage. Then she reached out and took it in hers.

Nicole walked over to exclaim about Jules's hair and dress, and pulled her into a brief hug. "I can't believe how long it's been. We were just saying it's such a scandal we don't get together more."

"It's life," Jules said. "It messes with your head."

Allie and Carter stood with Zoe, watching the reunion. Carter rested his hand lightly in the small of Allie's back. She leaned against him, allowing herself a moment of happiness.

As usual, Rachel was wise. It was time to leave the anger of their youth behind them. It was time for all of them to accept Jules as one of them again. To let go of the past.

It was time to grow up.

THIRTY-THREE

When Kyle, Gray, and Minal walked down to the party it was like walking onto a film set. Everything was just a little more perfect and beautiful than real life. The tables were topped with bouquets of white roses wrapped in deep green ivy and studded with red berries. Waiters in black with crisp white aprons swirled back and forth in a complex waltz carrying trays full of flutes of pale gold champagne. Lively music filtered out from the great hall, the quick, staccato beat reflecting the rhythm of Gray's heart.

A handsome dark-haired man, well over six feet tall, strolled toward them and it took Gray a second to recognise him as Maya's training partner, Seb.

Kyle clutched Minal's arm. "My God," he whispered. "Look at him."

Seb didn't seem to notice their astonishment. "Hey," he said, raising his voice to be heard above the growing crowd. "Have you checked out the great hall? It's…" His voice trailed off as he looked behind them. "…wild."

They all turned to see Maya walking toward them. She'd chosen a long dress the colour of fresh snow, and studded her blonde curls with jewelled hair pins that sparkled when she moved.

"Oh, Maya," Gray sighed. "You look perfect."

CODENAME FIREFLY

The other girl smiled at her fleetingly, before looking up at Seb with something like hope. He took her hand and bent over to kiss it, like someone out of a romance novel.

"You look absolutely stunning," he told her.

Her cheeks flushed pink, and she said something self-deprecating, but they could all see what was happening. And soon the pair had stepped away, talking in low voices.

"She fancies the pants off him," Kyle whispered to Gray and Minal. "When did that happen?"

"This is magic," Minal decided. "Winter Ball magic."

"Will all of us fall in love tonight?" Kyle asked, looking around as if the man of his dreams might appear without warning. "Please say yes."

They were laughing and this must have been why Gray didn't notice the waiter approaching until he was at her side, holding a tray. "Canapé?"

She flinched, caught off guard. But the others were too distracted to notice.

"Ooh, thanks. Is that Parma ham?" Kyle lifted one of delicate red and white swirls and popped it into his mouth without waiting for an answer. "Delicious."

Another waiter walked up with a tray of champagne. The three of them exchanged glances. "We're only supposed to have one glass," Kyle said, taking one. "But who's counting?"

"Probably everyone," Minal said, but she and Gray each took a glass, too.

Kyle held his up. "To surviving the party."

"To having fun," Minal corrected him.

The champagne was ice cold and delicious, but Gray silently vowed not to drink much of it. She needed to stay focussed.

"Is your mother here?" Minal asked.

Gray looked around. The atrium at the foot of the stairs was a mass of jet black dinner jackets and colourful evening gowns, but her mother would be easy to spot, with her retinue of security and staff.

"I don't think so. She'll probably be late. She always is."

"Look! Sophie and Caitlyn." Minal pointed to where the two girls stood with their night training partners. Sophie wore an elegant black sequinned dress slit nearly to the waist, revealing the entirety of her right leg when she walked. Gray noticed men swivelling to look at her. She was so tall that, beside her, Caitlyn appeared tiny, but her dark blue mini-dress made her seem incredibly sophisticated.

Sophie's gaze fell on Gray for only a second and then she turned away as if she hadn't noticed her. Caitlyn waved, but was immediately side-tracked by David, her training partner, who hurried toward her.

Only one of the night training group was conspicuously absent.

"Where the hell is Dylan?" Minal looked at the crowd around them.

Gray had been trying not to think about Dylan but now butterflies swirled inside her. Actually, where had he been all day? She hadn't seen him since training last night.

Before she could stop it, her mind began catastrophising.

He's avoiding me because he's embarrassed about the kiss. It was a mistake. He wishes none of it had happened. He's really in love with Sophie after all…

"He has to be here. Maybe he's in the great hall?" Minal suggested.

They began to move in that direction. Gray trailed behind reluctantly. She didn't want to go searching for a guy who didn't care enough about her to show up on the night they'd been training for all week. A night that could change all of their lives.

A man with heavily styled grey hair pushed past them, and for a split second her heart stopped. But it wasn't John Ashford. He would be here, though. That much was certain. And she had to be ready to face him without flinching.

Inside the great hall, the lights were low. Candles glowed on every surface. A six-piece jazz band was playing in a corner, and couples were already dancing in the middle of the room.

Minal touched Gray's arm and tilted her head at the dance floor. "Check out Sophie."

Gray looked over to where the girl was already dancing with a lanky dark-haired guy, with his back turned to them.

Kyle gripped her arm, "Wait, that's not Dylan, is it?"

Gray froze, staring at the pair.

Then the couple turned, and it wasn't Dylan at all. This man looked older than the students, his jaw chiselled, his expression rapt as he gazed at his dance partner as if he'd just won the lottery.

"I think he's one of the guards." Minal sounded scandalised. "I'm sure I've seen him around."

Kyle brightened. "Can we date guards? I just need some clarification because there are a few cute ones."

David walked over and said hello. The evening clothes suited him, bringing out the golden-blond of his hair and highlighting his chiselled features.

"It's quite a party," he said. He included all of them, but Gray thought his gaze lingered on Kyle, who had now pocketed his sunglasses and was working on looking as cool as possible.

Unfortunately, Kyle couldn't stop making awkward jokes that were in no way up to his usual standards.

Gray and Minal exchanged a meaningful look, but smiled encouragingly.

After a few minutes of chatter, David turned to Kyle and said in his slightly accented voice, "Do you want something to eat? I'm very hungry, but I don't want to eat alone."

"Food is all I'm here for." Kyle said it casually, but Gray didn't miss the way his eyes lit up. He turned to Minal and said quickly, "I won't go far. Don't worry."

She gave him an indulgent smile. "Have fun. I'll be fine."

As soon as the two boys were out of earshot, Gray and Minal turned to each other excitedly.

"Did you see Kyle melt?" Gray asked, beaming.

Minal started to say something in response but then she saw someone beyond Gray's shoulder and whatever she was going to say was instantly forgotten.

"Rachel!" she cried, rushing directly at a pretty woman who looked like a taller version of her and throwing her arms around her.

"There you are, Squirt," Rachel grinned, hugging her sister. "Still as calm as ever, I see."

Minal dragged her over. "Come and meet Gray. You'll love her."

Rachel gave Gray a look of instant recognition, but all she said was, "Hello. I'm Minal's calm older sister, Rachel."

Gray liked her instantly.

"Gray." She held out her hand. Rachel had a firm, no-nonsense grip.

"Where's Nicole?" Minal asked.

"I left her talking to old friends, while I searched for you." Rachel studied her. "You haven't grown at all."

"I'm sixteen," Minal reminded her. "I'm basically retirement age. My growing days are behind me."

With a laugh, Rachel said, "I need to say hello to some friends, but I want to talk to you. So don't hide from me. We're going to discuss security and whether or not you are old enough for this." She plucked the empty champagne flute from her sister's hand and put it on a passing tray in one smooth move.

Before Minal could say a word, Rachel turned to Gray. "It was nice to meet you. Keep an eye on this one for me, won't you?"

"I promise," Gray said.

A buzz of excitement grew in the hallway, and Gray turned to see people hurrying toward the front door.

"What's going on?" Minal asked, standing on her toes to try and see.

"I have a feeling I know," Gray said. "Come with me."

She and Minal followed the crowd toward the entrance, where a group had clustered around a new arrival. Gray made her way through the crush until she could see.

Her mother was being fussed over by dignitaries and staff, as a cluster of bodyguards in dark suits surveyed the crowd with suspicion.

Gray waited until there was a pause and then waved. "Hi Mum."

The crowd half turned to see her. Her mother held out her hands. "Darling! Look at you."

The people between made way for Gray to get through and hug her mother, who then stood back see her dress properly. "It's perfect," she announced. "I knew it would suit you."

"I love it," Gray swayed to swish the skirt. "It was the best surprise." She reached out a hand to where Minal stood. "This is my friend Minal. She's Raj's daughter."

"Oh my goodness." Her mother beamed at her. "You are so like him. And what a gorgeous dress."

One thing her mother was good at was making people feel comfortable, and in seconds Minal was excitedly telling the prime minister that she "loved her look". While they talked, Gray had a chance to notice how skimpy her mother's entourage was. Neither her ubiquitous assistant nor Gray's stepfather had come with her.

"Richard didn't come?" she asked, interrupting the two of them.

"He's in Zurich." Her mother's tone grew careful. "Some disaster or other at the office. He'll be home by Christmas. I'm sure he's looking forward to seeing you."

Gray made a vague sound. They both knew she was not a fan of her mother's second husband. For a while she'd even suspected him of being one of the people behind the attack that had nearly killed her. But her father and Raj had ascertained he'd had a legitimate reason to be in Parliament the night she'd encountered both him and John Ashford. They couldn't connect him to the plot.

All the same, she was glad he wasn't here tonight.

Her mother turned to Minal with that professional, politician's smile. "Darling, do you mind if I speak with Gray for just a moment? I won't keep her long."

"No problem." Minal, completely charmed, stepped back to give them privacy.

Her mother turned to say something quietly to the cadre of bodyguards behind her and then, leaving them by the door, ushered Gray away from the crowd, her expression growing grave. "Your father and Raj both assure me you're absolutely ready for whatever happens tonight, but I want to check with you personally. Are you truly ready for this? Because if you're not certain, my car and driver are outside and I can whisk you out of here in an instant."

There was a fine tension in the set of her face, and Gray realised her mother was nervous. She reached out to squeeze her fingers.

"I'm really ready," Gray told her. "I've been working hard and we have a plan." She glanced over to where Minal was looking around the room excitedly. "We're all ready. You handle much worse than this every day. And… I want to be here for you."

Red tinged her mother's cheeks, and she pulled Gray close. "If anything happened to you I'd never forgive myself."

Gray breathed in the familiar scent of her Chanel cologne. "Nothing will happen to me."

After a moment, her mother stepped back and gave her a sudden piercing look. "I know it's probably all in my mind but you look different. More grown up."

"Maybe I have grown up a little," Gray told her. Before she could say more, though, they were interrupted.

"Prime Minister." Allie approached, smiling and holding out her hand. "I'm Alyson Sheridan, the headmistress."

Gray's mother took in her form-fitting black dress and youthful face. "Oh, good Lord," she said, reaching out to shake her hand. "You're far too young."

"Mum." Gray was horrified.

"I'm sorry, but you sounded much older on the phone," her mother said.

Allie didn't seem to mind. "It's true, I'm quite new to this," she told her amiably. "But I know a great deal about this school. I'm an old friend of Raj Patel's, by the way."

"Oh yes, that's right." Gray's mother looked at her with new interest. "Lucinda Meldrum was your grandmother, wasn't she? What a woman!" She shook her head in admiration. "She's one of the reasons I decided to go into politics. She gave a speech called 'The Power of Empowering Women' ten years ago, and it changed my life. She described how much safer and wealthier the world would be if women were treated equally. I decided right then that I would run for office."

"She was my hero," Allie told her. "I think she would have loved seeing you as prime minister."

Just then, Minal reappeared at Gray's side, pulling her away. She tilted her head at the crowded hallway behind them. "Look who's here."

Gray looked where she indicated.

Dylan stood at the foot of the stairs. His black dinner jacket fit like a glove. The crisp, white shirt set off his brown skin. He looked as if he'd been born to wear that suit, and stand at the foot of that grand staircase.

"At last." Gray whispered.

THIRTY-FOUR

Across the crowded space, their eyes met. Gray managed to keep her expression cool as he made his way down the wide hallway to where they stood. He didn't look embarrassed or apologetic – it was as if disappearing for an entire day was absolutely normal.

And yet the crowded atrium around them receded as he looked down into her eyes. A short distance away in the great hall, the band finished a song with a flourish, and the crowd applauded, but the sound seemed to come from miles away.

"I'm going to go find Kyle," Minal said, tactfully. Giving Gray one last supportive glance, she began making her way through the crowd.

"I've been looking for you everywhere," Dylan told Gray. His eyes swept across her. "That… is one hell of a dress. You look fantastic."

The look on his face was pure admiration, but Gray was confused. "Where have you been?" she said. "I haven't seen you since last night."

She was trying not to look at his lips. Trying not to think of his hands on her back.

He had no such compunction, and his gaze strayed down to her mouth and back up to her eyes in a way that made her temperature rise.

"I'm sorry I'm late. I was working on a project today with Carter, and it took much longer than we expected," he explained. "We were setting some stuff up around the fence to make it easier for us to know if someone tries to break in."

Gray's brow furrowed. "Why were you doing that? Shouldn't the guards be doing that stuff?"

"They were there, too. Carter just asked if I could help." His voice was steady and convincing, but there was something about it that didn't make sense. He'd never worked with Carter before on things like this. But then, she reminded herself, these were unusual times. They were all doing things they wouldn't normally do.

"How did it go?" she asked. "Will it work?"

"Carter and Julia think it will. There are these super-sensitive sensors that get triggered by vibrations, so if anyone jumps over the fence they'll set off alarms—" He glanced over her shoulder and stopped mid-sentence. "Holy shit. The prime minister's here."

Gray burst into laughter. "Yeah, she got here a few minutes ago."

Her hurt and anger began to dissipate. It was hard to stay cross at Dylan.

"I'm sorry. I know she's your mom but it's so weird seeing her in person," he said.

"Come on. I'll introduce you." She reached for his hand. His fingers instantly closed around hers, as if he'd been waiting for an excuse to touch her.

Her mother greeted Dylan with her usual mix of friendly mother, campaigning politician, and who-is-this-boy-with-my-daughter caution.

"And where is that accent from?" she said, smiling as her eyes searched him for clues.

Dylan smiled nervously. "The States, ma'am. Texas, in fact."

"Texas? Goodness, you are a long way from home." Her mother's smile didn't waver as her gaze darted to their joined hands, and then to Gray's face.

Gray wanted to tell her mother that Dylan was doing night training with her. That he was the one who had got them all safely home from the chapel that night. But before she could say a word, a new group of admirers fluttered around them.

Gray and Dylan stepped back to give them space.

"Man, she is just like she seems on TV," Dylan told her, with a kind of stunned admiration. "She has this way of looking at you that wipes all the thoughts out of your head and makes you feel like an idiot."

"Yeah, she does that all the time. Drives me crazy," Gray said, fondly.

A passing waitress held out a tray of champagne glasses toward them. Dylan shook his head.

"No thanks, ma'am," he said politely. His accent made Gray smile.

They'd wandered as far as the door to the great hall, which was warm and crowded. Gray looked around at the beautifully dressed guests, wondering who was real and who was a security guard in disguise. Most, she knew, would be the latter. But many were also former students, who'd volunteered to be part of this.

Every so often she caught someone watching her, or talking quietly into a microphone. She knew cameras in every corner were recording the scene, and watching her and her mother closely.

She saw Julia standing across the room talking to Minal's sister Rachel and a beautiful woman in an amber dress. The bodyguard caught her eye and gave her a quick smile.

Dylan was still holding her hand and showed no interest in letting go. It was such a beautiful party it was hard to believe that trouble was out there, coming for them.

Then her eyes fell on a familiar angular face and her breath caught. John Ashford stood at the edge of the room, talking to another distinguished-looking man with silver hair.

Neither of them were looking at her, and she watched them surreptitiously. Each held a glass of champagne and they seemed deep in conversation.

She noticed that Julia had angled herself so she had Ashford constantly in view, and the realisation made her feel better. He couldn't do anything. He was surrounded by security and had no idea he was being observed.

The drummer tapped the cymbals twice, and the jazz band began to play Night and Day.

Dancers surged onto the floor. Across the room, Gray noticed Kyle and David dancing together, looking into each other's eyes. They looked perfect together, their steps in sync.

313

Dylan glanced from the dancers back to her. "Well, since this is a ball, I guess we might as well dance. What do you say?"

He had the most beautiful eyes. Warm brown with flecks of gold. Gray couldn't breathe when he looked at her like that.

"I'll step on your feet," she warned, weakly.

"Promises, promises." He pulled her closer, and swept her out onto the floor. His left hand was firm against her waist. His right hand held her fingers in a gentle grip. His steps were smooth and confident as he guided her around the floor.

"I don't know how to dance to jazz," she said, glancing over her shoulder as other couples swirled around them. "I only dance to regular music."

He gave a low chuckle. "All dancing is the same. You just listen to the beat and move where it takes you." He leaned closer, brushing her cheek with his and whispered, "You're doing fine."

The warmth of his breath against the sensitive skin of her ear made her shiver.

Gray had the sensation of the room around them sinking away until it was just the two of them alone on the floor, his arm around her, their eyes locked as they moved. Hell might come later, but for now they were together and everything was perfect.

"About last night," she said, her throat tightening.

"What about it?" he asked.

"I'm not sorry."

She expected him to say something like "Me neither" or "I feel the same." But he didn't. Instead he said, "Do you know the words to this song?"

She shook her head.

Leaning close, he began to sing softly. "Night and day... You are the one. Only you beneath the moon... Under the sun."

Goosebumps rose on Gray's back. She felt so lightheaded she thought she might actually pass out. Except that would be mortifying, so she willed herself to keep it together.

When the song ended and the crowd began to clap, the two of them stood in the middle of the dance floor, not applauding, not moving, barely breathing.

His eyes were electric. She couldn't look away. It was like they were sharing something without words. Something real and warm and true.

"Come outside with me," Dylan said.

THIRTY-FIVE

Talking to the prime minister gave Allie a curious buzz of energy. She reminded her so much of her grandmother. She had the same simmering confidence and fierce intelligence. The same manner of noticing everything and hiding that awareness behind a steady smile.

After they had talked for a while, Gray and Minal walked away. Spotting this, the prime minister stepped closer to Allie and asked, "Is everything in place for tonight?"

"Yes, Prime Minister. Raj's team has installed everything. The last pieces were put in place this afternoon."

The other woman gave a wry smile, and said, "Please, call me Jessica. I just want to know – are you confident about the plan? Will Gray be safe? Raj keeps telling me she'll be fine but I need your assurance."

Allie hesitated. All she wanted was to say "Yes." But her own experience wouldn't let her. More than anyone else, she knew how dangerous their plan was, and how easily it could go wrong.

"If she follows the rules we've set out she'll be fine. We have a safe room set up for her, and her bodyguard is nearby. But there's always an element of risk. We've done our best to minimise it. But… it's there."

"Understood." The prime minister gave her a considering look. "Raj was right about you."

Just then, one of her bodyguards motioned urgently for her attention. Before Allie could ask what Raj had said, she had walked away to speak with him and the moment was over.

A blast of freezing air signalled the arrival of more guests. Allie turned to see a couple talking to the security guards manning the entrance. The woman was stunning – small and incredibly stylish, in a white coat that looked like real fur. Her blonde hair was twisted into a loose chignon that drew attention to her sharply defined jaw and Nordic cheekbones.

The man wore a cashmere coat of such exquisite elegance it practically gleamed. He had a leanly muscled build and dark wavy hair. There was something familiar about the careless way he held himself, but he was turned away and she couldn't make out his features.

Still, he had to be someone she knew. She walked toward him, a welcoming smile already fixed in place. Their eyes met at the precise moment the guard at the door spoke into the microphone that fed into the earpiece she wore almost invisibly beneath her hair.

"New arrivals: Sylvain Cassel and Emily Blair. Identity checked."

Sylvain's vivid blue eyes met hers, and the moment froze in time. Allie was conscious that people were talking and laughing, drinks were being served – normal life continued. But she couldn't seem to move.

"Can I take your coat, sir? Madam?" One of the staff shattered the moment, moving toward the two of them, holding out her hands for the luxurious garments.

"Thank you." The woman had a British accent, very refined. She took off her coat as if she was removing her dress in a hotel room. Conscious of every move.

Sylvain shrugged off his coat impatiently and straightened his dinner jacket, which Allie knew would be Hugo Boss because he always wore Hugo Boss. She'd seen the pictures in the *Times* financial pages. She'd also seen photos of his Paris flat in a French décor magazine, and she'd seen images of him windsurfing off the coast of Nice in *Le Monde*. She'd seen all of this because she Googled him regularly.

The woman – Emily Something, she'd forgotten already – was looking at her oddly. Allie realised she must be staring.

Swallowing hard, she stepped toward them, trying to summon up her smile again. "Sylvain. Emily. Welcome to the Winter Ball."

The woman looked prettily confused, but Sylvain inclined his head. "Allie. It's been a long time."

His French accent was softer than she remembered. He stepped toward her with a swiftness she'd somehow forgotten he possessed, and in seconds he was so close she could smell his cologne – could it possibly be the same one he'd worn when they were teenagers? It had the same base notes of smoke and vetiver. The scent alone brought a rush of memories of his arms around her, his lips on hers. Kissing in the woods, in the summer house, in her bedroom, in his bedroom…

He leaned forward, brushing his lips lightly against her left cheek and then her right. She began to turn away just as he shifted to kiss the first cheek again and for a fleeting, breathless moment their lips nearly met. Startled, Allie jerked away.

"I'm so sorry," she said, a trifle too loudly. "The continental third kiss. I always forget it."

"The English are always in a hurry. They only have time for two kisses," he said, turning to Emily. "We French always have time for kissing."

He'd always been preternaturally mature. Now he'd grown into that. His face was longer, and his hair was cut shorter, highlighting those remarkable eyes. He was the same Sylvain she'd known at sixteen, only more so.

His date slid her hand into the crook of his elbow and said, "I'm half French, but I kiss like a native."

Something about her set Allie's teeth on edge. The affectionate smile Sylvain gave her only made that worse.

"Manners, darling. You haven't introduced us." Emily nudged him.

"Of course, I must apologise. Emily, this is Allie Sheridan, an old friend of mine from my days at school here." The blonde woman stepped forward and held out her hand. Allie shook it politely. "Allie, this is Emily Blair. My fiancée."

Allie's smile faltered. All her research – and none of it had told her he was getting married. But when she looked down, she could see a ring like a frozen teardrop on Emily's perfect finger – a diamond as big as the Ritz.

"You're engaged," she said, looking at Sylvain as if she might find something she'd lost in the fine-boned structure of his face. But there was nothing there at all. Not affection, not loss, not triumph. It was smooth and impassive. "My goodness. Congratulations."

A waiter came toward them with a tray of champagne flutes and Allie seized two glasses from it. "You must have champagne."

She handed the flutes to Sylvain and Emily, who accepted them without seeming to notice how flustered she was. She smiled so hard her face ached.

"Please. Join the party. Have a lovely time. There are so many people here you know, Sylvain. It's lovely to see you."

Then she turned and fled.

Fifteen minutes later, Rachel intercepted Allie as she spoke to staff in the kitchen about the next course of canapés.

"Head's up, Sylvain's here," Rachel warned. "And he's brought a super hottie with him who sounds like she stepped straight out of Windsor Castle by way of Buckingham Palace."

Leaning against the stainless steel counter in a quiet section of the huge kitchen, Allie said, "Show some respect, Rach. That's the future Mrs Sylvain." She took a long sip of champagne from the half-empty glass in her hand.

Rachel stared at her. "He's engaged?"

"Apparently." Allie plucked a tempura prawn off a passing tray and popped it into her mouth, chewing as she added, "It must be new; there's nothing about it on the internet."

"Well. Balls." Rachel lifted the champagne glass from her hand without asking permission and took a drink. "That is unexpected. How's the ring?"

"Oh, massive." Taking the glass back Allie finished it off, then she turned and summoned one of the waiters, holding up the glass. "More please." Impassively, he hurried over and carefully filled the glass to the top. Bubbles soared through the golden liquid. She barely waited until he'd finished before taking another drink.

"She's very pretty," she said, grimly.

"Stunning," Rachel agreed, intercepting the glass from her and taking another sip. "Is that smoked salmon?" They each took canapés from a passing tray.

Rachel looked around the industrial kitchen, with ovens the size of a small Volkswagen and sinks big enough to bathe in.

"The party is better in here," she observed. "Quieter."

Allie thought of something. "Where's Nicole?"

"Talking to Sylvain and the hot fiancée. You know she and Sylvain have been friends since they were tiny tots swimming in caviar, so they're catching up."

"Of course they are." Allie turned to look at her old friend. "How are you guys, anyway? Everything solid?"

Rachel laughed. "Ask me anything. No topic is too personal."

"Here. Have some truth serum." Allie handed her the champagne glass.

Rachel took a long drink. "Well, I have to say things have been a bit weird."

"Weird how?"

"Well, you know, I'm finishing medical school in Oxford, and Nicole's working in London, so we don't see each other as much as we'd like. It's been a little rocky. There was a third party for a while…"

Snatching the nearly empty glass from her, Allie raised it in the air and met the eyes of the same waiter. He brought the bottle over again and refilled the glass. This time though, when he had finished, he set the bottle deliberately on the countertop between them before walking away.

"Whose third party?" Allie demanded as soon as he was gone. "Yours or Nicole's?"

"I'm sorry to say, mine."

"Rachel!" Allie stared at her.

Rachel held up a hand. "It was stupid. I was lonely and there was this girl I know. A lot of cocktails happened one night and then other things. Anyway, I felt like an idiot."

"You are an idiot." But Allie softened the words by giving her arm a squeeze. "Does Nicole know?"

"Of course. We tell each other everything."

"And?"

"And… we're working on it. Spending more time together. Really listening to each other." She gave a half-smile. "It's helping. We're getting better."

"Good." Allie handed her the glass. "The thing we didn't realise when we were kids is that relationships are not a straight line to happiness. They're like a helter-skelter ride to happiness."

"That's it!" Rachel laughed. "You go round and round until you feel quite sick, but also exhilarated, and when you get to the end you just want to do it again."

They smiled at each other. But Allie's smile faded almost immediately. "He's engaged, Rach."

"Yeah." Rachel put an arm around her shoulders. "You know what? You're happy with Carter. If he's happy with what's her name, bully for him."

Allie knew she was right. But part of her had never fully let go of Sylvain Cassel. Choosing between him and Carter had been the hardest decision she'd ever had to make. Each of them had meant so much to her. She'd never regretted choosing Carter – and they were happy. But now and then, as she studied another picture of Sylvain on a random French website, a tiny part of her heart would whisper, "What if?"

Rachel watched her knowingly.

"Maybe it's time for you and Sylvain to have that talk you've put off for nearly seven years," she said. "Because it seems to me that neither of you should get married to anyone until you learn how to let each other go."

THIRTY-SIX

Julia circled the great hall, listening to the voices in her ear.

"No movement in sector two…"

"Sector three clear…"

Her eyes followed Gray and Dylan as they slowly turned across the dance floor. The band was playing Night and Day. Dylan whispered something to Gray, and her hand tightened on his shoulder, making tiny indentations in the smooth fabric of his jacket.

Julia's lips tightened. He was getting too close. This wasn't how it was supposed to go. He was supposed to keep an eye on her, not… this. Whatever this was. She'd have to have a word with him and remind him.

"We're here to protect her, not seduce her," she muttered.

"Who are you talking to?" Cameron walked toward her, smiling. Her bronze dress perfectly suited her warm brown skin, and matched her extraordinary eyes.

Julia still didn't know what to do about Cameron. She'd never been attracted to a girl before, and she wasn't sure what all of this meant or why it was happening now. All she knew for certain was that the bodyguard was astute and kind, that talking to her made her happy.

She glanced at Dylan and Gray. "I'm grumbling."

Looking where she indicated, Cameron said, "I see what you mean."

Zoe walked over to join them, her eyes scanning the crowded room, a small frown creasing her forehead. She looked so effortlessly sophisticated in her tuxedo. It was such a joy seeing her grown up – when Julia had left Cimmeria, Zoe had been barely thirteen. Smart as a whip but still finding her way.

"All the students are in place," she said. "No sign of trouble yet."

A voice in Julia's ear announced: "New arrivals – Sylvain Cassel and Emily Blair".

Sylvain. She hadn't seen him in so long. She glanced across at the door to the ballroom, but there was no sign of him.

Cameron nudged her shoulder. "She's talking to Ashford!" she whispered, eyebrows rising as she subtly pointed across the room. Jessica Langtry was standing just inside the door, talking to John Ashford. Her bodyguards were three steps behind her, giving her space.

Gray and Dylan instantly forgotten, Julia turned all her attention to the prime minister. She was talking quickly, her voice low. Ashford soon grew more animated, leaning forward when he spoke, his face purpling.

Lifting her wrist, Julia spoke into her microphone. "Swan is with Target in great hall. Does anyone know how that happened? Did he go looking for her?"

Carter's voice came through from the CCTV room. "Negative. She walked straight up to him."

Julia was bewildered. "What is she doing? Everyone in the great hall, be aware."

"Let's split up," she told Cameron and Zoe. "And get closer."

They divided, skirting the huge ballroom in different directions, staying a good distance apart. Julia was vaguely aware that the room was too hot. That the band was still playing Night and Day. That voices were talking in her ear.

Two dancers on the floor began to move in the direction of the prime minister. A couple at a nearby table turned casually. A waiter hurried through the door carrying an empty tray and began gathering used glasses and plates, his head tilted to watch.

There were at least ten guards in this room disguised as guests and waiters. Most of the other guests were ex-students, who had been told the basics of what was happening. In fact, only the prime minister, John Ashford, and a handful of others were actual guests by any normal definition of the term.

Suddenly, Ashford said something angrily, leaning closer to Jessica's face, and then abruptly stalked away. Whatever had passed between them, it had been unpleasant. His shoulders were tense, his hands clenched at his sides.

"Target on the move," a voice said in Julia's ear.

From across the room, Cameron caught her eye. Julia jerked her head at the deputy prime minister's back.

"Follow him," she mouthed.

Cameron nodded.

Julia headed straight for Jessica Langtry, who was sipping champagne and watching Gray and Dylan dance with a preoccupied look.

"Prime Minister," she said, as she approached.

Jessica looked at her blankly for a moment before recognition flared. "Julia. My goodness. I didn't recognise you for a moment."

"Yes, ma'am. Is everything OK? I saw you talking to Ashford."

"It's all fine. I just wanted to have a word." The prime minister set her glass of champagne down on an empty table. Julia noticed that her hand was as steady as a rock.

"Can you tell me what that word was, exactly? We have a very precise plan in place, and it hinges on Ashford having no idea how much we know." She was trying to keep her tension under control, but the withering glance she received told her the prime minister didn't like being lectured.

"We have plenty to argue about, I can assure you," the prime minister said. "None of which should worry you."

Night and Day ended and the crowd behind them applauded. Turning away from Julia, Jessica gave a tight professional smile and clapped politely. The bandleader bowed in her direction, and then lifted his trumpet and tapped out the beat of the next song with his foot.

Cameron's voice came through her earpiece, speaking quietly: "Target is in the hallway making a phone call."

Carter's voice followed: "Try to listen."

Cameron replied: "Copy that."

Zoe was standing in front of the back wall, her eyes searching the room.

Cameron's voice returned to Julia's earpiece. "The call was short. He said 'Do it now.'"

Julia's chest tightened.

"All guards on the fence, Code 2," Carter ordered. "Repeat: Code 2."

Code 2: Get ready.

Cameron: "He's heading for the back door – do I follow him?"

Carter: "Affirmative."

Julia hurried back to the prime minister, who was watching the dancers, and leaned forward to speak quietly. "Prime minister, we think it's starting."

Jessica nodded, her face giving nothing away – no fear, no doubt.

Julia motioned to the team of bodyguards who stood a tactful few feet behind the prime minister. "It's time. Get the prime minister to safety."

"Wait." Jessica grabbed her arm. "Are you ready? What about Gray?" She turned back to the dance floor, her eyes scanning the faces. "Where's Gray? I don't see her."

At that same moment, Julia heard Zoe's voice in her earpiece: "Where's Firefly?"

Her stomach dropping, she spun around to check the dance floor. Seconds ago, Gray and Dylan had been dancing right behind her. Now a new song was playing, and the crowd on the floor was swirling, just as they had been before.

But Gray and Dylan were gone.

THIRTY-SEVEN

Gray and Dylan walked across the great hall, hand in hand.

Gray felt strangely light, as if the ground beneath her feet had turned to billowing clouds. She'd never felt like this about any other guy. Jake had intrigued her, but he'd never made her feel so connected to him. With Dylan it was the way he looked at her, as if he found her somehow irresistible. And the way he talked to her, listening as if every word she said mattered. The way his fingers felt against hers – like matching pieces slotting into place.

The amount she liked him scared her. It was too much. If he let her down, it would crush her.

He cast a sideways glance at her. "Have I mentioned how amazing you look tonight?"

"You have, in fact." She glanced at his shoulders and across his torso, where the crisp fabric of his shirt lay flat against his chest. "You really suit a tux, you know."

His smile broadened. "You don't say."

They were headed toward the far end of the wide, formal hallway, where a door led out onto the terraced lawns behind the school.

"Should we go outside?" Gray asked, doubtfully.

"We'll stay by the doorway," he told her. "Just for two minutes. I just want to be alone with you."

The door was already open, and icy air flowed through, chilling the perspiration on Gray's skin after the dance in the over-heated great hall.

They weren't alone. A man stood with his back to them, looking out across the grounds, as if expecting to see something there.

At the sound of their footsteps descending the low stone steps to the garden, he turned. When his eyes met Gray's, she recognised him instantly.

John Ashford.

She drew in a sharp breath. Her hand tightened on Dylan's.

"You," she said, so surprised that no other words came to her.

He gave her a poisonous smile. "The thing about you, Gray, is you just keep making things easy for me. If your mother wants a war, let her have one."

He looked into the shadows behind her.

"Take her," he said.

There was a rush of air, a soft scuff of feet against stone. Dylan's hand let go of hers. And then everything went dark.

For a split second, Gray had no idea what was happening. The world simply disappeared. Someone grabbed her from behind, holding her arms and lifting her from the ground. She tried to scream, but the bag over her head muffled her cries as she struggled against the strong arms holding her.

A voice in her earpiece that she recognised as Carter's, shouted: "Code Nine. All students. Code Nine. Now."

Code Nine. Go into hiding.

But it was too late. They were already here.

Inside the ballroom, the band played on. The prime minister's guards had taken her away to the safe room set up inside the teachers' wing. At first she'd refused, but Julia had said sharply, "Prime Minister – we'll find her. You must be kept safe. Please let us do our jobs."

This had got through to her and now, at least, they could focus on other things.

"Get the students out of here!" Julia ordered. Her voice shook as she spoke into the microphone. She was running down the hallway, heedless of her dress. This was why she'd worn rubber-soled flats – they were as good as trainers. "Someone find Allie."

Suddenly Carter's voice came through the earpiece, talking rapidly. "We've got five large vehicles driving straight at the front gate. Everyone get ready. Code One. Code One."

Julia's heart began to race. It was happening. She skidded to a stop at the entrance to the dining hall, searching the crowd around the buffet tables, but there was no sign of Gray's blue dress.

"Where are you?" she whispered.

Minal, Maya, and Seb were standing by the cheese table, talking and laughing. The students didn't have access to the full audio feed that Julia received. They knew nothing about what was going on. Minal glanced up, her smile fading at the sight of Julia's expression.

At that moment, Carter's urgent voice came through everyone's headset. "Code Nine. All students. Code Nine. Code Nine."

The small bone china plate in Maya's hands slipped from her fingers and dropped to the floor, crashing into a thousand fragments.

Minal was still staring at Julia, realisation dawning. But there was no time.

"Go!" Julia said, motioning hard. "Go now."

In the great hall the band broke into Summertime. The singer crooned, "Summertime... and the livin' is easy..."

Seb grabbed Maya's hand and began pulling her toward the door. Minal spun around, looking, Julia imagined, for Kyle. He came hurtling through the door at precisely that instant, eyes wide. Relief suffused his face when he saw the others.

Alex still stood in the middle of the room, looking around frantically. Guards ran in all directions – some for the back door, others for the front.

Zoe darted across the room like a bird, grabbing the students and shouting, "Go!" at them, pushing them in the direction of the exits to the cellars. They began to run.

When she reached Alex though, he shook his head stubbornly, shouting something.

Zoe lifted her microphone to her mouth. Her voice came through Julia's earpiece: "Sophie's missing."

Julia swore, and ran for the great hall. First Gray and Dylan. Now Sophie. It was all falling apart. They'd told the students to stay together – was that too much to ask? As she raced down the hallway, she saw Kyle and Minal dive through the doorway down to the cellars. David and Caitlyn were right behind them.

Seb and Maya were disappearing through another door.

She couldn't stay and look for Sophie. She had to find Gray. She ran to the common room. It was empty save for staff manning the coat storage.

At the foot of the grand staircase, she paused. Where would she and Dylan go? Gray loved the library. Maybe there.

She sprinted down the corridor, calling into her earpiece, "Carter, where did she go last? Can you find her on the CCTV?"

Erin's voice came back to her. "Carter's coming down to help you. Hang on. I'm looking at the CCTV now. Give us a minute."

But Julia couldn't wait. She ran to the end of the hallway and shoved open the library door. The lights were on, but the room appeared empty. She was about to turn back and search elsewhere when she heard the faint sound of a muffled scream.

She sped into the room, scanning the rows of bookcases around her.

"Gray? Is that you?" she shouted.

The response was silence. And then, after a moment, the breathy sound of someone whispering, and a hint of a sardonic laugh.

"Dammit, Gray, this isn't funny," Julia said. But even as she said it, she knew it wasn't Gray.

"Lost your precious cargo, bodyguard? Tsk. That won't look good on your CV."

A tall, slim man, who Julia recognised as one of Cimmeria's security guards, walked out from the shadows. He had his arm around Sophie, who was struggling in his grip. Her glossy hair was tangled and it appeared she'd been crying.

"Julia, help!" she cried.

Julia stared at the guard, trying to remember his name. She'd rarely encountered him. He avoided patrol work. He wasn't one of Raj's guards – he'd been at the school when she started.

Someone on the inside.

"Let her go," she commanded.

He laughed. "You think you're in charge? You think you can win? I've got news for you. We're going to get that bitch of a prime minister and her spoiled kid. And then we're coming for everyone else. It's already over. Little Sophie here is just a starter."

"Maybe," Julia said. "But first you have to get past me."

His smile broadened. "That would be a pleasure."

He shoved the girl aside, sending her sprawling on the floor, and then he lunged at Julia.

She spun away, jumping up onto a chair and then onto a table, leaping down on the other side and whirling just in time to brace herself as he ran at her again.

He was fast. She feinted hard to the right, but still felt the air move as his fist barely missed her face.

Out of the corner of her eye, she saw Sophie dragging herself to her feet, teetering on her high heels, one hand clutching the side of her face.

He swung again and Julia ducked.

She tried to get her shocked mind to stay clear. He was a guard but he was working for Ashford. He must be the one who'd taken the dress from Gray's room. Perhaps he had opened the gate to let Ashford's thugs in. He had access and information.

She needed to get to her microphone, but she had to keep her hands up and her focus on the attacker, who was circling her, his eyes flat and predatory.

He aimed a kick at her head. Julia heard Sophie gasp but she couldn't spare her a glance as she dropped to the floor and rolled away, leaping to her feet, but miscalculating, coming up too close. He swung again and this time his fist connected with her cheek. Her head snapped back and she saw spots of darkness cross her vision. Her jaw felt as if he'd hit it with fire.

Before Julia could recover, he hit her again, this time connecting with her temple.

He was strong.

Dizzy from the blow, she jumped back, scrambling to put study tables between them, shoving them in his direction, throwing a heavy lamp at him with all her might. The lamp struck his face and he flinched, swiping it away. This finally gave her the chance.

Raising her microphone to her mouth she shouted, "Code red in the library. Code red." Her voice was thick – her face was already swelling, making speaking difficult.

Sophie had huddled by the librarian's desk, a look of sheer shock on her face.

The man ran at Julia, but she was ready for him and she leapt over a table, keeping space between them as she looked for something else to fight him with. Grabbing another heavy lamp, she brandished it like a club.

"Come on," she called, through swollen lips. "Do it."

Just then, the door flew open and Carter, Allie, and Zoe burst in. In a split second they took in the scene, and ran at the man.

Zoe was bullet-fast, and reached the man first, leaping into the air and aiming a perfect flying kick at his chest.

The man went down like a stone but rolled to his feet in seconds and raced to where Sophie cowered by the librarian's desk. Before any of them could react, he'd grabbed her with his left hand, pulling out a knife with his right.

Sophie screamed, her eyes wild with fear.

"Let her go." Carter held up both hands in a placating gesture. "She's not the one you want."

"I wouldn't be so sure." The man began backing toward the door, dragging Sophie with him. Her legs buckled and she sagged down. "Stand up," he snarled at her, tightening his grip. "Keep moving."

But Sophie didn't cooperate. As they inched to the door, she locked her gaze with Julia's. The bodyguard realised she was communicating. She was dragging her feet on purpose, buying them time to attack.

Carter glanced at Julia. She could see the question in his eyes. She nodded. Yes, she wanted to do this. Zoe didn't miss this exchange. Julia, Carter, and Zoe spread out, approaching him from three directions.

In tandem, all three broke into a run, hurtling straight at the attacker.

At the last second, Sophie spun free, right as Julia leapt, throwing herself directly at the man's knife arm.

From the other side, Carter and Zoe both lunged at him, leaving him confused and vulnerable. Julia grabbed his wrist as she landed, twisting it back with a quick, vicious motion. A snapping sound – like a branch cracking beneath an axe – split the air. The man screamed.

Breathlessly, Julia pulled the arm behind his back, while Carter grabbed the other arm.

Zoe grabbed Sophie, who had crumpled to the floor, and helped her up. "Are you hurt?" she asked, searching her for blood.

Sophie shook her head. "I'm fine. He didn't hurt me."

Zoe looked at Julia. "I'll get her downstairs."

"We've got this," Carter said, gripping the man tightly. "Go find Gray."

THIRTY-EIGHT

In the darkness, Gray could hear a fight. The sickening meaty noise of fists striking flesh. The oof of breath being knocked out of lungs. She heard a female voice shouting "Code One. Back…" And then an awful sound – a scream that was cut off and ended in a hideous gurgling sound.

The person carrying her held her arms pinioned at her sides. Whoever it was, he was moving at speed.

From somewhere nearby she heard Ashford's deep voice, which she remembered so well from that night in Parliament. "Get her to the car. It'll be waiting on the drive. And then take her out of here. Don't stop for anything until she's on the plane." He sounded winded and urgent but not at all panicked. As if kidnapping teenage girls was just something he did at parties.

Her attacker had her in a bruising grip across the chest that made it hard to breathe. He was much taller than she was, and much stronger. She knew five ways to fight off an attacker, but none for freeing herself from this kind of hold. She couldn't move at all. Her feet barely touched the ground. There was no way to brace herself – she couldn't move her hands.

It was all happening so fast. Gray had to make herself think. Where had everyone gone? Where was Dylan? He'd been right beside her.

In the distance she could hear the sound of car engines roaring. Whose cars? How had they got in?

Panic rose but she forced it down.

Think, Gray, she ordered herself. Think.

They'd practised this very thing – a stronger, bigger person grabbing them from behind. She remembered Zoe demonstrating what she should do.

Closing her eyes she lifted her feet from the ground, dropping her weight. She felt the man holding her stumble, heard his breath tighten as he struggled to recover.

He still had her arms in a vicious grip, but she could just about bend her elbows and jab them backwards into his ribcage.

Still struggling to hang onto her after the weight drop, the elbow jab made his breath hiss, but she couldn't get enough movement to do any real damage; he was holding her too tightly.

"Stop struggling," he ordered.

Still, Gray kicked backwards, aiming for his knees or his testicles. Either would do just fine. But again, she was stymied by the tightness of his grip and the lack of room that left her.

He lifted a hand off her arm long enough to punch her in the face. Her head snapped back against the hard muscle of his shoulder. The voices from her earpiece went silent.

Her neck made a crunching sound, and her nose throbbed from it. She drew in a sobbing gasp of breath.

"Try that again and I'll break your pretty little nose," the guttural voice said.

339

The engines were closer now. She saw light through the fabric of the bag covering her head.

"Help!" she screamed, writhing in his grip. "Someone help!"

Then the sound of a car door opening. "Here," the man said. "Take her. She's fighting like a bleeding tiger. Sit on her if you have to."

Someone else grabbed her.

"There. Get that."

She felt hands on her arms. She heard what sounded like tape being torn from a roll. She kicked hard at the hands holding her. "Let me go!" she demanded.

"Stay still, tiger," a new voice told her. She felt cold sticky tape being fixed to her ankles. But she kicked again before they could be bound together, flailing wildly. Her back was on something soft – the seat of a car, she thought.

They were going to take her somewhere – to an airport. And where from there? Who knew? She couldn't let them do that. She thought of Dylan. Of that gurgling sound.

She jabbed her feet into the stomach of the man who'd called her "tiger".

This time her feet made solid contact, and she felt his body sway from the force. Seizing the moment, she flung herself at him hoping to knock him down, but she couldn't see what she was doing, and she collided with a mass of fabric and muscle. She heard him make a startled breathless sound and then they both tumbled to the ground. Gray hit hard, her head banging against something metal with such force she saw flashes of light.

But she remembered her training, and she rolled away from where she thought her attacker might be. With her arms finally free, she ripped the bag from her head.

When her vision cleared, she realised she was halfway under a large vehicle.

A man lay sprawled a few feet away. Blood ran down his left temple, covering the side of his face. It looked like he'd hit his head on the car behind him. He wasn't conscious.

Quickly, she drew her feet the rest of the way under the Range Rover. She could hear people shouting, see them running by. The air smelled of exhaust – the car above her was running. She could feel the heat of the engine.

"What the hell happened?" someone said, standing over the fallen man.

"No idea. He was fine a minute ago," the man with the guttural voice replied. "Dammit. I should have stayed. She's a fighter, that one."

"Where's the bloody girl?" The first man's voice rose. She could hear the door above her being yanked further open. The vehicle sank a little as he climbed inside.

"Unknown." This voice sounded frustrated.

The car rocked again as the man stepped out of it. She saw both feet on the ground a few inches from her head. "She can't have got far. We have to find her."

Quietly, Gray slid across the cold earth away from the voices, moving to the opposite side of the car. There, she hid behind a tyre and looked out. The vehicles were in the drive, just at the edge of the forest.

Her heart felt like a stone in her chest. What the hell was she going to do? She was trapped.

The trees around them were draped in glowing fairy lights. About a hundred metres away, flaming torches lined the circular drive in front of the huge Gothic building.

The front door was closed, but there was no sign of panic. If anything, the school appeared perfectly normal.

Something in the air caught her attention – a faint sound. She held her breath to try and catch it. It was music.

Jazz music.

The realisation of what this meant sent ice into her veins. The band was still playing. The party was still underway. Did nobody know what was happening?

And where was Dylan? Was he hurt? Or worse?

He'd been right next to her. But she'd heard the sound of fighting before she'd been carried away.

Of course, other possibility was that he was working for Ashford. But that one was unbearable to consider.

It would explain a great deal, a voice whispered in her mind. His secrets. His disappearances…

No, she decided, emphatically. Not Dylan. Not ever.

Wherever he was, though, she had to assume nobody was coming for her. She'd have to get herself out of here. How, though? The lights made it impossible to run without being seen. And she was surrounded by Ashford's goon squad. They would find her eventually.

There was nothing else for it.

It was run or die.

THIRTY-NINE

The band was still playing in the great hall, although the room was empty when Julia ran by it. She found Rachel and Nicole clustered with Allie at the foot of the stairs.

As Julia neared them, Rachel surveyed her face with concern. "You're hurt."

"I'm fine," Julia said, shortly. "What's the situation?"

"Five vehicles came through the main gate." Allie reeled the information off, quickly. "About sixteen fighters. Gray and Dylan are missing. Cameron is missing. Ashford is gone. Everyone else is accounted for. Is Sophie OK?"

Julia nodded. "Zoe's getting her to safety. One of the school guards…"

"We know," Rachel cut her off. "Carter put out a warning."

"I'm going to check the front," Julia said.

"The front is well protected," Allie reminded her.

Julia didn't back down. "I'm still going to check it."

Rachel, Nicole, and Allie exchanged a look. It was Rachel who replied. "We'll come with you."

Nicole kicked off her heels and ran in her stocking feet. The others wore flats but couldn't keep up with Julia, who sped ahead, throwing open the door.

Outside, it was bitterly cold, and her breath rose around her in a cloud of steam.

The dancing flames of the torches placed symmetrically along the curving drive lit up the still night.

Five black Range Rovers stood in a line at the edge of the woods, facing the school like tanks, their headlights on. Some distance away, a huge tractor had been parked haphazardly on the lawn. Its tyres – as tall as a man – had gouged deep wounds in the grass.

With something that big they could have driven straight through almost any gate.

This was Ashford's army, then.

She could see no people in the glare of the headlights.

"Where are you, Gray?" she whispered.

"Back door." Erin's voice was loud and urgent in Julia's earpiece. "On the CCTV. Ashford went out the back door. Gray and Dylan went the same way. Cameron followed…"

Julia didn't hear the rest. She was already running. Behind her she heard Allie, who also wore an earpiece, shouting to those who didn't, "Back door."

She could hear their footsteps racing behind her as she hurtled past the kitchens and the closed doors that led to offices and hidden staircases.

Ahead, the back door stood wide open, letting the cold night air pour in. Julia flew through it, vaulting the short steps and landing, precariously but upright, on the frozen ground. She saw a flash of bronze on the ground, gleaming in the light that came through the open door.

"Oh no," she breathed, and hit the microphone on her wrist. "We need a medic outside the back door. Now."

Cameron lay on her side, her arms flung out against the earth.

Slowly, gently, Julia turned her over. She didn't seem to be breathing. Her warm brown eyes stared blankly at the dark sky.

Julia made an unconscious sound. She could hear footsteps around her. Someone leaned over her shoulder.

"We need an ambulance," Allie said to someone.

A figure appeared next to Julia and gently tried to push her aside, but Julia wouldn't budge.

Rachel knelt beside her. "I'm a medical student, Julia. Let me help her."

Slowly, Julia stood back, watching as Rachel felt Cameron's wrist, and then pressed fingers against the side of her neck.

They both saw the blood on the front of Cameron's dress

Crouching over the body, Rachel began performing CPR. But Julia knew – and was sure Rachel knew – it was too late.

All sound seemed to fade to silence. They'd failed. It had always been a stupid plan. They should never have tried. They knew better. *She* knew better.

Voices were shouting in her earpiece but she didn't want to hear any more. She didn't need to. She knew what they'd be saying.

They'd been outplayed. People would die.

Distantly, as in a nightmare, she watched Rachel kneeling over Cameron's body, breathing air into her lungs, then counting as she pumped her chest. Guards poured out of the building, racing past her. The scene would have looked bizarre if a stranger had stumbled across it. Some of the guards were in dinner jackets, others in ball gowns. Their faces were lost in the darkness.

With shocking suddenness, she saw it all. Everything Ashford had planned for tonight. Exactly what he meant to happen

Raising her wrist she said, "Lock the doors. All guards on the front lawn." Her voice was unnaturally calm.

Without waiting to see if anyone did as she'd said, she ran around the side of the sprawling building, vaguely aware that people were running alongside her. Past the darkened classroom wing, where the big windows stared blankly out across the woods.

As she emerged onto the frozen green of the front lawn, she saw the hulking black Range Rovers, exhaust rising from their idling engines.

Guards were already forming a human wall between the vehicles and the school building.

Someone brushed against her arm, and she turned to see Allie standing beside her with Zoe – both were watching the row of vehicles intently. On her other side, Carter and Sylvain stood side by side, still in their dinner jackets. Sylvain's face had a look of focus Julia remembered from when they were younger.

His blue eyes searched Julia's face, taking in the dried blood and bruises. "Hello Jules," he said. "This is like old times."

"Is Gray out there?" Allie asked.

"I think so." Julia looked back at the cars. "I thought they'd be leaving now, but they're just sitting there. If they've got her, what are they waiting for?"

"Maybe they don't have her and they are deciding what to do next," Sylvain said. "We should not let them make the decisions."

It was a good point.

Julia lifted her wrist again. "Gray could be in one of those cars. Find her. Now."

With that, the line of guards rushed toward the row of hulking SUVs.

FORTY

Gray watched the stretch of green she could see from beneath the Range Rover. Men kept walking by, moving fast. She could catch snippets of conversation as they spoke to each other in tense voices.

"…searched the tree-line…"

"…might be further in the forest…"

"…I don't care. Find her!"

She waited for what felt like forever, but might have been thirty seconds, her heart hammering against her ribs. Her head hurt and her neck ached. She felt strange. Dizzy, nauseous. But that, she guessed, was probably the adrenaline. Or maybe a concussion. Whatever it was, it wasn't going to stop her from saving herself.

She hadn't come this far to give up.

Staying where she was wasn't an option. At any moment they would think to check under the cars. They had to know this was the first place she'd go, surely? It seemed so obvious. But something was distracting them. She heard a shout, and then they all took off. She watched their feet fly by as they ran after something.

Finally, there was nobody in sight near her hiding place. This was her chance.

Using a move she'd practised a hundred times in the last few days, she rolled out from under the cars onto the open grass and leapt to her feet. She didn't pause to look over her shoulder, but broke immediately for the building, running as fast as she could.

When she was dragged from the building she'd lost her shoes, and the grass was ice beneath her feet. Stones dug into against the sensitive skin but she ignored the pain.

She'd been thrown into the last vehicle in the line of cars. She had to run past five more, and bypass a huge tractor parked in the middle of the lawn. Its tyres were each at least six feet tall. She made it as far as that before stopping to catch her breath.

The dizziness was back again, and the nausea. For a moment she thought she would actually vomit and she bent over, hands on her knees.

It was strange, but she could barely feel the cold. She seemed to be warmed from within.

When the nausea passed, she straightened again, getting her bearings. From here, she could see a line of people in front of the school building standing shoulder to shoulder. The sight made her heart leap. They had to be looking for her.

Facing them, stood a line of Ashford's men.

She searched for any sign of Julia, but it was hard to make anyone out amid the dancing torches and glaring headlights. Still, she thought she recognised the bodyguard's silver dress in the middle of the line.

Gray raised an arm above her head and signalled frantically, but her hiding place in the shadow of the tractor was too good. No one could see her.

Suddenly, a group of four men broke off from Ashford's group, and ran back toward the tractor.

Gray dropped down into a crouch behind the tyre.

She could hear the thud of their footsteps as they approached – see the clouds of steam their breath created in the cold. They were so close she could see their eyes gleaming above dark ski masks that otherwise hid their features.

But they didn't see her. They sped by, heading straight for the trees.

Gray sagged back against the cold metal of the tractor.

She was safe for now, but she had Ashford's men on both sides. She had to get out of here.

Desperately she looked again at the school building in the distance. She'd never wanted to be inside that building more. There had to be a way to get to it without being seen. Maybe she could run away from the building and then loop back to it from the side. But that would leave her in the open for too long. She wasn't fast enough to be certain she couldn't be caught.

She was trying to figure out a way when she heard more footsteps running toward her fast from the woods behind her.

Gasping, she spun around just as Dylan stumbled around the back of the tractor.

She stared at him in astonishment. There was blood on his face, and streaks of red on the once perfect white of his collar. One of his eyes was swollen nearly shut.

"Dylan!" She ran to him. "Where have you been?"

"There's no time." He was panting. Exhausted. It was the first time she'd ever seen him breathless. He was clutching his abdomen with one hand. But all he said was, "We need to run."

"You're hurt," she told him. "What happened to you?"

"I've been looking for you. I saw them take you, but one of Ashford's goons beat the hell out of me. By the time I got away, you were gone. I've been searching…" He shook his head, his lips tight. "We have to go. There are men in the woods looking for you. We're too exposed here. Can you run?"

"I can run," she assured him. "Which way, though?" she asked. "Ashford's got people in the woods and between us and the school."

"I've been watching Ashford's guys," he said. "I think I know what they're up to. If we run straight for the building we'll never get by them – there are too many and they're too good. So I think we should go through the woods." Unexpectedly, he flashed as near a wicked smile as his bruised mouth could make. "We know the woods better than they do."

They crept to the very back of the tractor. The only way to get to the forest was across a small stretch of open grass. It was the point where they'd be most exposed but they had no choice.

When they reached the back tyre, Dylan leaned out to check for trouble, and finding it clear, whispered, "Now."

They flew across the grass and into the protective shadow of the forest. It took only seconds to pass from the open lawn into the shelter of the trees. Gray had never been happier to find herself in those woods. It was hard to believe she'd ever been afraid of them.

They began to pick their way carefully through the bracken. There was no path, and they needed to move quietly. Ashford's men were in here somewhere too. Invisible and deadly. Twigs and fallen pinecones sliced at Gray's feet but she bit back the pain.

"Which way?" she whispered.

Dylan pointed right. "We're going to skirt the edge of the woods to the side of the school building," he told her quietly. "I don't think Ashford will have anyone around there."

It was a good plan. The only problem was the men she'd seen come into these woods a few minutes ago. They had no idea where they might be. Still, all they could do at this point was try.

Dylan went first, moving with swift grace, skirting the trees, and navigating the thick spikey bramble branches. Barefoot, Gray limped after him as quickly as she could.

They reached a fallen log, and Dylan leapt over it, reaching back to help her across. But the forest seemed to shift before her eyes, swinging left, then right, and Gray faltered as the nausea returned.

"Are you hurt?" He hurried back across, putting his arms around her before she could fall.

"I'm fine," she insisted. "Just a bit dizzy."

He touched her forehead and when he lifted his hand she saw the sticky blood on his fingertips. "You hit your head. Could be a concussion."

The concern was clear in his expression. But already the wave of dizziness was fading. She still had the strange sensation of being hot and cold at once. But she could stand on her own.

"I'm good," she insisted. "Let's go."

Still unconvinced, he stayed closer to her as they made their way through the dark. It was a still night. Gray could hear shouting from somewhere. Every step they took seemed amplified. The crackle of dried bracken fronds beneath their feet seemed as loud as a scream.

Gray's head had begun to throb. She still felt dizzy, although she said nothing to Dylan. They had to get to the school. To Julia.

To safety.

Dylan turned to her and pointed to a gap between two trees, whispering, "The path's straight ahead."

She nodded. They were almost there. But she felt so cold suddenly. And so tired. All of her strength seemed to have drained away. Every step took so much effort. Her feet seemed weighted down, as if the tree roots beneath her were reaching up to grab her and hold her in place.

She dropped back to try and catch her breath as Dylan stepped through the opening to the path.

He hadn't taken two steps when a man jumped out of the darkness and grabbed him around the neck.

Hidden from view by a cluster of trees, Gray froze. What was she going to do? The man was bigger than Dylan, and had the advantage of surprise. He could have broken his neck with one twist of his wrist.

Frantically, she looked around for a weapon – anything that would help.

"Where is she?" the man demanded. "Where's the girl?"

Dylan, his neck in a tight grip, gasped out, "She's right… behind… me."

Gray's breath caught in her throat. He'd betrayed her. Told them right where she was.

How could he? He couldn't be working for Ashford.

Not Dylan. Please.

The man twisted around to look in her direction. The second he was distracted, Dylan swung his right arm up above his head and broke the man's nose with the flat of his hand. Blood gushed down the man's face and he cried out in shock, instinctively releasing his hold to clutch his own face.

Freed, Dylan swung around smoothly with one foot raised, catching the man under the jaw with his heel and sending him flying backwards, into the base of a towering tree. His head struck the trunk with a grotesque thud. And he slid to the ground.

Gray watched this open-mouthed. She'd never seen anyone fight like that except Julia. It had been far more professional and accomplished than anything Dylan had ever done in training. It had been almost acrobatic.

She raced to his side. "Is he dead?"

"Unfortunately not," Dylan said tautly. "Let's go."

They followed the short path through the trees, their feet nearly silent on the compacted earth. Gray wanted to ask how he'd done that – where those fighting skills had come from – but there wasn't time. At least he wasn't working for Ashford – those doubts were gone forever.

She could no longer feel the pain in her feet, and her head felt clearer. They moved faster now that they were on a path, and within minutes the woods thinned and they began to see the lights of the school through the branches. At last they emerged at the side of the building, hidden from Ashford's crew.

In the distance they could hear the roar of engines and the sound of sirens, faint but growing closer.

"Is that the police?" she asked, hope kindling inside her.

"Doesn't matter," Dylan said, gripping her hand. "Let's just get inside."

With that, the two of them burst from the woods, and dashed toward the building.

The front of the building was to their left. The back to their right.

"Which way?" Gray asked.

"Go right," Dylan replied.

They were nearly at the first of the flaming torches, when they heard the sound of the Range Rover engines roaring into life.

They both skidded to a stop, turning to stare as the five hulking vehicles wheeled around and began speeding away toward the main gate, their tail lights burning crimson through the trees.

"They're going," Gray heard herself say, in disbelief.

Dylan put his arm around her shoulders, pulling her closer. Only then did she realise she was trembling.

"Let's get inside," he said.

They were stumbling toward the door when they heard a voice shout, "Stop."

A woman appeared ahead, dashing toward them. Through the haze of exhaustion, Gray recognised Julia's silver dress – so perfect earlier, it was now torn and dirty. When she stepped into the light, her face was more fearful and tense than Gray had ever seen it.

As soon as she recognised them though, some of that tension disappeared.

"Thank God," she breathed. "You're alive."

Wordlessly, Gray raced to throw herself into the bodyguard's arms, tears burning her eyes.

Without letting her go, Julia spoke into her microphone, her voice unsteady.

"Firefly is safe. Repeat. Firefly is safe."

FORTY-ONE

From that moment on, the night turned into a blur.

Almost as soon as the Range Rovers were gone, two ambulances arrived, followed a few minutes later by a stream of police cars. Guards in a variety of formal and informal dress raced around the grounds, talking into comms sets.

Moments after the police arrived, Gray's mother emerged from the safe room where she'd been hiding.

Gray, who was being checked over by paramedics, heard her voice through the open front door. "What I'm saying is, it's perfectly safe. I mean, my God, I'm surrounded by fifteen security guards. I insist on seeing my daughter."

When she noticed Gray sitting on the tailgate of an ambulance having her blood pressure taken, she burst into tears.

"Again," she said, folding her into her arms. "It's happened again."

"I'm fine," Gray insisted, embarrassed. "It's just a concussion."

By the time Gray and the paramedics finally convinced her mother there was nothing seriously wrong with her, Cameron was being moved into another ambulance. As the medics wheeled the stretcher across the gravel, Julia ran alongside it, holding the unconscious woman's hand. Her sadness was clear in the slump of her shoulders, and the way she stood in the drive after the emergency vehicle was gone, staring into the shadows.

Cameron's grave injuries put Gray's minor wounds into perspective. After that her mother stopped fussing.

Dylan and Gray had told Julia about the man who'd attacked them in the woods and soon police and Talos guards had formed a search party to look for him. Despite his injuries, Dylan insisted on going into the forest with them as a guide.

Gray stood on the front steps wrapped in a blanket and watched the flashlights flicker through the trees like fireflies.

Behind her, the doors flew open.

"There she is." Kyle walked out, grinning at her impishly. Minal was right beside him.

The three of them hugged for a long time, as the other students gathered around, talking excitedly. They were all grimy with cellar dust and thrilled to be free.

"How was the safe room?" Gray asked.

"Crawling with spiders," Minal said with a shudder. "But safe."

"I am never getting the dirt off this jacket," Kyle said, slapping at the dust with a grimace. David had come to stand near him and Gray noticed the two exchange a quick glance and a smile. It lifted her heart.

Uncharacteristically quiet, Sophie stood near Alex, occasionally resting her head on his shoulder. Hesitantly, he put his arm around her and she leaned against him. There was a bruise on the side of her face. Gray wondered what had happened to her.

But then they all had their scars now.

As the others talked, Maya walked over to stand next to Gray. For a long time she said nothing. Then, so softly that Gray might almost have imagined it, she said "I think you are incredibly brave."

Shouts from the forest distracted them, and Gray reached for Maya's arm, squeezing it unconsciously as they watched the torches converge.

"What is it?" Minal asked, joining them.

Gray explained what was happening. By the time she'd finished telling the story, the searchers began to emerge. In their midst was a man dressed all in black, his hands cuffed behind his back.

"We got one," Kyle said, with approval.

By then, though, Gray felt strangely exhausted. The paramedics had given her something for the pain, and all of it began to catch up with her. They moved inside, and gathered on sofas in the warmth of the common room.

She wanted to stay up and wait for Dylan to come back inside, but her eyelids felt heavy and she kept drifting off.

Sometime around one in the morning, she heard her mother say, "Take her to my room."

Someone picked her up and she felt herself floating.

After that, she remembered nothing.

When Gray woke, sunlight was pouring through the window next to the bed. She rolled over to check the clock but stopped, groaning as her head and neck protested. She waited a second for the pain to subside, and then turned.

Only there was no clock. And the window, which should have been high and arched, was low and rectangular.

Wincing, she pushed herself up and looked around. She was in a large, comfortable room. The bed was a four-poster, draped in white linen.

It was utterly confusing until she saw her mother's favourite suitcase leaning against the wall near the door.

There was no sign of her mother, and the building felt strangely hushed around her.

Gingerly, she eased herself up until she could swing her legs around and put her feet on the floor.

Everything hurt. Her nose, her eye, her head. When she reached the bathroom, the face that greeted her in the mirror was a mess. Her forehead bore a purpling bruise, and her nose was swollen to three times its normal size. A bandage covered a wound at her hairline.

"But I'm alive," she said aloud. And tried not to think about Cameron.

After a brief shower, she discovered her mother had left leggings and a warm jumper for her folded neatly on the chair, along with a chunky pair of ankle boots. She must have brought all of that from home, Gray realised, as she didn't have many of her own clothes at the school.

Her feet were still sore from the barefoot run through the woods, and she walked with her weight on her toes to ease the ache as she headed slowly out to find the others.

In the main hallway, she saw a few suitcases clustered near the door. All signs of the party had disappeared. The door to the great hall was shut.

"Gray!" Minal ran up to her, ponytail flying behind her. Dressed in jeans and a long sweater she looked very different, and it occurred to Gray she'd never seen her in normal clothes. "I thought you'd never wake up. Are you OK?"

Kyle was right behind her, looking a bit puffy-eyed but pleased with himself. "Girl! You have so much gossip to catch up on."

"Tell me," Gray demanded.

"The police are still outside," Minal said, excitedly. "They're searching the grounds with dogs."

"Cameron?" Gray asked.

The two of them grew sober. "They don't think she's going to make it," Kyle said. "I heard one of the guards say she lost too much blood."

Gray thought of Julia's pale face last night and her heart broke for her.

"Have they arrested John Ashford?" she demanded. "Please say yes."

They both shook their heads in unison. "They found the Range Rovers abandoned in a field about thirty miles away." Minal told her. "Apparently they were all stolen. And the tractor was stolen, too. That's still out front like the world's worst lawn ornament. Everyone keeps talking about how it was, like, organised crime, or something."

A group of bodyguards in dark suits came toward them and Gray saw her mother in the middle of the cluster, talking on her phone. Spotting Gray, she ended the call abruptly and swooped in to hug her.

"You should still be in bed! How do you feel?"

"Like I was in a car crash, but also hungry," Gray said.

"You look awful." Her mother tilted her chin to examine her more closely. "Your poor face."

"I'm not wild about my new look either," Gray agreed wanly.

"Well, I hope this is the last time." Her mother brushed a kiss on her forehead.

"Mum." Gray lowered her voice. "They haven't arrested Ashford?"

Her mother's face darkened. "They have to examine the evidence but so far there's nothing to directly connect him to the attack. The man they've caught is lying, just like the one who stabbed you in Oxford. He insists he did it on his own, which is patently absurd. So they have to go through all the evidence and try and prove he and the others were working for Ashford."

This was horrible news. They had to find proof. Somehow. Or this would never, ever end.

But her mother was still chatting in that determinedly positive way of hers. "You did brilliantly last night. Allie's raving about you to everyone." Her phone began to ring again and she stepped back. "I must take this, darling. It's all chaos because of last night. The press is losing its mind. Anna's trying to handle everything from London and it's a nightmare. We're going home in an hour. There are just a few things I have to do before we leave. Are you packed? No? You should get ready. There are sandwiches in the dining hall. Eat before we go. You missed breakfast entirely."

And with that she was off, the phone again pressed to her ear, bodyguards right behind her.

As soon as she'd gone, Kyle and Minal reconvened around Gray.

"Your mum is wild," Minal said with admiration.

"She's unbelievably glamorous," Kyle sighed.

"She's exhausting," Gray told them. "But I love her." Linking arms with them both she began pulling them down the hallway. "Come with me to the dining hall. I want to hear everything you couldn't tell me last night. But I need food." She glanced at Kyle. "Also, I need the gossip about you and David and I need it now."

He blushed. "I don't kiss and tell," he said.

"Yes, you do!" both girls chorused, and then they all burst into laughter.

"OK but I've only got an hour before the car comes," he warned them. "That'll never be enough time."

"I'm getting a ride with Rachel and Nicole," Minal said. "I think they're just waiting until things calm down here first." Looking at Gray she said, "By the way, I invited Sophie to spend the holidays with us, and she said yes. So it's all your fault."

Gray winced, "Sorry about that."

"Guys!" Maya ran up to them, already in her coat. "The car is here to take me to the airport. I just wanted to say goodbye." In skinny jeans and knee-high boots she looked beautiful. Her curls had been tugged back beneath a knitted cap, although some still escaped to frame her face. Her blue eyes found Gray, and she gave a shy smile. "I'm glad you're OK."

"I'm glad you are, too," Gray reached out to pull the Polish girl into a quick hug. "You're coming back next term, aren't you?"

"I hope so." Maya hesitated. Lowering her voice she said, "Can I talk to you for a second before I go?"

"Sure." Gray turned to the other two. "Meet you in the dining hall?"

"We'll save you a seat," Minal promised.

Minal and Kyle gave Maya goodbye hugs, and then walked down the hall, deep in animated conversation.

When they were out of earshot, Gray turned to Maya. "What's up?"

"It's Dylan." Maya spoke hesitantly. "There's something I should have said to you. I wanted to, but it didn't seem like my business, so I said nothing. But now I think I should have told you."

Gray's stomach lurched. She hadn't seen him since he'd gone into the woods with the police. By the time she'd gone to bed, he still hadn't appeared.

"What about him?" she asked. "Is something wrong?"

"No," the Polish girl assured her. "It's nothing terrible. It's just... I think he hasn't told you the truth about who he is. And he should. I can see things are happening between you and it's not right if you don't know who he really is."

Gray stared at her. "What do you mean? What are you saying? Who is he?"

"He's a good person. But he's not a student. Not really."

"Not a student?" Gray's brow creased. "I don't understand."

A man appeared at the end of the hallway and gestured for Maya to come. She lifted her hand in acknowledgement.

"I have to go," she told Gray. "Besides, it's not my right to tell you his secrets. But ask him. He'll tell you."

She began to walk away, but stopped and turned back to Gray with a serious smile. "I'm glad I know you. See you in January, I hope. If we all stay alive."

And then she was running down the hall, her steps light and eager. Ready to go home.

FORTY-TWO

Minal and Kyle both left for home soon after lunch. By then, the other Night School students had already departed. On her way to join Minal in the car, Sophie sought Gray out and gave her an unexpected hug.

"Thank you," she whispered fiercely, before walking away without another word.

Gray didn't know what to make of that. But she decided to chalk it up as a win.

After the others left, her mother sent a bodyguard to tell Gray to get packed, and she returned reluctantly to her room. The girls' dorm was empty now, and her footsteps sounded hollow as she walked down the hallway. It was the first time since she'd arrived that she'd gone up to her room without Julia checking it first to make sure it was safe. It felt strange.

Everything was right where it had been before she went down to the party the night before. Her makeup and hair supplies still lay scattered across her desk.

Dragging a suitcase out from under the bed, she began putting her things into it. She didn't have much – she'd leave the uniforms where they were until the next term. She need only pack the basics.

As she worked, Maya's words hung over her like a dark cloud. If Dylan wasn't who he'd said he was, who was he?

She thought of the way he'd fought the night before, the acrobatic swinging kick that had sent the guard flying through the air. The move had been like something from a movie.

Where did he learn to do that?

If he wasn't a student … what did that leave? Was he a guard? Something else?

If so, what?

"Who are you, Dylan James?" she asked aloud, as she zipped the suitcase shut.

"Nobody." The voice came from the doorway, and she whirled around to find him watching her.

His eye was still swollen, but it looked better than it had last night. His face was bruised, but he'd cleaned up. He wore jeans and a dark jumper in a soft, charcoal grey. His expression was deadly serious.

They stared at each other across the small room.

"You aren't a student, are you?" she said.

There was a long silence before he replied, his eyes steady as he considered his answer. "Not exactly."

Gray drew in a breath. Her pulse began to pound.

"Are you really from Texas?"

"Damn straight," he said.

But she was in no mood for humour. "Does that mean yes in English?"

"Yes, it does."

"Is your dad really attorney general?"

"William Tyler James, look him up." His voice was firm.

Gray was confused. "Then what isn't the truth? Who are you?"

"I'm Dylan James, son of William Tyler James. I'm from Houston, as I said." He paused before adding, "I'm also a trained bodyguard. And I'm nineteen years old. I graduated from high school two years ago."

She stared at him. "What are... You ... A trained... Nineteen?"

"All those things," he said, seriously. "Yes."

"I don't understand. What are you doing here?"

"It's a bit of a story," he warned her. But when she didn't speak, he explained. "My school in Texas is a member of an organisation which is related to Aurora, the group that runs this school. They work together from time to time. With everything that was going on here, they asked me to come over for a year and just help out."

"Help with what?"

"They told me the prime minister's daughter was coming, and that the Russians were trying to kidnap her. Or worse. They wanted me to stay close. Keep you safe."

Suddenly, it all made horrible sense. She backed up until she ran into the desk, and gripped it with both hands.

"So everything that happened with us was your job?"

"No," he said. "Not everything. That's the problem."

Gray shook her head. "Stop talking in circles. I can't handle it right now."

The sense of betrayal was overwhelming. All she'd wanted was someone she could trust. Someone she could believe in. She'd thought that was him.

He stood patiently in the doorway, his face hard to read.

"I just need to understand," she said. "Tell me the whole truth. Were you my friend because someone paid you to be my friend?"

"No, never." His voice was firm. "I was asked to be close, but becoming your friend was a complication I didn't foresee. Becoming more than that was a disaster."

Heat rushed to her face. "A disaster?"

His gaze didn't waver. "It's a disaster because it's not allowed. The guards, the security team – they want me to protect you. Not fall for you. But I did."

Gray didn't know what to think. More than anything, her heart wanted to believe him. But how could she? If he'd deceived her once, couldn't he do it again?

"Are you telling the truth now?" she asked, her lower lip trembling. "How can I trust you if you lied to me about everything?"

He crossed the room in three steps and stood in front of her.

She looked up into his battered face, her heart aching.

"You can trust me because you know I'm telling the truth. Look at me and tell me you think I'm lying now, Gray Langtry. Look at me and tell me you don't trust me."

A tear escaped and ran down her cheek. "I don't know what to think anymore," she whispered. "I'm so confused."

He held out his open hands. He was so beautiful it hurt her to look at him.

"I wouldn't lie to you, not about this. Everything I said to you, and everything that happened between us – I meant it. I care about you. I tried not to, but I do."

She thought of him stumbling out of the woods last night into the shadow of the tractor. Of the way he was always at her side when she needed him – from that first night in the woods when he wouldn't close the chapel door until she was inside, up until last night, when he'd nearly killed a man for her.

She bit her lip to make it stop shaking. "I believe you."

He took her hand, wrapping his fingers around hers. "That's all I want."

Then she stepped into his arms and let him pull her close. "Thank you for saving my life."

"Anytime." His voice was light, but she felt him press his face into her hair. For a long while they stood like that, holding each other.

At last, Dylan stepped back, clearing his throat. "Your mom's waiting downstairs. She said to tell you it's time to go. You all packed?"

Gray nodded, reluctant for the moment to end. She had so much to think about right now. She just wanted to be with him.

Soon though, he reached for her suitcase, picking it up as if it weighed nothing, and they walked down the narrow hallway in silence, and down the steps to the landing below. It was only as they crossed in front of the statues toward the main sweeping staircase, that she found her voice again.

"Are you coming back next term?"

"That's kind of up to you." He turned to look at her seriously. "If nobody finds out about us, I can come back undercover. But no one can know. You can't tell the other students – even your closest friends – who I am."

Gray's brow furrowed. "Maya already knows who you are. She's the one who told me."

"Maya, I trust," he said, simply. "I told her the truth early on, so she could feel safer. She's never told anyone except you. And that's only because she was mad at me for not telling you myself." He gave a wry smile. "I got quite an earful from her the other day about it."

"Minal and Kyle," she said, apologetically. "I told them we kissed."

He winced. "Tell them it was a mistake. Or swear them to secrecy about it. Either way, if any of the guards finds out I'll be sent home and they won't let me come back."

They paused at the top of the stairs. Below, Gray could see her mother waiting impatiently with a trio of bodyguards, Julia among them, her face impassive and exhausted.

She turned to Dylan. "I'll fix it with Minal and Kyle. Just come back, OK? I want you to come back."

By the time the motorcade pulled up to the tall, imposing gates in front of Downing Street it was already getting dark. Gray was half asleep in the back seat, with her head on her mother's shoulder.

Six police officers in neat black caps and dark jackets and Kevlar vests stood back from the gate, their eyes scanning the small crowd that was always gathered nearby.

Gray saw a sign that said, "JUSTICE FOR MYANMAR" and another that read: "GET LANGTRY OUT". Her mind still hazy with exhaustion, she wondered for a moment if the second sign was about her or her mother.

Seconds later, the motorcycle escort sped through the gate, with the car carrying the two of them right behind it. Gray turned in the seat to look out the back window and take in the view of Big Ben's spired tower on one side, and the London Eye Ferris wheel on the other. The wheel glowed red and gold, the colours of the holiday season.

For a second, the familiar sight felt almost like being home.

Seconds later, the bullet-proof silver Jaguar pulled up in front of the famous black door, with the number 10 right in the centre.

Her mother climbed out first. The machine-gun clatter of camera shutters was Gray's warning of what to expect.

When she climbed out after her, the clatter rose to a roar.

"Gray! Look over here! Gray! Gray! Prime Minister!"

The voices rose as the flashes sent bomb bursts of light into the dark lane.

Her mother had warned her this would happen, and as they'd planned, the two of them stood side by side, smiling stiffly at the gathered press. The questions came at them in a confusing rush.

"Are you OK?"

"Gray, what happened to your face?"

"Prime Minister, is the nation safe if something like this can happen to your child?"

"Prime Minister, will you resign to keep your family safe?"

At the last one, Gray felt her mother's body stiffen next to her. She reached out to take her mother's hand and turned to face the questioner.

"Langtrys don't give up in the face of violence," Gray said. "My mother isn't afraid. And neither am I."

As the reporters clamoured for more, her mother gave her a tight smile that said both "I'm proud of you" and "We did not discuss this, please stop."

She turned to face the cameras and in a voice that could silence a room of three hundred men the prime minister said, "Gray is doing well, as am I. She was attacked last night and could have been killed. I want everyone involved in this terrible crime to understand that, whoever you are and however powerful you believe yourself to be, we will find and arrest you. And we will bring the full force of justice down on you. Also, I will not rest until every family is safe. Until every child can attend school without fear. And every criminal meets the justice they deserve."

Typical Mum, Gray thought, fighting an unexpected urge to smile.

With that, the two of them ignored the barrage of shouted questions, and walked through the open door into the sheltering walls of Number 10.

EPILOGUE

On a rainy late December afternoon, Julia joined the flow of Londoners down the steps of Westminster station to catch the tube heading west.

It was quiet – most people were still away for Christmas, and there were plenty of seats. But she stood at the back, as the train rattled and sped through the darkness. Some people glanced up curiously at the young blonde woman in the black suit, but she didn't notice their interest. Her eyes were fixed on the dusty stone walls outside the windows, a blur of unseen things.

At Gloucester Road, she got off, and made her way up to the street, breathing in the cold, damp air with relief. Rain was falling harder now, but she pulled her hood up over her head and turned left, following the directions she'd researched the night before. It was a twenty-minute walk to her destination, but she made it in fifteen, pausing only to buy a bunch of vivid gold tulips from a flower shop on the way.

The modern building was on a busy street, and red double-decker buses rumbled by three at a time, belching exhaust as she waited at the crossing. The street would be leafy in the summer, but now it was lined with skeletal trees and patches of muddy green.

It had snowed on Boxing Day, but the storm hadn't lasted, and the rain had washed away the last bits of white, leaving only typical English grey.

The light turned green and she crossed to the building, making her way to the entrance. She followed signs for the lift and took it up to the third floor. Nobody was at the desk, and she walked by without encountering anyone.

The door to room 327 stood ajar. She tapped lightly with her knuckles and walked in.

Cameron's bed was a sea of cream and white. Tubes were connected to her arms, and machines buzzed and beeped around her.

Her eyes were closed when Julia walked in, but as she placed the tulips in a vase at the foot of the bed, they blinked open. Cameron smiled.

"You again," she said hoarsely. "You're a bloody stalker."

"Call the cops." Julia leaned over and brushed her lips against her forehead. "I brought chocolate."

"Oh, thank God." She lifted her hand. "Give it to me now. They don't feed me."

"They do feed you. I've seen them bring in food." Julia handed her a flat box, and pulled a chair closer. "You're just greedy."

Cameron handed the box back. "Take off the cellophane, would you? I forgot my scissors."

Smiling, Julia pulled off the plastic and opened the box before handing it back. The sweet scent of sugar and cocoa replaced the astringent smell of disinfectant that had filled the air.

C J DAUGHERTY

Cameron pushed a button and raised her head so she was sort of sitting up, and popped a chocolate into her mouth.

"Oh my God. It was worth getting stabbed for that."

"You're insane," Julia said, but she laughed. "How are you feeling today?"

"Alive. Grateful. Sedated." Cameron held out the box. "Take one. It's an order."

"You're so pushy," Julia said, but she took one.

"Raj came yesterday." Cameron chose another chocolate, holding it up to the light as if that could reveal what was inside. "He told me about Ashford."

"That bastard." Julia's body tightened. Even the mention of his name was enough to infuriate her.

"He said the police found no direct connection between him and the attackers," Cameron reported. "So far they've caught three of the men, and they all claim they attacked the school hoping to find cash. Without evidence, there's nothing they can do. He goes free."

"He's losing his job at least," Julia said. "The prime minister fired him the next day."

"Surely he's had enough?" Cameron closed the box of chocolates and set it aside. "He came very close to finding himself in prison for the rest of his life. He can't push this much further. He has to know we're watching him."

"He's so arrogant," Julia said with disgust. "I wouldn't put anything past him."

"But he doesn't know we've tapped his phones. We're watching his house. The Secret Service is watching him in Parliament," Cameron reminded her.

"No, he doesn't know. But it won't stop him. The people he's working for won't let him get away with failure," Julia said. "Raj thinks he'll try again."

"Let him." Cameron reached out a hand, tubes trailing. Julia took her hand. Their fingers tightened. "We'll be ready."

Julia's heart stuttered at her touch. She lifted Cameron's fingers to her lips.

"Yes," she said. "This time – we'll be ready."

ACKNOWLEDGEMENTS

My first thanks as always goes to the *Night School* fans who never stopped asking me to write a *Night School 6*. I couldn't go back to the same time, as that story felt complete to me. But one day it occurred to me that I could go back to the same *place*. And the *Number 10* series was born. So thank you to everyone who has written to me over the years. I'm very grateful to each and every one of you for being there in my inbox, on Facebook, on Instagram and in my book club. You make everything much more fun.

I also owe an incalculable debt to my editor, Karen Ball. We worked together on *Night School* back in the day, and were very happy to be reunited by *Number 10* and *Codename Firefly*. She's absolutely one of the best in the business and I am so privileged to work with her. More thanks go as well to Helen Grant, who copy edited the manuscripts and sorted out my commas. Helen is also an award-winning novelist, and her ghost stories are not to be missed! Thanks also to Shilpa Baliga, for her fine penwork proofing this book and removing all the remaining mistakes.

Huge thanks also to the small but mighty team at my new publishing imprint, Moonflower Publishing, especially to the multi-talented Jasmine Aurora, who was responsible for the fabulous covers and the interior designs of *Codename Firefly* and *Number 10*, as well as the gorgeous new *Night School* redesign. I cannot imagine what we would do without her.

Thanks always to my amazing agent, Madeleine Milburn, who fights like a tiger to make sure the books I write get into your hands.

And, as always, all my love and thanks to Jack Jewers. He is the first reader of every single book I write. My first editor. The one who keeps everything going.

Now, the bad news. If you're reading this right after Codename is released – in 2021 or 2022 – there's going to be a break in the series. I'm working on a new adult series called *Alias Emma* and it's going to take all of my time for at least a year or two. I will come back to Cimmeria, and Gray, Dylan, Sophie, Minal, Maya, and Kyle, I promise! But for a little while I've got to focus on the new thing. Don't forget about me while I'm gone. And I won't forget about you.

And, whatever happens… Keep breathing.

ABOUT THE AUTHOR

A former crime reporter and accidental civil servant, C.J. Daugherty began writing the Night School series while working as a communications consultant for the British government. The series was published by Little Brown in the UK, and went on to sell over a million and a half copies worldwide. A web series inspired by the books clocked up well over a million views. In 2020, the books were optioned for television. She later wrote The Echo Killing series, published by St Martin's Press, and co-wrote the fantasy series, The Secret Fire, with French author Carina Rosenfeld. Her books have been translated into 25 languages and have been bestsellers in multiple countries. She lives with her husband, the BAFTA nominated filmmaker, Jack Jewers.

Follow C. J. DAUGHERTY on…

- ⊙ INSTAGRAM_@cj_daugherty
- ▶ YOUTUBE_/nightschoolbook
- 🐦 TWITTER_@cj_daugherty
- f FACEBOOK /CJauthor

Join her book club at…
www.christidaugherty.com

Christi●Daugherty

Read book one...

When your mother is the prime minister and
someone wants to bring her down,
home is a very dangerous place.

Gray Langtry's life turned upside down the day her mother became
prime minister. Followed by the paparazzi and constantly protected by
bodyguards, she just wants to be normal, but normal is over for her.
Grounded at Number 10 Downing Street after a wild night with friends is
captured by tabloid photographers, she explores the secret government
tunnels beneath it. It's there that she overhears a plot to kill her mother,
and replace her with a new leader — one more amenable to Russia. The
only problem is, no one believes her. Only her friend, Chloe, and Jake
McIntyre, son of the leader of the opposition, will listen. They have two
weeks to find proof and stop the murder. And time is running out.

Allie Sheridan's life is falling apart.

She hates her school. Her brother has run away. And she's just been arrested. Again. This time, her parents are sending her away for a 'fresh start'. And yet, instead of hating boarding school, Allie is surprised to find she likes it. She's making friends. And there's Carter, a brooding loner with whom she feels an instant connection. But Cimmeria Academy is no ordinary school. Her classmates — and her teachers — are hiding something. And soon it becomes clear that this is a very dangerous place. And that nobody can be trusted.

Discover the million selling series that started it all.
All CJ's books are available in good book stores, or from
www.moonflowerbooks.co.uk